VOICE OF THE

JUST

The Blue Sapphire

Story

Allie Marie

VOICE OF THE JUST

This book is a work of fiction, and does not represent real events. Characters, names, places, and incidents are works of the authors imagination and do not depict any real event, or person living or dead.

VOICE OF THE JUST

The Blue Sapphire Story

Book 3 of the True Colors Series

Copyright © 2017 by Allie Marie

Published by Nazzaro & Price Publishing

Published in the United States of America

i

Allie Marie

DEDICATION

In loving memory of my mother
I miss you so much, Momma

ACKNOWLEDGMENTS

I have thoroughly enjoyed writing this series, and can only hope I've done justice to the extensive research I conducted. I also acknowledge that I may have created idealistic time lines to suit the plot and take full responsibility for that!

In this book, the mystery centers on Therese's desperate search for her mother. As I wrote the scenes, I thought so often of my own mother. Despite the years, I miss her every day. So in her honor, I also want to thank moms everywhere for all you do.

I owe a world of thanks to many people for their support and encouragement, or who inspire me.

To my husband Jack, for your unwavering love and support.

To my sister-in-law Ellia, for your creativity and thoughtfulness, and to my niece Becky for cheering me on.

To Nazzaro & Price, for giving me my start in the published world, with special thanks to Helen Brown Nazzaro for your wonderful editing, and to Julie Graham for your final eagle-eye proof.

To my "cover team." Once again, my model Elayna and photographer Sidnie created the perfect ghost. And to Carmin, who inspired Becky's last name. I love you girls!

To James Price, a special thank you for taking an idea and a photo and designing a cover that captured exactly what I imagined.

To Sandi Baum, for once more reading every word I wrote—and rewrote—and for keeping me focused. I appreciate your every comment and suggestion. My writing is better for your efforts.

To Laura Somers, your sharp eye and red pencil keep finding those pesky mistakes that still manage to sneak in. To Dawn for catching a few more along the way!

To musicians for the songs that tell the stories of life. A songwriter can tell a whole story in 250 words. It takes thousands for an author to tell the same story in a book.

To the Tuesday Morning Breakfast Club: Wilbor, Bob, Donnie, Sammie, Freddie, Wayne, Jimmy.

To Lauren and the members of the Windsor Book Club of the Windsor Branch of the Blackwater Regional Library, especially Mary B. You are the best. You are a fantastic reading group and cheering squad.

To the Artesia Ladies Group, thanks. Hope to see you all next year!

To Greg Parker at Arthur's General Store in Driver, Virginia for your support and clues about the Sleepy Hole Ferry.

To Audrey, Nettie, June, and Cathy of the Little Shoppes on High for your ongoing support.

To the Osfolk family, proprietors of the Bier Garden, the inspiration for the Bier Haus setting in my story.

To the Olde Towne Business Association and the Olde Towne Civic League for all you do to preserve the history and business of this district.

To my readers, because you make writing worthwhile.

I'd like to extend special thanks to the following for their invaluable insights for my research. Any inaccuracies are the result of my overactive imagination.

To Dianne Ringer for your valuable insight in developing Terry's professional persona.

To retired Portsmouth Police Homicide Sergeant W. C. Gavin and to Senior Forensics Tech T. McCurdy for answering criminal and forensic related questions.

To Catherine Wilson and Penny Gagnon for answering a multitude of questions about their ancestral DNA experiences. I also referred to these sources for information about ancestral DNA:

http://www.nij.gov/topics/forensics/evidence/dna/research/pages/mitochondrial.asp

http://www.dfs.virginia.gov/about-dfs/

To Philip M. Stoll, DDS, DO and to Wendy Schofer, MD for answering my many questions related to medical services. I'll be in touch for Book 4!

To RN Bonnie Bee, Krystal Leigh, and soon-to-be RN Allison Jo-Lynn for the help each of you gave me as I created Joan's medical scenario. To my dear friend Judy P. King, RN retired, and to all nurses everywhere, you are the backbone of the medical field. We don't thank you often enough.

My colonial characters were not too fond of the British, but we love our friends across the pond, especially Dave and Nicky, Rodger and Pauline, whom we met during their days with the Hampshire Constabulary Band.

Many Portsmouth, Virginia landmarks are mentioned in this story. While real cemeteries are mentioned, however, they are in no way the resting place for the fictional characters described in this book. You can find out more about Portsmouth's Olde Towne and other historic sites at:

http://www.dhr.virginia.gov/registers/Cities/register_P ortsmouth.htm

The colors of our American flag are a recurring theme of the <u>True Colors Series</u> because they represent each heroine's jewels as well as her persona. In researching the flag, I learned that its colors did not have the specific meaning with which they are today associated, but rather the colors of the Great

[1] 083-550 Our Flag - US Government Publishing Office

108th Congress, 1st Session H.Doc. 108-97

OUR FLAG

JOINT COMMITTEE ON PRINTING

UNITED STATES CONGRESS

Printed by authority of House Concurrent Resolution 139, 108th Congress

U.S. GOVERNMENT PRINTING OFFICE

WASHINGTON : 2003

Seal explain the meaning of the white, red, and blue.

Charles Thompson, Secretary of the Continental Congress, reporting to Congress on the Seal, stated:

"The colors of the pales (the vertical stripes) are those used in the flag of the United States of America; White signifies purity and innocence, Red, hardiness & valour, and Blue, the color of the Chief (the broad band above the stripes) signifies vigilance, perseverance & justice."

You can find out more about the American Flag at: http://www.senate.gov/reference/resources/pdf/ourflag.pdf

During my research about Olde Towne, some historic information was gathered from the following sources:

For the Pass House referred to during the Ghost Walk:
http://pilotonline.com/news/local/history/what-s-in-a-name-the-pass-house-in-portsmouth/article_103de0b6-cbf2-5f8c-b75d-22da9c2dcac7.html
by Meghan Hoyer
The Virginian-pilot
July 5, 2010

For the Ghost Walk:
The Annual Olde Towne Ghost Walk in Portsmouth takes place on the last Friday of every October. I've tried to capture the essence of my experience at this event while adapting it for my storyline. For more information go to
http://portsmouthghostwalk.com/
Information for some of the Ghost Walk vignettes discussed in this story come from the booklet *Ghost Stories of Olde Towne, Portsmouth, Virginia* by Doris Kuebler Leitner.

VOICE OF THE JUST

Books by Allie Marie

THE TRUE COLORS SERIES

Teardrops of the Innocent: The White Diamond Story
Heart of Courage: The Red Ruby Story
Voice of the Just: The Blue Sapphire Story

Allie Marie

THE PROPERTIES
After the Storm

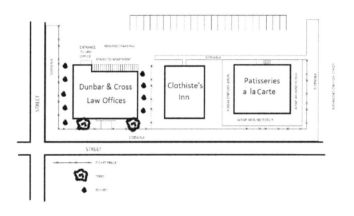

PROLOGUE

Theresé and the Blue Sapphire
Near Yorktown, Virginia, August 1781

The break of dawn brought forth no sunlight, but more of the storms that had plagued us for days. Storms that reminded me of the horrible night when British soldiers attacked and wounded our mother and grandfather. My brother's disguise as a British soldier gave us hope that they were cared for.

Thunder boomed in the distance outside as the rain eased. My sisters slept peacefully. Usually it was I who woke last, but I made up for it by working late into the night, sewing or writing letters dictated by soldiers who could not write.

This morning, however, I was up with my father. I prepared him a breakfast but, as he had done with too many of his meals, he pushed it to the side. He worried about his own father, but for my mother's safety, his concern nearly drove him mad.

My beautiful mother's sudden illness had forced us to seek shelter in our grandfather's house. But his wife, Abigail, our step-grandmother, had made it clear to us we were not wanted. When grandfather discovered his wife tried to poison my mother, he arranged for us to leave immediately in a wagon. Working with the patriots, he helped smuggle weapons and ammunition to the French soldiers supporting the Americans.

On that night, soldiers had gunned down my mother and grandfather before our eyes. My brother Louis, disguised as a redcoat, shot the attackers and sent us on our way while he stayed behind to care for our loved ones.

We had hoped for news of those we'd left behind before now. Nearly two weeks had passed without a word, unusual given the number of contacts my father had. I feared if he did not hear some word of Mama's condition, he would risk his life to go to Portsmouth to find her.

"Papa, please eat something," I begged as I pushed a plate of biscuits closer to him. My youngest sister Nicole and I had picked a basket of blackberries during breaks from the rain, and Marie Josephé had used them to add some taste to the flavorless firecakes we so often ate.

My father smiled and shook his head. "No, ma petit, I am afraid food is not on my mind." He rubbed his eyes and then pinched the bridge of his nose.

"Are you thinking of Mama?" I asked.

"Every moment I am awake, I think of your mama, and when I sleep, I dream of her. I long for the day when my beautiful wife and our daughters live together again in a grand house, where we can watch our girls laugh and play. To one day see you wear the pretty jewels that your grandfather and I wanted to surprise you with."

"Papa, they were so beautiful. It pleased Mama to show them to us. Nicole thought they were the continental colors, but Mama told us how you chose them for us."

I had told this story to my father a number of times but he seemed never to tire of it.

He said, "Diamond for our innocent Nicole, ruby for our brave Marie Josephé, and sapphire for our crusader, Theresé." He smiled, but the light did not shine in his eyes.

Thundering horse hooves signaled the arrival of a wagon. A driver's voice shouted, "Whoa!" as the creaks and groans of the wooden carriage came to a halt.

"Dear God, please let there be word," my father cried as he pushed aside the flap of the tent, taking no notice of the stream of water that poured from the shifting canvas. I stepped to the doorway, ignoring the drips as I watched Papa stomp through the mud toward the wagon. He reached it at the same time as several other soldiers from his brigade.

I recognized James, our brother's fellow spy, ensconced within the British Army at Portsmouth. He lifted the canvas covering the back of the wagon. Lizzie, our step-grandmother's unfortunate maid, scrambled over the sides, helped to the ground by my father. Her rain-wet hair dripped into her eyes, and her soaked clothing clung to her. Fresh mud clumped at the hem of her dress as it swept over the wet ground.

A small girl I had never seen before scrambled over the wall of the wagon and immediately wrapped her arms around Lizzie. Papa pointed toward our tent and gripped James's arm in frantic conversation.

Lizzie scurried toward the tent, the little girl in tow. I reached for a blanket and held it as she came to the door. The commotion had wakened Marie Josephé and she came to my side.

"Theresé!" Lizzie threw her arms around me and we held each other, unmindful of the wet. Lizzie embraced Marie Josephé next.

"We did not expect to see you, Lizzie. How did you come to be here?"

"My aunt has released me from my servitude. This child was sold as a servant to my aunt, and when I escaped, I brought her with me."

I hugged Lizzie again, and asked, "Then have you news of my mother? Can you tell me how she is? And Grandfather?"

The color drained from Lizzie's face and she said, "Your mother? Is she not here? I was told her family came for her."

My heart sank to my feet.

"She is not here, Lizzie." I answered.

My sister and I gripped each other's hand as cold, harsh fear washed over us.

CONTENTS

CHAPTER 1

Terry
Portsmouth, Virginia, present day

Terry Dunbar tapped the speed dial assigned to her father's cell number for the third time, and for as many times, received his voice mail response. She hung up without leaving a message, her stomach jolting with tension.

Her fingers flicked across the keypad as she sent text messages to her brothers asking for updates. Fear from the lack of news about her mother intensified with every unanswered query. She would arrive at the emergency room before they would have time to respond to her texts, but she had to distract herself somehow.

"Still no answer?" Terry's sister-in-law, Beth Dunbar, switched driving lanes as she spoke, the clacking of the turn signal the only other sound audible in the vehicle. "Maybe your dad had to turn his phone off in the ER," she suggested, trying to keep her fears in check for Terry's sake.

"More likely it's because that archaic phone he carries can't transmit from inside the building," Terry responded, prompting nervous giggles from the back seat where her friends Mary Jo Cooper and Stephanie Kincaid sat.

A night of fun had ended abruptly when Terry received the nerve-shattering call from her father that her mother was being rushed to the emergency room. The four friends had celebrated the long-awaited completion of their planned Bed and Breakfast in Olde Towne Portsmouth with a Girls' Night Out Slumber Party. They had gathered for delectable food paired with festive wine tasting. Beth, now three months pregnant with her second child, drank sparkling water in place of wine. After a lively game of poker ended with a hefty pot won by the rookie player, Stephanie, the women spent the next two hours on girly things like manicures and pedicures as they chatted and shared news.

Stephanie then brought them up to speed on the new findings of her ancestry research, which had brought her and the Dunbar family together in the first place. Now engaged to Terry's brother, Stephanie detailed more of the amazing ties that connected her to the Dunbar family in more than just social ways. After discussing the ghosts and strange occurrences she and Mary Jo had recently encountered, they were about to settle into their sleeping bags on air mattresses when the frantic call came from Terry's father that her mother was being rushed to the hospital.

The friends scrambled into clothes and piled into Beth's car for the twenty-mile drive to the Suffolk hospital.

Now the designated driver flipped the signal to indicate the turn into the ER parking lot. Beth entered the drop-off zone in front of the emergency entrance.

"Let me out here, please, Beth," Terry said, already unbuckling her seat belt.

"Go with her, Mary Jo," Stephanie urged. "I'll come in with Beth after we park."

"Thanks." Terry jumped from the car before Beth came to a full stop, Mary Jo in frantic pursuit.

The two friends reached the automatic door at the same time and turned to each other to clasp hands.

The glass doors parted. Terry squeezed Mary Jo's hand, then they dashed into the waiting room. Terry's head whipped from left to right as her gaze swept the room, then back to the left. Her brother Connor, holding his son, stood and lifted one hand. Four-year-old Tanner slept soundly, cheek nestled against his dad's shoulder. Connor shifted the little boy a little higher.

Charles Dunbar sat in a stiff-backed chair, perched on the edge as if ready to sprint at a moment's notice. His elbows rested on his knees, his hands scrubbing his face.

"Daddy!" Terry rushed to him, arms outstretched. "Mom? How is she? I couldn't get the phone calls to go through. What happened to her?"

Charles Dunbar rose from the thinly padded cushion and gathered his only daughter in his arms. He started to speak but his voice broke and he hugged Terry tighter. Fearing the worst news possible, Terry sucked in her breath and emitted a ragged, "No."

"She's okay so far, Terry," Connor broke in quickly. "The doctors are with her now, and they just let Gage go back there." He squeezed Terry's shoulder, then his dad's. Charles eased his hold on Terry to clasp his son's hand.

"I'm sorry I scared you, baby." Charles took a step backwards and cleared his throat. "I-I just…"

"Come sit down, Daddy," Terry said, drawing her father back to his chair.

Charles choked up again and Connor took over.

"Dad said she wasn't feeling well today." He spoke softly, shifting Tanner's weight to his other arm. "She was working on her high school reunion plans. You know how she gets when she's on a project, she doesn't eat right. She became a little nauseated at one point, but Dad got her to eat a little and rest."

Charles spoke next, voice stronger. "She kept getting up to go to the bathroom. Then she stumbled and I heard her knock something over on the sink, so I went to check on her. She was leaning on the counter for support, her breathing labored and her speech slurred when she tried to speak. I checked her pulse. It raced like a ticking time-bomb, scared the hell out of me. I thought she might be having a stroke, or maybe a heart attack, so I got her to the bedroom and called nine-one-one, then called Connor. He got there about the time the medics were putting her in the ambulance."

"Did they say yet what happened? Is it a heart attack or a

stroke?" Terry's own heartbeat pounded in her ears, and she was vaguely aware of her sister-in-law walking over to Connor. Mary Jo and Stephanie stood a few feet away.

Charles shook his head, his voice cracking again as he spoke. "I should have insisted she eat something, instead of letting her food sit."

"Stop that now, Daddy," Terry insisted. Her strong, strapping father suddenly seemed older and more vulnerable than she had ever seen him, his worry so intense that deep lines etched his face. She grabbed his hand. "You heard what Connor just said, she gets on a tangent with her projects."

"Not only that, Dad, you shouldn't give food to a possible stroke patient, so it's just as well. Let's wait and see what the doctor says."

The words were no sooner out of his mouth when the double doors leading from the emergency room to the waiting room opened. Anxious faces turned to the nurse entering between the partitions, who requested the family follow her to an interior waiting room.

Sudden fear pierced Terry and her heart seemed to fall to her feet. She slipped her hand through the crook of her father's arm, unable to prevent the thought that came to her mind.

Are they taking us to a private room to tell us Mom has died?

Charles clamped his free hand over hers and squeezed tight, his fingers ice cold. *The same thought must have crossed Dad's mind.* She inclined her head on his shoulder. Every member of the extended family remained standing, silently waiting.

"Please, God, let there be good news," Charles prayed out loud as the doctor stepped through the doorway, followed by Gage. She scanned her brother's face as Stephanie rushed to Gage's side, a sigh of relief escaping at his relaxed body language. Terry recognized the doctor as a family friend. He nodded as he walked toward them, and she scanned his face for a sign of the news he brought.

"Donnie?" Charles extended his hand to his long-time friend Donnie Stevens. "How is she?" The doctor shook his hand, and with his left, clasped Charles' shoulder in a sign of comfort, nodding again.

"She's resting at the moment." The doctor spoke as he accepted hugs or handshakes from his friend's children. "Sorry to see you under these circumstances, Charles. I wanted to come out myself to tell you we've stabilized Joan. We're still running a battery of tests, but we've ruled out a heart attack or stroke. The medics correctly recognized the signs of diabetic ketoacidosis."

"Diabetes? She's diabetic?" Charles asked. "She's never been diagnosed before."

"This is what we call Type Two Adult Onset. She's not making enough insulin to regulate her blood sugar. We're giving her intravenous fluids to offset dehydration, and we've got her on an insulin drip to suppress the production of ketone bodies. We'll monitor her every thirty minutes, and keep her under observation to prevent any complications and signs of infection."

"She cut her hand a while back and it still had not healed," Charles said.

The doctor nodded. "We'll treat her for that. This could be a one-time episode and may never happen again, but we want to rule out any other conditions."

"Will she have to be on insulin from now on?" Charles ran his hand through his hair.

"We'll know more after all the tests are analyzed. Often, this type of situation is a wake-up call. Type Two diabetes can be diet-controlled, or may only require oral medications. Worst case scenario would be insulin shots. Joan is in overall good health, so with some life-style adjustments, she may never have another occurrence. We'll get her set her up with a diabetes educator, a specialist who will help her understand this disease and develop lifestyle changes to manage her diabetes."

"She's gonna hate giving up her chocolate," Charles said, the tension lines easing from his face as his comment brought chuckles from his children.

The doctor smiled. "It's more about moderation and close monitoring. She may still be able to have an occasional treat, but this is something she'll be dealing with for the rest of her life. Let's get her through all the tests and see how she's doing. Because she was so severely dehydrated, we'll keep her here today, do what we need to do. She'll probably be released first thing tomorrow morning. They're getting a room for her now."

"When can we see her?"

"It'll be a few minutes before they move her. We don't have any other patients at the moment. You can come back in twos."

"Connor rode in the ambulance with her, and I was with her earlier," Gage said. "Someone else can go in."

"I'd like to go see her now," Terry said. She turned to her father and added, "Dad, I can't leave her alone tonight. I want to stay until they release her, even if I have to sleep on a chair in the waiting room. I want to be near her if she needs me."

Mary Jo stepped forward and hugged first Terry, then Charles. "Steph and I won't go in, Terry. We were just saying we shouldn't bother her now. It'll wear her out if we all traipse in to see her. Let her know we were here and we love her."

"I'll do that. Sorry to ruin our night, girls."

"Stop that now, Terry," admonished Charles in much the same tone his daughter had used earlier. The others nodded in agreement.

"I know, I know." With hugs and goodbyes all around, Terry drew her father toward the nurses' station. When the doors opened, she turned and blew a kiss to her friends and brothers.

As the doors shut behind them, she steeled herself to go toward the enclosure that held her mother.

"Dad, you go in first, and see Mom," she urged. "I'll give you a minute with her by yourself."

Charles patted her hand and slipped through the curtain opening. Her mother's warm voice greeted him, sounding strong.

Although relief coursed through Terry's body, she needed a moment to collect herself. Her knees turned to rubber and she gripped the edge of the counter. Tears burned and pooled in her eyes, and she squeezed her lids shut.

"You okay, honey?" A light hand touched Terry's shoulder. She looked into the concerned eyes of a pretty nurse with glowing skin the color of burnt umber.

Terry nodded and exhaled a deep breath. "I just needed a minute to collect myself before I see my mom. I wanted to give my dad a moment before I barged in."

"Your mom's doing fine now and she's kept us laughing with her jokes. She's a funny lady."

"She's my best friend." Terry's voice cracked.

The nurse patted her arm. "I know. I feel the same way about my mom."

"I've never been so scared in my life." Terry placed her hand over her heart and took a deep breath. She glanced at the nurse's name tag. *Cynthia Lynn, R.N.* Terry memorized the name to send a thank-you note later.

Nurse Lynn wrote on a clipboard and then slid it onto a shelf. She turned to Terry. "We're doing everything we can for her now. If she takes care of herself and keeps up with her medical treatment, she can manage her diabetes." The nurse reached for a small container and began writing on the lid. "We'll be moving her in about thirty minutes. If you need anything, let me know."

"Thank you, Cynthia, every one of you, for everything you do in this ER." This time Terry patted the nurse's shoulder. The half-second it had taken for her to notice the nurse's name and then use it brought a nod of appreciation.

With a sharp intake of breath, Terry steadied her nerves before stepping to the curtain opening. She glanced inside.

Joan Dunbar leaned back on the partially-inclined bed, her right arm tethered to tubes running from two bags of fluids hooked to an IV pole. Although she lay with her face away from Terry, she smiled. The curtain blocked Terry's view of her father standing at the bed, allowing only a glimpse of his arm and shoulder holding tightly to Joan's.

"Mom?" She poked her head inside.

"Come in, baby girl," Joan called.

Her mother's strong voice sent grateful tugs of relief washing through Terry. She slid through the opening and walked toward the bedside opposite where her father leaned across the rail. He held Joan's free hand pressed against his forehead.

Terry slipped her fingertips under her mother's, gently running her thumb across the skin. When her father glanced her way, she could see tears glistening in his eyes. He tried to wink, but instead caused a teardrop to slip out and trail down his cheek.

Seeing her mother and father so vulnerable floored her. She turned her back to reach for a chair, brushing at the tears sliding down her cheeks. She sat, then scooted the chair close to the rail.

"I'm sorry I gave everyone such as scare." Joan moved her hand, still encased in Charles's hands, and used her knuckles in a caress that stopped the teardrop rolling down her husband's cheek. "Looks like I'll be reducing my chocolate intake, though."

She pretended to pout and gave a playful wiggle of the fingers of her hand with the IV to greet Terry, wincing at the discomfort the movement caused, then continued. "Take that worried look off your face, my darling daughter. I'm going to be fine. But I'm afraid I ruined the plans for your surprise birthday party, baby."

Terry gulped back a sob, unable to speak over the lump in her throat. Finally, she managed to speak. "I don't care about my birthday, Momma, I want you to be fine."

Joan shifted in the bed and said, "Terry, I had a scare, I admit that, but from what the doctor says, they got me here in time. They'll get me to a room, do some tests, and maybe I can talk my way out of here before tomorrow. Why don't you two go home?"

"We'll stay here until you're settled in the room, Mom," Terry said, voice firm now. "It'll be a half hour before they take you up. But I'm staying the rest of the night, Momma, sleeping in a chair if I have to."

"I'm blessed to be surrounded by such a loving family." Joan's voice caught and she swallowed hard, then fixed a smile. "Did you girls have a fun night?"

"We did. The girls all send their love. They came with me but were afraid to tire you out, and said they'd see you later."

"Tell me what you did."

Terry willed her voice to be strong, to match the attempt at normalcy her mother was making. "Well, Stephanie claims she never played poker before, but she won almost every hand and cleaned us out. We also caught up on all the gossip and guess what? Chase proposed to Mary Jo on Friday. She kept the news to herself until she practically poked our eyes out with that new rock on her finger."

"Oh, I'm so glad those two knot-heads finally got their act together." Joan's face lit up with a happy smile.

"Of course, Stephanie also gave us an update on her genealogy research," Terry continued. "Then we analyzed the encounters she and Mary Jo have had with their ghosts. By the way, when I arrived, a freezing cold gripped the room but I couldn't find a source, and soon the temperature returned to normal." Terry paused to catch her breath, then added, "Finally, we settled on 'Clothiste's Inn' for the name of the bed and breakfast. I'll take care of the final details this week, so we can get up and running. And it might be fun to hold a costume party for Halloween in the house before we have guests."

"Hmm. Clothiste's Inn. I like that." Joan nodded in approval. "I really like that. I can already see how the place could be decorated for…"

"Mom, you're in the hospital. You need to take it easy."

"Oh, pooh." Joan rolled her eyes. "I had a wake-up call about my health and I'll have to change some things in my lifestyle, but there's no reason for me to take it easy. But thank you for worrying." Smiling, she settled back on the pillow, then sighed and closed her eyes.

"We're here, babe, if you need anything," Charles said. He settled his wife's arm by her side and leaned back in the chair, his hand still covering hers.

Mindful of the IV, Terry lightly clasped her mother's fingertips and rested her forehead against her mother's knees. Although her fears had moderated after seeing her mother, Terry's ears pulsed with the pounding of her heartbeat as she leaned forward. Hot salty tears pooled on the sheet.

She'd been lucky enough to be born the daughter of two parents who loved each other deeply and whose generosity spread to others less fortunate. From the time she could remember, her parents were always making someone part of their family. While raising their own three children, they were foster parents to Mary Jo. Charles became a surrogate father to Chase, the Dunbar brothers' childhood friend, now engaged to Mary Jo. And for a number of years Joan's cranky distant cousin Hannah had lived with them while she recovered from cancer.

A whole army of soldiers would be waiting on Joan Dunbar hand and foot.

Terry's eyes drooped, and she drifted into the twilight of sleep.

"I love you, Mom." She spoke aloud in her sleep. Joan brushed her good hand across her daughter's cheek, then slipped it back under her husband's gentle fingers.

Miles away, in the historic Olde Towne section of Portsmouth, a dingy gray mist swirled in the attic of the B&B newly-christened as "Clothiste's Inn." Resembling a swarm of angry bees, the mist twisted into the shape of a woman. The faceless form darted from side to side. Able to pass through most objects as if they did not exist, the raging image seemed imprisoned within the building, bouncing from one wall and crashing into the opposite.

A shimmering blue-silver light illuminated the attic, revealing the figure of a young woman in colonial dress. In a voice loud and clear, she declared, "I will find my mother."

As if sprayed with an effective insect repellant, the dirty whirl shrunk to a small stream that slithered into the unknown.

CHAPTER 2

After staying all night at her mother's bedside, Terry accompanied her through the hospital discharge process and then to the diabetes educator's office. She took notes throughout the conversation, loaded up on brochures and pamphlets about diabetes, then spent the entire evening searching the Internet. Joan had listened intently to the instructions and suggestions. She could still live a long and normal life if she followed the suggestions and made the necessary alterations to her lifestyle.

Returning to work on Tuesday, Terry had spent the morning in court. With only a muffin from Mary Jo's French bakery for lunch, she then devoted the entire afternoon conducting further research until she was convinced her mother was not in imminent danger.

"Ms. Dunbar?" Becky Cramin's voice followed the light tap on the door, just before she pushed it open and poked her head around the edge. Her fingers slid over the wall and found the electric switch, flooding the room with light.

Terry raised her head and blinked in surprise, her gaze shifting from the computer screen to her paralegal.

"Oh, my, Becky, I'm in the dark again." Terry said it more as a question than a statement. When she was involved in preparing a case, she often lost track of time. Working by the light from the computer screen, she rarely noticed when the afternoon sun disappeared and darkness engulfed her.

Becky walked over and set a cup of coffee on the edge of the desk with her right hand, then reached for a file folder and

11

a padded envelope she had tucked under her left arm.

"I don't see how you can work without overhead light, Ms. Dunbar. I have to admit that when I step in here, I'm always expecting to be attacked by killer mushrooms growing in the dark."

Terry inhaled an appreciative whiff of coffee before taking a sip. Then she set the cup down and leaned forward on her elbows and studied Becky, who shifted her gaze.

"Becky, we've been working together for nearly a year. When are you going to call me by my first name?"

The young paralegal's elegant cinnamon-colored skin took on a serious blush as she twisted a lock of honey-colored hair. She kept her eyes averted and stuttered, "I-I just can't. I admire you too much, but you're also my mentor and my boss."

"Well, start practicing now. We're going to be working feverishly on the Wheeler accident case starting next week, and I won't feel like I'm taking advantage of working you to death if we're on a first-name basis."

"I'll try, Ms.—I mean Terry."

"All right then, that's settled." With exaggerated motions, Terry dusted off her hands and reached for the padded envelope.

"Oh, my necklace!" she exclaimed at the sight of the jeweler's address in the corner. "I've missed my necklace. Thank you so much for picking it up for me, Becky." She fumbled with the sealed flap, managing to unfasten it enough to slip the contents through the opening. A long thin box fell into her lap.

"They sent it to another jeweler in Western Branch," Becky continued. "She had the expertise needed to complete such a delicate repair job on an heirloom like this."

With shaky fingers, Terry lifted the cover and drew the gold chain from the cotton lining. The precious metal warmed her fingertips, the gold cross dangling as she held the necklace to the light. A single sapphire stone rested at the juncture of the horizontal and vertical bars.

"It's perfect," she declared. "This pendant has been in my

mother's family for generations, passed down to daughters, then granddaughters. Mom gave it to me when I hung my shingle. We always thought it was a Celtic cross, but when I took it for repair, I learned it wasn't actually Celtic. Someone had added rings to give it that design. I've worn it ever since, until I snagged one of the bands on a sweater, twisting it away from the stipes. That's what they call the vertical part of the cross." Terry peered at the edges. "You can't even tell the circles were ever there."

"Martin said to bring it back if you weren't satisfied, but he also said he didn't think that would be the case."

"No, it's perfect. I like it better without the extra ring around it." Terry held the pendant up to the light, the familiar warmth tingling against her fingers. Light twinkled from the blue sapphire at the apex. She drew her other hand to her throat. Mysterious heat had often seemed to pass through the necklace, sometimes mild, sometimes irritatingly warm—occurrences that Terry had never shared with anyone.

How does one explain an inexplicable event?

"Are you all right?" Becky asked the question twice before catching her boss's attention.

"What? Oh, I'm fine." Terry shook her head to clear it. "Sorry, I'm just happy to have my pendant back. It's kind of my lucky charm." She set it back in the box and reached for a file labeled "Clothiste's Inn," hoping she appeared nonchalant under Becky's concerned stare. She continued, "So our Bed and Breakfast is up and running? Certificate of occupancy and everything?"

"Yes. I've got the website and social media pages finished and ready for you to look over before they go public. All the inspections are finalized and you have the CO. Now you need customers."

"I can't thank you enough for all the legwork you did for me this week, Becky. With the worry about my mom, handling these things for me on top of your normal duties took a load off my mind."

"My pleasure. I'm glad she's doing well. And I'm so excited

about Clothiste's Inn. I want to give my parents a weekend there when they visit, hopefully for Christmas. They haven't been back home for twenty years. They'll love the new places in Olde Towne, especially all decorated during the holiday season."

"The whole downtown area has changed and there is so much to offer visitors now. The Olde Towne Business Association and the Civic League work so hard to bring in new businesses. I love this time of year. We have less than three weeks before the Ghost Walk. Even though it's too late for Clothiste's Inn to be included on this October's tour, maybe next year we can participate. I just hope we get some business by Christmastime. The other owners of historical B and Bs in Olde Towne tell me they do a booming business in the summer, however, so maybe we will as well."

"Well, it's probably better to be low key this year, anyway," Becky said. "Has there been any more news about that skeleton the hurricane uncovered?"

Terry shook her head. "Not yet. We knew it would take a few weeks at the earliest to hear back from the medical examiner's office. At least things have calmed down, and all of the morbid ghoul seekers have left us alone."

Becky shivered. "Thank goodness for that. Are you going to be okay here? You didn't have much to eat today."

"Oh, I'm fine." Terry shrugged. "I work better on an empty stomach. I can always forage at the café if I get too hungry. Has Sandi left?" Sandi Cross was her partner in the small law firm of Dunbar and Cross.

"Sandi went straight home from court, said the case was continued until Monday and to tell you she was going home to have an antacid cocktail consisting of—and I quote—'liquid relief over ice.' I'll lock all the doors on my way out." Becky paused and added over her shoulder, "See you at your belated birthday party Sunday. I wonder how your mom's new sugar-free efforts will pan out for that."

"We'll find out. She's got Mary Jo whipping up sugar-free desserts. See you." Terry waved at Becky's retreating back, yawned and then stretched. She picked up the file and settled in the chair to review the paperwork for Clothiste's Inn. When the old house had come up for sale more than a year earlier, she and Mary Jo had jumped at the opportunity to purchase the property. The building stood between Mary Jo's café and Terry's law office, which had an upstairs apartment Stephanie rented. After overcoming a series of setbacks during the renovation, they were finally ready to open for business.

Terry flipped through the forms, pride coursing through her as she trailed her fingers across the business license that she would hang in the B and B office, the Certificate of Occupancy issued by the city inspections department, and the health permit from public health that would allow them to occupy the building.

The furniture had arrived and Mary Jo had taken photographs of the staged rooms for the brochure. Terry's busy schedule had not even permitted a glance at the newly-decorated rooms, but she had perused the draft with interest. Once she and Mary Jo had given the final approval to the pamphlets, Becky had graciously done the legwork to get them printed and distributed, and ads placed announcing the grand opening. Terry leaned forward, scribbling a reminder to obtain the temporary sign permits for promoting the open house in front of the building.

Grand opening! Terry sighed and sat back in the chair, perusing the utility company paperwork. All systems were go and they were ready to announce Clothiste's Inn open for business.

For a time, they'd wondered if the B and B would ever come to fruition. Due to a touchy legal issue, Mary Jo had suspended the remodeling during her deployment while moving forward with remodeling the café. On her return, however, she decided she wanted to continue its renovation in spite of the pending court case with her late fiancé's mother.

Then Hurricane Abby roared through in a path of destruction that toppled an ancient magnolia tree and unearthed an old skeleton underneath, causing further setbacks to the small businesses the Dunbar-Cooper partnership had established.

Terry's attention drifted from business forms, and she thought back to the day—was it really only a few short weeks earlier—when the strong Category 2 hurricane had torn through the East Coast. Her law office and the apartment received minimal damage, although during the height of the storm, Stephanie had had a harrowing encounter with a ghoulish specter.

But it was the Bed and Breakfast next door, and Mary Jo's French café to its right, that received the most extensive damage when the magnolia tree had crashed onto those buildings.

If it had not been for the priority attention her childhood friend Chase Hallmark had given to performing the repairs in record time, the businesses would still have been suffering from the havoc the storm created.

And then the bones were uncovered. Terry remembered the scene. During clean-up in the aftermath, a construction worker discovered a skeleton entangled in the roots of the fallen tree. She and Stephanie arrived just in time to witness the skeleton shift as dirt unsettled around it. It seemed to point an accusatory finger in their direction.

She shivered. In the past, several instances had occurred of a skeleton becoming uncovered during excavations, and were later determined to have come from long-forgotten family burial plots.

The Olde Towne section of Portsmouth, established in the mid-seventeen hundreds and the scene of significant events that transpired during both the Revolutionary and Civil Wars, had also experienced a deadly epidemic of yellow fever. The medical examiner had established that the remains were too old to have been associated with that event.

Although there were no signs of a family burial plot at this location, once the police and medical examiner's office determined the bones were not the result of a current crime, the construction work resumed.

As word spread of the discovery, crowds gathered for several nights in hopes of witnessing a ghostly event. Teenaged vandals caught up in the temporary frenzy caused yet another set-back to the restoration, extensively damaging the interior and exterior of the building. Chase stepped up to the plate, working his crew overtime, even stepping in to perform labor himself, until they finished the repairs and he announced the inn was ready.

The fear that had consumed Terry the night of her mother's medical emergency surfaced again. Shoving the business file aside, she pulled another folder from the pile on her desk and thumbed through the brochures she'd gathered so she could understand the disease better. Her mother was her best friend, and the thought of losing her brought her close to tears.

She glanced at materials she had already read several times, then closed the file. For the first time she noticed the pink "While You Were Out" slip informing her of a call from Detective Shellito, assigned to investigate the case of the old bones. Becky's neat handwriting asked Terry to return the call. She reached for her phone, only to draw her hand back when she noticed the late hour. Nine-thirty. *Too late to call.* She scribbled on a sticky note to call on Monday and to check on the status of the old bones, and stuck it on the receiver of her desk phone.

When the news media announced the discovery of the bones, the curious flocked to the area. For several days, the sightseers peered past the yellow crime scene tape and the mesh construction fence Chase had used to block access, in hopes of catching a glimpse of zombies or otherworldly beings. Disappointed when no apparitions appeared, the crowds lost interest and eventually stopped coming.

But the ethereal events they eagerly sought mostly manifested within the walls of the old house now named Clothiste's Inn. Both Stephanie and Mary Jo encountered young colonial ghosts begging them to find lost necklaces, but each also had encounters in the attic with an ominous spirit that seemed determined to keep them from finding the jewels.

Terry's stomach emitted an angry growl demanding food. She rose to her feet and patted her midsection.

"I hear you, tummy," she said aloud. She grabbed her purse and keys, turned out the lights, and headed for the back door. She stifled a yawn and arched her aching back. She was ready to head home when she realized the construction on the Churchland Bridge would send her the long way home.

It's late. I wonder if Stephanie will let me crash there for the night.

As if on cue, car doors slammed in the parking lot. Stephanie's infectious laugh drifted through the air, followed by a loud guffaw from Gage. Terry opened the door just in time to see Gage swoop Stephanie into his arms and swing her off her feet. Their laughter reverberated through the air, and he set her down again, pressing her against the side of the car as they wrapped their arms around each other in a passionate embrace. Stephanie laughed again at something he said, grabbed his hand and led him to the stairs out of her line of vision. Every few steps their footfalls stopped, followed by silence that Terry suspected involved a kiss, until they finally reached the top of the stairs.

Terry sighed. *So much for crashing at Stephanie's pad.* Then she smacked herself on the forehead. She had her choice of four beautifully decorated rooms in the B and B.

Decision made, she punched a number on her speed dial.

"Hiya, Antonio. It's Terry. I'd like a margarita pizza with just pineapple on it, crispy crust. For delivery."

"Hi, Terry, not your usual order, I see." The cheerful voice of the Italian chef crackled with laughter. "Tonight you are—how do you say—going rogue? Is that for delivery to your law office?"

"No, send it to the new B and B right next door to the law office. Tell the delivery person to come to the back door. And add a two-liter Pepsi, please."

"Got it. Be there in twenty."

"Make it fifteen and I'll add a huge tip."

"I deliver myself," Antonio laughed. The pizza shop was

right around the corner. "No ghosts are gonna get me, are they?"

"Not tonight, Antonio." They laughed again as they hung up.

In the attic of Clothiste's Inn, a gray mist formed, swirled once, and with a hiss, retreated.

Terry bypassed the B and B and walked straight to the café, rifling through the keys on her keychain until she found the right one to enter the back door. She flicked on the fluorescent lights, illuminating the kitchen in a silvery glow. The pristine kitchen gleamed. Terry walked around to the front of the refrigerated glass case to study the selections left over from the lunch hour. She passed her hand lovingly down the polished wood frame, remembering the heartache Mary Jo endured during the lawsuit.

Then Terry stooped to peer at the contents. "Rats, no *chaussons aux pommes,*" she muttered, pouting. The case contained none of the French apple turnovers that she favored but when her gaze dropped to the next shelf with four mini-éclairs on a doily on a china plate, she smiled in delight. "Aha, these will do." She returned to the other side of the case and slid the door to one side, removed the plate with the pinky-sized éclairs, then reached in for two cream puffs on a lower shelf. She popped one in her mouth, and closed her eyes, savoring the delicate cream dessert as it rolled on her tongue. She scooped up the saucer holding the remaining three puffs, a perfect accessory to the éclairs.

Binge time.

The sudden aroma of fresh-baked bread wafted to her nostrils and she inhaled deeply.

Mary Jo had sometimes smelled warm baked bread when a ghostly image appeared to her. Terry straightened, expecting to see the ghost of Marie Theresé, the young girl who had loved to bake for her family during the American Revolution. Through extensive research efforts initiated by Stephanie, Mary

Jo had learned the colonial girl was her sixth great-grandmother.

Terry spun around, gaze sweeping every corner of the room.

She was the only occupant.

That aroma must have come when I opened the case.

Terry said out loud, "Well, Marie Theresé, if you are here, hello."

Greeted by silence, Terry shrugged and popped another cream puff into her mouth. She wrapped the éclairs and remaining puffs in foil, rinsed the dishes and placed them in the dishwasher. Then she scribbled a note to Mary Jo apologizing for taking the leftovers, and locked up behind her. Her high heels clicked on the walkway as her long legs carried her toward Clothiste's Inn.

Out of habit, Terry touched her neck where her own heirloom pendant usually rested. She remembered then she had left the pendant in the box. She'd retrieve it first thing in the morning.

She missed her pendant!

At the back door, she paused with the key in the lock and her hand on the knob.

What would greet her when she opened it?

The last time she had entered the building, nearly a week earlier, was the night of the sleepover and before she heard the news of her mother's illness. She was carrying a bundle of sleeping bags. As she tried to cram through the doorway leading to the parlor, a blast of frigid air struck her, so cold that her breath formed vapors.

Only when Stephanie followed her into the house a moment later did the room quickly return to normal. They could find no explanation for the dip in the temperature on that occasion or others.

But despite all the lore about good and evil ghosts haunting the building, and the harrowing incidents Stephanie and Mary Jo had experienced, Terry had never experienced a moment of fear in the house. She pushed the door open with a determined flourish, flipped the light switch, and set the foil-wrapped desserts on a counter. Kicking her elegant pumps to the side, she inched toward the dining room, her purse slung over her shoulder with the fingers of her right hand resting on her pepper spray.

Just in case.

Crossing her left hand in front of her, she fumbled along the wall for the light switch. Prisms of light cascaded from the elegant old chandelier and danced on the wall. She passed the stately cherry dining table and hesitated before entering the parlor. She poked her left hand along the wall to flip the light switch before stepping over the threshold.

This time the temperature was perfect. Terry shrugged and moved further into the room, listening for any untoward sound.

Silence echoed, the only real sound coming from her heartbeat hammering in her ears. Her gaze swept across the recently-delivered furniture, observing nothing amiss in the room.

A pair of prim blue and white checkered wing chairs and a Federal blue sofa faced each other in front of the fireplace. Ruffled country curtains Joan had sewn framed the bay window, topping a wooden Venetian shade closed over the glass. She stepped to the window and fingered the ruffle of one tie-back panel, remembering her mother's enthusiasm at creating the frilly trim. Mentally she offered yet another word of thanks for her mother's steady recovery. She didn't know how she would cope if she lost either of her parents.

On the oak mantel above the brick fireplace, Mary Jo had hand-printed "Clothiste's Inn" on a sheet of paper and taped it on the mantel until they decided on the design of a permanent placard. Centered on the mantel, an ornate silver clock stood on four filigreed claw feet. A mother-of-pearl inlay surrounded the dial.

Two polished silver candlesticks bearing slate blue tapers flanked either end, standing like tall and stalwart sentinels.

Terry stared at the candlesticks. Although the room

remained comfortable, a chill washed over her. She studied the candlesticks. After Mary Jo had an encounter with the "evil" ghost in the attic, she'd uncovered a case containing more than a dozen pieces of handcrafted silver from the eighteenth century. Tarnished black and nestled in the old felt-lined crate, the pieces had been forgotten or misplaced for generations. A cryptic message left in the box stated that a great-grandmother wanted the pieces destroyed because the candlesticks frightened her. Someone in the family must have simply hidden the crate instead of destroying its contents.

Although she had not decided whether to leave any valuable heirloom pieces on display once the inn was open to the public, she agreed to use them for staging photos for the brochures.

Her gaze fell to the clock at the same moment three sharp raps at the back door signaled her pizza delivery had arrived. She went back to the kitchen door to find Antonio waiting on the stoop, holding up a pizza box in one hand and a plastic bag with the soda in the other.

"Why, you did deliver, Antonio," she laughed. She greeted the elderly Italian man with a kiss on the cheek as she held the door open for him.

"*Mia cara*, of course, only for you does Antonio deliver in person." He set the flat white box with red-checkered trim and the bag on the counter, the saucy aroma of the pizza filling the room.

"That smells delicious," Terry said as she sniffed appreciatively. "And of course, you are my favorite deliverer." She lifted a hand to rub her lipstick mark from his cheek and he sidestepped her with the agility of a man half his age.

"You must leave my badge of honor, *mia cara.*" Antonio smiled, his eyes twinkling in the glow from the overhead light. "If only I was twenty years younger. I would whisk you back to the old country and make you my wife."

"You are a rascal, Antonio." She reached into her purse and drew bills from her wallet.

"No tip, Terry, you are too good a customer," he

commanded.

"Oh, come on, Antonio, please, you brought this to me." Terry shoved the currency into his hand.

Antonio shrugged, sorted through the bills and returned a ten to Terry before stuffing the rest into his apron pocket. "I walk what? Five hundred feet? No need to tip. But *grazie, bella dona*."

Terry kissed the old man's other cheek. "Let's give them something to talk about, Antonio!" She laughed. "Ciao, *mio amico*."

"Ciao, *bella dona*. Lock this door immediately after I leave. And watch out for the *fantasmi*." Antonio whistled, the warbling shrill sounding more like a spacecraft than a ghost. Terry laughed and shooed him out the door, his tune filling the crisp night air. Then she locked the door behind him.

With a sigh, she leaned against the counter and flipped open the box with two fingers, her appetite suddenly waning. Antonio's harmless flirting had reminded her that she hadn't had a date in weeks, and she missed male companionship.

She bit into a slice, wondering what was wrong with her. It wasn't that she didn't have the opportunity to meet the opposite sex. She had her fair share of men hitting on her, whether she wanted them to or not, whether they were married or not. Considering that the majority of men interested in her seemed to be married—all of whom she sent packing—she had not been involved with anyone for nearly a year.

"What do you expect?" She spoke out loud, plucked a chunk of pineapple from the pizza and enjoyed the tangy taste. "You're the one who wanted to open your own law office. You're the one with no life now, working until nine o'clock every night."

She located a glass from the cabinet, poured soda, and then took a swig.

Not for one minute did she regret taking the chance to partner with her old college roommate Sandi. They met at William and Mary Law School, had become instant friends, and roomed together their final year. After graduation, Terry went to work in an Olde Towne law firm and Sandi in downtown Norfolk.

The ringing of her cell interrupted the reminiscing. It turned out to be a wrong number, but it was enough to break her from her reverie.

CHAPTER 3

Theresé
Near Yorktown, Virginia, August 1781

Theresé clutched at her throat. Anguish roamed over her father's face as James spoke. His voice inaudible to her, he raised his hand to Étienne's shoulder.

Her father clutched the younger man's arm, and with his free hand raked through his hair, unmindful of the rain pelting down.

"Papa!" Fearing the worst, Theresé sloshed through the mud and scrambled to her father's side, her tears mixing with raindrops. "What is it?"

Étienne gathered his eldest daughter close.

"We know not where your mother is," he choked out. "I must go look for her."

"No, Papa, it is too dangerous," Theresé cried.

"She is right, Captain," James added. "We've no idea what happened to Louis after we left Portsmouth. He would not tell me the reason he stayed behind, although I think it would be to cover our association. He only urged me to get away and said he would leave later. If he followed on horseback, he should have caught up with the wagon long before we reached the wharf in Suffolk."

"What could have happened to him?" Theresé asked.

James shook his head. "If he returned to the camp, they may still suspect him once my desertion is uncovered."

"Then I must be the one to go." Theresé said.

Étienne and James both started to speak. Theresé calmly placed a hand on each of the men's forearms.

"I am a girl. They will not look suspiciously at me. And I will go as the granddaughter of Phillip."

"She can do this, Étienne." James nodded. "She is the right person to go. The Brits have probably seen her in the market. Your father's role helping the Americans has never been uncovered, while his wife's loyalty to the crown is undisputed. No one will suspect anything. It will be far less dangerous for her than you."

"Papa, this is the only way," Theresé insisted.

Étienne's shoulders drooped. He hung his head for a moment, clutching his daughter's shoulder.

"I must go, Papa," Theresé repeated, her voice, calm and strong, her small hand covering her father's. A ray of sunlight beamed behind a dark cloud before disappearing.

She drew him toward the tent, where her sisters stood, waiting, fear shining in their eyes.

"I will go. And I will find my mother."

Terry
Portsmouth, Virginia, present day

Appetite gone, Terry placed her half-finished slice in the pizza box and tucked the lid into the bottom. She glanced at the pastries and found she had no desire to unroll the wrapping and taste the sweets. She smacked the foil packet on top of the pizza box with more force than she intended, wincing as the delicate confectionaries squished under her hand.

"Just great," she said aloud, shoving the two items into the refrigerator.

She checked the lock on the back door, grabbed her purse, turned out the kitchen light and headed toward the upstairs bedrooms. When she reached the staircase in the parlor, her gaze swept the pretty room with its colonial décor, and fell on the mantel. She frowned, hand poised on the newel post.

The silver candlesticks stood paired together on the left of the shelf, the clock resting more to the right than the center.

Terry squinted suspiciously and said, "I could have sworn

those candlesticks flanked the clock when I came in." Her voice echoed up the stairway. She stepped away from the post and glared, stood with feet planted apart, arms folded across her chest in defiance. "All right, ghost, show yourself," she demanded. She withdrew the pepper spray, finger on the notch.

Nothing happened. Terry stomped to the fireplace and stared. She moved one candlestick to the far right and centered the clock to its original place on the mantel.

She waited for nearly a minute, hoping to see—or sense—more activity. When no further otherworldly signs appeared, she flipped the light switch and skipped up the stairs, pepper spray at the ready. Her footfalls echoed on the wood treads until she reached the runner covering the hall of the second floor. She flipped on lights as she peered into each of the bedrooms Mary Jo had named for the significant eras that the house represented.

The Colonial, with three light blue walls and one dark slate blue wall against which the canopied bed stood, had quickly become her favorite. A slate wingback chair that her mother found in an Olde Towne antique store graced one corner; a hutch with mirrored dresser anchored the wall opposite the bed. Reflected in the mirror, she could see the door to the small *end suite* bathroom. A pair of spa robes hung from hooks on the wall.

In The Antebellum, elaborate chair railing divided the walls in half, with a lighter green on top and forest green below. Terry secretly called the room "Tara" because it reminded her of rooms in the grand house from *Gone with the Wind*.

Mary Jo had put a great deal of energy into coordinating the room schemes. The very fact that she had selected paint shades, matched prints for curtains and linens had been out of character. To Terry's knowledge, the straight-laced former soldier had always been more content with sporty, outdoorsy or natural surroundings. The woman who once happily wore combat boots now slipped her feet into more dainty footwear and embraced civilian life with gusto.

Terry peered into The Victorian, the largest of the three. Wallpaper design of cream background dotted with tiny mauve roses covered the walls. A dressmaker's dummy stood to the side of an oval cheval mirror. Fancy hats were hooked over the bed posts.

But she elected to bypass all the guest rooms as her crib for the night. These were rooms designed for romantic getaways, cozy places for lovers to share. She didn't want to sleep in any of them alone. She would settle for the innkeeper's suite downstairs.

She turned out lights to each room, and upon reaching The Colonial, the reflection of the fluffy cream-colored spa robes in the mirror caught her eye, reminding her she didn't have anything to sleep in. She snatched a fluffy white housecoat from the hook and gave the room a final glance before she turned out the light and stepped into the hall.

The hair on the back of her neck tickled against her skin. She rubbed her hand over her nape and fluffed out her hair with her left hand. The fingers of her right hand touched the notch on the pepper canister.

"If you're the evil one, you can slither back to your hellhole now," she called over her shoulder and marched down the stairs. She reached toward the light switch and paused.

On second thought...she withdrew her hand and left the light on.

At the bottom of the steps, she glanced toward the mantel and froze in her tracks.

This time the candlesticks stood side-by-side on the right side of the mantel, and the clock teetered near the left edge.

The air shifted, almost imperceptibly, and her head swiveled left to right as she swept her gaze around the room.

"Who are you?"

Warm air brushed her cheek.

"Are you Nicole?" Nicole was Stephanie's ghost, the youngest of the trio of colonial sisters that had made recent appearances. Through her ancestry research, Stephanie had determined that she was a direct descendant of the eighteenth-century girl.

Nothing happened.

Terry asked, "Are you Marie Josephé?" Marie Josephé, the middle daughter who loved to bake and wanted to fight the British soldiers, shared the same qualities as Mary Jo. Not only did the detailed research link Mary Jo to this ancestress, it also introduced her to family she never knew she had.

"Marie Josephé?" Terry repeated.

The room remained still.

Terry swallowed and her voice caught as she tried to name the eldest daughter of the family.

"Are you Theresé?"

The air trembled around Terry, and an invisible fingertip stroked her cheek.

"Can you show yourself to me?"

Nothing.

"Are you the same image I used to see when I was younger?"

The air erupted in wave after wave of unseen movement, ruffling curtains. The cover of a magazine on the coffee table flipped open.

"And are you trying to help me find you?"

The candlesticks rattled on the mantel; hands on the clock turned backwards; pages of the magazine fluttered from cover to cover. Overhead lights dimmed and over-illuminated, emitting a buzz that went from a low drone to a high-pitched hum and then to silence.

"I will find you, Theresé," Terry promised, her voice strong and clear.

"Find my mother." A girlish, metallic-sounding voice resonated through the room. In a somewhat clearer tone, the unseen speaker repeated the plea, "Find my mother," the last word fading in an ethereal sigh.

The candlesticks stilled. The magazine closed. The lights and clock returned to normal.

Terry stood motionless, eyes darting from side to side.

Waiting.

After five minutes of silence and inactivity, Terry gave up waiting for another sign, then debated whether to stay the night in the house following the events.

As a child, she'd had several encounters in this house with a colonial ghost, usually a young girl holding a book. Accepting the events as strange but ordinary, she had never encountered anything that caused her to have fear.

"I'm not afraid in this house," she declared to the empty room. "And I'm not leaving here tonight."

She headed toward the dining room. However, she left the lights burning behind her in the hall and parlor. She followed the path around the dining table, to the short hallway that led to the innkeeper's suite that would be her place for the night.

More functional than the decorated schemes of the guest rooms, the L-shaped suite had a sleeping area to the long side, a small sitting area to the short side, and its own bath.

Terry stripped to her fancy lace undies, slipped into the soft bathrobe, and lay there listening to the silence of the house.

Somehow, she fell asleep.

***

Cold air settled around Terry, and she snuggled further under the bedspread, teeth chattering as she wrapped the soft spa robe tighter. Her nose and fingertips became cold to the touch. The thin cover did little to ease the chill, and waves of shivers rippled through her body. Reluctantly, she eased from the warm spot where her body had curled. Bare feet hit the ice-cold floor and she hustled to the closet to search for extra blankets.

Finding none, she pulled the robe tighter and grabbed her cell. She reached for the doorknob and paused. Jiggling her right hand on the knob while holding her cell, she stretched backwards until the fingertips of her left hand circled the pepper spray on the end table. She stuck the canister in her robe pocket, her fingers still gripping hard.

A fresh blast of cold swirled as she opened the door and peered into the hall. Lights still burned as she had left them. She turned toward the right and followed the carpet runner leading to the kitchen, where she located the thermostat and glared at the dial.

She peered closer. The arrow indicated the temperature control was set at sixty-eight degrees. But the thermometer itself recorded the temperature in the room as forty-five degrees. She tapped the dial with a fingertip, then pushed the on/off switch several times.

An eerie silence surrounded her. A tinny-sounding thump startled her. A louder crash of metal followed from the direction of the parlor.

She stiffened her back and stared in the direction of the sounds, remembering that both Stephanie and Mary Jo had experienced unusual cold just prior to an unnerving encounter with an evil presence in the attic.

An acrid scent drifted to her nostrils, almost a smell of burnt matches mixed with metal. Terry stuck the cell phone in a pocket and withdrew the pepper spray to her left hand, careful to touch her finger to the notch to be sure the spray aimed away from her. She eased a carving knife from the butcher block. The metal blade seemed to screech as she extracted the knife from the slot. Gripping the wooden handle in her right hand, she tiptoed toward the parlor. Her gaze swept across the dining room before she stepped around the table and stretched her neck to peer into the parlor.

Nothing appeared amiss within her line of sight. She eased forward, stopping short at the wooden threshold between the rooms. Cautiously, she poked her head around the frame and glanced into the empty parlor. It was not until she stepped fully into the room that she noticed the changes.

Her ragged breath met the cold air and formed vapory wisps.

Torn shreds of the placard for Clothiste's Inn scattered the floor. On the mantle, one of the highly-polished candlesticks stood in the position she'd last seen it. The other was crammed upside down in the colonial coal hood, an authentic colonial scuttle standing at the base of the fireplace. A tapered candle, broken in half and held together by the wick, lay on the floor.

Flexing her fingers, tense from gripping the dispenser of the pepper spray, Terry bent to retrieve the candle and placed it on the coffee table. She glanced at the once-polished candlestick now upside down in the coal hood. A blue-black tarnish that resembled film from a smoking fire coated the stem from its base to the sconce.

She set the knife on the cushion of the wingback chair closest to her, and stooped to grab the toppled candleholder. She cried out the instant her skin touched the metal. A freezing-burning numbness not unlike touching damp fingers to a metal ice cube tray seared her fingers. The hands of the clock turned backwards, whirring wildly.

The clock hands stopped at three o'clock and chimed thrice, the arrow-shaped hands then continuing their spin backwards. A few seconds later the hands pointed to two o'clock, followed by two clangs.

Immediately, the hands shifted to the one o'clock position. A single echoing bong noted the hour. The room began to whirl around her.

Caught in a vortex, Terry seemed to spin head over heels in tempo with the movement of the clock hands. Her vision changed from color to grainy black and white. The hands on the clock whirled and stopped abruptly, both arrows pointing straight up. The timepiece emitted a series of twelve soulful clangs marking the midnight hour. A lightning flash shattered the darkness. The peals of a church bell took over the clock chime. A crash of thunder obliterated the twelfth toll.

Feeling light as air, she hovered near the ceiling, looking down on a dark passage lit by occasional bursts of lightning.

A woman's translucent shape entered the hallway, giving Terry the impression she'd just entered the film setting of an old silent ghost movie. The woman seemed weak, bracing her arm on the wall as she shuffled to the next room. She held her other arm close to her upper body. She reached the second room and gripped the doorjamb. A thin stream of light illuminated her form as she pushed the door open.

Terry stopped spinning, but she continued to float. Her fingers gripped the candlestick, no longer burning her skin. In fact, she couldn't even feel it in her hand. Unable to change her position to see into the other room, she glanced at the area below her. Lightning bursts provided enough illumination to make out the furnishings.

The scene resembled the upstairs hall of Clothiste's Inn. Similar but different.

The ghostly woman backed into the hall in trepidation. A second, older woman emerged from the room. Both women wore old-fashioned nightclothes. Their mouths moved in soundless argument and their faces twisted in emotion. The younger woman backed across the hall, her back striking the edge of a small table.

A flash of lightning crackled outside of the hall window. The older woman's face distorted as she shouted silently.

The younger woman flung her good arm backwards and steadied herself, brushing a candleholder. She reached behind her and forced the unlit taper to the side. Her fingers closed around the base of the silver stand.

The elder woman stepped closer. The younger used her good arm to swing the candlestick in a wide arc. It grazed the older woman's jaw. Incensed, she lunged forward.

The injured woman grabbed the other's throat with her good hand, her limp arm flailing at her side. They grappled until the older woman, hair spilling from her nightcap, broke free and pounced, knocking the smaller woman into a sitting position on the short hallway table. Her head cracked against the wall as she drew up her knee and thrust her foot into the older woman's stomach. They grappled back and forth, the younger using her good hand to rake her nails across the other's neck. The two women locked in a ruthless embrace, bounced against the wall, spinning back across the hallway to the opposite wall, and into the short banister at the top of the steps.

The silver piece slipped from Terry's grip and fell to the floor. The clatter reached her ears and broke the silence, bringing her back to the present.

The images disappeared, the black-and-white tones reverted to color, and the room brightened to normal light.

Terry whirled and spun to a stop in front of the fireplace. At her feet, the candlestick bounced three times in slow motion before coming to rest against a chair leg. Her hand burned, and she rubbed it along the robe. She glanced down, expecting to see marks where the silver had contacted her skin.

Her palm was clear, although it tingled.

With the exception of the candleholder on the floor and the ripped pieces of the placard, the room appeared as she first saw it.

Until the mirror over the fireplace quivered, first tapping, then knocking against the wall. The glass fogged with a dull gray mist.

Unseen fingers traced letters through the film. Terry stood transfixed, watching as each letter formed.

DIE FRENCH WHORE

Before Terry could react, the letters smeared in the way an eraser wipes a blackboard clean. New words appeared.

FIND MY MOTHER

The lights in the chandelier flickered. The sickening smell of dirty silver permeated the air and a stream of air brushed the back of her neck. She snatched the carving knife from the chair and whirled around on her heels, weapon and spray at the ready.

Her heart exploded, pounding a frantic rhythm through her ears at the sight of a trail of dirty mist gliding down the staircase, tentacles slithering through the rungs of the banister. The streaks gathered together and slid toward her.

Terry's jaw dropped and a gasp eked out before her throat

locked. She stood pinned in fear as the filmy mass slithered forward. She backed into the fireplace and her shoulder struck the mantel. She had no more room to move as the mist inched toward her feet.

Bric-a-brac around the parlor rattled as figurines danced on shelves and dishes clattered on tabletops. The chandelier dimmed and brightened.

Terry did what she should have done from the start. Tossing the knife on a chair, she leapt over the coffee table and beat bare feet to Stephanie's apartment door.

In Terry's office beneath the apartment, the slim jewelry box rattled on the desk. The cover bounced off, emanating a shine that lit the room. The necklace shimmied in the cotton lining, vibrating with a low hum. The blue sapphire stone radiated electric blue arcs as bright as lightning bolts.

The vapor whirling in Clothiste's Inn stopped in its tracks, and as if inhaled by a powerful vacuum, slid backwards up the stairs.

CHAPTER 4

Louis
Portsmouth, Virginia, August 1781

"Don't talk, Mother."

"She tried…to kill…Phillip," Clothiste whispered, voice breaking between gasps of breath. Tears trickled from her half-opened eyes, sliding along her temples to the floor.

Her jaw slackened. A gurgle rattled deep in her throat before the life ebbed from her body.

Louis gathered his mother's lifeless form, muffling sobs against her neck.

Low groans reached his ears. He glanced up the dark staircase. He could make out a form at the top of the steps.

"Who is down there? Help me."

He gently lowered his mother's shoulders to the floor. Her blood smeared his right hand, obscuring the emerald of the gold ring on his pinkie finger.

"Who is there?" The raspy voice strengthened.

"British soldier." Louis brushed his mother's cheek with his clean hand and stood up. He held the lantern higher and began a deliberate ascent up the stairway.

Abigail was sprawled on the top steps. Her head rested on the floor, her body aiming downward. One leg stretched before her. The other twisted at an odd angle, the heel almost reaching her hip.

Louis moved closer and shined the light.

"Never mind the whore at the bottom of the steps." Abigail gasped. "Do you know who I am?" She shifted and screamed in pain. "Do your *duty.*"

Louis stepped, careful not to touch Abigail's twisted limbs. He knelt beside her and moved the lantern close to his face.

"Do you know who I am?" he asked.

A trickle of blood seeped from a cut on Abigail's chin. In spite of the pain etched in her face, she glared insolently at Louis. "You were here the night my husband was shot."

"That is true. But do you *know* who I am?"

Abigail met his gaze with a sneer of contempt on her face.

Louis leaned closer and whispered, "I am Phillip's grandson. And the woman you call a whore is my mother."

He pressed his bloodied thumb and fingers to either side of her windpipe.

Her eyes widened in understanding as he pressed harder, harder.

***

The clock struck one. The storm had long since subsided, but rain still dripped from Louis's uniform sleeves, forming small puddles.

He stared into the lifeless eyes of his step-grandmother, the angle of the lantern light casting her face in jagged shadows. He felt no emotion, no regret, no guilt. He raised the lamp to shoulder level and glanced at the blood smeared across the knuckles of the hand that had once again killed another human.

But those other times had been in acts of war—this time it was an act of vengeance.

This blood did not come from the miserable figure slumped on the stairs, but from the woman at the very bottom. His beautiful mother Clothiste lay dead from an apparent scuffle with the woman she'd often referred to as the "Wicked One."

Louis knew the harsh life of an army camp follower had finally taken its toll on his mother. His father, Étienne de la Rocher, was a captain in the French army, serving with Rochambeau as Washington's army moved toward Yorktown. When Clothiste became extremely ill, Étienne had sent her to his father's house in Portsmouth. Abigail resented the presence of Clothiste and her three young daughters, forcing the two oldest to act as

37

servants in her home. When it was determined that Abigail had tried to poison her daughter-in-law, Phillip had arranged to get his family spirited away to safety.

Clothiste's ill health became further exacerbated by injuries received when rogue British soldiers shot her and her father-in-law, Louis's grandfather. There had been an attack which Louis suspected had been intended to flush out spies for the Americans. His grandfather was French-born but Anglicized by his British second wife. Because she held strong ties to the Crown and he was a respected businessman, Phillip had been able to maintain a strong cover as he aided the patriot army.

Phillip's network of contacts had warned him that some within the British army had raised questions about his household. On the night he had arranged for Clothiste and her daughters to depart, the unprovoked attack occurred.

Louis stood, cold gaze drifting to the form sprawled in its grotesque position. As he stepped over her body, his face contorted in contempt for the woman who had been so cruel to his mother.

Louis swept the light in an arc in the first bedroom, where his mother had once slept.

As he turned to his grandfather's room, he kicked a metal object. A silver candlestick rolled in an arc until it rested against a hall table with small knickknacks scattered across the top.

When he entered the second bedroom, his heart nearly exploded from fear. He rushed to his grandfather's side. The shaft of light from the lantern created shadows on the old man's face. The once robust and handsome man lay on his stomach, head turned to one side. Ashen flesh covered sunken cheeks framed by wispy clumps of his white mane of hair.

"Grandfather?" Louis dropped to one knee and shined the light closer. During the attack by British soldiers, one bullet had struck the older man in the lower back, another tore through his mother's shoulder. Louis killed both soldiers, and with the help of his friend James, managed to render medical assistance that had saved the lives of his family members. Shortly after the incident, Abigail and her maid Lizzie arrived from a trip and he was summarily dismissed from the house.

Lizzie had secretly kept him informed of their progress. Through her, Louis had learned that the doctors did not think Phillip would walk again.

He swallowed a lump in his throat. In a hoarse whisper, he said, "Grandfather?"

His grandfather did not respond, but the shallow lift of his shoulder signaled he was alive. Relieved, Louis repeated a little louder, "Grandfather?"

Phillip Roker, born Phillipe de la Rocher, groaned and shifted his face on the sheet. His eyes fluttered open and shut several times before he focused on his grandson.

"Louis?" Phillip's feeble voice wheezed and rumbled low in his chest like the dying note of a bagpipe, his lips so parched that tiny drops of blood seeped through the cracks. He tried to speak louder. "What-what are you…" He sighed, exhausted from the effort.

"Grandfather, something happened. Mother and Abigail must have fought each other. I found Mother at the bottom of the stairs, and Abigail at the top. Things are knocked over in the hall."

"I thought—I was—dreaming," Phillip whispered, his voice hitching in small gasps. "I heard—heard noise and shouting." He tried to lick his parched lips. Louis stretched his arm to grab the water pitcher.

Phillip's voice growled. "No, stop. I-I think it's—I think I've been drugged."

Louis said, "I will get water from Abigail's bedroom. That should be safe."

Phillip closed his eyes. As Louis rushed to the third bedroom the dull thud of his footsteps resounded in the hall. The lantern swayed against his arm with each rapid step, casting moving shadows on the walls. He steadied the lamp and then snatched the water pitcher from a table in Abigail's room.

Back in his grandfather's room, he stopped in his approach to the bedside and stared with concern at the motionless form.

"Grandfather?" The older man remained still.

If not for the trace of movement from the slow rise and fall of the bedcover, Louis would have thought his grandfather had died. But with sudden energy, the older man's eyes flew open and he struggled to speak. "Tell me what happened."

Louis relayed the story in rapid French. He paused when the older man's eyes closed, continuing only when Phillip regained strength and told him to continue.

39

The tolling of the half-hour shattered the silence.

Phillip remained still for several seconds. Then his eyelids flew up. In English, he said, "Here is what you must do."

Terry
Portsmouth, Virginia, present day

"Are you crazy?" Stephanie shrieked. "What were you thinking, staying there all by yourself?"

"No lectures," Terry warned. She was still out of breath from running up the stairs, shouting and banging on the door until a wide-eyed Stephanie and Gage appeared. In between gasps caused by cold and anxiety, Terry had blurted out a rapid description of the two situations that occurred, omitting the flashback revealing the fight between the women.

"I didn't go there looking for trouble, you know. I worked late and didn't feel like driving home. I didn't expect to run into ghosts." she added in an edgy tone.

"Well, why didn't you just come here?" Gage asked.

Terry shot her brother a withering look. "The way you two were entwined when you got home, I'm surprised you made it to the door before you—you know." Terry shrugged. "I thought you might do it right there on the steps."

Stephanie blushed and averted her eyes, grabbing Terry by the arm and drawing her into the foyer. "You're freezing. And you're barefoot! You really are crazy, woman." Her last phrase held more affection than annoyance.

Gage tightened his jaw and narrowed his eyes at his sister. "You two stay here, I'll go have a look and lock the place up."

"Like hell you will." Terry blocked the doorway. "I don't need you to charge in like a, like a…Ghostbuster or something."

"Oh, don't you two start squabbling like siblings," Stephanie scolded, failing to suppress a giggle that took the edge off her words. She grabbed a jacket from the hook behind the door, and tossed it to Gage before snatching her own. She said matter-of-factly, "Let's just all go check the place. But,

Terry, put these slippers on your feet, please." She plucked a pair from beside the couch and held them out.

"Thanks." Terry shoved her cold bare feet into the warmth of a pair of black slippers, wriggling relieved toes against the plush sheepskin lining. Then she jerked the door open and stepped onto the landing. Gage grabbed a heavy industrial-strength flashlight from a charging dock and the trio scuttled single file down the stairs.

On entering Clothiste's Inn, they found the kitchen awash in the lights Terry had left burning, the shiny surfaces casting a cozy reflection around the room. The temperature was comfortably warm, overtaking the chilled air seeping in from outdoors.

Once inside the kitchen, Gage none-too-gently elbowed his way past his sister and fiancée and stepped toward the parlor. Rolling her eyes skyward, Terry followed, with Stephanie in the rear. Nearly a half foot shorter than the siblings, she stretched on tiptoes to peer around their shoulders.

The parlor emitted the same welcoming glow as the kitchen. The polished silver of the candlesticks reflected the prisms twinkling from the chandelier light. Each holder bore undamaged candles, standing in their sentry posts at opposite ends, with the timepiece centered perfectly between them.

Only the tatters of the torn sign gave evidence to anything out of place.

Stephanie gasped and pointed to the carving knife still resting on the chair cushion.

Taking one long stride, Terry scooped the knife up by the handle, drawing a sheepish smile across her face. "I did that. I grabbed that in case I encountered a living person."

"What did you do, put it in the chair in the hopes a burglar would sit on it?" Gage asked.

"Oh, shut up," Terry snapped. Catching sight of Gage's scowl, she was glad she'd refrained from revealing the flashback scene, only describing the flickering lights, crazy clock, and the mist seeping in.

Stephanie stepped between brother and sister, too short to

41

block the steely glare each gave the other. Jaw firm, she said, "Tell us again exactly where you were and what happened."

Terry repeated her accounting of the first incident, pointing around the room as she described the displaced objects and the unearthly voice begging her to "Find my mother."

Then she detailed the second event, wrapping her arms around herself and shivering to simulate waking up in the cold. One again, she described how she had entered the parlor to find the sign torn to shreds, and the items rearranged on the mantle. She simulated gripping the candlestick and reacting to the ice-cold burning sensation to her hand.

"After that, the clock went crazy, hands whirling around. Lights flickered. The mirror banged against the wall, and writing appeared on the vapor covering the glass. Then that dirty white mist slithered down the steps. I swear it twirled into tentacles that were spreading toward me." She shivered.

"Did you get that metallic smell?" Although Stephanie had encountered the mist, she had not experienced the smell others had reported during an event.

"Yes, and it stunk, like a mix of old metal and burned matches. Now I know what Tanner meant when he had that one encounter with the mist and said it 'stink-ded.'" Terry yawned and smothered a small giggle. Tanner, her four-year-old nephew, had seen the young girls' ghosts on several occasions, and took their appearances nonchalantly, often referring to his friend "Nickel." The family thought he had simply created an imaginary playmate but soon came to realize she was Nicole, the spirit of the youngest of the colonial sisters believed to haunt the houses. Once Stephanie appeared on the scene, Nicole communicated with Tanner mentally and he had relayed the messages to Stephanie.

Later, Tanner's presence enabled the spirit of the middle sister, Marie Josephé, to appear to Mary Jo. This specter communicated mental messages directly to the modern woman.

As a child, Terry had often seen the oldest girl, dressed in colonial garb and carrying a book, but the specter always appeared from a distance and never spoke to her. Until tonight, she had never had an ethereal encounter as an adult.

"I felt the presence of a spirit tonight," Terry said. "The good spirit. A lot of things happened—the clock going backwards, the candle burning my hand…" She glanced down at her unmarked palm, and continued. "It reminded me of the encounters Steph and Mary Jo had after Tanner introduced the spirits. Hey…I just thought of something else. Somehow Tanner's the conduit that helps these restless souls contact us. I don't think this spirit will be able to materialize to me unless it's through him."

"Listen, that's enough of this woo-woo crap," Gage said, rolling his eyes skyward. "I'm gonna look around upstairs, then take my girl home and try to salvage what I can of my sleep." He stomped toward the stairs.

Although the subject of haunted houses often arose in the Dunbar family history, Gage had been a skeptic until little Nicole had appeared to him. Despite that one time, though, he avoided any discussions of otherworldly beings.

"They won't come back tonight," Stephanie said with conviction. She followed her fiancé up the stairwell, Terry on her heels. "I don't know why, but I just feel the—the good ghost and the evil one—they've exhausted their energy."

"I agree." Gage's abrupt tone indicated he agreed only to end the conversation as he stepped into the first of the three bedrooms.

Terry used the opportunity to grab Stephanie's jacket and pulled her back a few steps. She whispered, "Steph, we've got to talk as soon as we can. There's more to the story than what I told you."

Stephanie nodded. Terry stopped talking as Gage came to the door, turned out the lights of The Colonial room and exited.

"Hell, no wonder the ghosts are restless, every damn light in the house is on," he grumbled as he passed them.

"All the better to see them, brother dear," Terry shot back. She and her brother exchanged withering smirks before he disappeared into The Antebellum.

"Wow, I've never seen him so grouchy," Stephanie said, frowning. She kept her voice low. "As soon as he falls asleep, I'll meet you in your room and we can talk. I'm assuming you *are* coming to the apartment for the rest of the night?"

"You better believe it," Terry answered back, straightening knickknacks on a small table between the bedrooms. "I've had enough mayhem for one night."

Gage declared the final bedroom clear and flipped the light switch. Terry led the trio downstairs, and Gage flipped another light switch to off as he reached the bottom step. When he stepped into the living room to turn off the chandelier, he said, "I'll get Chase to check the electric hookups, make sure it's all safe and working properly."

"He'll punch you in the nose if you are questioning the quality of his work," Terry remarked.

"I'm not questioning it," he shot back, irritation in his voice. "But you said they flickered and dimmed. Better safe than sorry."

"You're right." Her brother's concern rose from his experience as a firefighter rather than workmanship. "I'll get my clothes," she called over her shoulder. She went into the bedroom and scooped her belongings into a pile. She fluffed the coverlet over the bed and turned out the light.

Reaching the doorway, she glanced over her shoulder.

Warm air brushed her cheek.

Terry nodded to the empty room and closed the door.

CHAPTER 5

"That can*not* be construction on a Saturday." Terry growled and burrowed deeper into the plush pillows to block the rhythm of banging hammers and the buzz of an electric saw. She and Stephanie had stayed up until five thirty, sipping tea and trying to make sense out of the encounters Terry had experienced. She was a night owl, and staying up until the crack of dawn never bothered her. *Waking* at the crack of dawn was another matter.

The incessant beating broke through her subconscious and she grabbed her cell phone to peer at the time.

"Ten o'clock!" Terry thrust the covers aside and scrambled to her feet. She didn't like mornings, but neither did she like sleeping the day away.

She threw open the doors to the closet. Empty hangers swayed. The only clothes she had available were the blouse and suit she'd worn to work, or the t-shirt and yoga pants she had borrowed from Stephanie. The sports outfit would have been fine if she had sneakers with her, but all she had were the furry bedroom slippers Stephanie had lent her, or her gray and white pumps. Neither slippers nor the pumps would work with the yoga pants, so she would have to wear her suit and heels. After dressing, she rummaged through her purse until she found her comb, and raked it through her tousled mane.

At one time, the apartment had been hers and everything she needed was at hand. When she had inherited the old house from her great-aunt Ida, she'd renovated the downstairs to house her law firm. She'd had the upstairs converted into a comfortable two-bedroom, two-bath apartment with the intent of living in it permanently. After a short period of time, she found that living a few feet away from her place of work meant she stayed too often and too late at her desk. A Navy couple had rented it until they were transferred to San Diego.

While the apartment was unoccupied, she or Gage sometimes stayed in it overnight, when they worked late hours. It was a long drive to their homes in the Driver area of Suffolk, where she lived in her parent's garage apartment, and Gage a house he was renovating. She had been about to advertise for new tenants when Stephanie agreed to rent the apartment on a short-term lease so she could continue her ancestry research.

Terry leaned toward the mirror to brush her cheeks with a stroke of blush. She reached for lipstick. The air around her rippled. She jumped at the sensation of a finger stroking her cheek. Without turning her head, she used the mirror to shift her gaze around the room.

She remained alone.

"It's just your imagination," she declared out loud, her glance still searching around her reflection. "You're thinking of Stephanie's encounters with the ghosts."

During the height of Hurricane Abby, Stephanie had uncovered secrets hidden in the old house, including a teardrop diamond necklace hidden in an antique colonial doll's dress. She found letters that indicated a family member had found the doll during the Civil War and hidden it with other family heirlooms when Union soldiers occupied the house. Painstakingly matching records with Kyle's help, Stephanie confirmed her long ancestry back to Nicole, the daughter of a French Army captain and a French-Canadian woman from Acadia.

Terry's mother Joan, already fascinated with family history, hired Kyle to research her family tree. He'd next uncovered Mary Jo's uncanny connection to the Dunbar family and traced her roots directly back to Nicole's sister Marie Josephé. And while he could trace Joan's family to the Civil War era, he had been unable to determine the possibility that Terry could be a descendant of the oldest sister, Therese.

If they confirmed that connection, it would not only tie the three modern day women to the colonial sisters—it would create a familial bond between them as well.

She paused and stared at her reflection in the mirror. *Pretty overdressed for a Saturday morning, Dunbar.*

Terry wished she had more interest in her family history, but there was too much going on in her current life to think about the past. She was pretty sure she could be persuaded if the researcher wanted to indoctrinate her.

Although she'd had quite a bit of contact with him in recent weeks and found him incredibly attractive, the scholarly Professor Avery had not looked her way—*that* way she wanted—even once. Her heart fluttered in her chest as the face that so resembled the movie character Indiana Jones flashed in her mind.

Good grief, I've got a crush on him.

She forced the lanky but sexy researcher's image out of her mind. She was thirty-one years old, for crying out loud. Too old for school-girl crushes.

Terry raked the comb one more time through the last of her tangles, wishing she had her hairbrush to do the job.

When she licked her dry lips, she wished for her toothbrush as well.

"You really ought to leave an overnight bag here if you are going to be sleeping in Olde Towne," she grumbled out loud. She gathered the housecoat from the B and B and draped it over the foot of the bed, making a mental note to bribe Stephanie to wash it for her before returning it to the inn.

She laughed. The last time she'd bribed Stephanie to complete a task, it had cost her the price of a pair of three hundred dollar shoes like the pair she slipped her feet into now.

A quick glance down the hall revealed the master bedroom door open and the bed made.

"Stephanie?" Terry called. Walking to the kitchen, her gaze dropped to a note propped on the small dining table. The note simply stated, "At the café. Steph."

Pâtisseries a la Carte. was a combination bistro and pastry shop, a dream finally come to fruition for Mary Jo. In the morning she served a variety of coffees and pastries. For lunch the menu featured soups, salads, and sandwiches

Terry closed and locked the door behind her, heels clacking down the newly-replaced staircase. She headed straight for the café. Her favorite meals were any she could avoid cooking.

In the rear parking lot, she found the source of the construction noise. Chase Hallmark, their long-time family friend, operated a jigsaw while Gage nailed picket strips to a brace. A gangly teenage boy bent over a workbench, carefully tracing a pattern onto either end of a two by four board. Then he measured from end to end and drew a line down the center of the board. He set the board on a stack near Chase, who was in the process of cutting another board. In a few seconds he cut out the designs at both ends, ran the sawblade dead center, and then tossed the two pieces toward Gage, at whose feet a pile of cut boards nestled. The boy went back to the workbench and pulled another two by four from the pile stacked by his bench.

"Good morning, fellas," Terry called as she stopped to admire the new fence taking shape.

Gage glared at his sister. "Morning, Sleeping Beauty. Glad someone had all day to sleep in." Brotherly sarcasm dripped in the words but Terry forgave him. The normally good-natured firefighter often worked for Chase part-time, but this day he looked particularly grumpy because of the ghost's nocturnal visit.

"Ooh, I tink somebody's still kwanky this morning," she replied in a Tweety Bird voice. Her brother ignored her with a particularly sharp rap of his hammer. She pinched his cheek and waved to Chase.

"We'll have the fence done today, Terry," the latter called before he turned back to the wooden plank to repeat the cuts.

"Thank you, Chase." Trees felled by Hurricane Abby had demolished the old picket fences around the house. Terry and her business partners decided it would be nice to extend the charming look around all three buildings of their complex.

Terry stopped beside the young boy and asked, "Hey, Kevin, what are you doing here? I thought you'd finished all your restitutions."

"Yes, ma'am, I've repaid everything. I'm earning some extra spending money now." Shortly after the work crew had discovered the skeletal remains, Kevin Clarkson, along with two other teenage boys, embarked on a vandalism spree in the Inn, throwing paint cans into walls, writing graffiti, and other mischief. Chase had caught the boys in the act, grabbing hold of Kevin as the other two had escaped.

Once all three culprits were identified, Terry and Mary Jo, as co-owners, and Chase, arranged a meeting with the boys and their parents. They decided not to press charges if the boys worked off the cost of the repairs.

Long after he'd made restitution, Kevin kept coming back, asking to do small chores. He had found a talent in wood working. He held up a board bearing lines he had measured. "I'm just doing odd jobs now so I can learn things until I am old enough to work for real. Mr. Chase won't let me handle the saws yet, but I'm gonna work with him next summer."

"I see. Is he paying you?" Terry asked.

"Yeah, I'm getting four bucks an hour," Kevin said proudly.

"Hmm. You got a dollar on you now?"

"Sure." Kevin reached a hand into a back pocket and pulled out a grimy dollar bill. Terry took it between her manicured fingertips.

"You've just paid me a retainer. You're my client now. Tell Mr. Chase if he doesn't pay you minimum wage, I'm taking him to court."

"Really? Cool. Hey, Mr. Chase…" Kevin called out.

"Yeah, yeah, I heard her," Chase interrupted. "When you turn sixteen next spring, I'll give you minimum wage. But for now, you get minion wage and it's four bucks an hour, like we agreed. Now get to work."

Terry winked and gave the dollar back to Kevin. "Settled out of court."

"Hey, Miss Terry," Kevin stepped away from his workbench and lowered his voice. "My court case for the petit larceny is coming up next week and I'm scared shitless. Sorry." A flush crept over his face at the slip of profanity, followed by a look of worry. "Is the judge gonna send me to jail?"

Terry didn't answer right away. Prior to the vandalism, Kevin had been caught shoplifting, and his father Jeffrey had retained Terry's partner to represent Kevin in court. Terry knew that the petit larceny charge was Kevin's first real offense, but figured it wouldn't hurt for him to worry a bit.

"Well, juveniles convicted of serious crimes aren't sent to jail, but to the detention center." Terry leaned toward Kevin, face serious. She looked into Kevin's eyes. He squirmed as she drew out the pause. Tears welled as he raised his gaze to hers. "The judge can be kind of tough because he wants kids to stay out of the detention center. He'll take into consideration that this is your first offense—that you were caught at, anyway."

Kevin dropped his gaze to his foot, his hand shaking. "I wish you were going to court with me."

Deciding he was sufficiently worried, she put her hand on his shoulder. "Ms. Cross will handle your case and you'll be just fine. You don't have a record, and other than the little stunt in my building, you haven't been in trouble. Although we don't necessarily want the judge to know about that, you've handled your restitution like a man. She'll be able to present a good argument for keeping you out of the hoosegow."

"The what?"

"Old-fashioned word for jail." She laughed and ruffled his hair. "Now get back to mending my fence."

"Yes, ma'am!" Considerably cheered, Kevin strode back to his bench.

"I've just given my client a crash course in fair labor standards, Chase," she called.

"Later, Terry," Chase called, waving her aside. His tone was good-natured, however, and she laughed as she walked away, heels clicking in time to the ping of hammers.

Then she remembered her necklace and turned in an about-face toward the rear entrance to her office. She called to Kevin as she passed back by him. "By the way, when's your birthday, Kevin?"

"April third, ma'am."

"You come see me if you don't get that raise," she said, winking.

"Woman, will you go away?" Chase said, picking up a board. "We men got work to do, right, Kevin?"

"Yeah." Kevin's spine straightened at being included with his two mentors. But he looked over his shoulder at Terry and with a grin, gave her a thumbs up.

Terry chuckled as she fished for her keys. Years earlier, Chase and Gage, along with Kevin's father Jeffrey, had gone on a similar vandalism spree. Jeffery's parents sided with their son when he denied involvement, and neither Chase nor Gage would rat him out. To make restitution, Charles Dunbar put the two boys to work all that summer.

Under his tutelage, Chase learned he had a knack for woodworking and developed skills that he turned into a flourishing home construction business in his adult life.

Terry passed through the kitchen and headed to her office. She strode to the desk, intending to retrieve the box and take it to the café.

Instead, she plopped into her chair and looked at the small white box. Frowning, she picked up the cover resting about two inches away from the base.

Didn't she replace the lid last night?

She fiddled with the cover. A vision flashed in her memory, of a young girl dressed in colonial clothes and carrying a book. During weekly visits to her great-aunt Ida's house, Terry occasionally encountered the ghostly form, sad and silent. Sometimes a tear shimmered on the translucent face. The apparition never spoke or moved, just faded in and out.

After the first occurrence, maybe when she was nine or ten, Terry told her brothers about the appearances. They teased her mercilessly and she finally stopped telling them. For a long period, Terry had no further sightings and forgot about the ghost.

Then, just before her sixteenth birthday, the ghost appeared on several occasions. In one instance, her nearly-solid form had stared down at Terry from the window of Great-Aunt Ida's house.

On another occasion, the translucent figure materialized near the old magnolia tree.

Terry leaned back in her chair and rocked with her eyes closed, the mental image of the beautiful old magnolia appearing in her mind. She and her brothers, along with Mary Jo and Chase, often hung around in the cool cave formed by the big leaves and massive branches. Protected from the sun and heat, the space under the tree was cool and bare. Sturdy lower branches formed benches big enough for Terry and the others to sit on. They played cards and discussed the teenage topics of the day.

On one particularly hot day, Terry had gone to the kitchen to refill a pitcher of lemonade. As she returned toward the group, the image of a young girl appeared in her path. The girl looked like she was sitting, but no chair existed. She held an open book on her lap and a quill pen in her hand. As Terry approached, the image faded away into tiny blue sparkles, like sapphire butterflies scattering in the wind.

An incident she never mentioned as she brought the lemonade to the group.

The memory of the sparkles brought her back to the present, her gaze falling to the box.

And she stared.

Were her eyes playing tricks on her or did she just see a smattering of the blue sparkles?

She shook her head. This was getting to be too much.

She removed the necklace from the box and held it up to the light, turning it so that it caught the facets of the dark blue stone and the gold of the cross. She loved that the jeweler had returned the cross to its simpler form.

A growl from her stomach reminded her she had not really eaten much the night before. She unclasped the chain hook and draped the pendant over her neck. The metal warmed her skin, a sensation she'd learned to accept.

This time, a little jolt of electricity prickled along her skin and gave her a start, as if the necklace was trying to tell her something.

She truly hoped she wasn't under some sort of trance. She glanced around the room, glad no one was there to see her. Surely, she'd be disbarred as a stark raving lunatic if anyone knew what thoughts had just crossed her mind.

Terry's gaze drifted to a file for an accident case she had coming up the following Thursday. She reached for the manila folder covered with scrawled notes written in various colored ink. Paper clips held notes at the top and on the right side.

She didn't expect the case to go to court. Her client had been rear-ended by a businessman texting his office, pushing the innocent driver into another vehicle in front. The insurance company had low-balled their offers, claiming the other driver had stopped intentionally. The accident, captured on an uninvolved driver's dashboard camera, showed the businessman was in the wrong.

She sighed. *If only every case could be as clear-cut.*

When her stomach growled again, this time with more insistence, Terry patted her stomach. "I hear you already," she said aloud as she pushed the file aside and got up. Work could wait until Monday.

The parking lot was empty as she exited the building, but the echo of hammers told her the crew was now in the front yard.

She paused at the rear entrance to the Bed and Breakfast, the events from the night before crowding her head.

Curiosity overruled hunger as she selected the key. Although the experience had unnerved her, she could not resist the temptation to look inside.

Strange events had never alarmed her. Even as a young girl, she'd accepted the ghostly appearances pragmatically.

Today, however, she entered on alert. Her eyes darted from side to side as her gaze swept the room. Comfortable room temperatures greeted her. She walked through the kitchen, past the dining room, and stood in the parlor facing the fireplace.

The room showed no signs of the phenomena of the night before. The mirror's glass sparkled, the polished candlesticks gleamed. The clock displayed the time accurately down to the minute. She drifted around the room, standing in different spots, tilting her head to study the silver holders, finally walking to the mantle. She stretched her fingers toward the base of the candlestick, pausing and flexing twice before pushing her hand forward and snatching the metal stand from the fireplace.

The temperature of the ornate silver remained normal in her palm. Silence surrounded her, broken by the occasional voice of the men working outside.

She glanced toward the empty staircase on the opposite side of the room. Sunlight poured in through the trio of small window panes in the front door, dust mites dancing in the beams.

Warm air brushed her cheek.

"Theresé?"

The warmth fluttered again.

"I'll find her, Theresé," she promised. She set the candlestick back in place. After a final glance, she exited the inn through the same door she had entered and walked toward the café.

On the mantle, the candlestick opposite the one Terry had touched darkened with angry tarnish, as if a storm cloud had floated in front of the sun and drained the sky of color.

Then the sheen returned.

CHAPTER 6

Terry finally entered *Pâtisseries a la Carte* through the back door to find the kitchen bustling with more activity than usual. A rumble of chattering voices resonated from the dining area in tune with the musical clank of dishes and silverware.

Standing sentry at the oven stood Hannah Jensen, her mother's diminutive but cantankerous cousin. At the ping of the timer, Hannah wasted no time unloading a tray of miniature tarts with one hand wrapped in a dishtowel as she shoved another tray in its place. She slammed the oven door shut and plopped the hot tray on the counter.

Barely five feet tall, Hannah sported spiked gray hair crowning her leathery tanned face. She had an unlit cigarette tucked behind her ear. Partial to vivid colors and t-shirts with snarky slogans, her neon pink tee today boldly proclaimed, "I ain't the Hulk but you still won't like me when I'm angry." She wore purple sandals with rainbow-colored socks.

"Good morning, Hannah," Terry said, kissing the top of the older woman's head.

"You too." Hannah rasped. She snapped the cigarette from her ear and headed for the back door. The woman refused to give up the habit, although she had slowed down considerably since she'd been reunited with the newborn son she'd given up for adoption years earlier.

Mary Jo bustled into the kitchen and carried dirty dishes to the sink. "Where did Grandma go?" she asked, inclining her head toward the tray of tarts and inhaling the aroma.

"Just stepped out to the smoking deck," Terry answered.

She still was not used to hearing Mary Jo call Hannah "Grandma." Although the two girls had been friends since first grade, Mary Jo had later lived with the Dunbar family as a foster child during her teen years. The family had only recently learned the astonishing news that Mary Jo was the daughter of the son Hannah had given up for adoption.

"Right under my very nose," Hannah had become fond of saying, always followed by a raucous laugh. A foot shorter than Mary Jo, she would then add in her raspy voice, "Or I should say, under Mary Jo's nose." From the age of twelve, Mary Jo had stood a foot taller than the little gnome of a woman.

"You seem able to say 'grandma' much easier these days," Terry commented.

Mary Jo nodded and rinsed the dishes before stacking them in the dishwasher. "It's becoming more natural." She washed and dried her hands, snapped on plastic gloves, and stepped to the food prep area where she glanced at order forms.

"The place is crowded." Terry plucked a miniature tart from the tray. "What's going on?"

"There was a charity golf tournament this morning. Some of the guys stopped by afterwards and they're making my cash register sing. Mary Jo laughed. She scooped chicken salad onto a plate, and arranged fresh fruit on the side. "Do you like that tart? We've been dabbling with some sugar-free recipes ever since your mom had that diabetic incident. We thought it would be good to add something sugar-free to the menu."

"You can't tell the difference. It's good."

Stephanie and Beth brought more dishes to the sink.

"You okay this morning, Terry?" Stephanie asked. "We got done talking so late, I hated to disturb you."

"Yeah, I'm fine. I slept pretty well. Did you tell them about last night?" Terry inclined her head toward Mary Jo and Beth.

"I did. I also checked Clothiste's Inn before I came over here, and everything was fine."

"I did too. Same."

"And we had our first inquiries about reservations for Clothiste's Inn." Stephanie said. "There's a naval officer…did he say he was a doctor? Anyway, he and his girlfriend are out front, and they were looking at the brochures." She lowered her voice and added in a conspiratorial tone, "By the way, Kyle is out there too."

"Really?" Terry feigned disinterest as she popped a second strawberry tart into her mouth, but she couldn't prevent her glance from darting toward the opening leading to the seating area.

"I think I'll go say hello to our Navy guy. I'm going to pick up his tab," Terry said, trying to keep her tone casual. "Can I get a chicken salad on croissant when things slow down?" Terry scooted past her friends and walked toward the French doors leading to the dining room.

Four men in colorful golf shirts sat at one of the larger tables, and she recognized fellow attorneys from other law firms. At two other tables, similarly dressed men and women chatted. Before she could sweep her gaze around the room to locate Kyle, one of the golfers shouted out her name and she walked in that direction. She managed a glance toward the bay window where two tables nestled in the space. A young naval officer and a woman sat at one ice cream parlor set, Kyle the other. He had an array of papers spread in front of him, and he peered intently at an old book, left pinkie placed on a page as he scribbled in a small spiral notebook.

Terry stopped at the table to exchange pleasantries with the four men. Each stood and greeted her with a hug, brushing their cheeks against her face. Two more golfers from another table walked over to where she stood, and the greeting routine began anew.

She tried to keep her attention on the light banter surrounding her, but her gaze followed as Stephanie set a to-go bag in front of Kyle. Stephanie moved between tables, collecting cups and plates until she made eye contact with Terry. With a pointed stare, she inclined her head toward the bay window where Kyle sat.

Terry ignored her future sister-in-law's signals and first approached the young couple's table to thank the Naval officer for his service, arriving just as the pair stood up. While he helped his companion into her coat, Terry swooped in and whisked the check away before he had the chance to pick it up.

"I hope you enjoyed lunch." She included the woman in her gaze and smiled.

The woman nodded curtly, eyes narrowed. She said in a clipped tone, "It was quite nice."

Terry turned back toward the naval officer and glanced at his name tag. *Lawrence.* "It's on me, Commander, in appreciation for your service."

"What? Oh—that's not necessary, ma'am." He shook his head modestly, a surprised look on his face.

Ma'am? MA'AM? He's my age, maybe a year younger. Terry ignored the slightly annoyed tone of her inner voice, flashed a grin, and said, "My dad is retired Navy, and our family supports our military as much as we can." She extended her hand.

"Thank you." The commander took Terry's hand in his own. A little jolt of electricity snapped as their palms touched and they both started in surprise.

"Sorry, ma'am," he said, dropping his hand to his side. "Must be static."

"Probably." *Stop calling me ma'am!* She smiled. "Again, it's just a small way to say we appreciate your service."

"Well, let me say thank you from my fiancée and me."

"Come back anytime."

"Yes, ma'am."

Grrrr, that makes me feel so old. Terry pouted inwardly, but smiled again and said, "Great. We look forward to seeing you again." She slipped the bill into her jacket pocket.

The couple headed for the exit. The bell tinkled merrily as the man opened the door and held it for his fiancée. The woman's voice drifted back as she snapped, "And where do you know her from?"

"Liana, you do that every time a woman says one word to me. You accuse…" The door snapped shut and cut off the last of his sentence.

Terry watched through the bay window as the couple walked on the sidewalk. The woman shook her head from side to side, shouting. Terry could not make out the words. The sailor jammed his hands in his pockets and stared straight ahead as they walked out of sight.

"Yikes." Stephanie walked around Terry and looked, then began clearing the dishes. "I saw that one coming. She's been snapping at him like that since they sat down."

"If looks could kill, Terry, you'd be a goner," one of the golfers chortled. Terry rolled her eyes skyward and resisted the juvenile temptation to stick her tongue out at the offending speaker.

"Then we'd all be dead," Stephanie muttered in an aside. "She's done nothing but glare at all of us."

"Poor guy." Mary Jo joined the circle. "That girl is green-eyed from head to toe. She pestered him any time one of us came near him. What did she think we were going to do, jump his bones in front of her or something?"

"I hope I never act like that with Gage," Stephanie said. She stopped at Kyle's table and asked, "Kyle, can I bring you some more tea?" When Kyle didn't answer, she headed to the kitchen with the dirty dishes.

"What did you say?" In a delayed reaction, Kyle broke from his transfixed stare at the old documents and gave Stephanie's retreating form a puzzled frown.

"She asked if you wanted any more tea," Terry relayed, waiting for him to look her way.

"Oh. I'm fine, thanks." His gaze met Terry's, and he shuffled papers on the small tabletop. "Uh. Oh, hi, Terry."

"Do you mind if I join you?" Terry said, plopping in the empty chair before he had a chance to answer.

"Not at all." Kyle shuffled papers to one side to clear space in front of Terry.

"So what earth shattering ancestry news are you working on for us now?" she asked. She wore a white open neck blouse under her suit jacket. Pretending interest in the pile of papers, some old, some new, she angled her body slightly for Kyle to catch a bit of her décolletage.

If you would only look!

"Well…" he began enthusiastically, pushing his laptop to the side. He flashed an endearing smile before sifting through papers. He grabbed a pile and slid it toward her.

She played with the necklace at her throat and leaned forward to study the copy of an old birth certificate, trying to ignore the scent of musty papers drifting toward her nostrils. She preferred Hugo Boss.

He straightened his shoulders and cleared his throat.

No! Don't talk about those old papers, just look at me!

"See here." Kyle tapped the document. "I've pieced together a bit more of the ancestral line of both Stephanie and Mary Jo. I am ninety-nine percent certain of their link to this French soldier Étienne and his wife Clothiste. However, if your mother's Wyatt family has any connection to them, I haven't found it yet."

Kyle pulled a family tree chart from his pile and traced his finger up a list of names of long dead ancestors, reciting connections.

Mentally, Terry wrinkled her nose. She didn't like old wood and paper. She liked new glass and sleek shiny surfaces. Her eyes glazed over as he talked, but she plastered an interested look on her face. As his fingers trailed over names, she concentrated on his hands. She liked this handsome ancestry geek—a lot—but she didn't seem ancient enough or dead enough to get his attention.

"Now, you see here," an oblivious Kyle continued. "I've managed to find the Wyatt connection for the Civil War-era cousins Emily Longchamps and Louisa Harris, who married cousins Thomas Wyatt and Edward. If your family is in the lineage like I believe them to be, it would be through Emily's cousin Celestine, who married Thomas's brother Frank. But I've run into a roadblock with information on Celestine that I just can't seem to break through. I found some Civil War records for Frank's side, but she remains a mystery. It's always so much harder to trace the females in the family."

You can trace all over me with your tongue. Terry stiffened. *Oh, please God, I didn't just say that out loud, did I?*

If she did, Kyle was unaware. He yanked another paper from the stack, but his mind was on how to ask Terry out on a date. He'd been wanting to see a movie at the restored theater where meals were served. He'd just about figured out what to say when the group of golfers stopped by the table on their way out the door to bid farewell to Terry.

When she rose to say goodbye, one of the men took her arm and drew her to their circle. They traded banter with her and brushed her cheek with kisses. She quipped to one of them, "Freddie, I'll remind you of this jovial exchange next week when we square off in the Wheeler case and I kick your butt."

"Bah," Freddie laughed. "You'll be hunting me down to settle out of court."

"Not a chance, but I will be expecting you to make me an offer I can't refuse."

Two other people rose and joined the group.

Kyle grew tired of the scene unfolding around him. With a sigh, he shut down the laptop. He left cash on the table with his check, slid his laptop in the case and crammed the papers in the outside pocket.

He glanced back once as he pulled the door shut, the tinkle of the bell lost in the din of chatter from the men surrounding Terry.

He turned to go back inside. *Forget it, Avery. A professor in khakis doesn't stand a chance against a lawyer in pinstripes—or golf shirt.*

Terry finally shooed the group toward the door and closed it behind them, the bell jangling cheerfully in the sudden quiet. She turned to face the ice cream parlor set where Stephanie gathered the dishes. Stephanie motioned with her full hands toward the outside, rolling her eyes in exasperation at her friend. Terry yanked the door open in time to see Kyle drive past the café.

Dammit all.

***

Kyle Avery took the corner a bit too sharply as he turned onto London Boulevard, sending his briefcase sliding across the leather seat. He winced as the case fell to the floorboard with a thud. That was the third time today he had dropped his laptop case.

Dammit all.

He took a deep breath and concentrated on his driving, trying without success to push the image of Terry's pretty face from his mind. He liked how she looked in the simple button-down blouse, professional but eye-catching. He remembered the top two pearl buttons were unfastened, the heirloom necklace resting at the opening. He hoped that she didn't notice his gaze drifting down a little further.

As did the wandering eyes of probably every other guy in the room.

He'd only been around Terry in public a few times, and she attracted men like the proverbial flower attracted bees. He'd made enough discreet inquiries to know she was not dating anyone exclusively, but guys were definitely interested in the tall, chestnut haired beauty. Feeling far out of the league of her admirers, he couldn't work up the nerve to ask her out on a date.

Shyness, unfortunately, was one of his strongest personality traits.

He hit the steering wheel with his fist, accidentally tapping the horn as he stopped at a red light. He lifted his hand palms up as the driver in front struck his head out of the window and glared.

Damn it. She took his breath away.

CHAPTER 7

Theresé
Return to Portsmouth, Virginia, August 1781

Étienne continued to resist Theresé's offer to return to Portsmouth.

"It is too dangerous," he insisted.

"But, Papa, I must go." Theresé took his hands in hers. "We must find out what has happened to Mama and Grandpapa, and whether Louis is safe. The rain has ended. I will be there by this evening, and get word to you as soon as I am able."

Étienne hugged his daughter and left to make arrangements. As Theresé packed a small satchel, Nicole followed her every move, tears streaming down her face.

"You have to go away because I stole the teardrop from Mama and now she cannot come home." Lips quivering, Nicole rubbed her fingers under her eyes.

Theresé knelt before her youngest sister, and gently wiped a tear. The memory of Nicole clambering from the wagon to find her doll brought back the sound of the gunshots and her mother and grandfather falling to the ground.

"You must stop saying that, little sister. Mama would be so sad if she knew you cried so. I will find Mama, and Louis, and Grandfather. I will look for your doll and the necklace you hid in her dress. Then there will be no more tears. Promise me." Nicole nodded but kept her face angled downward. Theresé touched a finger to Nicole's chin and gently lifted her head until their eyes met.

"Promise me, little sister?" When Nicole nodded, Theresé brushed a

63

knuckle across the small anxious face peering at her and captured another trailing bead. The teardrop glistened and Nicole tilted her head, a slight smile breaking her tense face.

"That looks like my necklace, does it not?"

"It does." Theresé touched the knuckle to Nicole's throat. "This will be where your teardrop necklace will rest one day. Now, no more tears."

A flurry of voices outside the tent signaled it was time and Theresé rose. Nicole wrapped her arms tight around her oldest sister's neck. Marie Josephé scrambled through the door and announced the wagon was ready. She joined her sisters as they clung together, then Theresé broke free, wiping a tear trailing down her cheek.

"Take care of Papa, Marie Josephé. And you help her, little Nicole." She smiled and picked up her bag. "I shall return as soon as possible. Now I must say goodbye to Papa."

Within two hours after James and Lizzie showed up at the camp, Étienne had arranged for Theresé to return to Portsmouth with a married couple supporting the cause. Like Étienne's father Phillip, Ian McDermott, a Scottish merchant and banker, enjoyed Portsmouth's long-established ties to Great Britain. While most business men openly upheld their loyalty to the Crown—and thus their coffers—some used the guise of commerce to covertly assist the patriots' efforts. Appearing as loyalists, such sympathetic merchants supported the cause by smuggling goods and providing supplies to the American Army.

In much the same way as Phillip, the Scottish proprietor McDermott operated as a middleman. Both men traveled frequently and were well known. With a lack of suitable commercial transportation methods and communication with outlying areas, middlemen coordinated the purchase of goods from overseas suppliers and in turn sold to farmers, shopkeepers and even the British military. This made it easy for both men to engage in activities that supported the efforts of the revolutionaries without detection.

The ride back to Portsmouth was considerably more comfortable than the one she had taken almost two weeks earlier, in the back of a wagon loaded with crates and a secret cache of firearms hidden below. This time, Theresé rode in the front of the wagon with the driver and his wife. They would take her to the Market Square in Portsmouth, and from there she would traverse on foot to her grandfather's home.

Although they were allies, she conversed very little with the couple. The less one became involved, the better.

Rainwater pooled in the ruts carved by wagons previously traveling south. The rain had cleared, giving way to a burst of sunshine. Blue skies were a rarity in the last weeks.

Therese turned her face toward the welcoming sun, warmth radiating to her bones.

Too late, she realized she had forgotten to ask if Lizzie knew where she could find Nicole's doll.

Her heart turned cold with fear of what she would find when she reached Portsmouth.

Terry
Portsmouth, Virginia, present day

The golfers' exodus nearly emptied the small café. Terry sat back at the table she had just shared with Kyle.

"He got away, huh, slowpoke?" Mary Jo asked as she straightened chairs around empty tables.

"Oh, shut up, Mary Jo." Terry glared, frustration all but shooting out of her veins.

"Tsk, tsk, somebody's cranky this morning."

"Now, Mary Jo, leave her alone." Stephanie set a sandwich plate in front of Terry. "We all had a rough night facing the newest round of ghosts."

"Always the peacemaker," Terry said with a smile. She took a bite from the sandwich.

Mary Jo plopped in the opposite chair. "So you had the same experience with the candlestick as I did?" she asked, referring to an encounter she had in the attic of Clothiste's Inn when she first found the silver pieces.

"Yep. Felt like an ice-cold burn, like dry ice. Remember how we used to touch Aunt Ida's old-fashioned metal ice cube trays and our fingers would stick to the bottom? It was like that sensation."

"I remember. And even though we knew it would stick to our fingers, we would touch it every time. And Gage got his tongue stuck when we dared him to lick the ice cube tray." Mary Jo and Terry burst into raucous laughter.

"What is so funny?" Stephanie's face registered distress. "How can you laugh about something like that?"

"Oh, poor Steph." Terry wiped a tear from her cheek. "Being an only child, you missed all the joys of sibling rivalry."

Stephanie shook her head in bewilderment.

"Tell me the details of last night," Mary Jo requested. "I want to hear it from you."

"Is our most cynical member now a believer?" Terry asked. She polished off the last of the croissant sandwich.

"No, but now that I've seen these things a few times myself, I have to accept something weird is going on. And I know exactly what you mean about the feel of that candlestick against your skin."

Terry relayed the previous night's incident again, ending with, "On my way here this morning, I stopped at the inn, and found nothing out of place. I even touched the candlestick, but it was normal. All normal."

"It's strange how these ghosts are telling each of us to find different things," Stephanie chimed in. "I had to find Nicole's teardrop. Mary Jo had to find her own heart as well as Marie Josephé's stone. Both turned out to reflect our personalities as well as our missing jewels. Now you've gotten the communication to find the ghost's mother. I wonder how this fits in with our messages." She grabbed a food order pad from her apron pocket and removed a pencil stuck in the rubber band of her ponytail, then jotted on a blank page.

"What do you mean?" Terry craned her neck to read what Stephanie had written.

"I'm not sure, but I think a pattern is beginning to emerge. We're dealing with spirits from the Revolutionary War. Depending on what information source you use, white on the American flag stands for purity or innocence, I found the white diamond, I'm the youngest of us three, and the youngest girl is my ancestress. I share my middle name with her. She never spoke to me, but communicated telepathically with

Tanner, who relayed her message. Her teardrops, shed by an innocent child, are represented in the shape of the necklace."

"Okay." Mary Jo and Terry agreed in unison.

"Makes sense so far," Mary Jo added.

"Then, on the American flag, red represents valor, bloodshed by war, and courage, which epitomizes Mary Jo's stoic military persona. Not only did she have to dig to find her necklace in the dirt, but she had to find her own heart within. And remember, although she'd seen signs of the ghost from a distance, it did not appear until Tanner was present. This time, the ghost spoke, but Mary Jo only heard the voice in her own head. So is it because she was an older child that maybe her spirit is a little stronger?" Stephanie scratched more words onto the small pad, flipping to start a new page. "Don't forget, we've traced the family roots and Mary Jo, which is a modern version of the named Marie Josephé, is descended from the middle sister."

"Well, this is making more sense, in a way," Mary Jo said.

"And to wrap up her connection, her necklace was shaped like a heart," Stephanie continued, scribbling again while holding three fingers upward. "Then we have the third sister, the oldest of the trio. The old letters I found indicated she received a sapphire necklace shaped like a cross…" Her gaze drifted to the pendant at Terry's throat. "You have yours back! It looks different without the bands encircling the arms of the cross."

Terry glanced at the pendant. "The jeweler I took it to explained that the vertical beam of the cross is called a stipes." She stressed the pronunciation of the unusual word as "sty-peez" and leaned back in her chair. "You would think by looking at the word it rhymes with stripes. The plural, interestingly enough, is spelled s-t-i-p-i-t-e-s and pronounced…I don't remember now. The horizontal is called the patibulum. Just in case you wanted to know."

"Well, I'm just learning something new every day. I don't know how you remember such stuff. " Stephanie leaned forward, lifting her own teardrop-shaped necklace. "Now, here

Allie Marie

is where I am going with this. We haven't documented Terry's connection to Clothiste and Étienne but we're pretty sure it's there somewhere." Stephanie stopped to scribble again and then looked up, excitement dancing in her eyes. "I've only known you as Terry. Is that actually your name?" she asked.

"No-o," Terry drew out the single syllable. "I was christened Teresa."

"Okay, okay." Stephanie stood, face scrunched in concentration as she wrote. "Teresa-Theresé. There you have it! I'm sure there will be a connection to the same ancestors, but we just haven't found it yet. And you haven't seen the ghost either. You could see her when you were younger, but now you can hear her *voice*. She's stronger than the first two sisters, maybe able to cross over to this side more easily. Don't you see the other correlations? Clothiste's letter described Theresé as speaking up for those who couldn't defend themselves. And here you are, an attorney—representing justice, the blue of our flag—and you speak for those who cannot. You have a blue sapphire necklace and received a message to seek something."

The three women looked at each other and said in unison, "Find her mother."

Stephanie's eyes grew wide, and she whispered, "Do you think that skeleton belongs to Clothiste? What could have happened to her? Did someone kill her?"

"Okay, okay." Mary Jo held her hands palms up, then rubbed her temples. "This is getting too deep for me. I am trying to go along with all of this mumbo-jumbo stuff, but it's so far out there. Can you imagine what people would think if they could hear us discussing ghosts and shit?"

"No, wait." Terry stood and paced, tapping her chin. She turned to Stephanie. "Was there anything in your ancestry research that indicated what happened to Clothiste?"

Stephanie shook her head. "No. Kyle found something in the research that indicated her date of death as seventeen eighty-one, but I don't remember where the record came from. But we have noticed a few errors in dates in the family tree so

68

far." She drew her cell phone from her back pocket and punched the keypad.

Terry snatched the phone from her friend's hands and held it to the light. "Steph, I am so proud of you! You've gone techno. You're even using your phone for your family tree."

"Yeah, well, call me enlightened." Stephanie recovered her phone and swiped the screen until she found what she was looking for. "And if Clothiste was born in seventeen-fifty, as I have recorded, she would have been very young when her daughters were born. Something is definitely wrong. Maybe Kyle and I can reconcile these mistakes."

"Women got married awfully young back in those days," Terry reminded her.

"And records weren't kept like they are today," Mary Jo added. "Kyle said it's not unusual to have several birthdates for the same person."

"That may be. Now this is going to bug me. I've got to check this out. Do you need any more help here, Mary Jo?"

"No, she doesn't," Hannah snapped as she walked to the table. "Beth and I have cleaned everything up while you three sat here yakking about ghosts and dead people. I'm out of here, Mary Jo, I'll see you Monday." She kissed the top of Mary Jo's head, and waved to the other two.

Beth came out to say her goodbyes, announcing Tanner had called three times. "He wants to know if it's time to go to Hollow-Scream at Busch Gardens, so we're going to take the blood-thirsty little ghoul again."

Terry glanced at her watch and grimaced. "Yikes. We *have* been yakking way too long. It's nearly two o'clock and half the day is gone. Sorry, Hannah, Beth."

Stephanie headed for the door and called over her shoulder. "Terry, I'm almost packed and ready to move out. Kyle should be able to move in as soon as you do whatever you have to do."

"Thanks. The inspector will be by on Monday. Don't wrack your brains too hard over those birthdates, Steph," Terry called to Stephanie's back as she disappeared out the door, the bell jingling merrily.

Mary Jo laughed. "She's obsessed with this ancestry business. So is Kyle."

"You don't have to tell me that twice. That's all he talks about. Mary Jo, I swear I might have to conk him on the head to get his attention."

"Oh, give it time, you'll think of something."

"I'm thinking. I'm thinking." Terry tapped her forehead.

"Well, go think elsewhere. I've got work to do. And if we are going to throw some sort of Halloween bash for the official open house for the Inn, we better decide in the next few days."

"That's it!" Terry slapped her hand on the tabletop as the thought occurred to her. "I have an idea forming. I'll tell you at the birthday party tomorrow."

"That's fine. Now get out. I'm closing shop and counting my blessings." Mary Jo walked to the cash register and punched the button that opened the drawer. The bell shrilled. She grinned and repeated the action several times, adding, "Those aren't church bells I'm hearing."

"I'm going." Ideas whirled through Terry's mind as she called out an absent-minded goodbye and headed to her car.

Terry called her mom. They'd always been close, but since the scare at the emergency room, she called to check on her three or four times a day. After her mother assured her she was fine, Terry asked, "By any chance, did you invite Kyle to my birthday party?" When her mother affirmed that she had and inquired why, Terry merely said, "Oh, I remembered there is an old leather case full of papers in the attic. I thought he might be interested in it. I'll let him know about it then. And keep your party hat on, Mom. I've got some great ideas for Halloween at the Inn."

"Sounds like fun. I hope you are not planning on severed limbs and fake blood."

"Not at all. How about a themed costume party spanning the historic eras of Clothiste's Inn? Colonial, Antebellum, Victorian?"

"Ooh, I like!"

"Great. I'll see you in a few, just wanted to check in before I hit the road. Love ya. Bye." She waited long enough to hear her mother responding "Love you back" before clicking the off button and putting her car in gear.

Zipping down the highway toward the Driver section of Suffolk, Halloween party ideas scrambled in her head. She loved the holiday, but had never cared for the terror forests her brothers and Chase had favored as older teenagers. She couldn't see the sense in going to a place where actors wearing distorted masks jumped from behind doors, or mannequins sporting sausages for intestines and ketchup for blood lined the rooms.

She recalled Aunt Ida's old trunk in the attic of the inn, nearly bursting at the seams with vintage clothing she and Mary Jo had played dress-up in when they visited. She couldn't remember the specific contents, but if nothing else, it probably contained useful props.

She slowed at the insufferable red light at London Boulevard and Effingham, racking her brain to remember what clothes the trunk held, without success. Undaunted, she then wondered if she could get Kyle's attention by inviting him to the attic to see both the old satchel of letters and the trunk.

His face popped into her mind and she smiled.

Almost as quickly, the face of the handsome naval commander with the jealous fiancée shaped in her mind and a small tingle surged in her right hand.

Startled, she shook her head to clear the man's sudden intrusion into her mental vision. Two annoying blasts from the driver behind her brought her attention back to her driving and she moved past the green light.

"What was that all about?" she wondered aloud, staring at her upturned right palm.

Slithering mist formed in the attic of the B and B, winding through the clutter, drifting around the trunk, and then swirling toward the faded leather case.

The swarm resembled angry bees as it circled the bag several times without touching it. Unseen forces blocked the mist from reaching the case.

The outline of a distorted human form rose toward the rafters. The figure gained vague arms, a neck, and a head. The neck elongated, the face had no features save for a cavernous mouth. The long neck craned and dipped near the trunk, and the mouth emitted a shriek each time the head dipped.

The figure shrank and absorbed back into indefinable shapelessness. In a frenzy of motion, the swirl bounced from roof joist to floor, from wall to trunk, but could not penetrate the invisible barrier protecting the leather case.

With an angry hiss louder than a burst of steam from a locomotive, the vapor shrank to a thin stream and broke into dirty particles that disappeared in the air.

***

Terry's twice-postponed birthday party wound down Sunday evening. The last of the guests had left. Kyle had been invited to remain behind with the family as they gathered around the fire pit for warmth as the sun dipped below the horizon. Cool night air wafted in slight waves, the scent of tidal marsh mixing with the scent of burning leaves and wood.

Under his mother's watchful eye, four-year-old Tanner waved two sparklers as he rendered his version of "Happy Birfday to Aunt Terry." After his brief performance, he bowed deeply as family members clapped and cheered. Terry whistled enthusiastically, as if her favorite singer had just personally serenaded her. Tanner handed the extinguished wire frames to his father, and then climbed onto Joan's lap, where he had already spent much of the evening. For the third time, he announced, "I don't want you to go to the 'hostabul' again, ever, ever, Grammie."

"Oh, God love you, Tanner Bear." Joan hugged him. "I won't. You're my best medicine." She and Tanner began singing "Old MacDonald" and the other adults provided the animal sounds.

Hannah stood beside Joan's chair, resting a protective hand on her cousin's shoulder. Her sweatshirt slogan today bore the words "Chocolate is a bean, therefore it's a vegetable and I can eat all I want" superimposed over a picture of a partially eaten candy bar.

"Poor little guy," Terry said in an aside to Mary Jo and Stephanie. "We **thought** he slept through everything that night, but apparently, he was more aware of what happened than we realized. Beth said he's wanted to call Mom every day this week, and he asks her if she is home and not at the 'hostabul.'"

"That episode gave us quite a scare," Mary Jo said. "Do you think she really is okay?"

"Dad says she has done well. She shopped for and prepared a whole new menu based on the doctor's suggestions, stays hydrated. She has to go back for a follow-up next week, but I'm starting to breathe easier. I'll keep an eye on her during the party preparations, make sure she doesn't overdo it."

"I really love the suggestion for a costume party based on the eras of the inn," Stephanie interjected. "I about peed my pants laughing so hard at the crestfallen looks on Gage and Chase's faces when you announced the plans."

Mary Jo chuckled. "They were hoping for a 'zombie' themed event, that's for sure."

"Well, our history professor's face lit up like Tanner's sparklers," Stephanie added. "I notice you had a lengthy conversation with him over by the river, Terry."

"Yeah, unfortunately it was mostly about American history. He knows so much about Portsmouth during the Revolutionary War. I had to mention the costume party again to bring him back to the present. It gave me the perfect excuse to mention that not only were there vintage clothes in Aunt Ida's old pirate's chest, but a bag full of documents. That started him on ancestry talk, but I promised him we'd check them out as soon as he comes back from Maryland. He's leaving tomorrow to get the rest of his things to move into the apartment."

"What bag?" Stephanie asked.

"Oh, I've been meaning to tell you about it. By the way, I found three autumn door decorations at the nursery in Driver. They'll match, and will be perfect for the law office, the inn, and the café." Terry allowed her plastic cup to slip from her fingers, causing the others to jump out of the way of the splashing beverage. She wiped the spilled liquid from the arm of her chair, offering a silent prayer of thanks that no one could see her blush in the waning light.

Her action had the desired effect, however, temporarily directing conversation away from the satchel and its possible contents. Her gaze drifted toward Kyle, kneeling beside her mother's chair, their heads nearly touching as they engaged in deep conversation.

"Don't try to change the subject. What's in the bag?" Stephanie asked after tossing the empty cup in the trash, her determination obvious on her face.

Guilt pricked at Terry in short stabs. She had known the old bag was in the attic since before the hurricane, but she'd kept it secret, waiting for the right moment to tell Kyle about it. Seeing Stephanie's excited response now enhanced her remorse and she prayed fervently that the satchel did not hold answers to the pressing questions of Stephanie's family tree search.

"I don't really know," Terry admitted. She laughed. "You're like a hound on the scent of a fox. It's just old and musty, full of faded papers, probably nothing important."

"*Everything's* important," Stephanie corrected. "I can't wait to see what's in it. Ever since I found that cache of old family letters that told stories from my ancestress Emily's point of view, I have been dying to find the missing responses from her cousin Celestine. Isn't it interesting that they are cousins by blood, and became sisters-in-law by marriage?"

"What are you three whispering about? You're missing the bonfire," Gage said as he walked to the trio. He wrapped his arms around Stephanie and nuzzled her neck.

"I just found out your mean sister has a satchel full of old documents and she is just now telling me about them," Stephanie complained, pretending to pout. She then turned her face to brush Gage's lips with a kiss.

"She's a bad sister," Gage said. "Come on, let's get warm by the fire and then we'll go home and make some fire of our own." He planted a kiss on his fiancée's lips, then brushed his mouth across her cheek to whisper in her ear. Stephanie's gaze grew dreamy as she listened.

"Oh, geez, get a room." Terry rolled her eyes skyward.

"We fully intend to," Gage said with a smirk, leading Stephanie toward the fire pit. By the time they finished a few more rounds of Tanner's songs, gray ash coated the glowing logs, the air breathing new life into the lava-red gleam as cool whiffs passed over.

"It's just about time to wrap this party up," Terry called out. Shouts of "Happy birthday" greeted her again, mixed with a loud "aww" from Tanner as he ran to wrap his arms around her.

She ruffled the little boy's hair and faced her family. "I just want to thank you all for a wonderful day. There's nothing that makes me enjoy my life more than being surrounded by my family and friends."

"Can't we stay longer, Mommy?" Tanner begged.

"No, sir, little man. It's past our bedtime." Connor scooped the little boy into his arms and swung him lightly in a circle as Tanner whooped.

"You get him too excited to sleep, Daddy, you can stay up with him," Beth warned, reaching for the little boy.

The firefighting brothers extinguished the pit fire, steam rising over the pit as water sizzled on the hot logs.

The usual commotion erupted as the family said goodbyes, with rounds of hugs and cheek kissing. Kyle was the last to reach Terry.

"Your mom was very kind to invite me to your party," he said "I had a great time. I always do when I'm with your family."

"Thank you for coming, Kyle. Just give me a call when you get back and we can go through the stuff in the attic."

"I can't wait to see if there are some answers to missing links," he said. He extended his hand. "Happy belated birthday, Terry."

"Thanks, Kyle, but you know Mom's house rule—no handshakes, just hugs." She pushed his hand to the side and threw her arms around him. Kyle seemed startled by her sudden move, but embraced her. She shifted to move just a little closer, enjoying the contact as she pressed into him. Not too hard, just enough. His hair smelled like camp smoke, and she nearly brushed her lips along his neck, stopping in time.

Had Kyle noticed her move? Had his arms lingered in the embrace or was it her imagination?

Geez Louise, I'm glad it's dark. What a fool I am.

CHAPTER 8

Terry's Monday morning commute went from bad to worse—before nine a.m.

She caught every red light along the route from Bridge Road in Suffolk, through High street in Churchland, and along London Boulevard during her rush-hour drive toward Olde Towne. As she endured the especially long-holding light at London and Effingham, a man walked up to her window and rapped on the glass. She rolled it down a few cautious inches.

"Yes?" she asked.

"Just wanted to tell you that your left front tire is going flat."

"Oh. Thank you, I'm almost at work, I'll check it there."

The man nodded and crossed toward the convenience store. The light changed and she had to wait for two cars running the red light to clear the intersection before she could proceed, only to get stuck at the next light signal.

"Aaargh," she growled in frustration. She glanced both ways on Washington Street, devoid of traffic. "There's nothing coming," she grumbled out loud, pounding the steering wheel. She made a mental note to call the city to see if traffic engineering could sync the lights for more convenient progress.

She entered the office parking lot only to find her reserved space occupied by a tan coupe. Seething, she parked in a customer space near the café, and got out, slamming the door. She stormed around the front and checked the left tire, which was indeed going flat. The head of a roofing nail protruded from the tread. She sent a text to Gage to ask if he could come change the tire for her. He sent a response that he was in a meeting and would come at noon.

As she entered through the private door in the back, Becky greeted her with, "Good morning and fair warning. Head straight for the coffee. I just brewed a full pot."

"It's not a good morning." Terry headed for the kitchen counter and grabbed a cup. "What's up?"

"You have a waiting room full of walk-in clients. And it's all my fault. It might be better to wait until Sandi gets in. You both…"

As if on cue, Terry's law partner Sandi Cross bustled through the back door. A divorced mother with a young daughter, Sandi elbowed the door closed, a stack of books in one arm and a bag adorned with the *Pâtisseries a la Carte* emblem.

"Good morning. The café just sold out of chaussons *aux pommes* thanks to *moi*. Help yourselves…what's the matter? Becky, you look so serious." She glanced from Becky to Terry.

"We are about to find out," Terry informed her as she grabbed another mug.

Becky seized the books slipping from Sandi's grip and said, "At church this weekend, there were several folks who were talking about a problem they've all had with the same car dealer. Actually, it's a used car dealer. Several of the church members have had their cars repossessed in the last few months, and some of those cases seemed pretty shady to me. I gave them your cards and told them I would mention the situation to you, to see if you could help. If you could, then I'd let them know. I had no idea they'd be waiting here this morning."

"All right, what have we got?" Terry asked, blowing on her coffee before she sipped.

"Well, I'm not sure all of the dealings are legal. I understand repo for failure to pay or what have you, but one of the ladies, a really sweet woman, said she paid her loan off early to avoid the high interest rate, and someone towed the car the day after her agreement was up. She's been getting the runaround ever since. She's been to one lawyer who wanted a thousand up front to take the case, and then to another who wanted twelve hundred. Another older gentleman's car was taken when he fell a few days behind for one payment. The third may be a legitimate tow because of non-payment in general."

Terry pinched the bridge of her nose. "Let me think here. I need to check my appointment book."

"I already did. You have an appointment at eleven with Mr. Wheeler for his accident case."

"I'm hoping they settle. Freddie Girard is representing the other driver. He knows his guy was in the wrong but I think he's going to hold out until the eleventh hour."

"I have juvvie court at ten," Sandi said. "Kevin Clarkson's petit larceny case."

"Oh, yeah, we talked about that Saturday. He's—and I quote—'scared shitless.' I hope he gets a break. He's turned out to be a really good kid." Terry sighed and turned to Becky. "I'll talk to them, but I'm not promising anything. How many are out there?"

"Well, there are three potential clients, and the accompanying family members." Becky grinned broadly. "You know my people, the whole brood shows up when someone is in trouble. Mrs. Belford's case is the most alarming. She's the one who paid in full." She handed Terry a file folder. "And thank you for talking to her."

"Well, like I said, I'm not promising anything." Terry rummaged in the café bag and removed a pastry in waxed paper. She sniffed appreciatively. "I'm officially in a bad mood and I need a morale boost. My morning has gone from bad to worse. I have a flat tire, and someone parked in my designated space."

"Do you want me to join you with the clients?" Sandi asked.

"No, you need time to get to court. I'll see what we've got." She headed toward her office. "Becky, give me a minute to get settled and I'll see Mrs. Belford in the conference room. And we need to get signs posted that designate our parking spaces and say unauthorized cars will be towed."

"I'll check with Chase and see who he recommends," Becky called to Terry's back.

Ten minutes later, Terry entered the conference room with a smile and offered her hand to the diminutive woman waiting for her. Thin, dressed in a blue flowered Sunday dress and small straw hat, the woman sat down.

"Thank you for seeing me, Ms. Dunbar," Mrs. Belford said. With features similar to Hannah and a much sunnier disposition, the older woman worried the snap on her black patent leather bag. "I know I shouldn't have shown up without an appointment, but I need to get my car back. It's the only transportation I have for me and my grandson."

"Well, let's see what we have. I looked at the papers you gave Becky. Can you tell me what happened?"

"When my husband died a few years ago, he left me with a nice Buick, but it was already old. It eventually broke down. I couldn't qualify for a new car loan. I'm on a fixed income and my grandson lives with me, so no bank would finance a new car. A little over two years ago, on September tenth, I went to O'Grady's Cars, out there on the highway. My brother-in-law went with me, and we found a decent sedan. It cost five thousand. The payment was four hundred and forty-seven dollars and some change each month. I rounded it up and paid him four fifty each month."

"I see he charged thirty percent interest. That's an enormous amount."

The old woman's thin fingers fiddled with her purse strap, veins protruding on the top of her weathered hands. She rummaged through her purse and drew out a pack of tissues. "I've never had credit in my name before and the banks would not give me a loan. I had no choice but to go to Mr. O'Grady. It was more than I expected to pay, but with caution, I worked out my other finances so I could afford the car. My son had been killed earlier in an accident and I'd hoped the litigation would be finished so that I could pay for the car before the loan period was up."

"I'm very sorry for your loss, Mrs. Belford."

"Thank you. Ms. Dunbar. When I got the settlement, I paid the car in full. I went to the office in person and gave the clerk the check for the balance. She was really ditzy. I had to ask her to stamp my loan application paid in full, and to get a written receipt. She finally wrote one out, said my loan was paid up and that I'd get the title in the mail in a few weeks. It never came and after a while I forgot about it. Then the day after the two-year mark, I woke up to find the car gone. I called the police to make a theft report. They put out one of those—what are they called, BOLO?"

Terry nodded as she scribbled on a legal pad. "Yes, short for 'be on the lookout.' Police broadcast the description to the officers on patrol."

"Well, an alert officer saw the vehicle being towed and stopped the driver. I understand that once they learned the car was repossessed, they canceled the BOLO thing. They called me back to tell me the dealer had repossessed the vehicle and where it had been taken. When I explained the situation, they told me it was a civil matter, not criminal, and I'd have to take the dealer to court. I went to see Mr. O'Grady first. He was so ugly to me. He accused me of faking the 'paid in full' stamp printed on the receipt, told me to carry my scrawny you-know-what back to the trash pile I came from. I went to the lawyer who handled my boy Eddie's case." Mrs. Belford dabbed the tissue to her eyes and cried silently, shoulders shaking.

Terry rose from her chair and walked to the other side of the conference table to sit beside the older lady. She put her arm on the woman's shoulder.

"Can I get you something, Mrs. Belford? Would you like a glass of water or a cup of coffee?"

"No thanks, just give me a moment." The shudders subsided and the old woman cleared her throat. She straightened her shoulders and said in a firm voice, "I'm sorry."

"It's fine. Continue when you feel like it."

"There isn't much else. As I mentioned, I went to the lawyer for Eddie's case. You know, Ms. Dunbar, he got an awful lot of money when they settled my son's death claim for five hundred thousand dollars. By the time he took his share, and the medical bills and funeral expenses were paid, I received less than one hundred and thirty thousand. He got more than I did, and so did everyone else." Mrs. Belford wiped new tears from the corners of her eyes, and continued. "When I took this to him, he told me it would be a difficult case and I'd have to pay a retainer of one thousand dollars. Plus more if it doesn't cover his hours and expenses. I don't have that kind of money. I'd put most of the settlement in a certificate of deposit, and I will pay a heavy penalty if I withdraw it before two years. Without the retainer, he wouldn't take the case. So then he recommended another firm but they wanted twelve hundred up front."

Tears welled in Mrs. Belford's eyes again. "May I use the restroom, Ms. Dunbar?"

"Certainly. I'll show you where it is. Please come back here to the conference room. I'm going to my office to make a call and see if I can get this straightened out over the phone." Terry guided the frail woman to the restroom. She asked Becky to bring water for Mrs. Belford to the conference room.

Once she settled at her desk, she grabbed the phone, using the eraser tip of her pencil to punch in the numbers listed on the paperwork.

Three rings later, she heard, "O'Grady's Sales and Finances. This is Winnie." The faceless voice dripped with an exaggerated cheerfulness.

Terry asked to speak to Mr. O'Grady and the cheerful voice sang, "Why, sure, honey, let me get him." A click put the call on hold, and Pat Benatar's "Hit Me With Your Best Shot" blasted Terry's ear. She grimaced and held the phone away from her ear, rolling her eyes skyward. Finally, a voice raspy from too many cigars or whiskeys—or both—echoed on a loudspeaker, "O'Grady."

Terry identified herself and offered a pleasant good

morning. O'Grady grumbled "Yeah, morning," in return.

"I won't take up too much of your time, Mr. O'Grady, but Mrs. Leslie Belford is in my office. Her car was repossessed but I think there may have been a mistake and I was hoping you could help straighten it out." Terry picked up her notes. "Mrs. Belford…"

"If the car was repo'ed, it was because the owner didn't make the payments." O'Grady interrupted.

"I understand if that was the case. But Mrs. Belford paid her loan off six months early. And according to your loan agreement, if she did that, she would not owe any interest and …"

O'Grady interrupted again. "Look, doll. What did you say your name was?"

Terry repeated her name.

"Well, Miss Dunbar, like I told you, we only repo when the owner fails to make payment."

"If you'd let me finish, Mr. O'Grady, I'm trying to tell you that in this case, the client paid the full amount about six months early. She has a paid in full agreement and…"

O'Grady interrupted again. "Belford was her name? You must be talking about that old lady. Nope, she didn't make the full payment." Papers rustled in the background. "But I told her I'd take fifty percent off her fees if she wanted to get her car back. She didn't want to."

"Well, Mr. O'Grady, I had hoped we could settle this easily as a misunderstanding. Mrs. Belford stands by her claim and she has the proof of payoff. That car only cost five thousand."

"You'd better check her papers, doll. She still owed a balance of three thousand dollars. Eight thousand dollars. That's what she signed for."

"Mr. O'Grady, you can't charge interest up front and then monthly…"

"Well, then sue me. It'll cost your client more to pay you bloodsucking lawyers and she ain't gonna win, so you just go ahead and give it your best shot, doll." He slammed the phone in her ear.

Terry smacked the phone in the cradle. "Oh, I will, O'Grady. I will." She took a moment to compose herself, then returned to the conference room where Mrs. Belford waited.

"I just had a rather unpleasant conversation with Mr. O'Grady," she said. "He says he offered to cut your fees by fifty percent."

Mrs. Belford sat straighter in her chair, anger darting from her narrowed eyes. "He most certainly did not!" Her eyes shimmered with new tears. "Are you going to take my case, Miss Dunbar? How much do you charge?"

"I still need some more information, but don't you worry about the fees right now."

Terry continued to review the figures and scribble notes. She put the pen down and scratched her head. "These figures confuse me. It looks like O'Grady charged you the full interest right up front and added it to the total, instead of amortizing it each month. I calculate it should have taken you twenty-four months at two hundred seventy-nine dollars and some change. At the payment he set, you had actually given him a little over eight thousand by the time you paid it off, which means he should have refunded you the amount over five thousand. But it also looks like he still charged you a monthly interest fee on the balance each month. My law partner is a whiz with numbers and I need her to review this for me, to give me the exact figures."

For the next half hour, Terry asked more questions and took notes as the soft-spoken Mrs. Belford answered. When Terry folded the cover on the legal pad, the older woman leaned forward and asked again, "Are you going to take my case, Ms. Dunbar?"

Despite her age, Mrs. Belford had a sharp memory, and spoke in a confident voice. She would make a good witness. And she had documentation.

And Terry wanted Shady O'Grady.

She looked in the diminutive woman's desperate eyes and took her hand. "Mrs. Belford, I need my partner's review, but if I'm right, I will take your case. I'll let you know this afternoon. In addition to your civil claims, I believe Mr. O'Grady has illegally seized your car, and it's possible he has committed other fraudulent acts. What I need now is for you to go to the police station and make a report. I'm not allowed to seek or file criminal charges but the detectives will help you."

"Will he be arrested?"

"First they have to determine if he has committed a crime and then prepare a case. The detective will consult with the Commonwealth's Attorney about the appropriate charges. But they will probably not arrest him right away. They will go for a direct indictment."

"What does that mean?"

"The case is presented to a grand jury. If the grand jury returns a true bill, that means they have heard sufficient evidence to believe he committed the crimes. He will be arrested on a Circuit Court bench warrant. But please understand that charging him criminally won't get your car or money back, Mrs. Belford. It is completely separate from the civil case. If we take your case, we will deal with the civil matter to recover your money and property. We will file certain paperwork with the court and O'Grady will be served with papers. He will have to appear in court to defend against these claims. There are some fees associated with filing these papers, including a fee for the Sheriff's Office to serve the papers. These fees should be less than one hundred dollars. I'll get an exact figure."

"I can pay that much."

"We'll deal with that later. Unfortunately, as I just mentioned, this won't get your car back right away. Civil cases can be a slow process. It may take a couple of weeks between filing and getting on the docket. Since Mr. O'Grady is local, we should be able to get him served with the papers fairly quickly, but I can't give a more specific time frame for the case. And most likely on the first docket date we will not go to trial anyway. Mr. O'Grady will ask for time to hire an attorney, and they may prolong it by asking for other continuances to try to drag the case out as long as possible. His attorney may demand what is called a Bill of Particulars, whereupon I will demand a Grounds of Defense. These are written pleadings each side must file. I would set forth the specifics of the claim for you, and his attorney would specify defense or defenses to the claim for Mr. O'Grady."

Terry took Mrs. Belford's hand in hers. "As I said, my partner and I will look over all of the details of your paperwork to be sure we will have our ducks in a row. We'll make a final decision and I will contact you right away."

Both women stood. Terry escorted her to the conference room door and shook hands. Mrs. Belford had a surprisingly strong grip.

"Try not to worry, Mrs. Belford. I'll work as quickly as I can."

The tiny lady gave her a warm hug. "Thank you so much. God bless you for your kindness." She walked down the short hall toward the waiting room.

Terry retrieved the file and turned to go to her office, nearly bumping into Becky coming from the reception area.

"How did it go?"

"I think she has a case. I called the car dealer, hoping it was a misunderstanding we could clear up. He was an absolute jackass. Now I want to take it on. I need Sandi to crunch some numbers for me, see if I understand Mrs. Belford's case correctly. I don't know what kind of case the other possible clients may have, but I'll tell you this right now. I'm declaring war on Mr. Shady O'Grady."

Becky nodded and placed another file on the table. "You go, crusader. That's Mr. Bates's file, the next one that might have a case. I don't think the third one is as strong. His appears to be repossessed for non-payment."

By the end of the next two interviews, Terry determined that Mr. Bates had a possible claim to defend. In his case, he'd never been late on the payments, but did pay the last payment one day late. Winnie the clerk accepted the payment along with a late fee of thirty-five dollars and stamped the receipt "paid in full." Mr. Bates woke up to find his car gone, and after calling police, learned he had suffered the same fate as Mrs. Belford. When he went to the dealership, O'Grady demanded payment of over one thousand dollars in fees before Mr. Bates could get his vehicle back.

The next gentleman had not kept up with payments and the car was repossessed for violation of the contract. But Terry wondered if there was something they could do to help, since the front-loaded interest and then additional accrued interest affected the man's ability to pay.

"This might be some kind of racketeering, or some kind of fraud. I'll bet he's also violating some kind of state law." Terry gripped her temples. "I have a headache. As soon as I meet with Mr. Wheeler, I think I'll slip out somewhere for a bite, see if I can make sense of this case." She stretched and rubbed her back. "I'm still so mad at that shyster that I could spit nails."

"Do you want me to get you something from the café?"

"Don't you dare tell Mary Jo this, but I'm in the mood for something home-cooked and fattening. I just want to slip away somewhere and eat mashed taters and gravy."

"Well, you know the perfect place."

"I do indeed. Mom's Diner. You want anything?"

"No." Becky patted her waistline. "I'm counting every calorie until my sister's wedding. I'll just have a bowl of lettuce and a piece of cardboard."

Terry laughed. Then she remembered her car had a flat tire. She grabbed her phone and tapped a message to Gage. He texted a return message that he was held up but would be there soon.

"Beck, can I use your car? Mine has a flat. Gage is on his way to fix it, but I need to go out now."

"Of course." Becky fished keys off her desk and handed them to Terry.

Terry still seethed at the rude encounter with the car dealer. She pointed toward the files. "Let Sandi know I'll get with her this afternoon. If I've correctly understood the numbers for Mrs. Belford's case, I'd like nothing more than to hit that crook O'Grady right in the wallet."

"Good. And I hope the rest of your day is better than the morning."

"Me too." Terry called over her shoulder. She left the building and walked to Becky's car just as Gage entered the parking lot. She remembered she still had her own car keys and dug them from her purse. When he pulled up beside her and rolled down the window, she handed them to him.

"Thanks for doing this, Gage."

"No problem, sis, I'm charging my lunch to you." He studied her face. "What's the matter? You look mad."

"Oh, I just dealt with a jerk this morning. I'll be okay. See you later." She kissed her brother's cheek. He then drove into an empty space beside her vehicle and got out.

"Uncle Gage! Aunt Terry!" Tanner burst from the back door of the café and jumped to the bottom step. "Whatcha doing?"

"I have to change Aunt Terry's tire. You want to help?"

"Yeah!" The little boy bounced up the stairs, yelling, "Hey, Mama! Can I help Uncle Gage change tires on the 'vertible?"

"Shhh," Beth cautioned as she came to the door, wiping her hands on a dishtowel. After she exchanged pleasantries with her siblings-in-law, she agreed to let her son join his uncle.

"You just behave yourself, young man. Gage, will you bring him inside when you are done?"

"Yeah, no prob. And will you make me up a special to go? Terry's paying." He inclined his head toward his sister, grinning mischievously.

Terry rolled her eyes. "Put it on my tab, Beth. See you later," She got into Becky's coupe. When she was sure Tanner was safely beside Gage and the way was clear, she backed out.

She rubbed her neck where the necklace suddenly turned warm against her skin, fanning the chain as she drove onto the side street.

She didn't look back.

If she had, she would have been startled at the appearance of a young girl on the stoop of the Bed and Breakfast. The girl wore a white shawl over a faded dress—a colonial dress, and held a book in her hands.

For a full minute, the figure stood still. The girl turned her face toward the sun, feeling warmth on her skin for the first time in two centuries. She looked at her hands. Solid flesh and blood, something else she hadn't experienced for so long.

Too soon, the translucency returned. Overwhelming sadness overtook her as she watched her form fade and she returned to the place of the undead.

CHAPTER 9

Theresé
Portsmouth, Virginia, August 1781

Halfway between Suffolk and Portsmouth, along the well-traveled King's Highway, the wagon ran over a rock jutting in the path. One of the wheels split, rendering the cart immobile. Nearly two hours passed before another carriage coming from the opposite direction crossed their path. Mr. McDermott left his wife and Theresé with the disabled coach and rode with the other traveler back to Suffolk.

Mrs. McDermott and Theresé made small talk while they waited under the shade of a huge weeping willow tree, sharing bread and hard cheese from a wicker basket Mrs. McDermott had packed.

"How long will you stay with your grandfather?" the older woman asked as she settled her skirts around her. The two women sat atop a piece of canvas from the wagon.

"I know not, Mrs. McDermott. Both he and my mother were gravely injured. My step-grandmother is not the kindest person in the world, and we are concerned about their well-being."

"We were shocked to hear about the incident. My husband and your grandfather are great collaborators in the cause, and he is certain the attack occurred because someone was trying to prove your grandfather as a traitor. It was very convenient that Mrs. Roker was out of town at the time, although Mr. McDermott says it is her fierce loyalty to the crown that has provided the protection Phillip needs to conduct his business without detection. Truth be told, I've never cared for her haughty ways," Mrs. McDermott said, wrinkling her nose in disdain. "And I don't even need to describe how the Scots feel about the bloody Brits."

90

Therèsé's smile at Mrs. McDermott's profanity faded quickly as she frowned. "My sisters and I found her quite unpleasant, but she seemed to especially dislike my mother due to some odd obsession about her French heritage. She did not allow us to speak French in her presence, and never introduced us as family when there were visitors. She forced us to act as her servants at times, especially when she had fancy dinners. I think she wanted to pretend great wealth by displaying a full staff of help. Little did the guests know her own husband's granddaughters served them beef and ale."

Mrs. McDermott snorted. "We heard she entertained the traitor Benedict Arnold and the general one evening."

Smoothing out a fold in the canvas, Therèsé nodded and rolled her eyes skyward. "I had the displeasure of serving dinner that night. Despite my step-grandmother's efforts to keep the conversation light, it always went back to the war."

Mrs. McDermott's petticoats rustled as she shifted uncomfortably. "In July, we were coming back from Richmond on the same day General Cornwallis crossed the James from his raid in Richmond. We were already on the ferry waiting, when several soldiers boarded and ordered us to disembark so the army could travel. My Ian has met the general several times and gives the appearance of a staunch loyalist. This proved beneficial as the general allowed us to remain on the ferry. He was actually quite personable, discussing his family and how much he missed them. He was rather dashing, even if he was a bloody redcoat."

Therèsé stifled a giggle and remained silent.

Mrs. McDermott fanned her face with her scarf. "My word! Tomorrow is the first day of September and it is still as hot as the height of summer." She settled her back against the tree and closed her eyes. "I fear we are coming to a climax in this war soon, and if Britain wins, there is no telling what shall happen to those who have supported the Americans in this battle." She mumbled the last sentence, ending on a light snore.

Therèsé sighed, relieved to avoid further conversation with the nice but chatty lady, and settled her head against the tree. Her father had assured her that the McDermotts were absolutely trustworthy, as loyal to America as he was, but cautioned her to avoid conversations that could reveal her brother's involvement with the spy ring.

Twice, other travelers coming from the opposite direction stopped and *inquired about the women's wellbeing. Mrs. McDermott roused enough to tell them her husband should be returning soon.*

Theresé watched warily. I wish they were heading toward Portsmouth instead of Suffolk.

But even if Portsmouth was their final destination, she would not have left the kind Mrs. McDermott alone.

A troop of red-coated soldiers stopped and circled the wagon. Theresé stiffened but Mrs. McDermott patted her hand and whispered, "The wagon is empty, dear. They will find nothing to arouse suspicion." The younger woman relaxed and studied the men for a sign of Louis.

One soldier walked toward the women. "Good afternoon, ladies. May I inquire as to what happened?"

"Our wagon struck something in the roadway and a wheel splintered. My husband went with another traveler for assistance and should return any moment." Mrs. McDermott scrambled to her feet and faced the commanding officer, her voice crisp with a far more Scottish burr than before the soldiers arrived.

"Then you would have no objection to a search of your conveyance." His soldiers had already lifted the canvas from the back. The captain looked over his shoulder and turned back to Mrs. McDermott with a slight incline of his head. "Our apologies, Madam. Supplies are being smuggled to the Revolutionaries and we must check out every possibility."

"Captain," Mrs. McDermott drew to her full height. "If you feel it necessary for your soldiers to suspect the conveyance of two women of proper Portsmouth society, by all means search for the cannons and other artillery we obviously have hidden in that small carriage."

Surprised by the tenacity the seemingly meek woman displayed, Theresé lowered her head to suppress a smile.

Before the Captain could respond, a soldier called out, "Clear."

"I presume you are satisfied, Captain, so I encourage you to be on your way before my husband comes across your men rummaging through our belongings. He will be having dinner tomorrow evening with General Cornwallis and I am sure there will be mention of this indignity."

The British captain stiffened. He bowed his head, and said again, "Our apologies for your inconvenience, Madam." He whistled and motioned for the men to return to their horses. He led the way as they returned to their path on the King's Highway.

"Bloody arses!" Mrs. McDermott spat out.

Therésé gasped in shock at the coarse language.

The older woman smiled and shrugged. "You should hear my husband's laments. His kin have fought the Crown since the days of William Wallace. Many of his Scottish brethren fear their profits will suffer should Virginia become independent. But my husband is not of that ilk of middlemen so monetarily linked to England that we want Virginia to remain dependent on the Mother Country. Mercy, I wonder what is taking so long," she said and nestled back into her spot, fanning her neck again. She sighed heavily, and drifted back to sleep.

Shadows grew longer as the sun lowered. By the time a light breeze alleviated the heat, Therésé too had surrendered to the temperatures.

She dreamed. A disturbing image formed. She roamed through an abandoned house. Dozens of doors lined halls stretching out like spokes of a wheel. The corridors widened inexplicably. Each door opened as she darted from side to side, finding only a dark void behind each.

"Mother?" Her voice resonated in the empty hall, seeming to fade through the emptiness behind each portal. She followed another hallway, doors opening to emptiness before slamming shut.

A light wavered at the far end of the hall. Odd noises echoed the length, a low, garbled clatter as rhythmic as it was bothersome.

The whinny of a horse awoke Therésé and silenced the chorus of sounds in the trees. The images in her mind disappeared as if swallowed by dark. She sat up and blinked in confusion.

Mrs. McDermott stirred beside her. Two fireflies chased each other in the field. Tree frogs renewed their chirruping from their secret places deep in the leaves above her head.

The horse hooves clomped closer, the squeak of the wheels matching time. A lantern swayed. Mr. McDermott jumped from the side and headed toward the broken wagon.

"We are here, Ian." Mrs. McDermott scrambled to her feet, huffing from the exertion.

Her husband shined the light in her direction and approached. "We have had several difficulties, my dear. Army troops stopped and searched us twice."

"We encountered one group ourselves." Mrs. McDermott fluffed her skirts with an indignant snap. She interrupted her husband's anxious

inquiries, stating that she and Theresé were fine. "Please fix this wheel and let us return to our travels. I shall tell you the rest as we ride."

Mr. McDermott nodded and turned his lantern to the rear axle of the wagon, and with the assistance of the two men who had transported him to the area, he replaced the wheel.

Finally, they were on their way.

Theresé paid scant attention to the goings-on around her. The images from her dream filled her thoughts, and she pressed her hand to her stomach. She shuddered and drew her thin shawl tighter around her shoulders.

She feared the dream was a premonition of something frightening to come.

Terry
Portsmouth, Virginia, present day

Terry slipped into a booth tucked at the very back of Mom's Diner, and flopped her yellow legal pad on the bench beside her purse. When the waitress walked toward her with a glass of water and a menu, Terry glanced at the girl's nametag and said, "Hi, Kelly. I noticed the chalkboard as I came in and already know I'd like the meatloaf special. Mashed potatoes with a gallon of gravy, and string beans. And rolls. I'm not counting calories today. Unsweetened tea with lemon, please."

The girl smiled and scribbled on her note pad. "That was quick. You'll enjoy the meatloaf. It's my favorite comfort food and it's especially good today."

"Thank you, Kelly." Terry smiled. She made it a practice to try to find out the name of every clerk or wait person who assisted her. Although the habit came in handy on the rare occasions she had a complaint, she found the small effort brought a smile to those serving her, and she was quick to call a manager to offer a compliment.

Mrs. Belford's case had gnawed at her during her drive to the restaurant. She picked up the yellow pad and her phone, switching the device to the calculator app. She tapped numbers and scribbled results on the paper, erasing and scratching out figures.

Math had never been a favorite subject in school. Trying to figure out the calculations on the agreement increased her headache. She rubbed her temples and texted Sandi. "Are you out of court yet? Totally confused with these figures on the car dealer and am furious at the ass who owns the business. Need your mathematical help."

At the answering ping, Sandi's message showed, "Still in juvvie. Long docket and judge in bad mood. Hope she doesn't take it out on Kevin. When r u gonna learn 2 abbrevi8?"

Terry responded, "You do the numbers, I do the spelling."

Sandi: "I 4got. L8R. Case just called. Pray 4 Kevin."

Terry smiled and slipped the phone into her purse. Fast on the keypad, she refused to use the text shorthand others used. She could tap out a sentence as quickly as others using symbols and letters.

She and Sandi were alike in many ways, with one big difference. Sandi could crunch huge numbers in her head, while Terry needed a paper and pencil at the least. Terry, on the other hand, could decipher a forty-character sentence in a game of Hangman with one or two letters, and often joked that Sandi spelled "shit" with two t's.

Kelly placed the special and drink on the table. "Enjoy."

"This looks great." Terry dug in with delight. True to Kelly's description, the country meal was satisfying. The tension in her shoulders eased and the distressing morning faded into memory as she savored each bite, the slightly sweet tomato base of the mixture blending with the meaty taste of the beef gravy.

She tried to ignore the yellow pad, but as an occasional thought crossed her mind, she used her left hand to scrawl a reminder while her right hand held a fork. Fairly ambidextrous, she often had to later decipher what she had scribbled with her weaker hand.

"I know just the person to call," she mumbled as she jotted "Call Briley." *Now, why in the world didn't I think of that earlier?* Briley was a long-time family friend and attorney, who had represented Mary Jo in a sensitive case where Terry was a witness. Della, the mother of Mary Jo's late fiancé had demanded not only possessions she was entitled to after his death, but several items belonging to Mary Jo. When Mary Jo had attempted to have the rightful property delivered, the vindictive woman had refused to accept it. Instead, she filed a claim to force Mary Jo to give up everything she had shared with Jay. Justice had prevailed and Mary Jo won the right to keep the disputed items, resulting in an even deeper divide between the two women.

Hmm. Maybe I should introduce Shady O'Grady to Della. They'd make such a perfect pair.

As if on cue Della Strong strolled into the diner. Terry groaned inwardly, the pleasant enjoyment from the meal ebbing away.

Della glanced around for an empty table. Her gaze caught Terry's, and she sauntered over, smirking.

"I guess you finally decided to get away from that French crap Mary Jo sells and eat real American food, huh, Terry?" Della asked, venomous saccharin dripping in her tone.

Terry didn't answer, but wiped the last of her gravy with a piece of roll and savored it. She dabbed a napkin at the corner of her mouth, and smiled. "Hello, Della." She snatched the check from the table, gathered her legal pad and phone and slid from the booth, motioning with her free hand toward the bench. "Be my guest."

"I'll wait until they fumigate the booth first," Della retorted.

Terry stopped and angled her head. "Tsk, tsk," she clucked her tongue. "I'm sorry I can't stay and speak longer with you, but I refuse to engage in a battle of wits with an unarmed person. Goodbye, Della."

Della's mad sputter followed Terry as she walked toward the cashier. Laughing inwardly, she paid Kelly and included a generous tip.

Maybe the day wouldn't be a total loss after all.

In a better mood now, Terry returned to her office parking lot and maneuvered into Becky's designated spot beside her own snazzy red convertible, now backed into its proper space. Terry circled the front and nodded approvingly at the replaced tire.

A note fluttered under the windshield wiper, and she retrieved it, smiling as she read Gage's scrawled note aloud. *"Hey, sis, here you are, all fixed and ready to go. Thanks for lunch. BTW, it cost you a dozen of those chosen oh palm things. That was payment for parking your car back in your space. I don't come cheap. Your loving bro."*

At the bottom, Gage had drawn a smiley face with devil's horns. Terry laughed out loud at her brother's comical reference to the French apple turnovers called *chaussons aux pommes*, one of Mary Jo's most popular pastries. Gage's endearing manner lifted the last of the gloomy feeling from her shoulders.

Glancing at her watch, she determined she had time to deliver the pretty door adornments she'd picked up at the country nursery in Driver. It had been a while since she'd stopped at the crossroads of the little community in Suffolk where she occupied a small apartment over her parents' garage. Autumn decor signaled the neighborhood was gearing up for the annual "Driver Days Festival" in a few weeks.

She gathered two arrangements and headed to the café first. In the kitchen, Mary Jo and Hannah mixed dough for the next day's treats. Tanner sat on a stool beside them, covered from head to waist in white powder as he stirred a bowl of dry flour.

"Hey, Aunt Terry, look what I gots," he said, holding up a miniature rubber spatula.

"Look what I *have*," Beth correctly gently as she brought dishes to the counter.

Tanner corrected himself. "I forgot, mama. But, look, Aunt Terry." He waggled the spatula in front of Terry. "I'm gonna be in Aunt Mary Jo's kids cooking school. All the little tools came in today."

"Well, congratulations, Chef Tanner." Terry ruffled his hair, raising a thin cloud of flour from his head. Terry brushed her hands and looked at Mary Jo. "So your kid's cooking corner is coming to life?"

"It is," Mary Jo said with a grin. Mary Jo waved in the direction of the designated room where visitors would soon purchase pint-sized cooking utensils for children. "We got the first supplies in today. *Le Petite Chef* is taking shape." She wanted to hold cooking classes for promising young bakers in the near future, but the recent hurricane had derailed those plans.

"Well, we've come a long way from Hurricane Abby and Storm Della, whom I just ran into a few minutes ago, by the way. Della, not Abby." Terry relayed the exchange in the diner.

"She just won't let it go." Mary Jo's tempo increased as she stirred the contents of her bowl, metal spoon clanging against the sides with each frenzied stroke.

"Well, we're not going to let her get to us." Terry held up the floral decoration, an oval wicker frame bearing cornstalk, Indian corn and colorful gourds entwined with orange ribbons. "Do you like this for the front doors of the buildings? I bought three."

"I like." Mary Jo said, echoed by Beth and Hannah.

"Great. I'll go hang this one on the front door, and take one to hang on Clothiste's Inn."

"Can I go wif you?" Tanner scrambled from the stool.

"Um…" Beth scratched her head and grimaced.

"I'm not going inside," Terry hastily assured her sister-in-law. Beth had declared the house off limits to her son. A few weeks earlier Tanner had gone upstairs to play in one of the empty bedrooms. A ghostly mist had swirled into the room and surrounded him until he screamed. Chase had reached him first, and with quick thinking, had turned Tanner into a hero by claiming the little boy's shouts had warned him in advance. Tanner relished the role.

"Can I go, Mama? I'm bored here." He tossed the spatula on the counter.

"Only if you stay outside with Aunt Terry," Beth ordered.

"Geez, I hope that will not be the reaction of kids in the cooking glass," Mary Jo pouted. "I'm bored," she mimicked in a perfect echo of the little boy's voice.

"All right then, Tanner, you can help me hang this." Terry held out her hand.

"Wait." Tanner grabbed a bag from the corner and dumped out toys. He scattered action figures and bright yellow characters until he fished out a miniature hammer. "You might need me to help hit nails."

"If all you people are so tuned to these miniature things for kids, why aren't you all having your own?" Hannah growled.

"Hey, I'm cooperating." Beth touched her tummy. "I've got my next bun in the oven."

"We're out of here," Terry said, pointing Tanner in the direction of the front door. She called over her shoulder, "I might have the oven, but I need a baker." The laughter of her family mingled with the musical notes of the overhead bell. She removed the summer wreath from the hook and replaced it with the autumn display. She followed Tanner onto the porch and shut the door behind them, admiring the display.

"Nice," she said.

"Yep. What can I hammer?" Tanner wielded the tiny tool like Thor.

"Nothing here. Let's go see about the Inn."

Tanner thumped two feet at a time down the steps and raced ahead of her on the sidewalk. He eyed the summer wreath hanging on the door.

"Aw, man it already gots…it already has a hook."

"Well, look here, this board is loose." Terry tapped her toe on a perfectly solid board. "Why don't you tap those nails down for me?"

"Sure!" Tanner dropped to his knees and banged haphazardly on the wood.

Terry winced, hoping the tiny hammer did not leave marks or Chase would skin her alive for marring his handiwork. She removed the older wreath and settled the new one over the hook. She took a step backwards to check the placement.

"Hello, lady." Tanner paused his pounding. "Who are you?"

Terry glanced around, then at her nephew. He returned his attention to pounding.

"Who are you talking to, Tanner?" she asked.

"That's pretty." A female voice spoke, almost in her ear. Terry whipped her head to the right and her jaw dropped.

She stared directly into the face of the colonial girl she had seen several times over the years. Usually sheathed in a shimmering translucent glow, this time the girl stood beside her in the flesh, clutching a book to her chest.

"I've been waiting a long time for you, Terry."

"What's your name, lady?" Tanner rose to his feet, stood in front of the girl and studied her face. "You look like Marie Jo-fess."

"I am Theresé, Marie Josephé's older sister. Do you remember Nicole? I am her sister too."

Tanner nodded his head sadly. Using his nickname for the youngest colonial sister, he said, "I miss Nickel. She never comes to play anymore."

Theresé knelt, eye-level with the little boy. "Nicole—Nickel—is very happy now. My sisters needed to be happy, Tanner, and you helped them very much. Stephanie found Nicole's teardrop and Mary Jo found Marie Josephé's heart, so they could move on to another place. And now—because of you, perhaps Terry will be able to find my mother."

"And I save-ded Uncle Chase when the bad ghost tried to scare him." Tanner waved the small hammer. "And if any bad ghosts come here today, I will hit them with my hammer. Bye, Terrace." Tanner dropped back to his knees and whacked imaginary nails. To his childish ears, the correct pronunciation of Theresé's name sounded like terrace.

Theresé rose to her feet and smiled wistfully at the little boy.

Terry watched the scene unfold, dumbstruck. She stretched her fingers and touched the specter's hand. Her hand did not pass through the image as she expected, but met the warmth of a human body.

"You are as real as I," she said. Her phone vibrated in her

pocket, followed by the shrill first ring.

"I am now. It does not last long." Already, the girl's form developed a silvery sheen. The second ring followed and her image faded, the porch railing becoming visible through her form.

At the third ring, she vanished.

"Help me find my mother, Terry." Her disjointed voice repeated the words, growing fainter until only the sound of Tanner's tapping hammer remained.

Allie Marie

CHAPTER 10

"This O'Grady guy has got to be one of the biggest crooks around." Sandi's voice rose in indignation as her fingers raced across the keypad of an adding machine, the stream of narrow paper curling into a bigger heap with each punch of the keys.

She looked up, brow wrinkled in concern as she yanked the paper across the serrated teeth and waved it. "Terry, he frontloaded the interest on Mrs. Belford's loan, adding three thousand dollars to the cost of the vehicle. Then he charged a monthly interest fee. The agreement clearly states that if she paid the loan off before the two-year mark, there would be no interest. She paid the balance six months early, and she has all her checks to show she paid more than five thousand, so he owes her a refund. Plus, she paid separately for the tax and DMV fees, therefore he can't try to claim she owes those fees as part of the payoff." Sandi scanned the figures printed on the paper, circled a group of numbers and pushed the paper toward Terry.

"So, I wasn't too far off with my estimates." Terry propped her right hip on Sandi's desk, swinging her leg as she squinted at the tape from the adding machine, totally confused by the stream of numbers in black or red. "We got hung up with the last of the preps for the Wheeler case, but I've asked Becky to check if he has any complaints with the Better Business Bureau. I doubt she had time before she left. So, does this look like a scheme whereby he charges the interest up front and the customers don't really notice what he's done? They later become caught up in the escalating costs?"

"It looks like it, certainly in Mrs. Belford's case. He might have quite a scam going on, overcharging people who may not be able to get a conventional loan, adding interest up front, and glossing over that in the loan agreement. People would never be able to pay a loan off this way. A smooth talker could easily crunch numbers so they made sense. High monthly payments set up a person struggling with money. They miss a payment and bam!" Sandi slapped the desk. "He tows the car, which he sells to someone else, and files a judgment against the original owner. This happened to the second client." She shoved the adding machine in her top desk drawer and cupped her chin in her hand, drumming her fingers before she continued. "It's like some of those auto-title loan companies, where people use their title to get an emergency loan, and if they can't repay it, they roll over to a new loan with new fees and interest, until eventually they can't pay and the car is repossessed."

"Or payday loan schemes where the customer borrows against their next paycheck," Terry said, "By the way, did I tell you I saw Della at lunch today? I think we should pair her on a blind date with Shady." Terry described the brief encounter.

Sandi threw her head back and laughed. "You are always so quick with the snappy comebacks. I seem to think of good comments hours after someone has insulted me." When her gaze dropped onto the Belford file, she tapped her desk. "This really pisses me off."

"Good. Me too. If we're satisfied, I'd like to take Mrs. Belford's case *pro bono*." Terry stood and straightened papers crunched when she sat on them.

"I'm in. I'll take this file and paper ream home with me." Sandi snatched the paper ribbon and waved it in the air, then stuck it in the manila folder. "I'd love to do it right now, but Leslie's got an indoor Pee Wee league soccer game at six and if I hurry I can make it. After dinner, I'll crunch every figure to the penny and we'll form our game plan tomorrow."

The two attorneys clasped hands and then embraced in a sisterly hug.

Sandi gathered her purse and the file. "You want to come

103

see Leslie's game?"

"Next time. I'm staying a while longer to look over the Wheeler case one last time."

"Freddie's just trying to make you sweat. He'll grab you at the door to court and offer your client the deal you want." Sandi referred to Freddie Girard, the opposing lawyer in the legal action.

"I know. But just in case, I'll be prepared. See you tomorrow." Terry followed Sandi through the kitchen, and locked the door behind her friend. She glanced around the small kitchen, hoping the coffee pot still contained enough java to fill a cup. The ever-efficient Becky had already cleaned the pot, and set the timer for the automatic brew in the morning. Terry grabbed a ginger ale from the refrigerator and walked to her office, using her free hand to flip light switches to illuminate the hall.

What a day. She plunked in her chair and held the cold can to her forehead. The day had worsened progressively. A burning sensation formed in the pit of her stomach and she sipped the ginger ale, hoping to soothe the churning.

The Wheeler file occupied center stage on her desk. She flipped though the file one last time, satisfied she had done all she could to prepare an airtight case.

Next, she glanced at her copy of Mrs. Belford's case, but without understanding the math she slapped it shut. Once Sandi confirmed the actual financial figures, she would attack the case with vengeance. She located Mrs. Belford's number and dialed. The woman's tentative voice answered.

"Hello, Mrs. Belford, this is Terry Dunbar. How are you?"

"I'm fine, Ms. Dunbar. I've been waiting to hear from you. I talked to the detectives today and filed the police report."

"Very good, Mrs. Belford. I wanted to let you know that my partner and I are taking on your civil case."

Mrs. Belford gasped, then sobbed quietly. "Oh, thank you. I feel certain you can help me. How much will it cost?"

"We are taking your case in what we call *pro bono*. We will not charge you. I don't want you to get your hopes up, but I think you have a strong case."

She checked her watch. Five-twenty. Taking a chance her friend Jonathan was still in the office, she called the detective bureau and followed the prompts to his extension. By the third ring, she prepared to hang up, when Jonathan's voice answered with a harried "Shellito."

"Hi, Jonathan, this is Terry Dunbar. Sorry to catch you so late, but I'm hoping you have a minute."

"Sure, Terry. Apologize if I snapped, I was on the cell phone with a useless caller yanking my chain. What can I do for you?"

"Actually, I'm calling for two reasons. One, to see if there's an update on the skeletal remains. And I know you're homicide, but there's a particularly troubling case I'd like to mention."

"Ok, first, I haven't heard anything from the medical examiner's office about the remains, but I'll call the M.E. first thing in the morning. Sometimes these non-active cases get pushed to the back burner. I'd say we should have an answer soon."

"Thanks, Jonathan. Now here's a case I picked up today." She relayed the details from the three clients. The scratching noises indicated the detective was writing as Terry spoke. When she finished, he gave a low whistle.

"A couple of our investigators have been looking at him for a long time, but never could get the goods on him. The few substantial complaints I have heard about were from people who hadn't made payments and their vehicles were repo'ed. I doubt if anyone picked up on the frontloading because O'Grady could always show proof of failure to pay. I don't deal with property crimes much, but this deal of adding the interest up front plus charging monthly has larceny by false pretenses or larceny by trick written all over it."

"Well, it's not the usual scam, is it?"

"No, it isn't. Everyone's gone for the day, and I don't see the on-call property guys in yet." Terry knew from previous cases that the Portsmouth detectives rotated to evening shift for the week they were on "callback," when they would investigate crimes that occurred outside of normal business hours. She heard the clack of a keyboard, and then Jonathan said, "Mrs. Leslie Belford? I see her report in the system. As you know, the property guys will work with the Commonwealth Attorney's office. They'll probably go for a straight indictment rather than an arrest warrant."

"Thank you, Jonathan. Since Mrs. Belford is my client, one thing I won't have to worry about is this creep asking me to represent him if he's charged with a criminal offense." They both laughed and exchanged minor chit-chat before ending the call.

Terry dialed another number. As her mother's voice resonated through the receiver, Terry offered up a silent prayer of thanks her mother was still with her.

"Hey, Mom, what's up?"

"Just put some finishing touches on party favors for my reunion." Joan's latest project involved making blue and orange tabletop arrangements for her 40th high school reunion from Woodrow Wilson High School.

"Have you decided if you are going to make the same things for Dad's class?" Terry's father had graduated the same year from Wilson's arch rival school, Churchland.

"I am. I've also decided that I will charge the orange and black double, and that will pay for my school's orange and blue favors." Joan's mischievous chuckle brought a smile to Terry's face. "So, how was your day?"

"Oh, Mom, it's been horrible." Terry gave a brief rundown of the events, skipping over the encounter with the ghostly image. Joan reacted with anger at the case with Mrs. Belford, asking a couple of questions that Terry scribbled on a sticky pad.

"Those are good questions, Mom. I've added them to my list."

When Terry next described the exchange with Della Strong, Joan clicked her tongue with annoyance.

"That was a good comeback, daughter. Proud of you. I

remember when Jay was alive, and she came to several events with him and Mary Jo. She never seemed particularly warm and friendly."

"I don't know what I did to make her so antagonistic towards me, but I think I've found her soul mate with Shady O'Grady."

Mother and daughter shared another laugh, then Terry said she would spend the night at the Inn.

"Honey, is it wise to stay there by yourself?" Joan's voice held a trace of worry.

"I feel perfectly safe there, Mom, in spite of some of the events that have occurred there. I feel protected, even, if that makes sense. And I won't be going up to the attic."

"I don't like it. I wish Stephanie was still at the apartment. When does Kyle come back?"

"He didn't really say. I know he wants to follow up on some more ancestry records, so I kind of expected he would move in as soon as he could. Tell you what, Mom. I'm going to grab a bite and if I feel like driving home, I'll let you know."

"Call me either way, honey. Love you."

"Love you too, Mom." Terry hung up. Before she could dial another number, the phone immediately rang. Mary Jo's number appeared on the screen.

"Hi, Terry! Guess what?" Mary Jo's voice rang with excitement, a far cry from her usual composed demeanor. Without giving Terry a chance to respond, she gushed, "I'm meeting my father tonight. He surprised us all by flying in for Mama's birthday. She just told me and we're on our way to the airport now. I'm so excited. Hannah—ouch, sorry. My *grandmother* just pinched me," Mary Jo said with a laugh. No one had known that Hannah had long ago given up a son for adoption until he had contacted her through Kyle's research efforts. Once the complicated case played out, Mary Jo also received the startling news that she was the granddaughter of the diminutive and cantankerous Hannah.

"Oh, how exciting, Mary Jo. I can't wait to meet him." Childhood friends long before the family relationship had been established, Terry and the Dunbar family had taken Mary Jo in as a foster child. The two women remained as close as blood sisters.

"Anyway, Grandma has talked to your mom and they're already planning a family gathering so we'll meet over the weekend."

"Oh, lawdy." Terry rolled her eyes skyward. There was nothing better than a family get-together to make Joan Dunbar and Hannah Jensen happy. Although distant cousins by blood, they too were as close as sisters.

"Okay, we're at the airport now. I'll call you later."

"Have fun." Terry hung up the phone and leaned back in her chair, reflecting on Mary Jo's difficult path to adulthood. They had been friends since first grade. Although she'd spent occasional sleepovers at Mary Jo's, most times the latter was at the Dunbar house because Mary Jo's mother Elizabeth worked evenings. Delayed one night by an unexpected winter storm, Elizabeth was not present when a fire broke out in an apartment below hers.

When firefighters found twelve-year old Mary Jo alone, Child Protective Services responded to take Mary Jo into their care. However, she had pitched such a fit that the Dunbars were called to the scene to calm her down. They agreed to take temporary care of her, and eventually became her permanent foster parents. She remained with the family until she joined the military. On return from a deployment to Afghanistan, Mary Jo received the startling news of her true relationship to Hannah and ultimately to the Dunbar family.

Terry propped her feet on a desk drawer and pulled a personal folder toward her. Joan had always been disappointed that her daughter did not share the same interest in the family tree research—until Hurricane Abby struck, felling hundreds of trees, including one in the rear of the café. Workers discovered the skeletal remains that now awaited disposition in the Medical Examiner's Office.

Since the discovery, she'd toyed with the idea of a DNA search to see if they could find a match. Documentation already linked Stephanie and Mary Jo to a French captain and his Canadian wife, believed to be the parents of the young colonial ghosts haunting the properties. Although Kyle suspected that she too was a descendant of the same family, the Dunbar connection had not been formally established. She'd sent in a sample, hoping that after the Medical Examiner's office released the remains, results would lead to a connection to the old bones through an ancestral DNA testing. Although she had the results, she found the material confusing.

She ran her thumbs over the letters she had handwritten on the tab: "DNA" in block print. A pamphlet fluttered from the file and she picked it up. She slapped the file closed and tossed it aside. She needed to close her eyes—just for a minute.

Kyle Avery's face was the last image that crossed her mind as she dozed.

***

Kyle Avery wished he had anything else on his mind but the rush hour traffic he'd caught on I-95. He'd planned to spend a few days in Maryland to move from his apartment, but instead moved in a single afternoon. The benefits of living in a furnished apartment left little necessity to own much property. He'd packed his few possessions, left a few small appliances and bath linens for the landlord, and prepared to return to Portsmouth Monday afternoon.

He made a quick stop at the university to donate some textbooks to colleagues. Upon his return to the parking lot, he discovered his car had a flat tire, as did his spare. He'd had to hunt around for someone to take him to a repair shop. About the time he replaced the flat and secured the spare in the well of the trunk, several other colleagues caught up with him and insisted he join them for a farewell lunch.

Returning to his vehicle and anxious to get on the road, he was further delayed by the unwelcome realization that he had locked his keys in the vehicle.

After thanking the campus police who helped him, he began his journey south. He encountered congestion at the usual bottlenecks along I-95 but once on I-64, traffic had flowed smoothly—until he hit the area around Fort Eustis. Then bumper-to-bumper traffic reduced his speed to twenty miles an hour, grinding to a halt a mile from the entrance to the Monitor-Merrimac Bridge Tunnel.

Kyle leaned forward and tapped his forehead on the steering wheel, then grabbed his phone. A quick punch of the number for the state traffic advisory confirmed his fears—a vehicle breakdown in the tunnel.

What a day. He settled back in his seat to outwait the standstill. *Maybe I should have waited a day or two to return to Portsmouth instead of making the roundtrip in one day.* He didn't know why he'd rushed back—or what had caused him to make the decision to pack up and leave Maryland in the first place.

Terry's face flashed in his memory. She was the reason why he was so anxious to return. The gorgeous lawyer with the mane of chestnut hair had caught his attention the minute he saw her.

But in her presence he turned into a shy awkward teenager.

I'm attracted to Terry. Kyle drummed his fingers impatiently. *Okay, very attracted. So is every guy who sees her.* In the short time he'd known her, he had watched how often men flocked around her wherever she went. It made sense. In addition to the lawyer's good looks, she worked in a predominantly masculine field, but she seemed to handle the attention with grace and ease.

She had to be the most genuine person he'd ever met, except maybe for her mother. The moment you met Joan Dunbar, you felt like you were part of the family. The daughter had certainly inherited that ability. He'd felt comfortable with the entire family at her birthday party.

And that, he discovered, was the uniqueness of the whole Dunbar clan, that endearing capacity to make strangers feel welcome.

It had been all he could do to keep his eyes off Terry

throughout the evening, but he tried. He became tongue-tied every time he had the chance to speak with her. All he could do was spout off details from Portsmouth's history or her family ancestry.

He'd caught Charles watching him speculatively several times. Realizing he was the subject of scrutiny by the father of the woman he planned to pursue sent adolescent angst coursing through him. Although he hadn't dated much since he'd started writing his book and conducting his research, he'd never had trouble getting a date.

Maybe he'd ask her to dinner when he got settled.

"She's got to think I'm a freakin' bore," he shouted out loud, and punched the steering wheel, then smacked his palm to his forehead. "Damn, it's like being sixteen again."

He saw movement out of the corner of his eye and turned to look into the face of the startled driver in the vehicle beside him. She stared in concern before averting her gaze and inching ahead in her lane. Kyle shook his head, sure he looked quite the fool talking to himself.

Vehicles moved forward and stopped. He turned his attention to his driving as traffic crawled through the tunnel and across the bridge before spreading out on the interstate. Speeds picked up and the rest of his commute proved uneventful.

He arrived at the law office parking lot twenty-five minutes later, just in time to see Terry withdrawing a bag from the trunk of her red convertible. She glanced his way as he pulled into the spot reserved for the apartment, her smile dazzling him as she waved.

The timing was perfect—if he could get up enough nerve to ask her to dinner.

CHAPTER 11

"I didn't expect you until later in the week," Terry called as Kyle got out of his vehicle. She looped the strap of a pink duffle bag over her shoulder, extracted a matching garment bag from the trunk, and pushed the lid closed.

"It doesn't take much to move out of a furnished apartment." Kyle tried to laugh as he walked toward the rear of his vehicle.

Ask her now!

But his mouth went dry and he lost his nerve. Instead he said, "I took a chance that maybe someone was still in your office. I figured if no one was here, I'd spend the night in a hotel and catch you tomorrow. I probably should have waited until tomorrow. I got delayed at the university, had a flat tire, locked my keys in the car, and hit gridlock most of the drive here."

God help me. I'm babbling.

Terry's smile overwhelmed him. "Your day sounds like mine, which started bad and progressed to worse. I'm not even driving home tonight, just going to stay at the Inn. But there's no need for you to go to the hotel, everything is ready for you to move into the apartment. Let me take my things inside and I'll get the apartment keys for you." Terry shifted the garment bag over the crook of her arm and took a few steps toward the bed and breakfast. She pivoted on one heel and faced Kyle.

"Have you eaten dinner yet?"

"No." The single word stuck in his throat like a wad of cotton.

"Neither have I. I was about to walk down High Street and grab a bite. Would you like to go with me? I'd love some company."

"Me?"

"No, I'm talking to the guy beside you." She jutted her chin toward his left shoulder.

Kyle reflexively swiveled his head to the left and Terry burst into laughter. "You *have* had a bad day if you fell for that," she said. "I'll be right back."

"I-I..." Kyle gulped and stood gawking as Terry dashed up the steps to the B and B, unlocked the back door, and entered the kitchen.

She flipped the light switch and paused, eyes darting from side to side.

Comfortable temperature and blissful silence greeted her. She sighed with relief and set the baggage containing toiletries and a suit for tomorrow on the kitchen counter. With a few long strides she passed through the dining room and turned the switch that operated the parlor lights from that doorway. Soft light washed over the room, revealing everything in order.

"Therèse?" she called softly.

No response.

A little disappointed, Terry flipped the light switch that illuminated the staircase. She continued to turn on lights as she made her way to the back door.

As the lock clicked in the door, the garment bag slid from the counter, pooling into a lump on the floor.

A light brightened on the dial covering the wall thermostat. The LED numbers slowly decreased: 68, 67, 66...

Kyle waited, leaning against the hood of his car, arms crossed. He straightened as Terry walked down the steps.

"What do you feel like eating?" she asked as he joined her. "There's Italian, continental, seafood. You name it, it's somewhere down here."

"Anything's fine. I don't think I've had a bad meal anywhere in Olde Towne. But some place quiet, if that's okay with you."

"Absolutely. And I think I know the perfect place, if you don't mind a short walk." They fell into step.

Kyle broke the silence. "Not at all. One of the weather reports I heard says a new tropical storm is forming in the Atlantic."

Can't go wrong with the weather. Or can you? Too late, Kyle remembered the devastation the area experienced nearly a month earlier and glanced at Terry as they passed a lighted storefront.

"I haven't had a chance to listen to the news today. I hope it doesn't follow Hurricane Abby's path of destruction. Olde Towne is just recovering." Terry seemed unperturbed and Kyle relaxed.

"I hope not. I like it here. Portsmouth has quite a bit of history, especially the downtown and Olde Towne areas," Kyle remarked.

"It really is a great little place," Terry remarked. "Sometimes the politics are…" she paused. "How can I say it diplomatically? The politics are—politics, that's the best I can say, because it can be a three-ring circus around city hall. And the city has its share of modern-day issues, but often gets a bum rap in the news."

"I like it here. This place got its name from Portsmouth, England. I've been there a couple of times."

"Really? Does it look like here?"

Kyle shrugged. "Not much. It's more British there." They laughed and he continued, "I have several friends in the Hampshire Constabulary. I met them years ago during an exchange program. Not only do the two Portsmouth cities have many similar street names, but the Hampton Roads area has a number of cities named after English cities."

Terry nodded. "Yep. Norfolk, Suffolk, Isle of Wight, Surry, to name a few."

Kyle stopped and pressed Terry's arm. He pointed downward to a white granite marker in the pavement, contrasting with the red bricks surrounding it.

"I read recently these markers designate the locations of significant squares of the old city and the original purpose. Our Portsmouth's boundaries were very limited back then, only about sixty-five acres, and its waterfront property was a bustling seaport in those days. The city founder, Colonel Crawford, named blocks according to the important function that occurred there. The city was laid out in a grid pattern, and like its namesake in the old country, it has a High Street, a King Street, a Queen and a North."

"You're right, these markers are popping up all around. I feel bad. I was invited to some of the dedications but always seem to have court on those days." Terry's glance followed Kyle's finger pointing at the engraved letters on the marker at her feet and she laughed. "Oh, look. 'Courthouse Square.' How appropriate."

"Sorry if I put on my professor hat," Kyle said. "I'm embarrassed to say I get carried away with American history, even more so now that I'm learning so much stuff about your mom's family tree."

"I'm actually enjoying your history lesson. Mom's been a bit frustrated with me and my siblings because we don't have the same interest in finding our roots. When we were growing up, we cared more about coming down to the riverfront for the Seawall Festival, which we no longer have, or going on the annual Ghost Walk."

"I've been reading about that event. Sounds fun."

"It is. My brothers and Chase outgrew it when they reached the age of slasher films. We thought of getting Clothiste's Inn included on the tour, but with the discovery of the skeleton after the hurricane, we decided it would be better to wait until next year so we don't attract a macabre crowd."

"Probably wise," Kyle agreed. He directed Terry out of the path of a puddle on the pavement. She didn't draw away, but slid her hand through the crook of his arm.

"But since you'll be living here, at least for a while, you need to experience it once." She stopped and swept her hand in front of a tier of signs citing the distances to Frankfurt and other locations. "And here we are at the Bier Haus." She led the way through a wrought iron gate and past the outside garden patio where blue and white checkered tablecloths covered the tops. Not merely checked, the slanted diamonds represented the patterns of the Bavarian flag.

At the hostess station inside they were greeted cheerfully by a young woman who escorted them to a corner table. She placed the menus down and discreetly slipped away as Kyle helped Terry remove her coat.

"This is really nice," he said.

"It's one of my favorite places. I feel like I step out of the rat-race when I come in here."

Terry sat in the chair Kyle held out for her. He politely scooted her close to the table, then hung her coat along with his jacket on a nearby rack. Instead of sitting opposite her, he took the seat to her right and sighed. "After the day I had, this is perfect."

Terry deliberately angled her knee so that her leg brushed his as he tugged his chair closer. She leaned forward and flashed an innocent smile. "Let's exchange our tales of woe and see whose day was worse," she suggested.

"You're on," he accepted, mirroring her movements. "You first."

"No, my idea, so you go first."

"All right. Get ready."

After they placed their orders, the normally reticent professor became more animated as he described his ordeals. He sliced his hands through the air to emphasize frustration with the flat tire, gave his forehead a light tap to describe his consternation with the locked keys, and rolled his eyes while relaying the traffic jams.

They'd never spent this much time alone before, Terry realized. She enjoyed watching the expressions on his face change. He relaxed as he recounted each phase of his day, using humor to unwind. His easy laugh mesmerized her. When he reenacted the scene where he banged his head on the steering wheel and imitated the alarmed look of the driver beside him, she laughed so hard she had to wipe tears from her eyes.

He lightly brushed his fingers across her forearm as he said, "Top that."

The simple touch sent a sensual shock wave through Terry, and she started to slide her hand toward his, when the waitress brought water glasses and a bread basket to the table. Despite the server's tactful movements, the mood shattered and Terry straightened her posture.

"Your turn." Kyle too had moved, leaning back in the chair as he slid his fingers away from her arm and to the water glass, tracing the path of a bead of water sliding down the stem.

Terry hid her disappointment by describing in animated detail her day of calamities.

When she finished, Kyle raised his glass in salute and said, "I have to say, your day was worse than mine. And I hope the cops nail that slimy car dealer."

"Me too. I just hope I can help Mrs. Belford get her money and her car back."

"I have a feeling you'll do it."

"Thank you."

Too soon, the waitress returned with their wine and food. Terry slid her fingers toward the wineglass. *Why didn't I pick some place with notoriously slow service?*

"So tell me about your family," Terry asked. "You already know so much about mine. What got you interested in family trees and all the nuts that fall from them?"

Kyle laughed. "Well, I'm an only kid, but my dad was one of eight brothers who live in and around Baltimore, so I have plenty of cousins. I grew up in Annapolis. I don't know why or how I got into the ancestry research. Dad owned and operated a marina but I was never interested in boats—or the Navy, much to his disappointment. I think he always secretly hoped I'd go to the Naval Academy." He shrugged. "I was always in awe of my grandfather, because he knew so much about his own grandfather, who had served in the Civil War and died fairly young. It was his widowed wife Annette who later married Arthur Wyatt, making him my step-great-great-great grandfather. Arthur would have been your fourth…" Kyle paused to count with his fingers. "Yes, your fourth-great uncle."

"We were fortunate to have four male descendants in a row, we can trace the Wyatts in my family quite far back. I know it's harder to trace female family members because of marriage name changes and all." Terry scribbled on a napkin, then held it to Kyle. She had drawn a rough family tree that indicated her male ancestors. She counted the lines and pointed to the name at the top. "Frank Wyatt is my third great-grandfather, right? And your third-great grandmother was his brother's second wife." Kyle nodded and she continued. "So, are we step-cousins like four times removed?"

"Something like that."

"See, that's already too much for me. Trying to figure out who is once or twice removed from the first or second cousin confuses me." She laughed. "I hate numbers anyway, and to tell the truth, I wasn't very fond of history in school."

Joining in her laughter, Kyle said, "I'll be honest, I have a computer program that helps me match up relationships. But your paper chart is useful tonight. As you said, I'm not related to the Wyatt family by blood, but through this grandmother's second marriage." He turned the napkin in his direction and added several strokes to the chart Terry had sketched. He printed his ancestress's name beside Arthur Wyatt.

"It seems you've inherited her penchant for genealogy." Terry smiled.

Kyle nodded, buttering bread. "And history. She definitely collected a lot of information in the mid-to-late eighteen hundreds that had both historical and genealogical significance. Ever since Stephanie and I made contact about the mutual names in our family trees, we've been on course with the research, which is not always the case in ancestry research.

We've established her link, as well as Mary Jo's, to the colonial ancestors Étienne and Clothiste. Now if I can just break through the brick wall holding me back from confirming whether your mom is related to the same French couple."

Another couple walked through the door and caught her attention. She grimaced and leaned toward Kyle. "Don't look now, but do you remember the couple who were having lunch at the café last Saturday? The guy was in uniform, a naval commander?"

Kyle inclined his head toward Terry. His brown eyes reflected gold specks in the glow of the candlelight.

"I remember them," he said.

"They just came in. She doesn't look much happier tonight then she did that day."

"She kind of picked at him a lot, if I remember right. Their table was next to mine and I couldn't help but overhear some of their conversation. I felt sorry for him and had to bury my nose in my papers to tune her out."

Terry smiled, remembering Kyle's startled look when she dropped into the seat at his table that day. "Yes. I came in on the tail end of their lunch. I'd picked up their tab to thank him for his military service, and he introduced her. She's his fiancée and didn't seem too pleased I'd stopped by to talk. Mary Jo and Steph also said she fussed at him through most of the meal."

Kyle turned his head casually toward the entrance, his gaze sweeping across the room before he faced Terry again. He scratched his chin pensively and said, "It doesn't seem like a good start to a relationship. I had a girlfriend like that once. We didn't last long."

"Ouch."

"Yeah." He shrugged and sliced his steak, then paused with a tilt to his head. "How about you? Any green-eyed monsters in your past?"

Terry paused and thought. "No, I can't really say that I've had that experience."

"Good. It's not a pleasant situation at all. It can kill your confidence, make you gun-shy."

Terry took mental note of Kyle's statement. *Maybe that's why he doesn't act interested.*

The waitress stopped by the table, set fresh glasses of wine at their table and said, "Compliments of the gentleman at the other table." She smiled. "Can I get you anything here?" Terry and Kyle both shook their heads. The waitress left and then in unison turned to the other table.

The commander, dressed in civilian clothes this evening, glanced their way. Kyle raised his wine glass in a salute and the Navy man nodded.

"I hope this doesn't cause any problems between them," Terry murmured as she picked up her glass.

"I was thinking the same thing."

They finished the meal in silence, declining dessert when the waitress came to the table. Kyle asked for the check.

"I'm paying," Terry interjected. "I'm the one who asked you."

"Nope, we agreed to compare our crappy days today, and yours was by far the worst, so I'm paying. This has definitely been the highlight of the day for me."

Terry wagged her finger playfully in Kyle's direction. "Me too. But next time it's on me."

Kyle wrapped his finger around hers at the knuckles and winked. "We'll see."

Terry's heart fluttered. Her day had definitely made a hundred and eighty degree turn.

After Kyle retrieved their coats, he helped Terry into hers and then they stopped by the

Commander's table.

"We'd like to thank you for the wine," Kyle said.

"My pleasure," Commander Lawrence said. He stood and shook hands with Kyle, then reached for Terry's hand. "I wanted to repay your thoughtfulness when Liana and I were at the café," he said. The static electricity snapped between them and Terry stepped back, laughing gingerly as she rubbed her palm on her sleeve. He raised an eyebrow as he glanced at his hand, and then touched his fiancée's shoulder. "This is Liana, my fiancée."

The woman extended her hand to Terry, nodding politely but indifferently.

Terry remained silent while the men exchanged a few pleasantries before they shook hands again. She said goodnight, and stepped into the foyer, Kyle joining her. Laughter and low music mixed with the occasional clink of glass drifted from the area of the wine bar.

"We should get the gang together and come back here sometime," Terry suggested. The bite of crisp October air greeted them as they strolled along the sidewalk.

The light aroma of burning wood drifted by. A crisp wind tossed leaves across their path, their shoes crunching the foliage.

"Autumn is here." Kyle sniffed the air appreciatively and zipped his jacket to his neck. "Are you up for a stroll?"

"I am." Terry inhaled the fall smells and smiled. "There's something about this time of year that I love. The crisp air, the excitement of autumn festivals, the anticipation of the upcoming holidays. From now through Christmas, this is my favorite time of year."

"No kidding?" Kyle bumped her arm with his elbow. "Mine too."

"Really?" Terry bumped her shoulder against his arm. "Okay, Halloween arrives first. Are you into the zombies and demons kind of celebration?"

Kyle winced. "Not exactly. Even as a little kid, my costumes leaned toward historical characters. Although one year I did dress as Jack the Ripper and another as Bluebeard the Pirate. So I guess I had gruesome moments in my own way."

"Blackbeard and Jack the Ripper, eh? You were a little ghoulish. Well, the Ghost Walk is coming up and you might enjoy that event. It's been popular for years and years. It's a walking tour of Olde Towne's historic district, with costumed characters spinning tales from porches and street corners. And

121

that reminds me. We're going to throw a Halloween-themed bash to commemorate the grand opening of Clothiste's Inn. I'm sure you'll be hearing about it from Mom, if you haven't already. She's all gung-ho."

Terry paused as they waited for a car to pass, and then they crossed the street. She continued, "Of course, it goes without saying that you're invited. If you're interested in an authentic-era costume, there's a trunk full of old clothes in the attic of the Inn. Which reminds me of another thing. The building that houses my office and your new apartment belonged to my great-aunt Ida. I inherited it lock, stock and barrel. She had boxes of old stuff in the attic. When we converted the house, we just moved stuff to the Inn because it was the last building to undergo renovation. I'm afraid I wasn't very concerned with those old things, and don't get involved like my mom or Stephanie. There is a weathered valise up there. I remember glancing through it once. It has old papers and maybe letters that might be helpful. And I apologize for babbling like that."

"Nothing to apologize for. I'm enjoying the insight. That valise sounds interesting. I'd like to look at it. Sometimes all it takes is one unexpected statement in a letter or journal that unlocks a clue," Kyle said.

"I learned that from Stephanie's experiences. I just don't get into the past that much."

"It's not for everyone." Kyle agreed. He stopped to gaze at the posters along the walls of the movie theater. "I read about this building," he said. "It's on the National Registry of Historic Places. It was renovated in the late eighties to bring back its original nineteen-forties art deco design, right?"

"That's right. I like it there. There's a dining area where you can sit at tables and enjoy the movie during dinner."

"Cool. I don't get much time to go to the movies, but I'd like to go once to see the inside." Kyle strolled a few more feet and stopped to peer through the wrought iron gate leading to the old cemetery of Trinity Church. In the path of a few of the lights from the church's arched walkway, the gray shapes of headstones stood out against the dark background. "This is another place I need to check out."

"The historian there is one of the most knowledgeable people about Portsmouth. But I don't think you'll find any Wyatt info. Mom's family is Catholic, not Episcopal, but you still might find historical information there. She and Dad were married in Saint Paul's, just a couple of blocks from here."

Kyle nodded. "Maybe there will be some church or diocesan records about earlier Wyatt marriages or baptisms." Kyle's phone chirped in his pocket. He glanced at his watch and smacked his forehead. "Holy crap! I was supposed to have an online chat with a researcher at ten tonight. We've been trying to hook up for weeks." He quickened his pace for a few steps and then slowed to normal, adding with a shake of his head, "That was rude of me."

"It's fine," Terry said. She sped up her pace and pulled him along, turning on Court Street. "I need to call it an early night anyhow. I'm staying in the innkeeper's suite at the B and B tonight. When the apartment was empty, I sometimes stayed overnight when I worked really late. Sometimes Gage used it as well, depending on his work schedule."

"Oh, I'm sorry to put you out. I can go to the hotel for the night. Or the Sea Siren's place where I stayed last time."

"Nonsense. You are the new tenant. Clothiste's Inn is another option for us now, so I'm fine."

They walked the last few blocks in silence, the echo of footsteps occasionally silenced by thick patches of damp fallen leaves. Terry considered telling him about the recent ghostly encounters at the inn but refrained. Instead, she opened the gate in the white picket fence surrounding the inn. A small wooden pathway separated her office and the B and B. She led the way, Kyle in step behind her. He walked with her to the back porch.

"Well, here we are," she said and withdrew her keys from her purse, fumbling to separate the door key from the rest. "Thanks for the company—and dinner."

"My pleasure." He took the key between his fingertips and turned the lock, his phone chirping again as he pushed the door open. "I'm really sorry to rush."

Me too.

"No problem, honestly," Terry said.

"Well, goodnight." Kyle stood, then leaned toward Terry. She angled her head in anticipation. Another chirp squeaked from his phone, and he straightened, brushing her cheek with a kiss.

AAArgh! Terry groaned inwardly but smiled and said, "Good night."

Kyle bounded from the steps, resisting the temptation to throw his phone in a nearby trash can as he passed it. He lifted his hand in a wave and took the apartment staircase two steps at a time.

Terry shut the door and locked it.

Her gaze fell upon the garment bag heaped on the floor. Hissing angrily, she grabbed the hanger, shook the bag and hung it on a hook by the door. When a shiver coursed through her, she realized the kitchen temperature matched the cold of the evening air outside. She withdrew her pepper spray from her purse and placed her finger on the nozzle.

"Therese?" she called.

Warm air brushed her cheek. The cold air dissipated.

A hand clamped on Terry's shoulder and she turned around with a shriek.

CHAPTER 12

Theresé
Portsmouth, Virginia, August 1781

By the time the arduous journey ended near the Elizabeth River in Portsmouth, twilight had fallen. A rising full moon lit the path.

After Mr. McDermott stopped and braked the wagon, he turned to Theresé. "Miss, I wish you would let me escort you to your grandfather's house."

Theresé shook her head. "It is less than a five minutes' walk and the moon is bright. The carriage would make noise. 'Tis better if we do not alert anyone."

The merchant helped his wife and Theresé from the seat and walked to the rear of the conveyance to retrieve Theresé's small bag. He set it on the ground nearby as Mrs. McDermott embraced the young girl, whispering, "Let us know as soon as you find your mother, and we will get word to your papa."

With a nod, Theresé reached for her bag. "Thank you both for your kindness. I will send word as soon as possible. I fear Papa may take a reckless chance to search for her if he does not receive word soon."

Mr. McDermott patted her shoulder and warned, "Stay close to the courthouse and avoid the area near the pub. 'Tis not safe there at night."

With another nod, Theresé dipped into a brief curtsy and skirted the wagon. She slipped into the long shadows between buildings on High Street and peered around the corner of one, pressing her cheek against the cool brick.

Four soldiers stood near one of the few street lights in the square, fat candles in lanterns illuminating the immediate area surrounding the men.

125

One carelessly leaned on the butt of his Brown Bess, bayonet stuck in the ground. The soldiers spoke in low voices, their murmurs drifting on the air.

From the shadows, a third soldier, obviously an officer, approached the men and barked an order. The relaxed men snapped to attention. Although Theresé could not hear the words, the wayward soldier recovered his weapon from its inappropriate station and moved it to the carry position. He paired with another soldier and they strode down the High Street. The officer joined the remaining two and marched in the opposite direction.

Boisterous laughter erupted from the pub on the opposite corner. Theresé pinned her back tight against the building, trying to gauge the distance she had to walk. If she could pass the tavern without a drunken patron detecting her, she could reach the alley that ran between the property lines of the private homes that dotted the side streets.

She moved in the shadows of tall trees, their branches blocking the moon and its reflection on her lighter clothes. She reached the tree closest to the pub without incident. She still had to cross a wide path of empty space before she could pass the pub and return to the shadows.

Through the open door, men in red uniforms brushed elbows with loyalists dressed in elegant velvet or merchants in white shirts and tan breeches. A soldier stepped outside the door, silhouetted in the light streaming from within. Theresé's heart froze when the soldier turned his gaze in her direction. He took three steps toward the tree. She shrank back, pressing her spine further against the trunk, straining her neck so she could keep him in her sight while staying out of his.

A serving wench skipped to the doorstep and called.

The redcoat gave one more glance in Theresé's direction before turning to the woman. The maid jumped from the step, yanked her skirts up, and dashed to the man. He scooped her up in his arms and she anchored her legs around his hips. The two engaged in a deep kiss as the soldier twirled. The wench broke free of his lips with a toss of her head, her bawdy laughter loud over the din of the pub. She dropped her feet to the ground and moved her body across his front with seductive sways of her shoulders. Then she dropped to her knees in front of the soldier. His sword clanked at his side.

Theresé gasped, the drop of her jaw so sharp she wondered if her skin stretched out of shape. Her cheeks blazed with embarrassment as the soldier's white breeches fell, the tops of his boots holding the material at his knees. The white of his exposed derrière reflected in the moonlight.

Theresé pressed her hands to her face and waited before she dared another look.

The couple stood and embraced. Encumbered by his dropped pants, the soldier shuffled forward in short awkward steps, pushing the maid backwards until they reached a clump of bushes under the window of the pub. Squealing and laughter mingled with the rustle of leaves as they disappeared into the brush.

A barrel-chested man in a dingy apron with a rag tossed carelessly over one shoulder, peered into the yard before stepping back inside and shutting the door.

With the door closed, Theresé now had a dark, clear path. She skittered across the yard toward the alley, giving the pub a wide berth, while avoiding the ribald couple in the shrubbery.

Twice she thought she heard footsteps behind her. Each time she stopped to listen. Only the chirp of insects greeted her. She ran down the alley, covering the short distance to her grandfather's house, the only private house with an outdoor kitchen in the immediate vicinity. She sighed with relief when she reached the small building with the upstairs loft she had once shared with her sisters and Lizzie.

Grandfather's house stood in darkness. Moonlight cast eerie reflections on unlit windows.

Theresé dropped her bag beside the stoop and ran to the back door of the main house. Finding it locked, she scampered to the front, only to discover that door also secured and the drapes drawn in front of the large window in the parlor. She knocked quietly, then pounded, stepping back and waiting.

Sweat beaded along her forehead. She swept her sleeve over her face to stem the trickle from reaching her eyebrows.

Heavy footfalls echoed across the deserted streets, the walkers invisible in the shadows as they moved closer. Slight clinks of metal rattled, and she recognized the soft slap of a military scabbard against thigh, matching the gait of the walker. She crouched, peering through the railing until a pair of soldiers stepped into the moonlight. They continued their patrol in the direction of the pub, once again swallowed by the dark swath of trees lining the street.

Theresé slumped to a sitting position, her thundering heart threatening to explode in her chest. She drew her knees close to her upper body and rested her face, tears mixing with sweat. When the moon slipped behind a cloud, she heaved a great sigh and pushed to her feet, seizing advantage of the momentary darkness and dashing from the porch.

She scuttled across the rear yard until she reached the outbuilding. Her fingers trembled as she searched along the window ledge for the key usually tucked in the corner. She traced the same pattern over the frame several times, to no avail. She flattened her back against the building and pressed a fist to her stomach.

Perhaps the key is not there because the door is already unlocked.

A prayer on her lips, she stretched her arm along the short space and turned the knob of the Dutch door.

With a soft click, the handle turned and she pushed the Dutch door inward, both sections moving in tandem. The design allowed occupants to open the top half for air while keeping the bottom portion closed, providing a barrier to keep children inside, and unwanted visitors—human or animal—out.

Theresé picked up her small bag. Moonlight cast a stream of silver through the high narrow window. The narrow strip of light fell across a section of the wooden table in the center of the room. Otherwise, darkness enveloped the room.

She stepped across the threshold.

A heavy hand clamped across her mouth. A strong arm grabbed her from behind, forcing her back against a solid form. She squirmed and tried to break free. The arms tightened and the assailant tilted backwards until her feet lifted from the floor.

"Silence," a gravelly voice commanded close to her ear, heavy breath brushing her hair. He dragged Theresé with him as he kicked the door shut.

The moon disappeared behind a cloud as Theresé struggled in the clenches of the faceless form.

Terry
Portsmouth, Virginia, present day

"Yikes!" Terry whirled and broke free of the grip on her shoulder, raising the canister to expel spray. She gasped at the sight of the flesh and blood girl standing before her. No haze shimmered around her, no eerie glow radiated from her.

But she wore a colonial dress.

"Who are you?" Terry gasped.

"I'm Theresé. I've been waiting a long, long time for you." Theresé stared at her hands, raising them toward the overhead light. "I'm solid," she added in awe. "I touched you."

"Did you *ever*." Terry removed her trigger finger and lowered the spray can as she blew out a deep breath. "I would have thought you were a three-hundred pound gorilla the way you clamped your hand on me." She patted her hand over her thumping heart and asked, "You are the sister of Nicole and Marie Josephé, correct?"

Theresé turned her hands palms up and back down several times before answering. "I'm sorry to have scared you. I am usually able to brush across your skin or to ripple your hair quite easily, but did not realize I had become—human again. It takes such energy to move through from the other side. I struggled to do that just now, so perhaps I used more force than I needed…"

Terry held her hands in a time out position. "Whoa. Wait. This can't be. Can it?"

The girl nodded, tilting her head down as she smoothed her hands over her skirts and lifted the apron. She rubbed her fingers over the hem and then shook the material.

Terry asked, "How are you here, in my time?"

"I know not how I come to be here. I have been trapped between this world and the world beyond for over two centuries." Theresé moved about the kitchen, running her fingers over the countertops, touching knobs on the stove, pulling drawers open. She walked around the small island cabinet and then glided to a stop in front of Terry, turning her head from side to side as she studied the modern woman's face. She placed her right fingertips on Terry's chin. "We don't really look alike, but I feel as if I am staring into a mirror." She touched her own cheek with her left hand.

Terry looked into blue eyes, so startlingly like Gage's. She stretched her hand and trailed her fingers down Theresé's face. "I used to see you when I was a little girl."

Shifting her weight from foot to foot with restless energy, Theresé nodded and touched the refrigerator door, then stepped toward the stove again. "I've seen many changes to the world I once knew." She walked back to stand in front of Terry. "I've appeared through the years to many in your family. Most were frightened of me. You weren't. You were always the strongest. I had to wait but I knew one day this time would come."

"Why now? Why are you here now?"

Theresé's gaze dropped to the pendant at Terry's neck. "The necklaces are together again for the first time in over two hundred years. We have the strength now, to find our mother, and we will all be able to rest in peace."

"Where are your sisters?"

"They are almost home, but still they are trapped between the two worlds."

"Okay, okay." Terry scrubbed her hands over her face, then ran them through her hair. *I'm talking to a ghost. Or maybe I'm crazy.* She paced in the opposite direction from Theresé. *I need to sit down.*

She swiveled on one heel. "I'm going to make some tea, and we're going to go in the parlor, sit down and talk. I must find out what's happening and why." Terry snatched the tea kettle from the stove and strode to the sink, clanging the kettle under the tap. As the pot filled, she turned and asked, "Can you drink?"

Theresé angled her head as she contemplated. She shrugged and said, "I know not."

"Well, there's only one way to find out." Terry set the pot on a burner with a loud thump, then snapped open a cabinet door and retrieved two mugs.

The colonial girl picked up one cup that bore an "I Love Olde Towne" slogan around the rim. "My father would have liked these. Our teacups were so small. He liked to drink tea but always wished the cups were bigger." Theresé raised her head, a surprised look in her eyes. "That is the first thought I have had about my father since I…" She shook her head as memory eluded her. "I don't remember."

Feeling silly, Terry asked, "Would you like sugar and cream?"

Again Theresé shrugged, and frowned in concentration. "I know not how sugar tastes in tea. I think we used honey or molasses to sweeten our drink, when we had it. These are not things I have thought of since…" Her chin quivered. "I must have died. But I don't feel dead."

The tea kettle began its low whistle, tempo increasing as the water grew hotter. Terry grabbed her duffle bag and ruffled through outside pockets. She pulled a baggie of homemade chocolate chip cookies from a side pouch.

She smiled toward the specter, who roamed the kitchen, touching appliances and gadgets.

"We might as well find out if you can eat, Theresé." Terry set the baggie on a tray, plopped a tea bag in each of the mugs, and made room for the sugar bowl. She poured boiling water into a whimsical apple-shaped teapot and arranged everything on the tray as Theresé continued her ramble around the room.

Terry carried the tray to the parlor room and placed it on the coffee table, aware of Theresé stopping behind her to touch or move something.

"This looks like my grandfather's house, yet it isn't his house." Theresé sat in one of the wing chairs, bouncing on the thick padding.

Terry poured water into two mugs and slid one in front of Theresé, wondering if it would have been wise to have brought a towel to the room—just in case. She brought her mug to her lips, set it down without sipping, and said, "When Tanner first told us about Nicole—he called her 'Nickel'—we didn't pay much attention. We thought he had conjured up an imaginary playmate, talking to her and playing games."

"Children sense things that adults cannot. Somehow they

bridge the gaps that we spirits cannot. Tanner could see us, and could communicate with each of us. He is a delightful child. When Stephanie came here, I knew right away that something would happen, though I knew not what it would be."

"Why did I stop seeing you as I grew older?"

"I know not. Perhaps the connection we needed was not strong enough. When your mother gave you that necklace, something changed in our worlds."

"How did you know that she gave me this?" Terry touched her necklace, the cross warm against her skin. "Are you always here? Do you see everything?"

"No. Something happens that makes it possible for us to return to this world from our own, but I have no explanation. May I try to drink this tea?" Theresé stretched her hand and stroked the handle of the mug before picking it up.

Terry lifted her mug, leaned forward and tapped the rim to Theresé's with a light clink.

The colonial girl wrapped both hands around the cup and brought it to her lips. After a slight hesitation, she sipped. Her eyes widened in astonishment, then delight.

"I can taste this! Awesome."

"You sound like a modern-day teenager." Terry laughed in surprise. "I would have expected you to have an accent."

"I learned to say that from Tanner. He is such a funny little boy. But I have learned many words…" She turned her gaze to Terry. "What do you call it—slang?"

Terry nodded, scratching her head in disbelief at her strange conversation with a ghost.

Theresé took another sip, sighed with eyes closed, and continued. "I learned slang from watching and listening to people who could not see us or hear us." She pointed to the small television atop a cabinet. "I can make my voice sound like any of those people who talk in that box. Marie Josephé and I had a gift for languages when we were young. She was the one who could imitate most accents, so much better than I."

"But you are not always…" Terry waved her hands around

her. "Around here? Around us, watching?"

"No, we cannot watch your world at will. But if something brings us to this side, we may appear at delicate times." She lifted her cup halfway to her lips and smiled coyly. "I saw you and the boy Chase kissing under the magnolia tree."

With a flush creeping up her neck, Terry cried, "We were like fifteen years old then."

Theresé merely shrugged, and took another sip.

Terry opened the bag of cookies and placed some on the tray. She said, "We now know you can drink tea, so maybe you can taste the cookie. These are called chocolate chip cookies. They have small pieces of chocolate, and are an American favorite. Try one."

Theresé studied the treat with interest. Tentatively, she took a bite and chewed, the sparkle of delight on her face turning brighter as she enjoyed the flavor.

"I have never tasted anything like this."

"It's from an old family recipe. My great-aunt Ida always had these cookies ready for us when we came here as children. This house has been in my family off and on for years. It was nearly destroyed during the Civil War."

"I remember that time. Sometimes, when I appeared, I could hear guns and cannons in the distance, much the way we heard them from our father's army camp when I was alive."

"Did you not ever live with your family in a home?"

Theresé shook her head, rubbing her temples as if bothered by a headache. "I do not remember much about my life. I've been trapped in the other world for many years. There are few memories of our past lives until we resolve what holds us here. My memories don't come back to me in an orderly fashion. Sometimes I might recall an incident that happened here in this house, but the next memory may come from my childhood somewhere else." She closed her eyes, a slight smile forming. "Drinking this cup of tea reminds me of a Christmas when my family was all together, in a pretty home. I am young, but I can see my parents, my younger sister, and my brother. Nicole was not born. We sat near a crackling fireplace, warm and comfortable."

Theresé stood and paced nervously, a frown etched between her eyes. "Then next I remember a cold winter, but nothing in between. Our home was a tent because we followed Papa's brigade as they moved from town to town in the battles to help the Americans. But when Mama became sick, Papa sent us here to Grandfather's house. This house, but different. I can remember that she was terribly sick, but not why. I know not what happened to her."

Unsure what to say, Terry bit into a cookie.

The colonial girl sat and took another sip of tea. Her voice echoed with sadness. "Then during that war, when soldiers in blue and gray uniforms fought. There was a period when three women cousins came together here. My sisters and I reunited somehow, in between our worlds. We rejoiced, thinking the time had come that we would be set free. We lost each other again. But we knew that finding the necklaces might be the key that could set us free. Nicole found her 'teardrop.' Marie Josephé her heart. We know where my necklace is. Now I must find our mother."

The antique clock struck midnight. Theresé set the half-eaten cookie on the tray, tears brimming in her eyes. One teardrop rolled down her cheek, and splashed through her hand. She stared as her skin turned translucent, and turned to Terry. "Find my mother. Please, you have to find my mother."

Before the twelfth toll of the bell, Theresé's form faded into a cloud of sparkling blue dust that disappeared without a trace.

For a full minute, Terry sat immobile, staring at the empty space on the sofa while doubting her sanity.

The only proof she had not been alone came from the partially-eaten cookie and extra mug opposite her on the table.

Fifteen minutes later, the clock chimed the quarter-hour. She'd had enough waiting and began cleanup, only to notice the lonely cookie with a bite missing. Remembering the bliss Theresé displayed when she nibbled the treat, Terry smiled. Compassion and sadness compelled her to keep the cookie, so she wrapped it in a napkin. Taking the tray to the kitchen, she placed the wrapped cookie in the refrigerator.

Finally heading to the innkeeper's suite, Terry left every light on in her wake. She locked the door behind her. After changing into her tee shirt and yoga pants, she placed the pepper spray on the table, rotating the can until the nozzle pointed outward.

Should uninvited visitors enter, it would only take one move for her to grab the can and spray, hitting her target. She slipped into bed and settled under the soft duvet, hugging it to her.

Brief images of her evening with Kyle flashed in her memory, her heart doing the now-familiar flip in her chest whenever he crossed her mind.

She could not concentrate on the evening, however.

Overwhelming sadness settled over her, and a tear slid down her cheek for the colonial girl caught somewhere between the past and the present.

CHAPTER 13

What is that noise? Terry buried her head further under the pillow to muffle the shrill sounds. After the fourth ring had pierced her consciousness, she wrestled her way clear of the covers and grabbed her cell phone, fumbling with the keypad.

"What?" she snapped.

"Well, aren't you all sunshine and rainbows today?" An amused Mary Jo spoke. "Where are you? I saw your car and just popped in the office. They said you hadn't come in yet."

"What time is it?" Terry mumbled. She squinted at her watch and cried, "Shit! Nine o'clock?"

"Exactly."

"I spent the night in the inn and overslept."

"I didn't even think to look for you there. Since no one had seen you this morning we got a little worried, especially when we saw the scratches on your car door. What happened?"

"Scratches? On my car?" Terry scrambled to her feet and threw a sweater over her shoulders, sliding her feet into her bedroom slippers at the same time.

"The driver's side looks like someone keyed it a half-dozen times."

"Aw, shit. I'll be right there." Terry hung up and dashed through the kitchen to the door. Outside, she raced to the side of her car and nearly tumbled into Mary Jo, who rose from a kneeling position beside the car door.

"Look at my car!" Terry cried.

Wiggly scrapes ran the length of her red convertible on the driver's side. She walked around the vehicle, snapping pictures with her cell phone from each angle until she returned to the damaged side.

"I'd guess someone ran a key or maybe a screwdriver down the sides," Mary Jo said, running fingers along one of the etched lines. Tiny flakes of paint peeled and she drew her hand back. "You don't suppose Kevin and his little delinquent buddies were at it again, do you?"

"No, no, I don't think it would have been them." Terry shook her head firmly. "They've been towing the line. This is—vindictive."

The two friends looked at each other and Terry said, "Della?"

This time Mary Jo shook her head. "She's petty and spiteful, but even she wouldn't do this."

Terry glanced at her watch. "By the way, I had a visit with Theresé last night that you will not believe. Maybe it's brought out our evil ghost for more mischief."

"What makes you say that? Although I've been wondering when our wicked specter would visit us again."

"I don't have time to tell you about it now. I've got to get dressed for work, and then call in a police report for this. Will you call Steph and see if we three can get together tonight? Maybe here at the B and B?"

"Sure. But make it at your parents' house. Chase is repairing something and I'm swinging by there. Hannah and Mom are going out with my father."

Terry grabbed her friend by the arm. "I forgot all about him arriving last night. Oh, I can't wait to hear about him. What did you think of him?"

Mary Jo sighed. She had a tumultuous family history and had only discovered her father's existence and her connection to Hannah.

"He's nice. You would not believe how tall he is, compared to Hannah. I'm going to take a few days off to spend time with him. Mom was so excited about his surprise visit. They had a poignant reunion."

"Wouldn't it be awesome if…" Terry began.

Mary Jo laughed and grabbed her friend in a hug. "Don't jinx it." She stepped back and smiled. "But the thought crossed my mind too."

***

Twenty minutes later, Terry applied the finishing touches to her makeup. She'd saved time by drawing her hair back in a bun before her shower, and now she simply pulled it through her hair band into a ponytail.

With a hasty shake of the duvet, she smoothed out the bed covers and then fluffed the sham-encased pillows into position. Everything else could wait until later.

She raced toward the back door and jerked to an abrupt stop in the kitchen. Wrenching open the refrigerator door, she stared at the baggie containing the chocolate chip cookies. The folded napkin rested beside it on the rack. She withdrew the paper linen and pressed it with her thumbs.

The half-eaten cookie was gone.

***

"Terry, sorry I couldn't get back with you sooner, last two days have been crazy here." Detective Jonathan Shellito's voice sounded tinny through the phone. "I called the medical examiner's office and they've finished their analysis of the bones. They're ready to release the remains for burial."

"What are their results?" Terry flicked on her desk lamp and pulled a legal pad closer to write as the detective spoke.

"I haven't seen the actual report, just what I gleaned during the phone call. The ME said the bones are well over two hundred years old, a female. She had broken bones in her neck and leg consistent with a fall, but beyond that, there isn't much to go on."

"What about DNA?"

"I asked about that. The bones were pretty much

unprotected all these years, but there are joints that mummified, and it's possible to get a sample. You can have it done through a certified private lab, which might be expensive though. An undertaker will have to arrange all of the transportation of the remains if that's what you decide to do. Or someone from the lab may be willing to go to the mortuary."

"I'll find out what I need to do to set that up."

"Okay. And Sergeant Lewis will be calling you to follow up on the car dealer. He thinks your client may have just what his office needs to break this case."

"That's good news. I also had to make another report today. My car was vandalized."

"Your Maserati?" Jonathan whistled through his teeth. "Man, I hate to hear that. I totally envy you that car."

"Apparently, someone else does. Some asshole scraped stripes down the passenger side. It didn't come from someone sideswiping it in the parking lot. These lines are wavy, like they just walked back and forth scratching with their tool of destruction."

"Any idea who could have done it?"

"No, not really anyone I could name. Too much is going on. I'm going to have security cameras installed to cover my buildings and the parking lot."

"Probably wise. You've had your share of incidents there recently."

"We have. Jonathan, thanks for giving me the heads up on what's happening with the remains."

Terry and the detective exchanged a few more pleasantries before she hung up the phone and tackled the next file on her desk.

She still had a full day of work ahead of her.

***

Terry sat in a line of traffic held up by road construction on her way to her parents' house. The two-lane road that once meandered through farmlands and forests had given way to a new four-lane highway. She drummed her fingers on the steering wheel, and zipped ahead when the flagman waved her on.

"I've been here before."

Terry swiveled her head, jerking the steering wheel. Her right front tire left the pavement. She regained control and straightened the vehicle. She eased onto the shoulder, her heart thumping, and then turned right into a nearby parking space. She stared at Theresé in the passenger seat.

"You've got to stop scaring me like this." Terry placed her hand over her racing heart.

"I'm sorry," Theresé said. "You were thinking of me. Your thoughts can sometimes bring me to you now. I do not understand how or why." She settled in the seat and ran her fingers over the creamy leather. "These horseless carriages have intrigued me since I first saw one. I believe the father of your great-aunt Ida bought the first vehicle for your family, but it did not look like this."

"What did you mean, you've been here before?"

"Not here, exactly. Near here." Theresé's brow wrinkled with concentration. "I came to find Mama. I crossed the ferry near here. Sleepy Hole, they called it. What a funny name."

Terry smiled. With a tilt of her head, she studied the colonial girl. "You look different today, Theresé. More grown-up."

"I seem able to remember a little more each time. It hurts very much to go back and forth between our worlds." Theresé tapped her thighs in a nervous tattoo, and then gripped her forehead. "I remember why we fled Portsmouth. My mother's life was in danger. I know not from whom or why. We had to move quickly to get her away from my grandfather's house. He arranged for a wagon. A fierce storm rose the night we were to leave, with lightning and thunder. Rain soaked through our clothes and we had to tramp through the mud. The wagon waited to take us—somewhere. Where? Mama was supposed to go with us. Then there was a horrible incident outside Grandpapa's house." The colonial girl clamped both hands over her mouth and shook her head, eyes distant as she tried to capture the memory.

Goosebumps crept along Terry's skin and she shivered. She turned the car's heater to a higher level.

Theresé continued. "British soldiers confronted us, and gunfire exploded. Something happened to Mama and she couldn't go with us. We had to leave her." She shook her head, eyes widened. "We left, but thought she would be safe. She was with Louis. My brother. He was a spy for the Americans. He forced us to leave. I remember the driver took us to the river, where Papa arrived to take us to the camp near…Yorktown? Was that the name? We went to the camp and waited for news of Mama and Louis. For days, we heard nothing. Then we learned later that Mama was not at the house in Portsmouth…but who told us?"

Theresé closed her eyes, then snapped the lids open. "I know this makes no sense. My memories jump forward and backward in time, out of order. But I remember now who brought the news to us. Lizzie. It was Lizzie, the maid for my step-grandmother. We were surprised when Lizzie arrived at the camp, and we asked about Mama. She said my step-grandmother told her the family had come for Mama. But that had not happened."

Theresé struggled to remember the story of how she traveled to Portsmouth.

"We crossed the James on the ferry to Sleepy Hole. I remember it because of its funny name I had never crossed the river in the real ferry, only in small boats under cover of darkness. Why do I recall such a trivial thing as that, yet I cannot remember what happened to my mother?" She frowned and pressed the back of her hand to her lips, eyes closed in concentration.

Terry asked gently, "Try to think what else happened when you got to Portsmouth."

"Something happened to me there that frightened me

terribly."

An incoming call sent Terry's phone into rings and vibrations. She and Theresé both jumped in their seats. Therese's solid form disappeared in shimmery waves as she whispered the words, "But I do not remember what."

Then the passenger seat was empty.

Stephanie's number appeared on the keypad and Terry punched the answer key. Her heart pounded. "Hello?" The word stuck in her throat like dried cotton.

Stephanie answered. "Are you all right, Terry? Gage and I just drove past your car. Did you have a breakdown?"

Just mental.

"No, I'm fine." Terry cleared her throat.

"It looked like you were talking with someone when we passed."

Just a ghost.

"Um, I was on my phone." Then Terry dropped her voice to a whisper and said, "Not really. Don't say anything to Gage. I'll see you at the house and tell you. But you're not going to believe who was just riding with me."

"Come to the Driver General Store. We're stopping there now. And why are you whispering? Only I can hear you."

Terry laughed nervously and clicked her phone off, put her car in gear, then drove west.

The panic in Therese's voice disturbed her. Something horrendous must have happened to the family during the Revolutionary War.

She willed Theresé to return but to no avail.

When she reached the fork splitting King's Highway and Nansemond Parkway, a local historical marker caught her attention. She pulled sharply into a small parking lot on the right and scrambled from the car.

After checking for traffic, she sprinted across the road. She stopped in front of two historical markers posted at the intersection, and snapped a photo of the one describing General Cornwallis crossing by ferry. The way was clear of oncoming traffic and she scooted back to her vehicle to drive the short distance to the general store's parking lot.

Fall decorations graced the front of the old building. Pumpkins and cornstalk decorations gave testament to the harvest season. Two large signs advertising the upcoming "Driver Days Festival" filled windows on either side of the door.

Terry's heels clacked as she crossed the rustic wooden porch. When she opened the door, the hinges squeaked in protest.

The scent of aged wood immediately greeted her the instant she stepped through the door. A few pumpkins and other Halloween knickknacks scattered between the decorations added to the quaint atmosphere.

She breathed deeply, associating the dusty but pleasant smell with her many childhood visits to the old store. Often on Sundays, her parents loaded the family into the station wagon and took long drives through the once-rural roads of Suffolk. If she and her siblings managed to get through the ride without crying "I'm bored," or "Are we there yet?" their parents rewarded them with a stop at Author's General Store for ice cream.

Commercial and residential development in the area had since displaced the country atmosphere. The general store no longer bustled with the activity it once enjoyed when Terry was a child. But the scents, the creaks of the planked floor, and old brand memorabilia lining the walls still sent her back in time.

Terry waved to the owner as she strode over to a small wooden table where Gage and Stephanie stood looking at packages of bread and rolls. "Hi, guys," she said brightly as she came between them.

"Are you okay?" Stephanie asked. "You look as if you've seen a…"

"I have."

"Aw, man, please." Gage rolled his eyes skyward. "Please, no more woo-woo shit."

"Yes, woo-woo shit," Terry said. "And I'm talking to your fiancée, not you."

143

"Then don't let me stop you. Mom is fixing sloppy Joes for dinner. Said to let you know." Gage picked up three packs of hamburger buns.

Stephanie gave him a peck on the cheek and said, "I'll be right out, baby." With a wink, Gage kissed Stephanie on the cheek, glared at his sister, and then stomped to the counter to pay.

Terry turned on her heel to follow her brother. "I'd rather tell this to everybody all at once."

"Oh, no you don't." Stephanie grabbed Terry's sleeve and pulled her back toward the refrigerated display case. "Tell me now."

Terry briefly described her encounter with Therese in the car. Then she pulled out her cell. She scrolled to the photo she had just taken.

"Therese talked about being on the ferry with the funny name of Sleepy Hole. I remembered this marker at the fork. It commemorates the site of the Sleep Hole Ferry, which operated about three miles from there. The sign describes occasions when Benedict Arnold and Cornwallis crossed here. They would have traveled to Portsmouth along the King's Highway." She pointed to the door. "That road out front is named for the original King's Highway."

"She might have been somewhere near here during her lifetime," Stephanie said, excitement rising in her voice.

"There must be some connection. Why else would Therese appear to *me*?" Terry shook Stephanie's arm.

"Kyle and I sorted through more family papers today, trying to find some connection to your mom and the family of Clothiste and Étienne. If you are a descendant of Therese, however, we haven't been able to find the link."

"Come on, let's get home." Terry stopped short as she watched a vehicle pull up outside. "Isn't that Kyle's SUV?" she asked.

"It is."

"Hmmm." Terry paid scant attention to Stephanie's words and craned her neck to peer through the window. Gage and

Kyle engaged in conversation at the bottom steps, illuminated by the porch lights. She reached for her purse, dug the phone from the pocket and tapped the keypad.

"Hey, Mom, it's your favorite daughter," she said, laughing when her mother responded with, "You're my only daughter."

"That's beside the point. Gage says you're making sloppy Joes tonight. How many people can you serve?"

"I made several batches so I could freeze some for another meal. Why?"

"Mom, I hope you aren't overdoing yourself." Tears burned at the memory of her mother attached to tubes and monitors in the emergency room. She squeezed her eyes shut and said, "Shouldn't you take it easy?"

"Nonsense, I'm monitoring my sugar and doing everything the doctor tells me, which did not include becoming a couch potato."

Terry laughed. "Well, that's a good idea. We're near the general store. Kyle just drove onto the lot. If you've made plenty, can I ask him to join us? I've got some news to share and it may be good for him to hear it too. And I'll call Mary Jo. If everyone is together, I'll only have to tell it one time."

"Well, sure. But Mary Jo is already here with Chase. He's been installing an electric door on your dad's garage."

"That's right. See if they can stay too. It's important. Thanks, Mom. Love you." She dropped the phone into her purse.

"Pretty smooth," Stephanie remarked.

"What?" Terry asked.

"Don't play coy with me. I saw your eyes light up when Kyle pulled in here. And I've already heard about your date last night."

"It wasn't a date," Terry denied, then added, "What did he say?"

"It's the most animated I've ever seen him, Terry. I think he described the Bier Haus right down to the decorations on the wall. He enjoyed the walk. He said he peeked into Trinity churchyard through the wrought iron gates and wants to check

Trinity Church records but I've already done that."

"Oh." Terry paused, hoping she appeared casual. "Is that all?"

"And he mentioned you ran into our Navy couple."

"Ah, yes, we did. Steph, I have to tell you something weird. It's the second time I've met that man, and each time we shook hands, I had that spark. Like you and I had when we first met, remember? And you and Mom always have when you touch each other. I wonder if we have another lost relative in the pile."

Stephanie shrugged. "With all of the mysteries we've encountered in recent weeks, nothing would surprise me anymore."

"True." Terry craned her neck to peer through the window, watching her brother and Kylee step over to her driver's door and study the scratches.

"Kyle mentioned that he liked the restaurant and wants to go back soon."

"Oh," Terry said again. She led Stephanie across the weathered floor and extended her arm to pull the doorknob on the wood slatted doors. Rusty hinges squeaked in protest as the door swung open.

Stephanie burst into laughter. "And all other conversation paled in comparison to the many times he mentioned how much he enjoyed the evening with you." She pushed Terry through the doorway without waiting for a response.

CHAPTER 14

Kyle hadn't planned to stop at the general store at all, until he spotted Terry's snazzy convertible parked in front. At the last minute, he'd whipped into the lot and parked beside Gage's truck.

He figured he could pick up sandwiches and chips to take home for dinner.

Or at least that would be the excuse he would give for stopping in.

He encountered Gage outside. They engaged in discussion and Gage showed him the mysterious scratches on Terry's car. When the store's old door squeaked, his heart danced with a little flutter at sight of Terry stepping onto the wooden porch, Stephanie close behind.

"Didn't I just see you with your nose buried in old records?" Stephanie laughed.

"Yeah, you did. I just stopped to grab some sandwiches to take out. I haven't had time to shop for groceries."

"No need for that," Terry said as she walked to her car. "I have a lot to tell everyone, and you may be interested in some of it. Mom's got sloppy Joes on the stove and I can fill everyone in on all the news at once."

"If it's not an inconvenience, I'd like that. I haven't had a sloppy Joe in ages."

"Then, let's head to the house," Gage said, opening the passenger door of his truck for Stephanie. "I hear four sloppy Joes calling me." She scrambled in, her infectious laughter muffled as he closed the door.

"See you at the house, then." Terry smiled at Kyle.

"Sure. Thanks for the invite." He moved his mouth as if to say something else, then clamped his jaw shut.

Dammit. Say something. Anything.

He mentally shook his head and clambered into his vehicle, managing only to say, "I'll follow you."

Not what I wanted to say.

Terry paused for a split second, then nodded. She opened the door to her own vehicle.

Dammit.

***

When the group entered the Dunbar home, their collective arrival sent the family's twin Irish setters into fits of joyous barking. The dogs yelped as they wound their way around human legs, nearly tripping Stephanie in the process. Gage steadied her and gave the dogs a "Radar— Roscoe—sit!" command. The pooches plopped their butts on the floor for all of three seconds before heading for Terry. She patted each on the head, and both dogs rolled on their backs in twin poses to expose their bellies for scratching. Laughing, she knelt between them and tickled both at the same time.

Once the hubbub of greetings simmered down, an unfazed Joan shooed the men to the family room, assuring them she would arrange for plenty of cleanup for them to handle later. The two pets, now content with scratched tummies, padded behind Charles and curled on their dog beds by the fireplace.

Terry set her purse on the counter and headed to the sink to wash her hands as Mary Jo dug through the cutlery drawer. Terry leaned toward her and whispered, "Mary Jo, it's been so busy today I didn't have a chance to ask you how the meeting with your father went."

Mary Jo set plates around the table, and paused, eyes glistening. "Terry, he's wonderful. It's hard to believe he's Hannah's son. And he's so tall, at least a foot and a half taller than she is. He was married for a while but divorced years ago. They never had any children. After he retired from the Navy last year, he got into the family tree thing as a retirement hobby. His research led him to contact Kyle." Mary Jo sorted silverware as she talked. "I think it's been good for my mother to see him again after all these years. You remember how we learned that her mother intercepted his letters to her and prevented my mom from contacting him?" Terry nodded and Mary Jo continued, "By the time Mom realized she was pregnant, it was too late and his family had moved. She never knew he had written to her and he never knew I existed."

"That's so sad, but it's wonderful you've found each other after all these years. How long is he staying in town?"

"He has to go back to California on Sunday. Not knowing how things would be, he only planned a short trip for this visit. We are already talking about him coming back to spend Thanksgiving with us."

Stephanie picked up a basket of hamburger buns from a nearby cabinet and said to her friends, "By the way, has it ever occurred to you guys that Kyle is our human connection to our families, in much the same way Tanner connected us to our ghosts and our ghosts are our other-worldly bond to each other?"

"What do you mean?" Terry paused, holding a plate in mid-air. She glanced toward the family room. Kyle leaned against the fireplace mantle and conversed with her father. The family's two Irish setters crowded contentedly at his feet. He bent to stroke the ears of first one, then the other.

Her heart skipped a beat.

He belongs here.

Stephanie set the basket on the table, and turned to face Terry. She ticked off with her fingers. "Well, we know our ghosts connect each of us in some way to our direct ancestors and Tanner seems to be our link to them. And Kyle, an outsider like me, came into the picture. He made the first contact when he found my family tree and helped me trace my heritage to Nicole and her parents, Clothiste and Étienne.

Then he was the catalyst for Mary Jo learning she is a descendant of Nicole's sister Marie Josephé. And if he finds your mother's connection to them, Terry, that will establish your link to Therese."

"Hmmm, interesting. I never thought of it like that," Terry mused.

"Thought of what?" Joan asked as she set a hot pad on the table. Terry repeated Stephanie's observations as she walked with her mother to the counter that separated the kitchen and family room. Joan listened, then picked up the crock pot bubbling with tangy sauce. Terry grasped the handle of the ice tea pitcher.

"That is an interesting point of view," Joan agreed. "Let's talk more about that later."

She set the crock pot in the center of the table and clapped her hands to signal for her family to gather round. The flurry of human activity heading for the table set the dogs barking. She gave one sharp command that quieted the four-legged noisemakers but was less successful with the two-legged.

Finally, the matriarch of the Dunbar clan claimed victory over the humans and the room fell quiet.

After grace, only the clink of silverware and glasses filled the room as the dining ritual began.

Terry broke the silence. Handing a platter of French fries to Stephanie, she said to the family around her, "I've had quite a start to this week." She then gave a brief accounting of the fraud case she and Sandi had undertaken. Her friends and family broke into cries of disgust and indignation.

"I hope you nail the bastard to the wall," Charles said. Joan, instead of admonishing Charles for his language, echoed the sentiment.

"I hope we can. Mrs. Belford's case is the strongest," Terry explained.

"No wonder you seem so distracted," Joan said, patting her daughter's hand.

That's because of this man sitting beside me. Unconsciously—or maybe deliberately—Terry bumped her thigh along Kyle's. He did not move away, and the warmth of bodies through cloth sent her senses whirling.

"Terry?" Mary Jo repeated her name two more times.

"I'm sorry." Terry shook her head and settled back to reality. "What did you say?"

"Tell them about the vandalism to your car."

Mary Jo's comment immediately sent the family into a flurry of questions.

Terry held up her hand to offset the inquiries and explained the damage she had found on the car.

"There's no way to know who did it or when, but we need to get security cameras to cover all three businesses. I hope you can install them, Chase."

"We'll check it out tomorrow," he promised. "I hope you reported it to the police."

"I did."

"I don't think you should stay at the inn anymore," Joan said.

"I'm fine, Mom. I'm perfectly safe. I look in all the nooks and crannies and I sleep with every light on. Could someone pass me another roll?" She took the opportunity to change the subject. "There's other news. I spoke with Jonathan today. He's the detective investigating the bones. They've finished with the remains at the crime lab." She relayed the information he had provided, finishing with, "The bones are likely from one of our ancient family members, but even if they're not, I want to arrange for a proper burial. And he said I could arrange for DNA testing as well."

"I can help with that," Kyle said. "I've got some contacts at a private lab."

"Kyle, thank you so much for all you've done." Joan said. She stacked her plate on top of her husband's, then paused. Her gaze drifted over the family gathered at the table. "Tell the family about the online records you found for my great-great grandfather, Frank Wyatt."

All eyes turned to Kyle and he nodded, holding up a cautionary palm. "I found death records for a Frank Wyatt in

151

the old Norfolk County vital statistics, but don't know for sure if it's the right one. I'm also planning to visit the Catholic cemetery to look around. Sorry, the name of it escapes me."

"All Saints," Charles interjected. "It's near downtown, kind of between Olde Towne and the Norfolk Naval Shipyard. It was developed in the eighteen-eighties as Saint Paul's. It's been through several name changes before being renamed All Saints. It's the only Catholic cemetery in the city, so it might be worth checking out. The Wyatts were a long-time Catholic family, and my father, his father, and his father before him, have all been members of the local council of the Knights of Columbus almost since its inception in eighteen ninety-nine."

Kyle nodded. "What I really hope to find is some record of Frank's wife Celestine. We know her maiden name was Longchamps. If she was indeed the cousin to Stephanie's ancestress Emily Long, then we will be able to trace her back to the same ancestors, Clothiste and Étienne."

Terry had considered revealing the visits from the specter of Theresé but decided the past few days of her life had been filled with too much drama. She wanted to discuss something that would take her mind off old bones, scoundrel car dealers, and ghosts.

So, she smiled brightly and said, "I'm getting excited about the grand opening for Clothiste's Inn. We have about three weeks to get ready. Has anyone thought of what costumes they will wear?"

***

The dinner ended later than planned, and while Joan rode herd on the men to clean the kitchen, Terry pulled Mary Jo and Stephanie to the side.

"I don't want the guys to hear this right now, Mary Jo. Nor Mom. Steph already knows." She quickly explained how Theresé seemed to take on a human form, first at the Inn and then in her vehicle. "I think it is painful for her to travel through time, or whatever her spirit does to transport back to this side. She remembers bits and pieces of her past life each time she appears, but not in an orderly fashion."

Mary Jo rolled her eyes skyward. "The only reason I believe you is because of my own visits from Marie Josephé. Otherwise, I would say this is getting ridiculous and go have your head examined."

"Hey, she *at*e the cookie and *drank* the tea. She was as real as you or I. I'm going to be working late for the rest of the week, so I plan to stay at the inn. Can you guys meet me there tomorrow after I get off work? I want to see if anything changes once we are all there together."

"Much as I'd love to play 'Ghostbuster' with you," Mary Jo said, the slight sarcasm not lost on Terry. "Tomorrow's out. I'm taking mom and my father to dinner in Smithfield. How about Friday?"

"Friday would be better for me, too," Stephanie said. "Gage has to be at some meeting to discuss plans in case this new storm develops into a hurricane." She shuddered. "Oh, I hope we don't go through another Hurricane Abby. We just got back on our feet." Worry lines furrowed her brow as she added, "Are you sure you should stay at the inn alone?"

Terry shook her head firmly. "I feel safe in that place, even if something evil exists there as well."

"I still don't like it," Stephanie said.

Terry hugged her future sister-in-law and said, "Answers might be at our fingertips." She shifted her attention to Kyle, now engaged in lively conversation with her mother. Joan handed Kyle a covered bowl as they walked to the front door.

Kyle took the container, kissed Joan's cheek and lifted his coat from the peg by the door.

Terry called, "Hold on, Kyle," and scooted through the dining room, grabbing a plastic bag from the counter.

He turned, one arm through a sleeve. The majority of the jacket dangled on the floor. He waited as she took several long strides to catch up with him.

Shaking the bag of hamburger buns she held in her hand,

Terry said "I'm sure that's a bowl of Mom's sloppy Joe mix. You'll need some rolls for that." She grabbed the slack jacket. Kyle transferred the container to his other hand and slipped his arm through the sleeve she offered.

Kyle smiled. "At least now I'll have one decent meal in the fridge until I can get to a grocery store. Thanks for inviting me tonight."

"It's always a pleasure." She slipped her hands into her sweater pockets. "Did you notice the banners and signs advertising the Driver Days Festival this weekend when you were at the general store?"

Kyle laughed. "I did. And your mom's been telling me about it."

Terry nodded and waved toward the dining room where Joan's craft projects competed with boxes of family records for space on the huge formal table. "It's like an old-fashioned country festival, only small scale. Mom's church group has a booth of homemade crafts and they donate their proceeds to their charities."

"She told me that too. We're often in here working on our projects at the same time. She's easy to talk to, and amazing. That woman moves non-stop."

"That's Mom. I swear, she can be on vacation and she's already planning the next one in her mind."

Kyle smiled. "I can see where you get your energy."

Terry nodded and walked to a tall easel. Two poster boards taped together leaned against the frame, marked with hand-written notes, circles or colorful arrows pointing to other names. "You've added more names to Mom's tree."

"A few." Kyle trailed his finger along a branch of lineage. "Whenever I verify ancestors in the lineage for your mom's tree, I scribble on sticky notes and place the name in their proper familial position on this chart. Then I'll add the information later to a genealogy program on my computer. Your mom's dream is to have a family tree chart professionally printed once she's traced the family line as far as she can."

"I'd love to give her that for a Christmas present." She

brushed her fingers over new names.

Kyle's gaze followed Terry's outstretched arm and nodded. "The Wyatt lineage is well documented, but I've exhausted the leads for her great-great grandmother Celestine. I've found nothing in the Portsmouth court records for her, either maiden name or married. I'm going to search the Archives of the Library of Virginia next. It might mean a short road trip to Richmond."

Terry hesitated, then plunged ahead with her next thought. "Um, Kyle, maybe I could help you with some of the record search while I'm off. I have a case to litigate that may last a couple of days, but after it's over I need to take some time off, recharge my batteries before I sink my teeth into the Shady O'Grady file." She laughed. "I probably need to stop referring to him by that name. I don't think it would look good to accidentally refer to him as Shady in court."

They walked toward the front door. Laugh lines creased Kyle's face as he chuckled. "Good idea."

"So, I'd be happy to go to the cemetery with you."

"Great. I'd be glad for the company. Your mom will be happy to know you are interested in the limbs of your family tree."

Terry straightened his scarf and brushed a kiss across his cheek. "Maybe she'll put me back in her will," she laughed. She waved once and shut the door quickly on the cold air, leaning pensively with her back against the doorjamb.

Watch out, Mr. Avery. It's your limbs I'm interested in.

***

Such a warm feeling enveloped Kyle that he had nearly reached his apartment before he realized he had forgotten to turn on the car heater.

Even when he parked and stepped from the car, the crisp autumn air snapping at his face failed to catch his attention.

The only thought running through his mind was that he

was falling hopelessly in love with Terry Dunbar.

CHAPTER 15

Terry slapped the desk phone into its cradle and shot a fist in the air.

"Yes!" she shouted.

Becky scuttled from the reception area to find her boss dancing a little jig beside the desk and cried, "What is it, Terry?"

"The Wheeler case is settled! No court tomorrow!"

"Congratulations." Becky extended a hand and pumped Terry's enthusiastically.

Sandi's heels clicked across the wood floor as she ran from her office, calling, "Do I hear exuberant voices in there? Did Freddie agree to settle?"

"He did." Terry spun once more and plopped in her chair. "And a whole lot closer to my figure than his. Mr. Wheeler has been so nervous about the case. When I told him the offer, he was thrilled and said 'go for it.' Let's celebrate."

"I can't," Sandi and Becky said in unison.

"Aw, come on."

"I can't tonight, boss," Becky said. "I have a hot date and I need to jumpstart my prep." She fluffed her hair.

Terry pretended to pout and turned soulful eyes to her partner.

Sandi raised her hands palm up. "Leslie has her soccer game tonight. She's been asking when were you coming to see her play. Why don't you join us?"

"Not tonight. When is her next game? Tell the munchkin I promise to make that one."

157

"I'll check the schedule and let you know. I'm sorry."

"Oh, it's okay. I probably need a night to myself anyway. Maybe I'll just go soak in a hot bath or something."

After her colleagues apologized again and left, Terry sat at her desk for a few minutes longer. She ran her hands along the keyboard to her computer, typing the letters "cmswjfpsjdps" aimlessly, just to give her fidgeting fingers something to do. She then unlocked three paperclips that had become tangled, rearranged the pens on her desk caddy, and lowered her head to the desktop with a groan.

Finally, she snatched her cell phone from the desk pad and punched the keypad. She tapped fingers, wincing as the dial tone shrilled in her ear before changing to a ringing tone.

On the third ring, Kyle answered.

Terry plunged right into conversation. "Hi, Kyle, it's Terry. I was wondering if you wanted to meet for dinner tonight. I'm staying at the inn again. I'm too tired to drive home."

"Oh, man, Terry, I wish I could. I'm in Newport News, meeting a friend." Terry's shoulders drooped when she heard Kyle's answer. He continued, "In fact, it's the colleague I mentioned who may be able to help us with the DNA analysis on the remains. He's in town for a conference. I'll find out what we need to do and let you know tomorrow. Are we still on for the ancestry search?"

"Absolutely. Thank you for contacting your friend. That's good news, Kyle." She hoped she covered the disappointment in her voice. "I've called the funeral home to make preliminary arrangements. They'll retrieve the bones once the medical examiner's office releases them. It should be no later than Friday. I explained about the DNA and they said the lab tech can take the samples right there this weekend. Then we will have a simple interment. It doesn't seem right not to give the person a final resting place."

"Well, I'm pretty sure Eric can help us, if he'll be here. I'll let you know."

"Thank you, Kyle. I appreciate your help."

"One more thing, Terry," Kyle added.

"Sure, what is it?" she asked.

"I'd like a rain check on that dinner. Maybe tomorrow night?"

Terry answered, "You've got it."

After she hung up, Terry pumped her fist in the air and then spun in her chair. Once the spin ended, she flopped back and let out a growl of disappointment mixed with fatigue.

She straightened weary shoulders and pushed buttons on her phone.

"Sandi? Change of plans. Where's Munchkin's game? I'm heading your way."

***

After the soccer match, Terry joined Sandi and her daughter for a pizza celebration. Long after the mother had taken the sleepy little goalie home, Terry remained behind, nursing a glass of wine. The pizza parlor was halfway between her apartment and the B and B. She debated whether it would be just as well if she went to her own apartment. A nice hot bath and a cup of tea would be just right.

But if you go back to the inn, you might see Kyle when he comes home.

Deferring to the voice of reason, she paid the tab and walked into the brisk fall air.

She drove back to Clothiste's Inn and parked, noticing the rear porch light had burned out. She glanced around the parking lot before exiting her car, holding the building key at the ready.

She took the steps with a wary eye on her surroundings, unable to shake the sudden sensation that she was being watched. The lock turned with a click and she opened the door cautiously, anticipating a cold blast of the erratic temperatures that often greeted her.

The temperature was comfortable and she welcomed the warmth. She checked the door locks behind her and then flipped light switches as she entered each room to glance inside.

Satisfied to find nothing amiss, she settled in.

An hour later, she emerged from the soothing bath, wrapped in a cozy bathrobe. She headed for the kitchen to heat water for tea, carrying her cell phone and her pepper spray. She set them on the counter and turned to the stove, jumping back in surprise.

Theresé stood beside her, a demure look on her face.

"May I have some more cookies?" The colonial girl smiled.

Making the now familiar movement of tapping her hand over her heart, Terry wagged the index finger of her other hand at her visitor. "Theresé, if you keep doing that, I'm going to pass out right in front of you."

Laughing out loud now, Theresé picked up Terry's cell. "I've seen so many amazing things come to this world, inventions we would have never dreamed possible in my lifetime. I remember when your ancestors got a strange black box that hung on the wall over there." She pointed to the wall near the back door. "The family was very excited to get it. They could talk into it. When it made a ringing noise, it meant someone was on the other side."

"I remember that old telephone. It had a rotary dial and a shrill ring when someone called." Terry pointed her index finger and drew several half-circles in the air as if dialing from the old-fashioned phone.

Theresé imitated Terry's movements. "I even tried to use it once, to see who they spoke to." She then traced her fingers across Terry's cell phone. "And now you carry this small black box everywhere you go and talk into it. How wonderful it would have been if we had these things in my lifetime."

"Who did you try to contact with Great-Aunt Ida's phone?"

Theresé shrugged, then frowned with the effort of concentration. "My mother, I think. But there was no one for me on the other end."

"Have you ever appeared to other family members like you have to me?"

"We have all tried to make contact through many generations of your family. I cannot see my sisters in the limbo we are in, but I know they have come back and forth in their time. We don't always appear to the same people in your family. I don't know why. Some people have seen our images and were frightened away, never to enter the house again. Some we could communicate directly with, as we all did with Tanner."

Terry nodded. Her pendant turned warm against her skin. She twisted the chain as she tried to recall the history of the three cousins in the eighteen-hundreds. Two women married Wyatt brothers, and one married a Wyatt cousin. That was all she could remember.

Why didn't I pay more attention when Stephanie and Kyle discussed these things?

Standing abruptly, Theresé began to pace. "But I think the time is right now and you will be the one to help us. I can remember more clearly things about that time we lived here. I want to tell you about them. On the night we left, little Nicole forgot her 'baby.' It was just a very old doll. Marie Josephé had painted a new face and I sewed a dress for it. It was Nicole's only toy, and she grieved its loss for many years. Almost a century later, I visited the woman who lived here at that time. She had a French-sounding name, similar to my mother's. I felt a strong connection to her. She wore my cross then as you do now, another century later." Theresé's gaze dropped to the pendant at Terry's throat. "The soldiers in blue came to the city. When she hid her family treasures from the soldiers, she found Nicole's doll hidden away. She put the doll in a metal box and placed it with the other valuables."

"That was the box that Stephanie found during the storm," Terry said as more of a question rather than a statement. Her fingers brushed the necklace, increasingly warm against her skin.

Theresé nodded. "From the time of that other war, the one between the blue and gray coats. When this woman and her two cousins gathered together, I thought the evil spell would finally be broken and free me and my sisters. But when the family retrieved their treasures, the little metal box was overlooked. I tried to tell her. I rattled dishes, I dropped books, and I moved things around." She glanced toward the fireplace, uncertainty flickering across her features. "Perhaps I moved that clock?"

As if on cue, the hands of the clock snapped to the midnight position with a loud clack. The twelve mournful tolls of midnight began.

At the end of the first bong, a candle fell from one of the silver holders. Terry stooped to pick it up and the second chime rang. As the sound of the third toll rang out, Terry stood to place the candle back in the stand. The clock pealed the fourth chime at the moment when Terry touched the base of the candlestick.

Theresé screamed, "NO!" and grabbed for Terry.

The lights in the chandelier flickered. Blue sparks snapped and flashed around the room. The hands of the clock spun around the face wildly, the hour hand moving counter-clockwise and the minute hand clockwise. The tempo of the chimes clanged with the resonance of a dozen church bells.

The blinding sparks swirled into a whirlwind that drew Terry and Theresé into the current of air, the women spinning head over heels in opposite directions.

The cobalt gleam that enveloped the room faded to a grainy black and white scene. In the middle of a dizzying spin, Terry flung her hands out and caught Theresé's wrist. The two steadied and faced each other as they floated toward the ceiling, watching the scene unfold below them.

At the base of the steps, a woman lay crumbled on the floor, a soldier in a British red coat kneeling at her side. A lantern on the floor at his knee cast a yellow tint to the bleak scene

The woman's lips moved, but the incessant clang of bells drowned out her words.

The soldier jerked his head abruptly and angled his face toward the top of the stairs. He snatched the lantern and held it upward. The light swung with the momentum of movement, illuminating the angry lines etched in his face. Blood covered his right hand.

With purposeful strides, he ascended the stairway.

As if tethered on a line above him, the two women drifted upward with each step he took. Livid energy pulsed around Terry, rippling through her body. Her hands still gripped Therese's wrists, but Terry could neither move her limbs nor speak. She tried to look toward Therese's face, but her gaze locked on the soldier's back as he bent over a woman sprawled at the top of the steps.

He raised the lantern and moved his other arm, but she could not see what his hands were doing.

The soldier rose and walked toward a room with an open door.

The swirling force propelled Terry and Therese s through the doorway. Terry was unsure if they went through the actual opening or passed through the walls themselves, but the spinning stopped. She and Therese floated to the ceiling with hands still interlocked, and looked down at the scene below them.

A man lay on his stomach in the bed, so still that Terry wondered if he was alive. The soldier dropped to one knee and shined the light closer to the figure in the bed.

The old man managed to lift the fingers of one hand weakly, and the younger man inclined his head closer to hear the whispers. He nodded and touched the shoulder of the bedridden man. Then he picked up the lantern and walked from the room.

Although the lamp had provided the only light in the room, a strange halo of gold light swathed the bed even after the soldier left.

The soldier returned with a pitcher. He poured a small amount of water onto a cloth and gently patted the old man's lips. The elder gentleman moved his lips to speak, and once again, the soldier dropped to his knee and placed his head close to listen.

Still swaying in suspended animation, Terry and Theresé spun slowly above the immobile figure.

Terry witnessed the exact moment that the old man died—his spirit rose from his lifeless form and floated away, awash in gold light that blinked shut in an instance.

From the darkness, a new vortex swept the women into a turbulent whirl as the scene disappeared.

Then the colonial girl and modern woman stood once again in front of the fireplace. The hands of the clock clicked into the position at 12:30, and then with a snap jumped to a stop under the number 12.

The crashing cacophony of bells tolled the final stroke of midnight.

Terry held the candlestick in one hand. She dropped it to the floor, the clang echoing in the silent room. When looked toward Theresé, she gasped with concern. Theresé had aged into her mid-thirties, and stood frozen in place, eyes glazed in a trance-like stare.

Terry trembled, unsure if it was from cold or fear. Her heartbeat thundered in her ears. She shook the colonial girl's arm. "Theresé! Can you hear me? What did we just see? Who were those people?"

Tears rolled down Theresé's cheek. "My mother lay dead at the bottom of the steps, my step-grandmamma at the top. That was my brother Louis, dressed in the British uniform. And Grandpapa, dying in the bedroom."

"Once before I touched this candlestick and saw some of those images." Terry said. She skirted the silver holder she had dropped, and walked to the fireplace where the other half of the pair stood inoffensively. She flexed her fingers along the base, and turned to Theresé. "Will it happen again if I touch this one, or only when I touch the one on the floor?" Before Theresé could answer, Terry grabbed the standing silver base and waited.

Nothing happened. The precious metal column remained cool to the touch.

Terry set the silver stem back on the mantle and continued

to speak. "On the other occasion when I touched that candlestick on the floor, I saw parts of this same scene, but it must have been just before they fell. Those two women had a violent struggle. I could not hear any sounds of their speech or movement. The younger one struck the older with a candlestick."

Terry's gaze dropped to the silver holder on the floor. "Then they continued to struggle. The younger woman fell to the bottom of the stairs. The older woman took a step down toward her but she slipped into a crumpled position with one foot horribly bent under her. I think what happened tonight was the culmination of the first events I saw."

"I too could hear no sounds." Theresé's face tightened in physical pain, and she pressed her fingertips to her eyes before speaking again. "In the short time we lived in this house we learned that my step-grandmother Abigail was a cruel woman who forced her niece into servitude. The niece, Lizzie, was an indentured servant. She once told me the story of how her aunt lost her fiancé to a French woman and hated all things French, especially the women. Abigail set her sights on my grandfather with the notion that marrying a Frenchman earned her revenge on the French woman who stole her fiancé. By all accounts they had a fairly friendly marriage in the beginning. Abigail was as shrewd in business as my grandfather. They prospered, and later moved to America." Theresé pressed her fingers to her temples. Light from the chandelier played on the traces of gray in her hair. "My mind is such a jumble. It hurts to think."

With a light touch to the elbow, Terry guided Theresé to the sofa and gently forced her to sit. She dropped beside her, remaining silent.

After a few minutes, Theresé continued. "Lizzie's mother owed a great deal of money to Abigail. When she could not repay the loan at the agreed time, she had to send her daughter to America to work off the debt. She warned Lizzie never to call Abigail by her pet name of Abby, as her family and fiancé called her. In her nervousness on arrival, Lizzie forgot and greeted her as 'Aunt Abby.' My step-grandmother beat her black and blue, and warned her never to let it happen again."

Theresé pressed her hands over her heart and said, "I am sorry if my memories do not return in an orderly sequence. My thoughts are clearer and stronger, but they are out of order. I hope what I tell you now makes sense, because it happened before this scene we witnessed tonight. I told you we lived in the French Army camp, first in New England. Slowly we moved with Papa's garrison to Virginia. Mother became very ill and Papa arranged for us to be taken to his father's home. We knew very soon our step-grandmother did not want us in her home, but she had no choice other than to allow Mama to be nursed here. Abigail forced my sister and me to work in the household alongside Lizzie. Mama got sicker. Grandpapa discovered that Abigail was slowly poisoning her. He arranged for us to be taken back to the camp. British soldiers attacked us as we prepared to leave. Mama and my grandfather were shot. Louis sent us away and helped them."

Terry nodded. "Yes, you've told me that."

Theresé paced nervously, wringing her hands. "I'm sorry, these memories just keep repeating in my head. I eventually made it back to Portsmouth." Theresé clapped her hand to her face. The clock chimed a quarter after midnight.

Her image began to fade.

"Theresé, don't go. Tell me what happened. Please stay with me. Try to remember." Terry begged.

Blue shimmer washed over Theresé. She turned a translucent arm outward. "Find my mother, Terry. Please find her." The ghost's disembodied voice broke into a sob.

The blue light faded and Terry stood alone in the empty kitchen.

***

Just after midnight, Kyle parked in the space beside Terry's red car. He got out and faced the back of Clothiste's Inn.

Lights blazed in all the rooms except one.

He recalled the exhaustion in her voice when they spoke earlier. With all the willpower he could muster, he resisted the temptation to knock on the door.

She's probably sound asleep.

He walked toward his apartment, wondering if he would be able to do the same.

CHAPTER 16

"Theresé?" Terry called softly. "Theresé, can you hear me? Please return if you can."

Silence.

Hoping that the colonial girl would reappear, Terry waited another ten minutes to no avail.

Resigned, she gave up, left the lights on throughout the building, and went to bed.

She played games on her cell until the low battery warning appeared. After plugging the phone into the charger, she tried reading a magazine. She thumbed through a few pages, then tossed it aside. Mrs. Belford's case with creepy Shady O-Grady came to mind, but she didn't want to think of work and the pending matters she had ahead of her.

That left thoughts of Kyle to play around in her head. Every time he popped into her mind, she forced him away.

She liked him, wanted to be with him. He seemed to like her too, but he hadn't even asked her for a real date.

"Tramping through cemeteries and rifling through old files does *not* count as a date, Mr. Kyle Avery!" she grumbled out loud.

In the past weeks, she'd been so busy she hadn't much time to wonder why Kyle wouldn't make a move. He'd briefly mentioned a jealous girlfriend. Could he be reluctant to engage in another relationship?

Maybe his mind is cluttered with so much old stuff it doesn't occur to him to ask me out.

Well, she'd fix that. She'd make the next move, she decided.

Somehow.

An idea struck her. She snapped her fingers.

Great-Aunt Ida's old trunk! After they finished traipsing around mossy old cemetery stones and searching musty records, she'd take him to the old attic. Under the guise of looking through the trunk for costume accessories, she'd "inadvertently" stumble across the valise full of old family documents.

Bingo! She clapped her hands together. She'd earn his undying gratitude for her contributions to his research.

A pang of guilt shot through her. She'd come across that trunk weeks ago when she was in the attic with Stephanie and Mary Jo. Instead of calling Stephanie's attention to it, she had shoved it further back among the clutter with the express intention of attracting Kyle with it.

"Okay, they've been working on other documents," she rationalized out loud. "So they probably wouldn't have had time to look through the case yet anyway. They'll have it soon and can start fresh."

The antique clock struck four.

Sleep continued to elude her. When her mind cluttered to the point she could not sleep, she made notes. It seemed she could fall asleep as soon as she compiled her thoughts. She kicked the covers aside and grabbed a yellow legal pad from her briefcase. She would detail everything she remembered from her previous encounters, as well as tonight's incident. Stephanie had created a chart identifying the common elements that occurred to the three women and entered new events as they occurred.

Scribbling furiously, Terry compiled a record of her recent conversations with Theresé. She detailed conversations down to Theresé mentioning the arrival of the first telephone, even seeing the pre-teen Chase and Terry exchanging a kiss near the old magnolia tree. Several times when Terry wrote down the incidents in the order Theresé's rambling had stated, she found it necessary to scratch through a sentence and place it in the proper sequence.

169

She took pains to note every detail of the mysterious visions after she picked up the candlesticks. Her recording of events concluded with Theresé's return to Portsmouth.

It occurred to Terry that sudden noises, like the ringing of a phone or the clang of the clock, caused Theresé to disappear. The look of fear on Theresé's face indicated something traumatic must have happened near the clock—or perhaps at a particular hour. Midnight? She underscored that observation.

Next, she noted that Theresé seemed to age each time she reappeared, and that her recollection of events often fell out of line chronologically.

But what was Theresé unable to finish telling me?

Terry put the writing tablet aside, yawned, and stretched. A slight shiver washed over her. She pulled the covers over her legs, pausing with concerned expectation.

Would the room's temperature drop further and precede a new flurry of ghostly activity?

When the temperature remained constant, Terry relaxed and slid under the covers.

Peaceful slumber still eluded her. After tossing and turning, she kicked the blanket to the side and scrambled from the bed. She unlocked the door and poked her head around the frame.

Waiting.

Temperatures remained steady. No shimmery lights or ethereal voices greeted her. Nothing fell from shelves.

She shuffled to the kitchen and filled the tea kettle with water. As it heated, she paced between the parlor and the kitchen, hoping for a sign of Theresé.

Terry glanced at the candlestick still on the floor, and opted not to pick it up.

"I'm not in the mood for evil spirits," she announced.

The tea kettle blasted its whistle. She fixed a mug of orange flavored tea and sauntered back to the bedroom.

She set the steaming ceramic cup on the nightstand, settled under the covers, and yawned again.

Before the drink had a chance to cool, she had fallen asleep.

***

Terry woke and glanced at the clock on her cell phone, sure she had overslept. It surprised her to note it was only seven.

She dressed, taking extra time for her makeup and hair.

"Watch out, Kyle Avery," she advised. She then straightened her room, took the cup of tea to the kitchen and zapped it in the microwave. While it heated, she found the plastic bag of chocolate chip cookies and shook them at the empty room.

"Theresé, come have some tea and cookies."

No response.

Sipping the tea, she read through the notes she had prepared. Satisfied she could add nothing more, she pushed the tablet aside. After a peek at her watch, she hastened to wash and dry the mug.

Without sparing a glance toward the parlor, she left the B and B and followed the walkway to the café.

Hannah leaned in her usual position against a pillar of the porch, arms crossed. Instead of the customary burning cigarette jutting from her lips, she held an unlit one between her fingertips. As Terry approached, Hannah uncrossed her arms, revealing the message on a bright yellow sweatshirt. On the front, a screen print of a large green doorknob placard bore the words "Do Not Disturb." It looked like a hotel privacy card dangling from Hannah's neck.

"Are we already cranky this morning?" Terry asked affectionately as she hugged the older woman.

"Damn right," Hannah said. "I've decided to quit smoking and its affecting my usual sunny disposition."

Terry laughed out loud. "Is that why you are holding that unlit cigarette?"

"I am. I'm testing myself. If I don't light it, I'll take it as a sign I can do it."

"You can do it." Terry kissed the choppy locks on the crown of Hannah's head. "I know you can. I want to see that sunshine you've been hiding all these years."

Hannah's gravelly laugh followed Terry as she walked through the door into the kitchen. The scent of cinnamon and apple permeated the air. Stephanie stacked dishes at the sink. Mary Jo transferred flaky pastries to a cooling rack.

"Morning, girls. Mmm. That is the perfect autumn smell," Terry said as she sniffed in appreciation.

Stephanie stopped and inhaled. "I never grow tired of that scent."

Terry motioned for her two friends to come closer. When they grouped together at the end of the counter, she showed them the notebook.

"I had a really intense incident last night. Theresé visited me in her human form. Those damn candlesticks sent us back in time. At least one of them did. One seems to be a dud."

"What happened?" Stephanie asked.

Terry shook her head. "I don't have time to talk now, but I wrote down every single thing I could think of. I'd like you both to read my notes and then tomorrow we can analyze everything. I'm meeting Kyle in a few minutes. We're going clue-hunting."

"You don't sound enthusiastic," Stephanie said. "I could go with him if you'd rather not go."

"No," Terry said, too quickly. "I mean, I've taken the day off so it's no problem. I haven't really pulled my share of this ancestry research anyway."

"Well, you picked a good day for it. It's supposed to be in the upper sixties."

"Good. See you later." Terry snagged an apple pastry from the rack. She strolled to the dining area. The front door opened. The musical bell overhead jingled as Kyle pushed through the opening. The strap of a camera case draped over one of his shoulders, a backpack dangled from the other. Both hanging articles bumped the doorframe. He wobbled and steadied. Catching Terry's eye, he winked and grinned boyishly.

Flutters danced in Terry's tummy as she smiled in return, taking in his khaki pants, jacket, and white shirt.

He looks like a Boy Scout on a mission.

They exchanged greetings, and Terry asked him if he wanted breakfast.

"No, I had coffee with some pastries. Hannah sent me home with a box full yesterday."

Terry polished off the apple turnover she was holding and dusted her fingertips.

"Then let's go! What did you have in mind first?" she asked.

"Well, there are a couple of places. I definitely wanted to take a walk through the…" Kyle pulled a notebook from his jacket pocket and read from it. "Cedar Grove Cemetery. It was established in eighteen thirty-two. It's the oldest city-owned cemetery in Portsmouth. Did you know it's listed on the Virginia and national registers of historic sites? There's another cemetery not far away that was established in about eighteen-fifty. I was able to locate partial headstone listings online but didn't find any familiar names. Still, I'd like to have a look around."

"Would you like me to drive my convertible?" She jangled her keys in front of Kyle.

Kyle's face lit up like a boy in a toy shop. "Aw, man, I've been dying to ride in that car."

Terry resisted the temptation to shout, "Why haven't you told that before?" Instead, she smiled and said, "Maybe I'll even let you drive."

"How about on the way back? I don't know my way around the city enough to drive to these places."

"Deal. Which one first?"

They settled on Cedar Grove and Terry drove the short distance to the historical site. Outdoor temperatures climbed quickly, and midway through the walk around the cemetery grounds she shed her jacket and tied the sleeves around her waist. Kyle seemed unaware of the temperature as he photographed ornate headstones and markers, respectful of the somber surroundings.

"This cemetery has some amazing examples of funerary

architecture." He pointed to a mausoleum. "Look there, that is Greek Revival. And over there is a Victorian crypt. This is worth the visit just for the historical art and monuments here, but I'm looking specifically for markers from the Revolutionary War era."

Terry drifted away and plopped onto a bench in a small park. The sun dipped behind a cloud and the landscape turned gray. Stone markers, polished obelisks, sculptured memorials, crosses—even flowers—drained of color. She shivered and shook her head to keep fanciful thoughts from forming.

She glanced toward Kyle, sheepishly realizing he knew so much more than she did about her own hometown. Because she worked in Olde Towne, she was aware of the many locations that were included in various preservation registries. She rarely took into consideration their historical significance.

Using her cell, she accessed a website about the cemetery. She noted a reference to public burial grounds not being established in Portsmouth until 1832. Prior to that many families had burial plots in their gardens until the practice was outlawed in that same year.

Did he know this? She started to call out to Kyle, only to observe him far across the burial grounds snapping photos. She cut and pasted the information into a text message and sent it to her phone to show him later.

She lost track of time as she read more history of the cemetery. A forerunner of modern public parks, the cemetery became a favorite spot of locals during Portsmouth's Victorian era. Families often gathered together and picnicked on the grounds.

She thought of the woman's remains buried for so long under the magnolia tree.

She must have been buried prior to eighteen thirty-two. Who was she?

Terry ambled from the park bench, reading headstones as she progressed toward Kyle.

Kyle joined her where she stood at a simple marker overshadowed by a nearby ornate monument. "This is quite an interesting place," he remarked.

"I have to admit, I never realized how interesting it could be to stroll around an old graveyard like this. When you look at headstones, do you ever wonder about the dead person, how they might have died, or how their family must have felt?"

"I do. Especially when I'm looking at the grave of a young child, or if two people share the same date of death. Did they die in an accident? Did you notice that many death dates here occurred in eighteen fifty-five?"

"The yellow fever epidemic?" Terry asked, thanks to her just-concluded web search.

"Yes!" Kyle nodded. "Crew on a ship bound for New York were infected and the ship harbored in Portsmouth. The captain ignored orders to keep the hold sealed. Thousands of people in Norfolk and Portsmouth died."

Terry nodded. "At St. Paul's on High Street, there's a monument to one of the priests who died helping victims during the epidemic."

Kyle scribbled in his notebook. "I'll check it out sometime." His stomach growled and they laughed.

Terry patted her tummy. "I think my apple pastry has long since disappeared. How about we grab a quick bite and then head over to the Catholic cemetery?"

"Sounds good to me."

"Let's go to my favorite hot dog joint. Llewellyn's. I haven't been in ages. The place doesn't grab your eye when you first go in there, but you can't beat the food."

They walked through the gates to the street. Terry stopped to let a jogger pass. She did a double take, as did the runner. He took two more steps before he pivoted and jogged back to the couple.

"Hello there, Commander," she called.

"It's nice to see you again." The Navy doctor extended his hand. "If we're going to run into each other like this, we should be on a first name basis. I'm Kirby."

"I'm Terry, this is Kyle." The familiar jolt of electricity jolted through her as they shook hands.

"My goodness, that happened again," she said. She

175

narrowed her eyes as she studied his uneventful handshake with Kyle. "Kirby, are you of French descent by any chance?"

He pondered a moment and said, "Not that I know of. As far as I know, I'm English and Irish, with a bit of Italian thrown in. Why?"

"Just curious." *How can I explain that every time sparks fly, I meet a new member of my family?*

"I've been wanting to research my family history, though, but never seemed to have time."

Terry smiled and said, "Well, Kyle's the right man if you're ever in the market. He's working on my mom's tree right now, which is why we came to the cemetery."

"Oh, yeah? You got a card, Kyle?"

"Only from my university." Kyle scribbled in his notebook and tore the page in two, handing one half to Kirby. "Here's my cell and email. Give me a shout. I'll be glad to help you get started."

"Thanks, man, I will. Well, I've got to go. I'm on my lunch break. By the way, my girlfriend and I are looking forward to staying at your Bed and Breakfast. I've just come back from a deployment and we thought it would be a nice location to be together when she gets some time off."

"We'll be glad to have you," Terry said.

The doctor raised his hand and resumed his jog.

Terry looked at her hand. "There's something about him," she mused out loud as she raised her gaze in the runner's direction.

Startled by her words, Kyle's heart plummeted. *Is she interested in him?* He stumbled.

Terry grabbed his arm, catching a fresh whiff of his cologne as he steadied. Firm muscle rippled in her grip as he steadied, and she slid her hand to the crook of his arm.

She glanced at the runner and wagged her finger. "There's something about that man, Kyle. I have a feeling he's connected to the family in some way."

Kyle's gaze followed Terry's finger, but he couldn't focus. Relief flooded over him.

With her hand pressed firmly on his arm, his heart somersaulted.

The encounter convinced him the time had come to make a move on Terry Dunbar pretty damn quick.

The thought terrified him.

***

"Good choice for lunch." Kyle patted his tummy, a satisfied look on his face.

"I can't believe you ate four hot dogs in one sitting."

"That sitting lasted two hours," Kyle pointed out matter-of-factly.

The faded sun created a dusky sky, the crisp chill of autumn descending around them.

"Temperature's dropped quite a bit," Terry said as they walked to her car. She handed Kyle her keys and walked to the passenger door. "We'll pass the Catholic cemetery on the way back to the apartment. It's not a huge place, so we could probably finish looking through it quickly."

Kyle grinned and settled his long frame behind the wheel, running his hands around the rim. "This is one sweet ride," he said.

"I got such a great deal on it. I successfully litigated a personal case that enabled me to make a substantial down payment, and mortgaged the family farm to finance the rest."

"I hope it wasn't with Mr. O'Grady."

Terry laughed. "No, it wasn't. I'm sure if Shady got his hands on a car like this, he'd keep it for himself. I can't wait to tackle Mrs. Belford's case." She caught another whiff of Kyle's cologne as he put the car in reverse and angled his body to look out the rear window.

She closed her eyes. Every fiber of her being jolted with awareness of the man beside her. Her fingers itched to stroke his jaw and turn his face toward her so she could kiss him. All day, his scent had nearly driven her crazy every time she came within close proximity of him.

In the restaurant, they'd sat side by side on unsteady barstools at the counter. They often bumped knees or thighs as they rotated the stools from side to side in conversation.

More than once, Terry twirled and pressed her thigh alongside his. Once when she leaned across him to reach for a straw, the stool wobbled and she placed one hand on his shoulder, brushing her breasts lightly against his upper arm. She resisted the urge to bury her nose along his collar and inhale the cologne.

The waitress delivered their food and they rested their hands on the countertop at the same time. The hair on the back of his hand tickled hers.

"Which way?" Kyle asked.

"What?" Terry gazed around, realizing they were in her car, not the restaurant! "Oh, I'm sorry. I was daydreaming. Turn left."

Kyle waited for a break in traffic to enter the roadway and follow her direction.

His question brought her back to the present. She told him to turn left. A few minutes later she directed Kyle to the quiet lane under the wrought-iron arch displaying the cemetery name. He parked.

As they had done previously, they separated and drifted through rows of headstones. Kyle snapped photos. Terry walked around until she found the one she was looking for. She knelt and straightened a floral arrangement tilting in a vase.

Kyle joined her, his shadow falling across a pink granite marker bearing the name of Sadie Wyatt.

"This was Great-Aunt Ida's older sister. I barely remember her. She was almost one hundred when she died."

"This name is ringing a bell with me," Kyle said. He took shots of the headstone, then snapped his fingers. "Before Stephanie was born, her birth mother Jessica recorded some contacts she'd had with someone named Sadie Wyatt. I'm pretty sure it was how we verified Stephanie had found the correct Wyatt branch. We've been concentrating so much on finding the French connection we've overlooked this possible Wyatt link. Are there any other Wyatts buried here from your family?"

"I don't know. Aunt Ida is buried in another cemetery, where my dad's parents and some of his side are buried." The perfect opportunity presented itself to Terry and she added, "About that valise is in the attic of the B and B. Maybe some of its old papers could be helpful. I've been meaning to get it for Stephanie. I need to look through some vintage clothing from an old trunk anyway and she's been after me to find that case. Would you like to meet me there later today and look for it?"

Kyle agreed and they set a time to meet at the Inn as they walked toward Terry's convertible.

Terry drove onto the highway, elated at the prospect of enticing Kyle's attention with the old papers.

A sudden chill sent shivers down her spine, erasing the sense of elation. She tapped the button to turn on the heat.

She could not shake the foreboding feeling.

CHAPTER 17

Terry's glance locked with radar precision onto the target she sought: her great aunt's antique steamer trunk with a rounded top. Metal rivets secured discolored brass strips designed to reinforce the corners. On the front, two lion's head plates, dotted with pits and green tarnish, sported rings through the noses to secure chains.

Originally located in Aunt Ida's home next door, the "treasure chest" had been the focal point of many a swashbuckling buccaneer adventure when Terry and her brothers had visited as children. Smiling at memories from her childhood, Terry pushed aside boxes to clear a path to reach the trunk. The vintage clothing contained within could be the mother lode of paraphernalia for a costume party.

The faint odor of mothballs mixed with traces of the flowery scent that reminded her of the diminutive great-aunt who had been so generous in bequeathing her estate.

"Aunt Ida, thank you for everything you left me. There was a bit more than you bargained for," Terry said, looking skyward. She rummaged further through layers of clothing protected by tissues, laying aside items she thought could be used for the costume party.

She paired a white ruffled batiste blouse with a red and black checkered taffeta skirt. Perfect for the Civil War era attire, it would be less wieldy than a hooped skirt.

Next she uncovered a stiff black crinoline. Laughing out loud, she fluffed the starched netting and said, "This might work for Stephanie as a southern belle. There's no way that

Mary Jo will ever wear that stiff petticoat for any costume." She placed it with the checkered skirt.

Unfolding the next layer of tissue, she clapped her hands. Still talking out loud, she said, "Aha, now there's something Mary Jo might wear." Terry shook the folds from a black taffeta skirt lined with a single flounce at the hem. Further rummaging uncovered a high collared white blouse trimmed in a thin line of black lace. Long sleeves, puffed at the shoulders, ended in a lacy point at the wrists. Shiny black buttons lined the front of the trim-waist.

"Add a fancy corset, some high-heeled boots and a bowler or top-hat with netting and voila! She's the perfect steampunk Victorian gal."

Enthusiasm took over, and before long, Terry had uncovered more petticoats, velvet cloaks, lace gloves, and shawls. A small enameled box held a half-dozen colorful lace folding fans. Although she hadn't found a colonial gown, she had the accessories to start putting an ensemble together.

Careful to replace the protective tissues of the remaining clothes, Terry shut the lid of the old trunk. She gathered the larger dress pieces and took them downstairs to the living room, smoothing the material over the backs of the chairs and sofa. She retrieved a plastic dishpan from the kitchen and trudged upstairs once more. In the container she placed the smaller accessories and the box of fans.

She stumbled over the foot of an old-fashioned coat rack, which wobbled and sent a cascade of old hats around her. She reached up in time to keep the stand from hitting her in the head. The second target of her search—the small satchel—snagged the claw foot of the rack and wedged against a crate. The top arms of the rack tilted perilously.

She reached for the musty leather case and dragged it over the clutter. The temperature dropped noticeably and she shivered in the sudden chill. Vapor formed as she breathed through clenched teeth. A strange odor, like tarnished silver, assaulted her nose.

She turned toward the stairwell, banging her shin on a crate.

Looking down at the toe of her boot as she rubbed her leg, she noticed a dirty silver mist swirling through the clutter, wending its way through the labyrinth of boxes until the mist obscured the floor. Then the meager overhead light went out.

Below her, the door at the base of the stairs slammed shut, leaving her in total darkness.

She flicked the flashlight and swept the beam over the floor. The murky haze reached her feet, a thin tempest swirled into a human outline, a neck forming, followed by the shape of a skull. The banshee bobbled forward toward Terry's face, silver-red eyes glowing above a cavernous mouth that emitted a screeching hiss.

Terry stumbled backwards over the pouch, landing on her rump. The light beam wavered until she steadied her hold. She fumbled in her jacket pocket to withdraw her pepper spray. Leaning on her left elbow, she depressed the nozzle of the canister with every ounce of strength she had. The filmy stream of capsicum cut a path through the apparition.

The figure shrieked and shrunk toward the clutter.

Heavy footsteps thumped up the stairs from the first floor, growing louder as they reached the landing below. "Terry, are you up there?" Kyle's muffled voice called through the door. He rattled the knob and pounded.

"I'm here, Kyle," she shouted, struggling to her knees. She inhaled the burning taste of the pepper spray and coughed.

Two heavy thuds preceded the sound of wood splintering. The light flickered on. Kyle bounded up the steps and dropped to his knees beside Terry, calling. "Are you okay? What happened?"

Terry realized she'd held her breath after the last fit of coughs. She let it out with a long whoosh, then gulped deeply, causing another round of hacking.

Kyle helped her to her feet, clearing his throat as he breathed in spray. Lightly coughing, he shouted, "Let's get out of here."

Terry reached for the satchel. A thin curl of the dirty gray haze slithered from under the clutter, weaving between her feet and drifting toward Kyle. Before she could open her mouth to warn him, a new wave of the acrid metallic smell overpowered the trace of capsicum. Another fit of coughing racked her body as she flailed her arm in vain, pointing to the mist curling around his feet in an angry rush.

Too late.

Kyle's eyes widened as he caught sight of the mist. He stepped to one side and stood locked in stunned stillness as the haze curled around his torso and whirled in front of him.

The vapor twirled into the feminine shape wearing a colonial-era dress. The specter's back was to Terry, who could make out gray hair spiking loose from a bun at her neck.

Her nearly human hands reached out and shoved him. He struck the side of his head on a rafter and he reeled, pain etching his face. He stumbled as he stepped in front of the stairwell shaft.

The female form lost the last of its translucence and turned a solid angry face toward his before raising her hands to shove Kyle again.

"No!" Terry screamed and pushed the form to one side, squirting pepper spray wildly.

Kyle teetered and Terry clutched him by the arm, bracing herself to keep them both from falling. The pair stood toe to toe, bodies leaning backwards like dancers engaged in an odd jitterbug.

The acrid air burned their lungs, and they both coughed.

Terry tossed the can to the side and held Kyle's arm with both hands. The metal can rolled past Kyle's feet and clanked down the steps. Kyle flung his free hand to grasp the flimsy railing at the stair opening.

The wood rail cracked and broke in his grip. Terry stared in wide-eyed alarm, struggling to hold him. His feet dropped one step lower and his arm slipped from her grasp. The momentum forced Terry backward and she stumbled over the leather bag.

Kyle hovered, arms flailing, and fell backwards.

Somehow, he did not fall. Unseen forces supported his

weight. He steadied and gripped the railing, heaving his body forward. His knees hit the top of the stairwell. Tears streaming down burning eyes, Terry scrambled to her feet and tossed the bag down the stairwell.

"What the hell was that?" Kyle asked. He held his hand over his nose and mouth, eyes darting from side to side in search of the image.

Holding her breath to avoid inhaling more pepper spray, she gasped "Let's get out of here before we choke to death."

They scuttled down the steps, Terry in the lead, stopping to pick up the spray can and the satchel.

At the bottom, light from the hallway beamed through the broken door. Terry eased through the split without turning the knob.

Kyle followed, pushing a splintered piece aside to make a bit more room. As he took the leather bag from Terry and led her to the next flight of stairs, he said, "I'm sorry about busting through the attic door."

"Don't worry about that. I just wish I could have seen you kick through it. You were like Indiana Jones to the rescue."

"You know, my students have called me that for years," Kyle admitted.

"I hope you won't be offended but we've kind of nicknamed you that too." Terry grimaced, glad Kyle was walking behind her and could not see her guilt-ridden expression.

Air was clearer on the first floor. Kyle opened the front door. Terry grabbed a box of tissues from the foyer table and joined Kyle on the porch, ignoring the cold air. Her eyes still watered, and she dabbed at the corners with another tissue, careful not to rub. She offered one to Kyle.

"I've never seen anything like that." Kyle glanced toward the attic. Interest mixed with hesitation. "I didn't know whether to run from it or study it."

"It seems to be getting stronger, like Therese is." She coughed again. "I feel much better now that we are out of the confined space. I kept my eyes shut when I sprayed, but I still breathed in some of the residual effects. Let's go outside for a minute," She cleared her throat with a most unladylike sound and spit into the bushes.

"That stuff does sting a bit. I'm glad we didn't take a direct hit. Are you sure you're okay?" Kyle asked, then blew his nose.

Under the porch light, she noticed the blood stains on his shirt and said, "I'm more worried about that bump on your head than about me. I hope you don't need stitches." Using two fingers under his chin to turn his face to the side, she gently dabbed a fresh tissue to the wound. The tissue held a slight trace of blood.

"Maybe the pepper spray cauterized it." Kyle laughed, winced, and then took a step back.

Terry placed a hand on his shoulder to steady him, jump-starting the sexual tension she had experienced all day. A sensual shiver coursed through her when she touched his skin, warm through the cotton shirt cooled by the night air. Her hand shook from standing so close.

The man could be bleeding to death and I'm getting turned on.

A slight whiff of his cologne competed with the smell of pepper still burning her nose. Shaking her head to concentrate on tending to his wound, she steered him toward the door. "Let's go back inside. There's still a trace of bleeding, but I think the worst is over."

Kyle gripped Terry's wrist and drew her hand away from his head. The unexpected movement startled her.

"Did I hurt you?"

"I want to know what's going on here. What was that apparition up there, and what kept me from falling?"

"Can't we talk about that tomorrow? It's late and we need to clean up. And we really need to tend to that wound. There should be a first aid kit at the apartment."

"I'm fine. Stop changing the subject. And you're not staying here tonight."

"Well, I'm not driving home in my Maserati with this stench on me," Terry stated emphatically.

"Get your things," Kyle commanded and reached for the

door handle. "You can shower at the apartment. But you're not staying here, and we *are* going to talk about this tonight."

***

In record time, Terry stepped from the guest shower in her former apartment, dripping water on the clothes she'd shed and left heaped beside the tub.

She wrapped her hair in a towel. After dressing in a white blouse and jeans pulled from the bag she'd hastily packed, she wiped water droplets from the sink and mist from the mirror.

She examined her make-up free face in the mirror. Red-rimmed eyes gave testament to the earlier effects of the spray. Her eyes no longer watered but she still had to clear her throat often.

The skin under her nose was tender from the constant use of tissues. She could only imagine the results of a full blast of pepper spray to the face.

Brushing her wet hair into a ponytail, she then twisted it into a bun and secured it at the nape of her neck. She stepped back to study the results.

Not the most glamorous image she'd ever portrayed.

Under ordinary circumstances, being ordered around by any man would have put her back to the wall. She would have stubbornly done exactly opposite of his command. But in all fairness, Kyle had witnessed too much paranormal activity to be satisfied with waiting until morning for an explanation.

She scooped up the discarded clothes, sniffing the slightly peppery smell that clung to the clothes.

Under no circumstances would I have ever exposed my prized convertible to the slightest hint of residue from that pepper spray!

She dumped the load into the hamper. She'd gather everything in the morning to take to the dry cleaners.

Hopefully, the effects of the spray had been contained in the attic. She'd have to check in the Bed and Breakfast to be sure.

When she finally stepped into the hall, the pleasant scent of cooking greeted her. She padded to the kitchen, expecting to see a freshly-showered Kyle at the stove.

He stood with his back to her, wearing the same white shirt stained with dried blood droplets. He looked over his shoulder and said, "Hey, I've got your mom's sloppy Joe sauce heating. It's about all I can offer you if you want to stay."

"I will. But I'll finish here while you shower."

"Thanks." Kyle tapped the spatula on the side of the frying pan and set it on the stove. He turned around and faced her, his Oxford shirt unbuttoned to reveal a ripped six-pack she had no idea he possessed. Terry hoped her eyes didn't pop from her head—even worse, she hoped she didn't drool. Stepping aside to let Kyle pass in the narrow space between the bar and the wall, she backed into the edge of the counter.

"Be right back," he said and headed down the hall.

Terry peered around the wall in time to catch him peeling the shirt off before he entered the bedroom.

It was official—she drooled.

She returned to the stove, stirring the hamburger mix with more force than necessary.

Wow!

From the moment she'd first met Kyle, he'd intrigued her. He was tall, slender, and endearingly shy. Not to mention a bit all-thumbs at times.

But never in her wildest dreams did she imagine the buff physique hidden under his oxford shirts and khaki pants.

Terry shook her head to prevent lascivious thoughts from forming. She removed the saucepan from the heat and arranged hamburger buns on the plate.

She rummaged through the woefully bare refrigerator. A small gray box emblazoned with the *Pâtisseries a la Carte* logo sat on the top shelf. No doubt Hannah had sent Kyle to the apartment with a well-stocked care package.

Peeking inside the café box, she smiled at the variety of pastries from which to choose. Below, a pizza box from Antonio's took up the shelf space. She opened the lid. Half a pepperoni pizza resided in the box.

She discovered cucumbers and tomatoes in the salad bin. After washing the vegetables, she sliced them and arranged them in layers on a plate. Then she pulled plates from the cabinets and forks from the drawers and set the table.

As she turned around, her gaze fell on a shirtless Kyle walking toward her. Freshly-showered and in jeans, he sauntered past her with a sheepish look on his face. "Sorry, I need to get a fresh shirt. I haven't even unpacked yet."

He dropped to his knees in front of two suitcases by the door, and rummaged through one, pulling out clothes.

Terry brought a closed fist to her mouth and bit the knuckles, regaining her composure a second before Kyle stood. Out of the corner of her eye, she watched him shake out a white cotton shirt and slip his arms in through the sleeves.

She glanced toward him as he turned to face her. He settled his collar around his neck before reaching for the first button. She almost bit her tongue, and dropped the fork she was holding. With a loud clang, it bounced across the plate and fell to the floor at their feet.

They both stooped for the utensil, bumping heads.

"Ouch." Kyle tapped his temple.

"Let me look at that," Terry commanded, ignoring the sharp pain in her head. She yanked a chair from under the table and pressed Kyle's shoulders until he sat. She ran her hand gently across his hairline. When she withdrew, her fingertips bore a slight hint of blood from his temple.

"We must have opened the wound again." She grabbed a napkin and dabbed lightly. "It's already stopped bleeding, though."

"I put antiseptic on it after my shower," Kyle said, standing. "Are you okay? That was quite a knock."

"I'm fine. There's a fresh blood drop on your collar now." Terry touched her fingers to the spot. The base of her hand rested on Kyle's shoulder, his skin warm under her fingers. The close contact was almost more than she could bear. She let her hand drop, stopping right at his left pocket. His heart raced under her palm, in step with the thundering of her own. Her gaze dropped to the exposed chest muscles a mere fraction from her fingers.

Kyle slid his hand to her neck and drew her close. He titled her head until their gazes met.

Their lips touched in soft warmth. Terry had never known a kiss like it. They parted lips and stared, Kyle's eyes smoldering but locked in her gaze. Still holding her neck with one hand, he wrapped his other arm around her and pulled her body closer.

The air sizzled with the undercurrents of sexual awareness.

Terry melded her body to his, one hand on his arm, the other skimming his bare ribcage under the open shirt. He jumped lightly, his breath hitching.

His next kiss scored with the heat of a dormant volcano erupting. Terry's hands slid on either side of Kyle's neck, fingers trailing his neckline as they sought the shirt collar. She pushed the sleeves down his arms and pressed her lips to the indention below the collarbone. He broke the embrace long enough to shake the cuffs from his wrists and toss the shirt to one side.

His arms cocooning Terry, he pressed her against the wall in the hallway and rained kisses along her collarbone. The feathery touch sent sparks straight to her toes. With her back flattened against the cool plaster she became even more aware of the heat radiating from his body to hers.

A heat that she was certain would soon scorch the wall behind her.

She trailed her left hand up his neck until her fingers curled through his hair. She skimmed her right hand along the side of his face and kissed him. His tongue touched hers.

The simple action seemed to send lightning bolts of sensation straight to her core.

Still locked in an embrace, Kyle backed Terry in the direction of his bedroom. At the door, he stopped.

"Are you sure about this?" he asked.

In answer, Terry pulled him over the threshold. *I've never been surer of anything in my life, Kyle Avery.*

He scooped her into his arms and carried her to his bed.

She melted onto her back, dragging him with her. He fumbled with the tiny metal buttons on her blouse. She drew her fingers over his and tried to work the buttons herself. When the stubborn fasteners refused to push back through the buttonhole, she clutched the fabric and ripped. Two buttons near the neckline broke from the threads holding them and skipped across the hardwood floor with light tic-tac sounds. The next two remained in place, leaving just enough room to pull the blouse over her head. She raised forward and dragged the hem over her head.

She reclined, Kyle moving with her. She arched her hips, the pressure of his erection sending riveting thrills through her. Her hips swayed, matching his motions.

The friction of clothes heightened her arousal. She skimmed her hand between their torsos to reach for his zipper.

With lightning speed, they shed the last of the barriers between them and returned to their reclined positions.

Linking fingers with hers, Kyle brought both of her arms over her head. With his left hand lightly pinning both of her wrists, he used the other to brush hair away from her face. He stopped and rolled to his side, fumbling for the trousers he had shed. He withdrew a foil packet from his wallet and set it on the table. He moved over her, swaying forward in sensual moves as his lips found hers.

Terry arched her back, extracting her hands from his clasp. She stretched her arm until her fingers touched the foil packet.

He kissed her shoulder, and her fingers ripped the foil. While his tongue trailed across the swell of her breasts, steady hands sheathed him.

His lips found a nipple.

Need tore through her. She skimmed her fingers along his jaw. His kisses trailed upwards until his lips found hers again.

They took each other in a synchronized ballet, slow sensual moves that built to a crescendo of pleasure.

***

Booming cannons echoed in Kyle's ears. Blazing fireworks flashed behind his closed eyelids. Thoughts collided in his befuddled mind.

Was it New Year's Eve? Fourth of July?

He collapsed in a heap, dimly aware of his surroundings but acutely aware of the woman beneath him. He turned his head and kissed Terry's shoulder. She emitted a sound somewhere between a moan and a purr, the trembling sigh vibrating in his ear.

"Am I in heaven?" Terry asked. "'When the Saints Go Marching In' seems to be roaring in my head."

"I don't know where you are, but I'm in the middle of a fireworks celebration myself," Kyle said. He stretched on his back and pulled Terry into the crook of his arm. "I think John Phillips Sousa's band just marched through my head."

Terry laughed. She shifted her body and settled her head on his shoulder. Her palm rested on his chest, fingers splayed. His racing heart thumped against her hand.

Kyle closed his hand over hers. He liked the comfort her touch brought.

Her breathing slowed, each exhale sending tickling whispers across his chest. She shifted closer and sighed. Steady breaths signaled when she had fallen asleep, wrapped in his embrace.

He brushed his lips across her forehead and closed his eyes.

Woman, do you know what you've done to me?

His heartbeat settled and his breathing waltzed with hers.

CHAPTER 18

The distant clink of glass roused the sleeping couple. When the tinkle repeated, Kyle sat upright. They looked at each other in the sliver of light shining through the window, then scrambled from opposite sides of the bed.

Terry draped the sheet around her. Reaching the window first, Terry peered between the blinds and asked, "Did you hear that too?"

Kyle pulled on his jeans. "Something woke me. Breaking glass?"

"Maybe. I don't see anything moving out there."

"I'll be right back." Shirtless and barefoot, Kyle ran from the bedroom.

"Wait for me." Terry followed. Tightening her grip on the sheet around her, she shuffled to the living room just as Kyle yanked open the front door and disappeared down the stairs.

She grabbed his coat from the rack on the door and slipped into it, letting the sheet pool at her feet. When she stepped out onto the landing of the stairwell, her bare feet slid on a thin coat of moisture. She steadied, dancing from foot to foot on the cold wood as she peered. Vapor formed as her warm breath mingled with the cold air. Rear porch lights illuminated the parking spaces closest to the buildings, but darkness engulfed the back portion of the property line.

Light reflected on his bare chest as he stepped onto the parking surface and checked around the buildings. He looked up toward the apartment, then crossed to Clothiste's Inn, where he repeated the movement. The inn blocked her view of the café as he headed there, but she heard him stumble and curse as he returned along the narrow boardwalk linking the buildings. He jogged up the steps.

"All the windows seem okay in the buildings." His breath formed ragged clouds as he puffed. "Damn, it's cold out here."

"Maybe someone was putting trash to the curb," Terry suggested. She took two long strides on tiptoe to get back inside the apartment, Kyle right behind her.

"There'll be frost on the pumpkins tonight," he predicted as he shut and locked the door.

Terry stepped to the side, still clutching the material of his jacket around her. "I was out there thirty seconds and I'm frosted," she laughed, shuddering.

Kyle laughed, but stopped when his gaze dropped to her bare legs. The jacket hem just grazed the tops of her thighs, barely covering her assets.

Also aware of the shortage of material, Terry stooped, bending her knees to one side to retrieve the sheet. As she rose, their eyes met. She noticed the pulse in his neck, and the bob of his Adam's apple as he swallowed.

Kyle took the bed linen from her hand and let it fall to the floor. He backed her against the door, and in slow tantalizing strokes, parted the jacket. His cold fingertips touched her warm skin as he ran his hands up her hips, along her sides and over her breasts.

The contrast in temperature sent Terry's senses into instant overdrive. Her breath caught in her throat. Kyle's lips sought her collarbone. He pressed his cool face against her neck, nibbling along her jaw line to her ear.

Terry ran her hands across his sinewy back, impressed with the rippling muscles usually hidden under the loose white shirts and khakis the scholarly professor wore.

"I can't get over how ripped you are," she said, her hands sliding down his sides. She hooked her fingers and ran them around the waistband of his jeans until they met at the unsnapped button above the zipper. Kyle inhaled sharply and she nipped his neck.

"I work out on occasion," he said matter-of-factly as he walked her backwards until the backs of her legs touched the sofa.

"On occasion? It looks like you live in the gym." She shrugged the jacket from her shoulders and unzipped his fly in one fluid movement.

"It builds stamina," he said, nuzzling her neck as he leaned her toward the cushions.

Marching bands collided under a brilliant fireworks display.

***

Terry stood in front of the microwave, wearing Kyle's shirt and nothing else. She punched buttons to reheat the dinner they'd missed. Kyle, shirtless and wearing jeans zipped but unbuttoned, leaned against the counter. She told him of the strange incidents she had recently encountered ending with the incident in the attic.

"It terrified me when you were pushed backwards. I thought for sure you were going to fall down the stairs," Terry said.

"I did too. I could feel hands push me forward until I regained my footing. Did you see anything behind me?"

"The specter took on a shape, but it was like her hands were solid."

"I've never seen anything like that…thing."

"I guess we've all seen it now. It started out in this slithery mist. It wound its way around my feet. Stephanie first, then Mary Jo. It even showed itself to Tanner once, streaming around his feet. It formed into an almost-human shape this time, though."

"I don't know much about the phenomenon of ghosts. I never really believed in them, but I know people at the university who have claimed to see spirits roaming the old buildings. Until today, I've never seen anything…" Kyle seemed to struggle for the right word.

"Otherworldly?" Terry offered.

Kyle nodded. "Yeah, otherworldly works. Knowing the occurrences that have happened to your family in the last few months, I can't help but think there's something to this theory of people trapped between life and death."

Terry shrugged. "They've been around the family for ages. I guess we take it all in stride." The microwave timer sounded and she retrieved the sauce dish. "Smells good," Kyle said. He opened a bag of potato chips.

"I can't believe it's only eleven-thirty. It feels like it should be four a.m." She scooped sloppy Joe mix onto buns. Steam rose from the plate of sandwiches she placed on the table.

"I'd say we got a little sidetracked," Kyle smiled. He slipped his hand over hers.

Terry leaned in for a kiss. Then she said, "By the way, I wanted to mention something I learned at the first cemetery this morning. Apparently family plots in personal yards were common until eighteen thirty-two, when the first public cemetery opened in Portsmouth. So that would mean the bones from the magnolia tree must have been buried before then."

"That makes sense. Good point. By the way, Eric, my friend I met with the other night, can help with the DNA if he can get a sample from the remains. He said he could go to the funeral home Saturday if you arrange it."

"Oh, thank you. I'll make the final arrangements and get back with you. Do I have to go too? I don't think I want to be there."

"No, you won't have to be there. But he'll need to get a living sample, perhaps from you or your mother."

Pausing with a chip in hand, Terry said, "I've already had that done, right after the discovery. I just got the results back."

Kyle set down his sandwich. "Really? What did it say?"

She looked at him, an incredulous look on her face. "Are you kidding me? All I can tell you is that I am eighty-nine percent European. I tried to understand mitochondrial, Haplogroups, genomes, coding regions." She shook her head.

"If you don't understand the topic, how the hell did you remember those terms?"

"I am the queen of words. Hated math in school. Second to math, I hated science."

"I liked history and geography best myself. Well, having those results in hand is going to save a lot of time. Can I look at them?"

"Absolutely. I'll bring them to you after work tomorrow. Mom had the testing done a year or so ago, but never did anything with it. Would it help to have theirs as well?"

"Even better. With these reports, Eric may be able to determine if you share a common ancestry by comparing your DNA to that from the bones. If nothing else, I'm gaining valuable insight into materials for my book." He had taken a leave of absence from his university to conduct research into amateur genealogy. When Terry's mother hired him to research her family, she also allowed him to use the experiences as part of his research.

"I'll drop mine off tomorrow."

"I won't be home until late. I'm leaving your parents' house to meet Eric and a couple of his colleagues tomorrow evening." Kyle's voice held a hint of regret. He ran his fingers across Terry's hand. "I can cancel."

"No, that's not necessary. I'm getting together with Mary Jo and Stephanie tomorrow evening anyway. We've got a lot of catching up to do. I'll drop it off in the morning before you leave."

Kyle polished off his sandwich and said, "I promised your mom I'd stop by the festival in Driver on Saturday. Want to meet me there, then maybe go to dinner after?"

"Sounds like a plan." She jumped up to clear the table.

"I'll take care of that." Kyle grabbed the plates from her hands and took them to the sink. "I'll finish in the morning."

Kyle's actions moved him up a notch in Terry's esteem. Her gaze followed him as he walked to the sink.

He does have a great butt.

To his back, she said, "I need to go now."

He returned to the table and reached for the rest of the dinnerware. He glanced toward her and said firmly, "You're not going back to the inn tonight."

Terry opened her mouth to speak and he cut her off. "You're staying here with me." He crossed to the sink and set the dishes down with a thump.

Terry raised her hands palms out. "Okay. I'm staying here."

He angled his head over his shoulder and raised an eyebrow. "Guest bedroom or mine?"

"Yours," she said without hesitation.

Kyle extended his hand and she took it in hers. Her heart flip-flopped against her ribs. She practically floated as she walked beside him down the hall.

In her opinion, Kyle just rocked the dial on her esteem meter.

***

Terry eased back the covers. She wanted to reach the inn before the staff arrived at *Pâtisseries a la Carte*. Kyle grabbed her and snuggled close. Despite his protests and obvious morning signal that he was alert and ready, she laughed and scooted to the edge of the bed. He managed to grab the hem of her shirt—his actually—and pulled her backwards. He nuzzled her neck and mumbled, "Morning."

"Gotta go." She scurried from his reach.

Trying to grab her again, he missed and fell on his side across the mattress. He pretended to pout and said, "Aw. C'mon, stay."

She laughed. "No way. If I'm lucky, I'll beat Mary Jo and Hannah before they arrive to start their morning baking and they won't see me slinking into the inn." She scrambled into her clothes, her back to him.

Kyle swung his legs over the side of the bed, pulling the sheet as he moved. The linen barely covered his lower body.

"I'll come with you."

Terry glanced in the mirror at Kyle rising to his feet behind her. The sight of his toned chest and chiseled stomach kicked in her drool factor.

"It's better if you don't. I'm only going into the innkeeper's room, nowhere else. But I promise to call if anything looks out of order when I enter." She grabbed her purse. Sidling up to Kyle, she cupped his chin in her hand and smiled. "However, I could be persuaded to stay tomorrow night—if you're interested."

For an answer, he weaved his fingers through her hair and drew her closer, until their lips met.

The sheet fell to the floor.

His interest poked her hip. "We'll see you tonight."

Terry's laughter trailed behind her as she darted from the room and gathered her belongings. She scanned the parking lot. Neither Mary Jo nor Hannah's cars were in their spaces. Terry slowed her pace and walked to the Inn. She unlocked the door and cautiously pushed it open.

Normal temperatures greeted her. She peeked into the parlor. The period clothing was still draped over the backs of furniture in the same way as she'd left them.

The candlestick remained in the spot where she'd dropped it. No trace of pepper spray lingered downstairs.

Finding nothing amiss, she walked to her room. Kyle's spontaneous send-off had recharged her intellectual batteries. She showered, mentally listing the steps to prepare Mrs. Belford's case. First thing, she would file a Warrant in Debt for the money owed and Warrant in Detinue for his illegal possession of her car. O'Grady's mocking voice played in her ears and she rubbed her scalp vigorously to clear her mind. How she hoped the police could arrest him, and wished she could be there to witness it. She prayed for a fast court date for Mrs. Belford's sake. If she had to answer a Bill of Particulars or file a Grounds for Defense, she would be ready.

Battle plan etched in her memory, she dried her hair and then dressed. She slung her purse over her shoulder and headed for the back door. In one hand she toted the heavy satchel, the other, her briefcase. She stopped at the back door and paused.

What else?

Coffee—of course—then war on Shady O'Grady.

It was Friday. She hoped her week would end on a less chaotic note than it began.

She was in for a rude awakening.

***

Terry stepped onto the porch to see a car stopped in the middle of the parking lot, the driver's door hanging open. Mary Jo stood at the trunk of Terry's convertible, bent with hands on knees.

"What's the matter?" Terry called in alarm, scrambling down the steps. Her long legs gobbled the pavement as she ran to her car. Shards of red and frosted glass dotted the asphalt near the rear of the convertible.

Both taillights had been broken. Someone had etched fresh scratches on the trunk. The rear tires were flattened.

Terry cried out in anger, "What the hell?"

"I always pass that car with a touch of envy and noticed the damage as soon as I drove by," Mary Jo explained. "I couldn't believe it."

"We heard glass break last night, but we thought someone was breaking in. Kyle checked the windows of the buildings, but I doubt he even thought of the vehicles."

If Mary Jo wondered why Terry knew Kyle had checked the buildings, she gave no indication. She merely stated, "You're up early."

"Long story. I had another encounter with our evil spirit but everything is okay," Terry said. "Just make sure the wine is in abundant supply tonight. I've got a lot to tell you and Steph." She handed the leather satchel to Mary Jo, and reached into her handbag for her phone. "Will you give this to her? It's full of old papers and shit she'll appreciate. I've got to report this damage."

"Terry, you probably should put the police on speed dial." Mary Jo chuckled, but her expression was not amused. She shook her head.

"I already did. I'm becoming such a regular customer I need a direct line," Terry said dryly.

Once again, she filed a police report. After taking photos to document the damage, she finally entered the office.

She fixed a pot of coffee. While it brewed, she started her computer.

She made notes for the insurance company. They probably weren't going to be happy to get her call when they opened. Gage had arranged for a fresh paint job and planned to take her car there himself.

The next note she scribbled in capital letters: HAVE SECURITY CAMERAS INSTALLED TODAY. She underlined today for emphasis.

The scent of fresh coffee reached her nostrils about the time she had downloaded the photos to the file with the other damage and stormed to the kitchen. She grabbed a mug from the cabinet, plunking it on the counter with such force that it broke in two. Disgustedly, she tossed the two halves in the trash and rummaged for another.

Armed with a cup of fuel, she retreated to her office to prepare her case against Dennis Arnold O'Grady.

That thought brightened her day.

CHAPTER 19

Ready to relax with her friends for the evening, Terry walked into the kitchen of *Clothiste's Inn* just in time to see Mary Jo transfer pastries from a box to a plate, and close the lid. Stephanie flipped through a binder of pages encased in protective plastic sheets.

Terry leaned on the counter near Stephanie and said, "What kind of goodies are we having?"

"Antipasto tray. Wine. A variety of pastries and canapés I'm trying out for the ribbon-cutting." Mary Jo ticked the list off on her fingers. "If we run out of food, we can order pizzas from Antonio's."

"Suits me." Terry shuffled forward, her foot nudging the old red leather satchel. She pushed it with her toe, and said, "Hey, Steph, did you find anything interesting in this old suitcase?"

"Did I ever!" Stephanie cried. She leaned down and picked up the bag. Fingering the worn wooden handle of the battered leather satchel, she reached inside to withdraw a stack of letters tied with a bow. With narrowed eyes, she shook the envelopes at Terry, the papers gently rustling with the motion. Then she reached inside and brought out a wad of tissue.

"Look at this." She shook the paper until a gold ring rolled into her palm and held it out. "This looks like a man's signet ring, except instead of initials or a seal it has prongs. One is broken. It must have held a stone at one time. Hold it, see how heavy it is."

Terry obliged and plucked the ring, then immediately dropped it back into Stephanie's hand.

"It's warm."

Stephanie nodded, glancing toward Mary Jo. "We had the same reaction when we touched it too. I don't know why, nor do I know who owned it. It was the only thing in the case that was not part of a written document. Terry, I just can't believe you knew this case was up there in the attic the whole time."

Terry gave a sheepish shrug of her shoulders. "Sorry. I just kept forgetting about it. I hope you have found some clues." Guilt still nipped at her for keeping the satchel from Stephanie, so she changed the subject. "By the way, what did you think about my report on the ghostly visits?"

"Let me answer that," Mary Jo said. She tapped the legal pad that contained Terry's written notes. "Compliments on a very detailed report. I want to know more about this kiss with Chase–the kiss that your ghost witnessed. You've teased me with that interesting tidbit before, on our last girls' night. Then I read that little snippet in your notes that your *ghost* saw you planting one on him. Spill the beans."

Terry waved her hand to as if to brush Mary Jo aside. "Sheesh, what's with you? And that's not what my notes said. Besides, I couldn't have been more than fifteen back then. You and Chase weren't even an item in those days. We shared one kiss under the magnolia, testing the waters so to speak."

"Hmph." Mary Jo removed the cellophane from a plate of cookies with more force than necessary.

"As I remember it, he's a great kisser." Terry mused. She cupped her hand in her chin, an exaggerated dreamy look clouding her eyes.

Mary Jo slapped *a Pâtisseries a la Carte* box on the table and opened the lid, tearing the cardboard in the process.

Terry winked at Stephanie, smiling when Mary Jo plunked éclairs onto a platter with short choppy movements. Waiting nearly half-a minute, she finally added, "But we just never felt any spark."

"Like I care," Mary Jo said. She leaned against the counter, arms crossed and back erect in a stiff pose.

Stephanie burst into a fit of giggles. "Oh, you care all right. I can see why Chase gave you that nickname 'Coppertop.' Right now, your face matches that red hair right to the roots."

Mary Jo pursed her lips and tried to remain angry, but soon joined the other two women in laughter. She poked her finger in Terry's direction. "Well, just see to it you don't try to test any more waters, Theresa Dunbar."

Terry poured wine into flutes. "I've got oars in my own waters, thank you very much," she said self-contentedly and immediately regretted it.

Stephanie pounced beside her and grabbed the taller woman's arm, eyes wide.

"Did you and Kyle finally…"

Having to abandon her smugness, Terry straightened and sipped her wine. "That's not what we're here to discuss."

"Oh, we're here to discuss the ghosts all right," Mary Jo said as her fingers wrapped around the stem of a glass. "But after that, we'll talk about where your oars have been."

"All right already." Terry frowned in annoyance. "All of those notes brought you up to date on all of the incidents, except for last night. I went to the attic." She pointed toward the ceiling.

"You went up there alone after everything that's happened?" Stephanie shook her head, then reached for an éclair.

"I may be encountering some strange events here, but I know I'm safe. Let's go to the parlor and I'll tell you. There's a lot to show you, too." She picked up a tray and her glass. Mary Jo managed to grab the wine bottle and her glass with the fingers of one hand and a plate in the other. Stephanie balanced a plate on top of her notebook and led the trio single file.

Setting the binder on the coffee table, Stephanie noticed the candlestick still on the floor where Terry had dropped it. "What happened?" she asked, stooping to pick it up.

"Don't touch it! Leave it there for the moment." Terry

grabbed Stephanie's shirttail and pulled her back. "Take a seat and I'll explain everything."

Her friends sat, food and drink forgotten. Terry described the encounter in the attic up to the point when the spirit reacted to Kyle's arrival.

"The banshee turned almost humanlike and pushed him. It was like unseen hands supported him until he regained his footing. He banged his head on a rafter but is otherwise all right." Terry ended her story at that point. *The rest of the night is my business.* "I couldn't see behind Kyle, so I don't know whether Theresé saved him or what."

"It's amazing to think that Theresé comes to you as a living, breathing person now," Stephanie said.

"It is, but I think it's painful for her to cross from her limbo to the present," Terry said. "I haven't seen her for a while now. She disappeared just before she could tell me what happened to her when she returned to Portsmouth. I wish she could come back and finish the story. Maybe it is what keeps her from crossing to the other side."

Terry stepped in front of the candlestick, eyeing it warily. She crossed her arms in front of her. "It's been there since I dropped it. I don't know if I want to touch it again."

Stephanie moved to a similar pose, followed by Mary Jo, who slipped her hands into the back pockets of her jeans.

The three women studied the innocuous stand.

"Shouldn't we pick it up?" Stephanie asked. "It can't remain there forever."

Terry rubbed her fingers. "I don't want to."

"Me either," Mary Jo agreed.

"Should I? I'm the only one who hasn't touched these mysterious candlesticks."

Terry shook her head. "I don't know, Stephanie. It's an incredibly unpleasant feeling, that icy cold burn. And the visions are terrifying."

"Hold on a minute." Stephanie grabbed her binder and flipped through the pages.

"What are you looking for?" Mary Jo asked.

"That note that was with the silver you found it in the attic when you had your encounter. Aha, here it is." She removed a photocopied page and waved it.

"This note was written by Mary Jo's ancestress Louisa, cousin of my third great-grandmother Emily. She wrote to Frank Wyatt. Remember that he married Celestine, Emily and Louisa's cousin. Even though we can't trace Celestine's heritage yet, we're pretty sure she will be a descendant of Clothiste. Almost positive, in fact."

Terry peered over Stephanie's right shoulder and read the note out loud. "Great-Grandmother had a terrible episode last night. She says this silverware is haunted and frightens her. She wants it destroyed, but it is much too valuable to destroy. The candlesticks especially seem to frighten her. Can you please hide it all with your things until—?"

"Until what? Her death?" Mary Jo asked, leaning over Stephanie's left shoulder.

"That's what I thought," Stephanie said. "But who is the great-grandmother? This note is not dated. We know Marie Josephé died in eighteen forty-three, Nicole in eighteen fifty-nine. We don't know when Theresé died yet."

Stephanie walked a few steps to stand in front of the candlestick again. "I have a theory. I think the great-grandmother mentioned in the letter is Theresé. Mary Jo, when you had your incident with the candlestick, you did not have a flashback like Terry did, but the banshee materialized before you and the candlestick passed through it."

Mary Jo nodded and Stephanie continued. "Then, Terry, when you later touched the candlestick, you actually witnessed the event where Clothiste swung it and struck Abigail. Correct?"

This time Terry bobbed her head.

Stephanie circled the candlestick once. "Then I was the one who handled the candlesticks when we decorated the inn. Nothing happened to me then, and I touched both of them. So what I am thinking is that Marie Josephé and Theresé had knowledge of the incident but Nicole, being the youngest did not. So it will be safe for me to touch it."

"Well, that sounds logical," Terry agreed. She stepped to one side of Stephanie, Mary Jo the other. "But it causes an awful feeling, Steph, and I don't think you should chance it."

"I'm going to see." Stephanie rubbed her hands along her jeans, then flexed her fingers. She bent her knees, and with her hand inches from the silver piece, said, "Grab me if you see me getting sucked into a time warp or something."

She wiggled her fingers and took a deep breath.

Then she gripped the silver stem and lifted the candlestick from the floor.

She shrieked, her body convulsing. A low hissing sound filled the air as she gripped the candlestick in both hands, twisting from side to side.

Terry and Mary Jo grabbed her shoulders, shouting her name and shaking her.

Stephanie bowed forward, then straightened. She pulled away and set the candlestick on the mantle. She turned to her friends and burst into laughter, nearly doubling over with the effort.

"You should see your faces," she cried, a tear sliding down her cheek.

"What!" Mary Jo swatted Stephanie across the shoulder. "I cannot believe you just did that."

"I'm sorry, I couldn't resist." Stephanie gulped for air.

"Oh, you wicked, wicked girl." Terry gave her a little shove.

"I just told you my theory that Nicole being so young, she maybe never learned about the mystery." Stephanie wiped her eyes and sat down. "Do you think I would have touched it if I thought I would experience what you did?"

Terry gave Stephanie another light push. "Of course you would have. And that was not one bit funny. You scared the bejeebers out of me." Terry wore a peeved expression as she sat in one of the wing chairs.

"I'm sorry, really I am. It's not like me to do something like that."

"And that's the only reason we will forgive you. Let's

change the subject." Mary Jo turned her back on the candlestick and picked up the steampunk dress Terry had earmarked for her. "I love this idea of the 'industrial-Victorian' style. Does this have a crinoline?" she asked.

Terry tossed a small throw pillow in Mary Jo's direction. "I would have staked a paycheck that you would balk at a crinoline."

"Shows what you know." Mary Jo laughed as she rummaged through the stack of petticoats.

The friends forgot about the mysterious candleholder as they tried on the clothing Terry had retrieved from the attic. Each one tried each dress before agreeing Terry had selected the right style for the women's personalities.

"One last thing to finish tonight," Stephanie said. She grabbed the binder of ancestry notes. Terry and Mary Jo leaned backwards with exaggerated groans.

"Stop it," Stephanie commanded. "Now, Terry, in your notes, Theresé said something significant." She wagged a finger in the air to emphasize her thoughts. "This colonial woman Abigail, the stepmother-in-law to our Clothiste—she hated the nickname Abby. Does anyone see the irony that Hurricane Abby struck at just the time we were discovering secrets in this old house?"

Upstairs, a trail of gray mist swirled. The evil specter tried to form but could not fight the force generated by the three necklaces together for the first time in centuries.

"Hurricane names are selected well in advance," the ever-practical Mary Jo said, pouring wine in each of the glasses. "I think I read somewhere the list covers six years of storm names."

"That may be, but why did this particularly named hurricane occur this year? To bring me here?" Stephanie asked.

"I don't know," Mary Jo waved her hand. "To quote Gage, it might be that 'woo-woo shit.'"

"But I see Stephanie's point," Terry interrupted. "And it

makes sense. We are all three descendants of the same eighteenth century ancestors, Étienne and Clothiste, and for the first time in over two-hundred years these three jewels are together again."

In unison, the three touched their pendants.

The trail of haze slithered toward the stairs.

On the kitchen counter, the wadded tissue containing the ring curled open. The surface of the old ring took on a green glow where an emerald once rested.

Combined, the True Colors were too strong.

The fog dissipated.

Unaware of any disturbance upstairs, Terry continued the conversation. "We know each girl experienced something here that has prevented their spirits from finding peace. Are we close to solutions that will let their spirits finally rest?"

"And what about the evil spirit?" Stephanie added. "Something prevents her from peace."

"Maybe she has a guilty conscience and can't rest." Mary Jo popped a canapé in her mouth.

"Maybe when we get the final results of the old bones, they will all rest. By the way, have you ever been in the Cedar Grove cemetery near the Naval Hospital?"

"They call it the Naval Medical Center Portsmouth now," Mary Jo said. "It hasn't been the Portsmouth Naval Hospital for years."

Terry shrugged. "I know. Old habits from Dad's days there. Anyway, Kyle and I tramped through the cemetery. Did you know that in the Victorian period people actually considered it like a park? Families would picnic there and everything."

"Eww." Stephanie grimaced.

"I agree. I sat on a wrought iron bench while Kyle browsed. It left me a bit melancholy, wandering among headstones. Especially the ones for children. Some died so young. And so many deaths occurred in eighteen fifty-five. Thousands died during the yellow fever epidemic. You should check it out.

Maybe the Victorians had something."

"No thanks." Mary Jo and Stephanie said together.

Stephanie added, "I've already looked through there. When I first came to Portsmouth, I looked. Once was enough. Now let me tell you the progress I've made in the last few days. There were about fifty letters in that satchel, Terry, plus a few family documents and some loose pages with French writing, which may have come from Clothiste's journal. If you remember, I'd found several pages of notes she had written in that metal box. I specifically looked for any responses from Emily. Let me start with this one, from Celestine to Emily." She cleared her throat and began reading.

My sweet cousin Emily,

I write with hope that you are in good health. Here, all is as well as can be expected.

This letter comes with both good and bad news. Do not worry, we are all safe, so put any concerns aside for now.

First, I must share my exciting news. I am to have another child! The doctor has just confirmed my suspicions. It is not a good time to be with child. There is so much need for medical staff for the wounded soldiers that a woman in childbirth is cared for last, if at all. Indeed, Cousin Louisa has allowed her house next door to be used to care for some of the wounded, and for that reason I was able to seek the doctor's confirmation.

That leads to my second news. Union soldiers all but took over our house for several days. I know Frank's brothers support the Union cause whilst he remains neutral. These men are not good men like our husbands and their brother Arthur, or their cousin Edward. The ones who came here were horrid, horrible creatures, marking my beautiful floors with their careless boots, breaking things. We did have enough time to hide the valuables in a small cubbyhole in the attic of Arthur's house next door. This is where Frank had hidden the silverware that once frightened my great-grandmamma, God rest her soul. She has been gone several months now and I still miss the elegant old lady.

But enough talk of the sad times. Here is my final piece of news. When Frank shoved the silverware and valuables in the cubbyhole, he struck something. He looked around and found a small tin box, with a small child's doll. It must be from colonial days, but it is in rather good shape. There are pages from a diary, written in French. I am most keen to translate them, so at the first opportunity I shall test my French and decipher them. I cannot help but wonder who owned these things from so long ago.

Write soon, dearest cousin, and send me news. I so look forward to your move here someday.

Celestine

"You'll have to refresh my memory, Stephanie," Terry said when Stephanie finished reading. "All I remember is that you found some letters and the doll in the metal box during the hurricane, but none of the details."

"That's what I'm trying to tell you." Stephanie's voice rose with excitement. "Remember, what I found in the old metal box was my ancestor Emily's responses to Celestine. They only gave us one side of the correspondence. Celestine's other letters may give us many more clues. I still have to look through dozens more and add to the file. The family histories have a lot of gaps."

Stephanie turned the pages to another letter encased in plastic protective sheets. "That letter you just read from Celestine starts a period of correspondence that occurred during the Civil War. Bear with me and just read Emily's answer." She withdrew a photocopied version of the letter and handed it to Terry.

This time Terry read aloud, eyes darting from side to side as she skimmed down the lines.

Dearest Cousin Celestine,

I am so delighted to hear you are with child and that young Henry will have a baby brother or sister. I wish I could have been there to see your face when you confirmed this wonderful news, but my own confinement keeps me homebound. This baby is due in a few weeks, and I am so excited. I wonder what we each will have. Maybe our children will be able to play together someday. If I have a girl, I shall name her Madeline Nicole. If it is a son, well, of course he will be Thomas!

It is hard to believe you have lived in Virginia five years now! I know the climate is so much warmer and you love your life there, but I miss you every day.

It is calm here in New Hampshire, maybe even in all of New England, as the conflict does not touch us quite as severely as it does you who live in the south, and I listen for news every day, as there are many units from New Hampshire fighting for the Union.

I was saddened to hear Union soldiers occupied your house for a time and caused some damage. That must be horrible.

But how clever of you to hide your valuables while the soldiers were there! Have you been able to retrieve them yet? I am most intrigued by this secret compartment you have discovered, and the items you found already hidden.

It is hard to believe that a small doll and some French papers could have been placed there almost one hundred years ago, and no one had found them! I am anxious to hear more about them. Why were they in that space in the wall? Do you suppose a servant girl, one who may have had to sleep in that garret many years ago, hid them?

I pray your own precious property shall be recovered soon and placed back in your home.

Now this war has started, pitting man against man, brother against brother. We are fortunate it did not cause our men to take opposing sides, and Frank has been neutral, even with Thomas and Arthur in the Union Army. Indeed, this dreadful war threatens to take a terrible toll on both sides, and I fear for you and Frank and young Henry so close to it all. I hope the fact that you have family in the North never causes you grief.

I will try to send you news when the baby is born. Thomas and his parents all send you their best regards, and say they will write when they can.

Dearest cousin, please write soon and tell me how you are.

Much love,

Your cousin Emily

"Celestine started to answer Emily with this letter but something interrupted her." Stephanie handed another photocopied letter to Terry to read aloud.

My dear, dear Cousin Emily,

Your recent letter did so much to cheer me up. It is good to know all is calm there at home. How funny I still call New Hampshire "home," even after living in Virginia for five years. I do like it here, very much. But my fondest memories are of the fun we had growing up together. I so look forward to your visit when this bloody war is over. (Forgive my coarse language, dear cousin!)

Today I am not feeling well at all. The shipyard is burning and although a distance away, we can smell the horrible smoke even here on our street. I pray desperately that the fires do not burn their way to us. The Union soldiers have retreated to Fort Monroe, however I fear this is just the beginning.

But I must tell you of the excitement we have had, in spite of this awful war. I have had someone help to translate one of those French papers I found. I will tell you about it later in this letter, but it is from our great-great grandmother Clothiste. I am so ashamed I did not pay much attention when my great-grandmother Nicole and yours talked of their beautiful and courageous mother and the mysteries surrounding her. I remember they smelled of rosewater, and I hated that smell as a child. However, I have come to enjoy it as I have grown older.

I think back to when we were children and we sat near them, making faces and mimicking them. What horrible little monsters we were! I wonder if we will live to be two old biddies ourselves. I shall watch my grandchildren like a hawk to see if they are making fun of me.

But if I had paid attention, perhaps I would recall more about Clothiste and her daughters. Could it be true they were once spies for the American army? How intriguing!

I will finish this later. There is some commotion outside…"

Terry glanced up, then handed the copy to Stephanie and said, "Okay, I remember you telling us about finding the letters to Emily. This is interesting but what does it tell us?"

"Don't you see, Terry?" Stephanie tapped the book to emphasize her excitement. "Celestine's letters fill in blanks. And most exciting, this would have occurred about the time the Naval shipyard was burned. Our families witnessed historic events in Portsmouth during both the Revolutionary War and the Civil War, and we have stories written in their own hands as proof."

"I get all that. But how does it tie in with our mysteries?'

Stephanie rolled her eyes skyward. "I don't know all of the answers yet. But by compiling the significant information from the family correspondence, I've found lots of clues. For instance, I learned that my ancestress Emily's father had changed their family surname from the French 'Longchamps' to the anglicized 'Long' in order to get work on the railroad, while her cousin Celestine's family had retained the name. So right there we have solved one piece of the puzzle in my ancestry."

Terry nodded. "I wish I shared the same enthusiasm you, my mom, and Kyle have. I'll just leave all of this to you guys and you can give me the condensed versions when you figure it out. And I've had my limit of ghosts and dead people for this day."

"Me too." Mary Jo yawned. "I'm going home and try these clothes again. Then I'm going to jump the fine bones belonging to Chase Hallmark."

"And I hear my firefighter calling me." Stephanie sighed, a slight smile curving her lips.

Terry looked at her two friends, full of love. A light tug of envy pulled at her. She fought to keep a petulant note from creeping into her voice as she said, "Well, go on home and have hot sex. See if I care. I'll just stay here like Cinderella and clean the place up."

"Wish I could feel guilty but I don't." Stephanie hugged her, gathered the bag in which she had placed her costume, and bolted toward the back door.

Mary Jo also hugged Terry and said, "If you sleep alone, it's your own fault." She followed Stephanie's path.

Terry cleared the tables and loaded the dishes in the dishwasher. She placed food in the refrigerator and noticed the bag of chocolate chip cookies that Theresé had enjoyed so much.

"Theresé? Are you there? Can you come back?"

Silence.

She sighed. Tires crunched on the pavement outside and headlights shined through the window over the sink, she peeked out. Kyle's vehicle occupied its parking space. The headlights went out.

She tossed a dishtowel to the side.

To hell with the clean-up. I'm not sleeping alone tonight.

***

Terry curled beside Kyle, nestling her head between his arm and chest. He propped one arm under his head and used his other to draw her closer. He traced lazy circles on her upper arm.

"I have to admit something," she said.

"Hmmm? Tell me."

"I tried a lot of subtle ways to get your attention when we first met."

"Oh, yeah? Like how?"

"Oh, I don't know exactly. Standing close to you, brushing against your arm. One time I practically thrust my boobs in your face in the cafe."

"I remember."

Terry threw a leg over Kyle's thighs and settled on her hip beside him, bracing her chin in her hands as she rested on his chest. She stared into his eyes. "What do you mean, you remember? I didn't think you even noticed. In fact, I almost wondered if you were gay."

Kyle burst into laughter and hauled Terry on top of him until she lay splayed across his torso. He shifted his hips purposefully.

"And happily for me, you most certainly are not." She smiled as his arousal pressed against her thigh.

He toyed with a lock of her hair, his eyes closed. "I definitely noticed you that day," he said. "But you were surrounded by every other guy in the place. They were like a pack of hounds."

"No, they weren't. They were just a bunch of colleagues celebrating together."

"Yeah, right." Kyle kissed her forehead.

"Be that as it may, I couldn't seem to catch your eye. I figured I was going to have to bash you over the head to get your attention. I even began to consider the trench coat and high heels thing."

Kyle raised his head from the pillow and looked her in the eye, one eyebrow lifted in a sexy arch. "Really now?"

"Yes, really now."

"I'm kinda sorry I didn't wait a little longer to get your attention," he said.

"And miss all this great sex we've had?"

"There is that." Kyle slid his hands along her sides and across her butt. "Do you think you could try that trench coat and heels thing for me someday?"

Terry pondered for a moment and said, "Not a chance now. You'd know what I was up to if I showed up in a tan canvas overcoat." She moved her shoulders seductively as she pressed against his body and kissed his neck. "And I can't have that."

"Aw, rats," Kyle said. "Can't I earn some extra credit points or something?" His mouth found her breast.

Terry trailed her tongue upwards until the tip found his earlobe. He shivered and tightened his hold.

"Don't worry," she whispered and nipped his skin. She slid across his body. "I've thought of something you can do to earn a lot of points."

CHAPTER 20

Kyle arrived at the Driver Days Festival later than planned, missing the kick off of the hometown parade. Events were in full swing when he headed to Joan's craft booth. He noticed Terry standing out of her mother's line of vision. Joan was engaged in animated conversation with a customer, but Terry fixed an intent gaze on her mother. In the unguarded moment, concern etched her face.

While the daughter assessed her mother, Kyle took in the sight of the beautiful lawyer dressed in a long coral sweater over tight jeans tucked in brown leather boots. She ambled to the front of the booth and leaned her elbows on the table, swaying her hips from side to side as she waited to greet her mother. Terry was the complete package, something he had never had before. An unexpected hitch in his chest startled him.

He was totally in love with the woman. Had been since he first laid eyes on her.

He let his gaze run up mile long legs until they settled on her shapely butt, imagining her in a trench coat and stilettos for his benefit. *Gotta work on my brownie points.*

Joan stretched across the table to brush a kiss on her daughter's cheek, catching Kyle's eye. She waved him over.

A warm flush wrapped around his neck and he wondered if he had unconsciously conveyed his lascivious thoughts. He sauntered toward the booth in his most confident gait, ready to shout out apologies for ogling the daughter if the mother called him out.

Terry turned and glanced over her shoulder. Her hair cascaded in waves along her arms and she curved her lips into a flirtatious smile as she walked toward him.

He gulped, losing his poise. He stubbed his toe on probably the most miniscule rock in his path, shuffling his feet to regain his footing.

He gave a half smile and stood in front of Terry. *So much for suave and debonair, Professor Klutz.*

However, Terry's welcoming kiss sent his confidence soaring—straight to his crotch. As his lips met hers, he opened one eye and stared straight into Joan's interested gaze.

Oh, God, does she know her daughter and I are doing it? As Terry pressed closer to him, he tried to back away, desperately hoping the stacks of wreaths on the table hid any signs of his increased confidence.

Or worse—does Charles suspect? His confidence wavered.

"You missed the parade," an oblivious Terry said when she at last peeled away from him.

"Sorry. I got into some records and lost all track of time. Hello, Joan." Kyle met her gaze, the flush creeping under his collar. If Joan had any inkling of the extent of his relationship with her daughter, she didn't show it.

"Hello, Kyle. I hope you are going to buy lots of goodies from my booth today."

Guilt caused Kyle to read more into her message. He cleared his throat and glanced around at the floral displays, with no clue what to select. "Um, that hanging thing with the Thanksgiving corn on it looks nice for my aunt. That Halloween centerpiece would be good to send to my mom. And I'll take that Christmas wreath there. Oh, two of those stockings striped like a candy cane would be good for my cousin's new twins." He withdrew his wallet, prepared to spend every cent he had.

She knows.

"Excellent choices. I'll bag them and keep them here so you can walk around the festival. You can get them later."

Kyle handed her several bills. "By the way, Joan, you'll be

pleased to know why I was late. I finally found some news on Celestine Wyatt."

"Really? Tell me, tell me." Joan leaned on her elbows in anticipation. "It always seemed to me that her paper trail ended rather abruptly."

Kyle nodded. "I know why now. She became a widow in eighteen-ninety. Because we've been searching under her maiden name of Longchamps or her married name of Wyatt, I never could find death records for Celestine Wyatt. First thing…Stephanie found enough references in that satchel full of old letters to ascertain that at the time Celestine buried her husband Frank, she also had two other graves moved that were at one time buried on the grounds of Clothiste's Inn."

"How intriguing," Joan said. "I wonder who might have been buried there."

Kyle shrugged. "Stephanie didn't find any references to them yet. But a most interesting clue came to light. It turns out, a few years after Frank Wyatt's death, Celestine married a man named Ellis Harper. Searching for the name Celestine Harper, I found several references in old Norfolk County records, including some property transactions in the years after Frank died. Her own death record reveals she died in nineteen-thirty-seven, and she's buried in the Catholic cemetery. Now that I know her second husband's name, I can follow up on more records next week. Maybe I can find out whose graves were moved to the cemetery."

"So, does this link my family to Etienne and Clothiste?"

"I'd say without a doubt you are descended from them."

"That's so exciting!" Joan stretched across the table and threw her arms around Kyle's neck. "Are you and Terry coming to the Brunswick Stew Fest tonight? I'll be late but Charles will be there, stirring the pot."

"Is that the Knights of Columbus thing?" Terry interjected.

"Yep."

"Sorry. I forgot all about it, but Kyle and I made other plans."

Customers gathered around the booth and Kyle stepped

back, relieved he would not have to face The Parents that evening. Joan had already turned her attention to a customer looking at autumn decorations.

"I love this orange and blue theme," the customer said, fingering a door wreath. "They were my school colors."

"You must be a Wilson grad," Joan said with a laugh. "I've made a slew of these for my reunion."

"Yep. P-town born and raised. Got my fortieth reunion next month. Hard to believe."

"My fortieth is coming up too." Joan's eyes grew wide as she scooted around the table. "Judy? Judy Parker, is that you?"

The customer's eyes grew wide with recognition. "Joan Wyatt! How long has it been?" The two women squealed in delight and hugged each other.

"I'm Dunbar now," Joan said.

"I'm Judy King now. I haven't gone to the earlier reunions, living out of town. I'm excited to be here this year." The women hugged again, and began chattering with excitement.

"Well, Mom's lost to us now," Terry said with a laugh. She tucked her arm through Kyle's and pointed toward the row of food trucks. "Are you hungry?"

But she lingered at the booth for a minute longer, watching. Worry lines etched her forehead.

Kyle patted her hand. "Don't worry too much. She's taking good care of herself. We talk about it sometimes when I'm doing the family research."

He plucked a small blue flower from Terry's sleeve and held it up. It was the blue of Joan's school colors. "This attached itself to your sleeve when you leaned on the counter." He tucked it behind her hair. "It seems like she has really enjoyed the preparation for her reunion. She's kept me up-to-date on the events they have planned and it sounds like a lot of fun. You know, I've never gone to any of my reunions, either high school or college."

"Really? Why not?"

Kyle shrugged. "Never felt inclined. I was the classic nerd in school. Not shunned or bullied, just invisible. Which suited me fine at the time."

"Well, I went to my tenth-year reunion. There are plans for a fifteenth next year."

"My college reunion is coming up in November. Who knows, maybe I'll go if you'll come with me. What an entrance I could make with you on my arm." His brow furrowed as he guided Terry toward the sandwich truck.

"What's the matter?" Terry stopped and glanced into his eyes.

"How much does your mom know about—what's going on between us?"

Terry shrugged. "I don't know. I suspect she has some idea since I am spending a lot more nights in Olde Towne. Why?"

"Just wondering. Does your dad own a shotgun?"

Startled, Terry stared for a moment. Then they both burst into laughter.

"Don't be silly." Terry smiled and bumped his shoulder. Kyle draped his arm around hers. They strolled around the main intersection of the small community known as Driver, blocked off from traffic for the festival. During the weekend-long event, visitors could enjoy a county fair atmosphere reminiscent of a bygone era. Despite the industrial and urban invasion mere miles away, the sleepy little crossroads remained suspended in time. Worn buildings mixed with newer shops; a feed and seed shop bore the last few traces of the former farming needs of the community.

The scent of popcorn mixed with the sweet smell of cotton candy and sautéing onions and peppers. The lazy autumn breeze rippled banners proclaiming curly fries, roasted corn on the cob, burgers, hot dogs and sausages with all the fixings. A band on an outdoor stage belted out a bluegrass number. Nearby, a giant inflated replica of Mr. Peanut stood sentry over the grounds. The famous icon represented the Planter's Peanut Company, whose founder had settled in Suffolk.

Kyle stopped at a booth loaded with candy apples and sniffed appreciatively. "I haven't had a candy apple since I was a kid. I loved that hard, crunchy cinnamon covering."

"I favored the caramel apples myself, with peanuts on top," Terry said, peering at the case holding the treats. "I haven't had one in ages either. What say we indulge our inner children? My treat."

"And afterward, cotton candy too? We can't have one without the other."

Terry laughed. "You sound just like Tanner. Or Gage." She ordered one of each of the candied apple flavors, handing the red one to Kyle. They continued to walk around the displays, stopping to admire craftwork or check items for sale. Terry offered her caramel apple and Kyle leaned forward to take a bite. He then extended his red candied apple to her. She had to hold his wrist steady in order to bite through the hard coating. Small shards of the crystallized glaze broke and landed on her chin.

Kyle brushed them away and leaned in for a kiss.

Terry obliged, and brushed her tongue across his, sharing the cinnamon flavor.

"Get a room!" Gage called out as he and Stephanie strolled up.

Stephanie bumped her elbow against his. "Be nice."

Terry rolled her eyes in an exaggerated movement. "Stephanie, your beloved baboon has been acting like that since we were kids." Brother and sister pushed each other playfully.

Stephanie crossed her hands in front of each other to signal a stop. "Well, I want total peace and harmony between my maid of honor and my groom."

"So you've set the date?"

"Yes, the Saturday between Christmas and New Year."

The women hugged at the news and the men shook hands.

Stephanie continued. "We're going now to an appointment with the priest. We're just planning for a small ceremony, and then we'll have the reception at your parents. Your mom says it's perfect timing, in spite of being only two months away."

"She'll be in her glory. It's the first Christmas since the house was restored, and she's been dying to decorate for the holidays. To get to have a wedding reception there will be the icing on the wedding cake. She'll love it."

"I've got it made. She wants to handle the decorations, and Mary Jo wants to cater. All I have to do is show up in my bridal gown—if I can find one I like."

"Shopping trip on the horizon," Terry said with a twirl of her hand.

The two couples chatted briefly and then said their goodbyes. Gage draped his arm around Stephanie's shoulder and they disappeared in the crowd.

"They are such a perfect match." Terry sighed as her gaze followed the couple. "I'm really happy for them. Even if I question Stephanie's taste in men."

Kyle threw back his head and laughed. "I wish I'd had a sister to spar with growing up. Must have been fun between you and Gage."

"Well it wasn't always fun, but I do have the best brothers a sister could want."

They strolled around the grounds toward the general store. A miniature train puttered across the parking lot and circled to a stop on one side of the building. Consisting of a bright blue engine, two yellow boxcars, and a red caboose, the tiny vehicle snaked its way through the festival grounds while tots and toddlers waved at passersby.

"Aunt Terry! Mr. Kyle!" Tanner's high-pitched voice called out.

Terry laughed as the little boy scrambled from the caboose and ran toward her, arms outstretched. Beth scurried close behind, her eyes on her son in the throngs of people.

"How are you, little man?" Terry cooed as the little boy planted kisses on her cheek. She kissed his cheek in return, suppressing a laugh as Tanner wiped the cheek she'd just kissed.

"I'm fine. Hi, Mr. Kyle. We're gonna go see Daddy's fire truck. Wanna come wif us?" Bouncing with energy, Tanner tugged on Kyle's hand.

"Well, sure, why not?" Kyle obliged and let Tanner lead the

way.

"You hold Mr. Kyle's hand tight, young man," Beth cautioned. She and Terry greeted each other with a hug, then strolled toward the area where a fire truck and rescue squad were stationed for emergencies.

"I think your baby bump is finally showing," Terry remarked.

"It is." Beth rubbed her rounded tummy. "And the morning sickness has finally subsided. I've extended my belt as far as it can go, so I'll be in stretch pants soon. I told Mary Jo I was thinking of coming to the Halloween party at the inn dressed as a pumpkin, but she says I have to dress in an historical era ensemble. Maybe I could go as the Hindenburg?"

The two sisters-in-law burst into laughter. Then Beth leaned closer to Terry and whispered, "Tanner's taken a shine to Kyle. He asked me if Kyle was going to become his new uncle. Is he?"

"I don't know about that, but we're good. Slow but steady." Terry lowered her voice and continued. "I think I've fallen for him, Beth, and it scares the hell out of me." She glanced toward Kyle, talking with Connor as Tanner held both men's hands. Her heart did a little flutter as she wondered what it would be like to see her child holding his hand. "I just don't know if I'm ready to say it—or if he's ready to hear it."

"Just relax and take it as it comes." Beth squeezed Terry's hand. "You'll be fine."

"Time will tell." Terry sighed. "And why were we whispering? No one could hear us."

They giggled again. Beth said, "We sound like Wilma and Betty in the Flintstones." Arm in arm, they joined the men by the fire truck.

Before she could draw Kyle's attention away, the roar of motorcycles thundered in the distance, signaling the arrival of the participants in the motorcycle run. Tanner jumped up and down in excitement, until finally Connor scooped the boy up and propped him on his shoulders. The little boy waved a small American flag as each motorcycle zipped past, occasionally rewarded by an extra rumble as the rider turned up the throttle in salute and the crowd cheered.

When the welcome silence followed as the last biker rode out of earshot, she was ready to leave, but Kyle pulled her in the direction of the antique car show. Dozens of restored and vintage autos lined a cordoned area, hoods gaping open like beasts awaiting a meal as spectators strode from one to another.

Once again, Kyle proved himself to be more than a nerdy history professor. As knowledgeable about old cars as he was history and ancestry, he held his own in conversing with owners over the merits of a 1955 Chevy versus a 1968½ Cobra Jet Mustang.

"A one half?" Terry asked.

"It got the one-half designation because it came out in April of nineteen sixty-eight," Kyle explained. "Did you know that the first Mustang was introduced at the World's Fair in New York in sixty-four?"

"Really? I did not know that. I always thought I would own a vintage Mustang one day, but my Maserati was a once in a lifetime deal and it won me over."

"Well, that is for sure one sweet ride. Still—I wouldn't mind one of these babies in my driveway." Kyle poked his head under the hood of another car, and Terry stepped back. She took the opportunity to study his jean-clad buns. When he raised his head and whacked it on the hood, she shook her head and smiled. When he stepped to the other side and thumped his knee on the fender, she could not help but laugh out loud.

Kyle gave a helpless shrug as he laughed with her.

To other people's eyes, the nerdy professor may seem to be a perfect klutz. I know the man's choreographic abilities in bed.

The thought brought a blush to her cheeks. But she felt so much more than a sexual attraction to Kyle. She pressed a hand below her fluttering heart.

Have I really fallen in love with him?

Her cell chirped, indicating an incoming text message. She

slipped it from her pocket and out of habit glanced at the screen before opening. Instead of a phone number, the words "out of area" displayed on the face.

She clicked on the text icon and read the message: *You bitch.*

The sensation of eyes boring into her back overtook her, chasing her tender thoughts of Kyle from her mind. The hairs danced on the back of her neck, sending a cold shiver coursing through her. Whirling around, she scanned the throng of people crossing in front of her. Her gaze landed on a stocky figure disappearing into the crowd. She didn't recognize the man, but he moved in a furtive manner.

She took a step forward to follow him. Two shrill blasts stopped her short, as a golf cart loaded with ice wound its way through the pedestrians, clearing a path.

Her phone chirped again. The new message flashed on the screen: *You'll get yours.*

The golf cart passed. She pushed her way through the throng, looking for anyone with a cell phone in their hand.

Only every other person in her vicinity seemed to be talking on cell phones or tapping keypads.

She could not find the man she had seen earlier.

She shoved her phone in her pocket and walked back toward the auto display looking for Kyle, dismissing the messages as a prank.

But she could not shake a sense of foreboding.

***

Terry's cell rattled against the wooden nightstand. She poked her hand under the covers and grabbed the phone. The second shrill ring disturbed Kyle and he turned to encase her in his arms.

"Speaking," she mumbled in reply to the voice asking for Ms. Dunbar. She rested her head on the pillow, eyes closing.

"Are you serious?" Terry practically shouted into the receiver and sat bolt upright. She drew her knees to her chest and tucked the sheet around her. Kyle sat up beside her, pulling the sheet to the side and kissing her bare shoulder. She held a finger up.

"You're kidding me, right?...That is fantastic news, Mrs. Belford! Thank you for calling me...I'm really happy for you...Good-bye now."

Terry hung up the phone and rolled over, straddling Kyle. She rained excited kisses along his face.

"Whoa! Who was that on the phone and can she call you every morning?"

Terry laughed. Her lips trailed his jaw. "That was Mrs. Belford. Do you remember me talking about her? She was the widow that Shady O'Grady swindled."

"I remember you talking about the case."

"Well, her car was illegally repossessed and she had no other transportation. She's had to depend on neighbors and friends to take her and her grandson places. She bought a raffle ticket at her church and guess what?" Before Kyle could answer, she planted a kiss on his mouth. Then she pulled back and continued, "She won the grand prize! A Ford Fiesta. It'll be perfect for her and she'll be able to get it by the middle of the week. Her case was so frustrating but there wasn't much we could do. I've filed the papers but it could take months to get to trial. Even if we win our civil case, there isn't any guarantee she would get the car back. He could have sold it or..."

Kyle touched his finger to her lips and she blinked.

"Do you ever slow down?" Kyle asked. He twirled a lock of her hair around his fingers.

"Slow down?"

"You go non-stop. Like a whirlwind." He traced circles across her forehead. "And this mind is always in motion."

"Can't help it. It's in my nature." She wiggled suggestively. "But if you really feel like I should slow down—or stop, then..." She rolled over and flopped on her back, limp hands at her side. Eyes closed, she broke into exaggerated snores.

Kyle flipped on top of her. "Time's up, woman. You've

had enough rest."

Terry growled one more snore before Kyle silenced her with his lips.

And the whirlwind awakened.

***

Terry shook out her mane of hair and hung up the blow dryer. The pleasant smell of frying bacon reached her nose and she inhaled in appreciation. She still marveled at the good news Mrs. Belford's call had brought…not to mention the lingering glow making love with Kyle gave her.

All in all, it was a smashing start to a Sunday morning.

After dressing and then straightening the bathroom, she strolled down the hall. Kyle held his cell phone between his chin and shoulder as he transferred bacon from the frying pan to a plate covered with a paper towel. "She just came in, Eric. I'll pass on the information. Thanks so much for all you've done…Yeah, man. Catch you soon."

He hung up and set the phone to the side. He glanced at Terry. "Eric has the DNA results. They don't match."

"What do you mean?" Terry sank to a chair.

"The woman's DNA is not a match to your family," Kyle repeated. He turned off the frying pan. "He's one hundred percent certain the bones do not belong to Clothiste or anyone in your family. There are different types of genealogical tests that can be conducted. For instance, there are ways to test for the Y chromosome which is passed on from father to son, usually along with the surname. You have an excellent pattern in your family. Your grandfather Peter is at least the fifth male Wyatt descendant in a row." Kyle opened a bottle of water and set it in front of Terry.

"Okay, I'm following you so far but don't get too technical."

"Another way to test is called mitochondrial DNA, passed from mothers to both genders of her children. Males carry it

227

but it is only passed on by female offspring. Neither your mom nor you match the DNA from the bones. You are not related to the person buried under the tree."

"You mean they belong to a stranger?" Terry asked.

"Right. It boils down to this. Eric is convinced that the person who was buried in that old grave is not related to your family. Maybe it was a second spouse or an in-law who died and was buried on the property, but she was not a blood relation of your ancestors."

"I thought for sure we would learn we were related. I had hoped we could prove they were Clothiste's and perhaps end Theresé's limbo here on earth. What do I do now? I keep hoping Theresé would appear one more time. Maybe she could remember more of her story and I could help her find her mother."

She looked at Kyle with a sad smile. "I must sound like a lunatic to you, talking about ghosts and limbo."

Kyle laughed. "Hearing most of your family discuss these sightings so nonchalantly, I've learned to listen without judgment. Up until a few days ago, my pragmatic and methodical nature kept me focused. But after we had that incident in the attic, I'm more inclined to accept that something can keep souls from passing to the other side. Whether it is something I ever write about in my future book remains to be seen."

"Well, should you decide to include it, you'll have a wealth of material." She paused and pressed her fingertips to her temples. "What a morning! Is it okay with you if I try to get my family together this evening? There is so much to discuss and I'd rather tell everyone at once."

"Of course." Kyle squeezed her hand reassuringly. He had never seen a family sort through an issue with the orderly sharing of information, family discussion, and offering of suggestions the way the Dunbar clan did at a summit.

CHAPTER 21

On Friday morning, the interment took place in a single plot Terry had purchased. Dark storm clouds loomed overhead, casting the cemetery in gray bleakness. Even the flowers at various headstones seemed drained of color in the gloom.

The small party walked through the dried leaves to the graveside where the priest waited. The funeral attendants had already lowered the simple coffin into the vault and waited a discreet distance away. A single flower spray stood to one side of the opening. Gage had arranged for a chaplain from the fire department to conduct an interment prayer but could not attend the service due to work.

The chaplain nodded as Terry, her parents, Hannah, Mary Jo, and Stephanie clumped together. Kyle and Chase remained a few paces in the background.

After reading a few passages from a Bible, the chaplain stepped closer to the grave and raised his palms skyward.

"Lord, we know not whose mortal remains are committed to this grave, but we pray the soul has found its way to Your heavenly home. May You grant this unknown woman mercy, and may she rest in peace. In Your name, we pray. Amen."

A current of air rolled through, stirring leaves and pulling several flowers from the wreath. Terry shifted her scarf to block the wind. The chaplain greeted each family member, who expressed thanks.

"It's too cold to delay you, Chaplain," Terry said. "But you are welcome to come back to our café for something to eat."

He shook his head. "Thanks, but I do have another funeral to attend."

Chase and Kyle both declined and said their goodbyes. Her parents excused themselves as well. Joan had a routine doctor's appointment. She kissed her daughter's cheek. "Thank you for doing this, honey. I don't know if we'll ever learn that woman's identity, but maybe her soul will rest in peace."

"You would have done it too, Mom," Terry said. She hugged her father. "I love you guys."

As her parents walked toward their vehicle, she glanced back toward the gravesite. The workers had already begun to shovel dirt into the opening.

She linked arms with her friends as they walked to Mary Jo's car in silence.

A sliver of sunlight beamed through the clouds. Mary Jo checked for traffic and drove onto the main road, saying, "I saw the weather report. It's supposed to warm up during the day, and they predict a clear evening for the events tonight."

"After this, it seems kind of morbid to go on the Olde Towne Ghost Walk tonight."

"You've been looking forward to it ever since you came to Portsmouth," Terry said. "Look at it this way. It fits right in with the history and mystery of the district and will be all the more impressive for you and Kyle."

"We'll see." Stephanie's voice held a touch of uncertainty.

Mary Jo pulled into the parking lot and stopped. "I'll drop you two off," she said. "I need to make a store run."

Terry and Stephanie scrambled from the vehicle and with a wave went their separate ways.

∗∗∗

"I haven't been on that in more than ten years." Terry laughed when they'd completed the tour. She walked with Kyle and Stephanie. Leaves crunched under their feet as they crossed the green of the park where warm cider was being served to patrons of the tour. A costumed musician strolled the perimeter while playing bagpipes, the mournful notes adding to the haunting atmosphere.

Terry handed cups of warm cider to Stephanie and Kyle before taking one for herself. The musician had exchanged her bagpipes for a dulcimer set up on a stand, and the gentle pings of the chords lightened the mood a little as Terry blew on her drink. She inhaled the scent and sighed. "Oh, this taste brings back memories. When I was a kid, I never paid attention to the historical aspects of this tour. I was always bracing for one of the three stooges to pull a prank. Gage was always ready to sneak behind a bush and let out a howl or creepy laugh."

"If he had pulled that tonight, I swear I'd divorce him before we're married."

Terry giggled and bumped Stephanie's shoulder. "He adores you. He'd never pull such a prank on you."

"Well, just the same, I'm going to look around before I sit at the table tonight."

The trio laughed. Kyle took the arms of both women and led then across street, passing by another group just ending the tour. Terry said, "So you're the historian, Kyle. What was your favorite part of the tour?"

He said, "Well, I have to say I liked the costumed reenactments throughout the walk. Some of the actors really got into character, like that woman looking for her missing husband. But I think I liked the Union soldiers at the Pass House because they really played to the crowd. The little girl in our group was cute when he asked her if she had a pass and she handed him a gum wrapper."

"That reminds me," Stephanie said. "Just this morning I came across some of the letters from our Civil War era cousins, and they talk about the Pass House." She tossed her empty cup into a container. "One of the women, I don't know which off the top of my head, was quite vocal about an encounter she had with the Union soldiers who commandeered that residence and turned it into a pass house. They required residents to swear allegiance to the Union and to obtain passes before they could travel to Suffolk or Norfolk. She had some choice words about the matter."

"That would be interesting to read. How about you, Stephanie? What did you like about the tour?"

"I like the start at Trinity Church. It was the first cemetery I visited when I came to Portsmouth to search my ancestry. I think it sets the mood for the group to pass under the arches of the church walkway out to the cemetery, where the colonial character talked about the mysterious death of...what was the guy's name?"

"John Braidfoot," Kyle supplied.

"See what a history professor he is, Stephanie?" Terry asked. "Kyle hasn't been here very long yet he can name people buried more than two hundred years ago."

"Well, you have to admit that the story held our interest about how the ghost told Braidfoot he would die in a year and he did." Stephanie laughed. "Wasn't it funny when the guide asked the young girl in our group to read the headstone, and the date was one year after the ghost' delivered her message. She must have jumped three feet when he told her she was standing on John's grave."

The small group laughed and strolled toward the Bier House restaurant where they were to meet Mary Jo, Gage, and Chase. Stephanie continued, "I got cold chills when they talked about the house where they found a skeleton in the yard during renovation. That hit too close to home. When the actor told us about the young couple uncovering bones I thought he was going to mention the inn."

"I did too. I'm so sorry about that." Terry said. "I forgot about that story or I would never have suggested we stay on the tour."

"I'm okay, really." Her breath formed vapors in the chilling temperature. "I wonder why that guy wanted to keep the bones he found? I was so glad when we buried ours this morning. Do you suppose we will ever know for sure who they belonged to?"

Terry sighed. "I don't think so. The DNA tests says we do

not match. But I think we would have sensed they belonged to—family ghosts. Does that make any sense?"

Stephanie burst into laughter. "We're talking about ghosts and you ask me if what you said makes sense?"

They looked at each other. Snickers escaped before turning into full-blown laughter.

"Oh, Jiminy Cricket, let's get out of here." Stephanie wiped tears from her eyes as she and Terry regained their composure and they turned onto High Street. Music and laughter drifted from the Bier Haus outdoor dining area. Gage leaned against a blue signpost proclaiming Frankfurt was 6650 kilometers away.

"You ghouls ready to start goblin?" he quipped as he held a hand toward Stephanie.

Stephanie kissed him and answered, "I'm starved. Look, here come Chase and Mary Jo."

After the three couples exchanged greetings, they entered the wrought iron gates. The hostess guided them to a table, where she distributed menus in English and German.

"Before we start, I've got one thing to say," Stephanie said. All eyes turned in her direction, and she continued, "For the next two hours, let's have no talk of ghosts, bones, or things that go bump in the night. Agreed?"

***

Later, after saying goodbye to the other couples, Terry and Kyle walked the short distance to the apartment hand-in-hand.

"That was good," she declared. "And we managed to get through the night without mentioning any of Stephanie's taboo topics."

"It was. Do you know everyone in Portsmouth?"

She laughed. "Why do you ask that?"

"I don't think we have been anywhere yet that we don't run into someone you know."

"Oh, that's just because we are downtown. I see a lot of the same people time after time." Terry glanced at her watch as they stopped to allow a group from the Ghost Walk to pass. She said, "That must be one of the last tours." They continued their stroll.

"It was well-done," Kyle said. "I've walked similar tours in London and DC. And Mary King's Close in Edinburgh. Interestingly enough, that historic part of the city is called 'Old Town' without the 'e' at the end."

"Really? And how does our tour compare to theirs?"

"Well, they're all different, of course. London's is based on Jack the Ripper, obviously, so there's that element of the macabre added to the Victorian setting. And the Edinburgh one gives a sense of the seventeenth century lifestyles, including the crowded and sometimes bleak conditions compounded by the plague. It was an informative but melancholy tour." They were in front of Clothiste's Inn and Kyle nudged Terry to walk past the picket fence to the porch. The motion detector turned on an amber porch light, bathing the area in soft light. He sat on the top step and drew Terry beside him.

"But there are reasons I like the Olde Towne Ghost Walk the very best."

Terry gave his knee a flirty little bump. "And those reasons are?"

Kyle smiled. "There's really only one," he said. He kissed her. Then he reached into his pocket and withdrew a blue velvet case, tinted to a jade green because of the tawny light. He flipped open the lid to reveal a sapphire in a solitaire setting.

Terry's breath caught in her throat. Kyle said, "I've been carrying this with me for a week, waiting for the right time and place. I don't want to wait any longer. I know it's not the traditional diamond, but you're not the traditional woman. I wanted a sapphire to match your necklace." He removed the ring from the slot and took Terry's left hand in his.

"I love you, Terry Dunbar, and want to marry you. Will you be my wife?" He held the gold band between his thumb and forefinger and slid it just past Terry's fingernail. He paused and looked into Terry's eyes, waiting.

Terry felt her jaw drop as she pulled her gaze from his and glanced at their hands. Tears stung her eyes and she swallowed a lump before she gave a quiet but firm, "Yes." Kyle moved the ring past her knuckles, brushed his fingers over it to ensure it was in place, then kissed the finger bearing the ring.

"I love you, Kyle!" She threw her arms around his neck. "And yes, I will marry you."

The sensor timed out and the porch light went dark as the young couple locked in a steamy embrace.

"Let's go home," she whispered.

Kyle's phone rang and he answered, "Hey, Dad, what's up?"

Although the voice was muffled, Terry could sense the speaker's agitation.

"What?" Kyle jumped to his feet, triggering the motion sensor. Terry stood beside him and touched his arm. "How is she?" Kyle listened, frown lines on his face. "Leaves at five forty-five? And gets in when? No, it's no problem, book it and I'll catch it. How's Mom holding up? Okay, good. I'll see you in the morning...Same to you, Dad. Tell Mom I love her too." He shoved the phone back in his pocket while his other hand raked through his hair.

"What is it, Kyle? What happened?"

"My grandmother's been sick and my parents were visiting her in Holyoke. She fell tonight trying to get out of bed and broke her hip. They're taking her to surgery, but the doctors are concerned because of her age and weakened condition. Mom's brother works for the airline and said there's one seat left on the five-forty a.m. flight to Boston. I have to go up there, be with them."

"Of course you do. I wish I could go with you." Terry took his hand and they ran up the stairs to the apartment.

"I'm sorry this spoiled my proposal."

She touched her fingertips to his lips. "Don't say that. I know all too well the shock you feel. Mom's emergency is still too fresh in my mind to shake. We'll do whatever it takes to get through this." She took the keys from his trembling hand and opened the door. "You need to pack a bag and try to get some rest. I can drive you to the airport. We'll need to leave by three-fifteen to make your flight."

Inside, she wrapped her arms around his neck and touched her forehead to his. "Do you mind if I don't tell anyone about our engagement until you come back. I'd like us to tell the family together."

Kyle nodded. He knelt before his suitcase still sitting by the door and rummaged for clothes.

Terry locked the door on the dark cold night.

CHAPTER 22

Terry's week, busy as it was, seemed to drag by. She missed Kyle but was relieved to hear that his grandmother had survived the surgery for the broken hip and improved daily.

Although they spoke and texted several times a day, a realization struck her like a bolt of lightning. He'd become such an integral part of her life. She wanted to be with him every moment she could. A dozen times a day her gaze dropped to the unusual engagement ring. She had trouble focusing on court and missed the first time her client's name was called.

After the case ended, she scurried from the court house and jumped into her car. Dark gray clouds hung low in the sky. The temperature had dropped considerably. She didn't wait for the heater to warm up, but drove straight to the law office parking lot.

The bone-chilling air tore through her again as she got out of the car. After she grabbed her purse and briefcase, her leather-gloved hands fumbled to get the key into the lock.

She burst through the law office door, welcoming warmth greeting her. Not even stopping to shrug out of her coat, she raced to the door of Sandi's office.

"Sandi!" she called. "I just ran into Detective Sergeant Lewis. Guess what? Grand Jury returned a True Bill today. The Shady has been indicted on the criminal charges."

"Wow, that was fast!" Sandi jumped up with such momentum that her chair rolled into the wall.

"Will he be arrested today?" Becky asked as she joined

Terry at the door.

Terry added, "Probably. Or he'll turn himself in. But he'll make bail. He has money and the charges are not violent ones."

"I guess time finally ran out on him. Are you okay? You look like you are freezing."

"It's cold as shit outside." Terry drew off her gloves and stuffed them in her coat pockets.

"Break out the long johns. The weatherman just said we might get some flurries tonight. There's still some coffee in the pot."

"Thanks. I'm good. I saw a few stray flakes on the way here from court."

"Oh, another thing. Terry, you really must have a guardian angel watching over you. I've got more news for you."

"Give it to me!"

"Mrs. Belford's civil case is set for preliminary hearings in two weeks."

"You're kidding." Terry and Sandi spoke in unison.

"Nope. Set for the sixteenth. O'Grady's not going to be a happy camper."

"Well, I don't trust him. You be careful."

Terry nodded, then shrugged. "Kyle comes back tonight. His grandmother is out of danger and on the road to recovery."

"I'm so glad. I know you'll be glad to have him home," Sandi said.

"I will." Terry smiled. "And for a final piece of good news…Mrs. Belford won a new car!"

"What?" Sandi asked.

"How?" Becky asked at the same time.

Raising her hand to quiet her friends' excited questions, Terry told them of the call from Mrs. Belford.

"That has to be the best news yet," Sandi said.

Terry nodded and glanced at her watch. "It's almost two o'clock. I have an idea. Do we have any appointments on the afternoon agenda? If not, I say, let's shut down."

"You don't have to tell me twice, boss," Becky said. "We don't have anything scheduled this afternoon, but you do have a full day coming up tomorrow. I'll set the answering machine and close up shop."

"I agree." Sandi shut down her laptop and stood, stretching her back. "All in all, it's been a good week so far. We've settled two cases, got two new ones, O'Grady was indicted, Mrs. Belford has a brand new car, and we get to party at the inn this weekend. I'm looking forward to it."

The phone rang and the three women turned their heads in the direction of the reception room.

"You guys go on," Becky said. "I'll get it. If it's important, I'll let you know."

"I'm going to the café first, in case you need me. It dawned on me that I haven't eaten. What better place to forage then *Pâtisseries a la Carte*? See you guys tomorrow."

"See if they have any asparagus soup left. It was terrific," Sandi called.

Terry tossed her briefcase on her desk and switched off lights. She passed by Sandi's already darkened office. With a wave to Becky, she bundled up and slipped out the door to the café.

Both Stephanie's and Mary Jo's cars were in the lot.

Terrific! She could bring her two best friends up to date at once.

***

"That asparagus soup—*c'est magnifique!*" Terry kissed her fingertips appreciatively as she pushed the second empty bowl to the side. "Perfect with a BLT." She polished of the last bite of sandwich.

"That was the last of it," Stephanie said as she scooped the plates away.

"Leave them in the sink, Steph," Terry called. "I'll clean up."

239

Mary Jo straightened in her chair. "Whoa, who are you and what did you do with my friend Terry?"

"What? You think I can't do dishes?"

"You are the girl who always paid Connor to do your shift in the kitchen."

"So? This place was spotless when I came in, and you were ready to leave. You took care of me, so the least I can do is clean up. Besides I need to kill some time before I pick up Kyle from the airport."

"Ah, the truth shall set you free," Mary Jo said with a laugh.

Terry laughed, then sobered. "His grandmother came home from the hospital and the doctors expect her to make a full recovery."

"I'm so glad. And I know you will be glad to have him home." Stephanie dropped back in her chair.

Before she could answer, Terry was interrupted by her phone chirping with an incoming text.

"Asshole!" she exclaimed when she glanced at the screen.

"The unknown texter again?" Mary Jo asked.

"This one was blank. I've gotten two blanks and a half dozen messages that say something like 'Bitch' or, "You'll pay."

"You can't block him?"

"No, the number doesn't show up so there's nothing to block. The police and phone company suspect someone is using an international phone while here in the United States. Somehow the caller is able to text without the number showing up because it pings back to the service somewhere overseas."

"It's creepy." Stephanie drew her sweater closer.

The phone chirped with a new text.

The three women looked at the phone before Terry snatched it from the table. She sighed in relief when she saw Kyle's number.

She read the message out loud. "Stuck at Logan. Flight delayed indefinitely. Plane has not even arrived. In line to try to get ticket changed to last flight to Washington. I'll get a car and drive home. Call you as soon as I know something."

"That sucks," Mary Jo said.

"For sure." Terry's fingers tapped a response. *It's cold here. I'll be waiting to warm you.*

Kyle responded immediately. *Trench coat and heels?*

She typed: *Sorry, no trench coat.*

Kyle: *Aww darn.*

Terry glanced down at her favorite Manolo Blahniks, and smiled as an idea formed. *A cashmere overcoat is way sexier than a canvas trench coat.*

She looked up to see her two friends watching her intently. "What?" she asked innocently.

"What's going on in that mind of yours?" Mary Jo asked.

"Nothing."

"Hmmph." Scrunching her face into a Hannah-like smirk, Mary Jo jumped up and scooted chairs around tables.

Stephanie leaned on Terry's table. "Have you told him you are in love with him yet?"

"What? Who says I'm in love with him?"

"Your face does. Every fiber of your being says that tonight. Do you need one of the ghosts to conk you on the head before you tell him?"

"It-it's not that." Terry stuttered.

"Don't waste time, Terry." Stephanie covered Terry's hands with hers. "You've got something now. Something good, like Gage and I have. Like Mary Jo and Chase. Like your parents. Grab it and savor every minute life has to offer you."

"That's deep stuff, Steph." Mary Jo kissed the top of her friend's head. She glanced at Terry. "But I agree."

"Okay, you two, back off. Leave me alone and get out of here before I change my mind about cleaning up." Terry stood up and shooed her friends to the door. They laughed and hugged, before stepping out into the cold.

"It's snowing!" Stephanie called out. A thin layer already coated their cars' windshields.

"Be safe going home," Terry called, peering at the swirl of scattered snowflakes. "You know how a quarter-inch of snow affects drivers around here." She closed the door on her friends' laughter.

She made short work of the kitchen clean-up. After a final look around, she slipped into her off-white cashmere coat and tightened the belt. A quick glance down at her hemline and the delicate toes of her high heels brought a sly smile to her face.

Sorry, Kyle. Only cashmere will do.

Another idea struck her. She rummaged through cabinets until she found a box of crackers. A search of the refrigerator revealed fruits and several kinds of cheeses. Terry selected a clump of green grapes, and then cut wedges from blocks of brie, Camembert, and Swiss. She swiped four mini éclairs from the refrigerated glass case. She arranged everything on a small platter, covered it in plastic wrap, and paused. She peered at the small wine rack where Mary Jo kept champagne on hand for mimosas.

No Dom Pérignon, but two bottles of sparkling Brut nestled in the wrought iron holder.

Terry removed one bottle and placed it beside the platter. Upon second thought, she grabbed the other bottle as well. She located one of the gray shopping bags with the café logo emblazoned on the front and loaded the goodies in it. With a final glance around, she grabbed her purse and headed toward Kyle's apartment.

The flurries had increased. A dusting of snow covered the convertible's windshield. Halfway to the apartment, she remembered she did not have the spare key. The day she had taken Kyle to the airport, they had scrambled from the apartment so quickly that she'd left the key on the dining table.

Terry pivoted and headed for Clothiste's Inn. *I'm lucky to have options!* Slight change of plans but same expected outcome. She balanced the shopping bag in the crook of her arm and dug through her purse with her free hand until her fingers touched the keys. She put the platter and bottles of champagne in the refrigerator, and ran back to her car to get her overnight bag from the trunk.

Her cell phone pinged as she bustled through the door. Kicking the door shut behind her, she pulled out her phone as she set the case on the counter. Scrolling to the text icon, she clicked on the envelope. "Out of area" appeared on the screen, with one word in the message box.

Bitch.

"You asshole." She hissed the word through clenched teeth and jammed the phone in her pocket.

Almost immediately, the phone rang. She looked at the dial and her mother's number came up. With relief, she hit the answer button.

"Hi, Mom." She headed toward the bedroom, telling her mother she would be staying at the inn as she waited for Kyle.

The back door failed to shut completely. A short burst of wind pushed the door inward a fraction. The latch disengaged from the strike plate, and the door settled against the frame.

***

Kyle called a few minutes before six. The flight to Norfolk was cancelled because the incoming plane was stranded by the weather. He'd managed to get the last seat on the last flight to Dulles, scheduled to arrive just shy of eight p.m. Several other passengers on the same flight agreed to share a rental car to the Hampton Roads area rather than risking becoming stranded.

"The pilot just announced that skies are cloudy in Dulles but they have no snow yet. If all goes well, and the roads are okay, we should get home between one and two."

"Darn. I have champagne chilling and everything," Terry said.

"Let it chill while you keep my bed warm."

"Well, I'm actually at the inn. I left my key when we rushed to the airport but I didn't go get it. If I go into my office for any reason, I will wind up working. So I'll just warm the sheets for you here." She ran her fingers along the strap of the lace bra. *And heat up other things.*

"Can't wait to get there," Kyle said, his voice husky.

"Drive safe," Terry said. She nearly added the words, "I love you."

But those were words that needed to be said face-to-face. Instead she said, "I have to turn my phone off for a while. My battery is low and I don't have a charger with me. I'll turn it on at eight. You should know your travel conditions by then. Bye, Kyle."

She snapped the phone shut. With a sigh, she pushed the off-button and picked up the remote.

She fell asleep during the news.

***

A short stocky man circled the block several times, passing the law office parking lot. The fancy red convertible sat alone, dusty white with a covering of snow. He eased his car into a space along the curb, ignoring the "Decal Parking Only" sign.

Cops weren't going to be checking windshields for parking decals in the snow.

He grabbed the Phillips-head screwdriver from the console. It would create such pretty scratches along car doors painted cherry red.

Not another creature stirred. Snow tended to send southeastern Virginians into a panic, and most had headed home early. It was perfect. If he hurried, he could do what he wanted and his footprints would be covered quickly. He scrambled from the car. A clump of slush slid from the door frame and slid down his collar. He clenched his fingers around the screwdriver.

That bitch.

He could have been home long ago, warm and dry like everyone else. Instead he had to sit in that holding cell for hours, beside common criminals, until he made bond.

That had to be worth a nice twin track around her whole car tonight.

For good measure, he pulled out his phone and tapped out

a text message.

Bitch.

He hit send.

∗∗∗

Terry burrowed further under the covers, the tip of her nose cold to the touch. She fumbled for her cell phone. She remembered she'd shut it down, and traced her fingers along the edge until she located the on button. When it powered up, she glanced at the time and tossed the covers.

Ten o'clock!

The screen showed eighteen percent battery. She scrolled through the log for Kyle's number.

"Terry!" Kyle answered on the first ring. Other voices chattered in the background. "I've been trying to call you."

"I still had the phone off. I fell asleep. Where are you?"

"We're on ninety-five, just passed Alexandria. We got in on time and got the rental fairly quickly but it's really slow-going right now. A few accidents and stranded vehicles here and there. I hope we make good time. Our car has a shitty heater. We're nearly frozen already."

"I'll warm you up when you get here." Terry's voice lowered in a sex purr. "You can call me on the inn's landline if you need to reach me."

"I don't have it."

"I'll call you from it in a few minutes. Hurry but be safe."

"Sounds good. Especially that warming up part."

Smiling, Terry hung up and slid from the toasty covers.

She shivered. Lace lingerie might look great, but it was totally ineffective against the cold. She slipped into the cashmere coat, startled by the cold satin lining. Her skin quickly warmed the material. She reached for the matching thigh-high stockings and rolled one up each of her long legs, then preened before the door mirror.

Kyle might arrive encased in ice, but after one look at her, he'd be thawed in no time.

She used her toes to stand the high heels into upright positions and slid her feet in. Turning side to side in a saucy twirl, she licked her finger and tapped it on her butt, hissing between her teeth.

The finished look should bring him to the boiling point.

Her breath came out in sudden vapors. Shivers ran down her spine and she pulled the coat tighter. Even the warmest thought of Kyle could not stop the chills.

Cold temperatures! That could only mean one thing. A ghost was outside.

She tightened the coat around her and grabbed the pepper spray from the nightstand. She jammed the canister in her pocket and inched the door open. As far as she could tell, all of the lights still burned as she'd left them.

"Theresé?" She called. No answer, no welcoming warm stroke brushing across her cheek.

The hallway was freezing, colder than she ever remembered. She gulped and said, "Abigail?"

Had she really expected a response? Other than the grotesque forms Abigail had taken in the attic, she'd never verbally communicated with Terry.

Terry inched her way along the wall, looking for the thermostat. She stood at the door to the kitchen, and her gaze fell to the wide-open back door. She raced forward and pushed it shut. With a click, she secured the lock and stepped back.

A hand clamped on her shoulder.

"You don't scare me, Theresé. I've gotten used to you." She laughed. As she swiveled her head, her gaze swept across the floor. Her smile faded.

Too late, she noticed the wet footprints.

The hand moved from her shoulder and across her throat.

This was no ghost.

CHAPTER 23

"You bitch." Spittle struck Terry's cheek as the voice hissed in her ear. The burly hand squeezed her windpipe. Terry clutched at the man's coat sleeve, trying to wedge her fingers under his to break the grip. She squirmed and the hold tightened.

Something sharp poked her right cheek. Terry rolled her eyes sideways but could not see what the man was holding.

The grip tightened once more, then loosened. "I'm going to move my hand, but if you make a sound, I'll ram this screwdriver through your face. Do you understand me?"

Terry nodded. The man slipped his hand from her throat but moved his arm across her shoulders. Her head lodged in the crook of his arm as he pulled her closer to his chest. She could turn her head enough now to see the yellow handle of the screwdriver clenched in his grip.

"Who are you? What do you want?" she gasped.

"I'm your worst nightmare, doll," he snarled.

Terry recognized the voice and cold nerves knotted in her gut.

Dennis O'Grady pressed the screwdriver into her cheek again, then trailed it down to her jugular vein. He rested the tip against her skin. Blood rushed through her veins so rapidly that her very heartbeat ticked against the point.

O'Grady shoved her forward. She splayed her hands ahead of her but missed the counter. Her right cheek hit the edge and she tumbled to her knees.

"Just what I like. A bitch on her knees." He rubbed his

crotch. "Got something for you, doll." He grabbed Terry by the hair and pulled her to her feet. He slammed her hip against the counter and pressed his body into hers. He clamped one hand at her throat again. The can of pepper spray dug into her side, out of reach.

"You cost me a lot of money today, doll. And to make up for it, I'm just gonna help myself to some of those fine antiques you have in that living room." He trailed the screwdriver along her jaw and down the collar of her coat. He used the tip to push the lapels aside. His eyes bulged at the swell of breasts over the lace bra.

"Well, well, well. What have we here?" Still gripping her neck, he squeezed her windpipe and ran his tongue down her cleavage.

She swung blindly, raking her fingernails across his face. "You filthy little bastard!" she gasped. She shoved O'Grady and dashed around the counter. She made it through the dining room before he caught a handful of hair and yanked her back against his shoulder. He wrapped his arm around her neck and leaned backwards, his shorter stature forcing her to bend with him. Increasing pressure against her throat, O'Grady dragged her to the living room and shoved her toward the fireplace. Knickknacks rattled. She stared into the glass front of the clock as it tottered in front of her, and then steadied. She turned and faced O'Grady, her shoulders digging into the mantle as she moved back as far as she could.

Calm down, Terry! Think! If she could keep his eyes distracted, she might be able to reach the pocket with the pepper spray.

"These candlesticks are pure silver, very valuable. Take them." She raised one hand cautiously and pointed behind her.

He held the screwdriver like a sword. His gaze roamed over the gap exposing the thin lace bra and thong, then trailed up and down each leg. His chin glistened with spit, and he brushed his hand to wipe it.

She ignored the lewd stare.

"Watch what you do, doll. They took my gun when I got

busted today, but don't think I can't do damage with this. Any sudden moves and this blade is gonna pierce your throat like a dart going through a pumpkin. Got that?"

Terry nodded.

"Now move slowly and put those candlesticks on the table. Easy now."

Now would be a good time for you to appear, Abigail. Terry grabbed the closest candlestick, hoping to feel the burn that seemed to precede Abigail's appearance.

Nothing happened. She set it down on the coffee table and straightened. She reached to the left, allowing the coat to part further. O'Grady's gaze dropped to the gap and she slipped her right hand into her pocket, fingers wrapping around the canister. The nozzle pointed in the wrong direction. It would take a few seconds to rotate the can so that she could spray outward when she raised her arm.

In the meantime, her left hand touched the base of the second candlestick. This must be the one—the haunted one. She braced for the burn.

The burn that did not come.

O'Grady grew impatient. "Stop stalling, doll. I'll take the clock too. And that necklace. After that…" His eyes roamed her body again.

"You're not getting my necklace, you bastard." Terry withdrew her hand with the spray. Her shaking fingers pressed the nozzle. Her aim struck too low, sweeping across his lower face and neck.

He coughed as a wave of propellant struck his chin and sputtered, "You bitch, I'll kill you." He flicked his wrist and sent the screwdriver sailing.

Terry sidestepped just in time. The blade pierced the wooden mantle over her right shoulder. She crashed into the coffee table, knocking the candlesticks to the floor. One rolled under her foot and she kicked it aside.

O'Grady caught her coat sleeve and tugged her back. She turned and aimed her left foot, planting the well-pointed toe of her shoe right to his balls.

He doubled over and fell to his knees, yanking her down with him. She wriggled her shoulders free, not caring that shedding the coat left her nearly naked.

She glanced at Shady, ready to press another burst of capsicum directly to his face. He knelt frozen in place, eyes wide, jaw slack, hands cupped over his crotch.

Beyond the pain, however, sheer terror gleamed in his eyes. A pungent stench reached Terry's nostrils. Instead of the pepper sensation she expected from the spray reaching her, the odor of sulfur permeated the air.

Smoky mist wound around furniture, past her legs, over the coffee table and stopped in front of O'Grady. The haze spun and rose. The elongated, faceless head formed and stretched, the cavernous mouth shrieking into the face of the cowering man.

He tried to scream but only a squeak crept out. He keeled over in a dead faint.

As fast as the vapor had rolled into the room, it dissipated, all traces of the pepper spray disappearing with it.

Eyes on her attacker's prone figure, Terry fumbled with the old-fashioned rotary phone on an end table, poking her shaking finger in the slot at the number nine. In seemed an interminable amount of time before the dial slid back to its original position. She flicked her wrist twice to complete the call to 9-1-1.

***

Terry barely had time to throw on some clothes before the police responded to her frantic call. Police responded rapidly to find O'Grady still crouched in a fetal position, hands covering his crotch. It had taken two paramedics and a police officer to strap the whimpering, writhing man onto a stretcher. His eyes darted frantically from side to side as he begged the police to keep the ghost away.

Two police officers looked at Terry with quizzical

expressions.

She shrugged. "People say this house is haunted."

The emergency responders wheeled the gurney to the ambulance. One officer then climbed into the back of the ambulance.

The snow had stopped, long since. Tire tracks left crisscross marks across the pavement. Seeing a pattern of footsteps around her car, Terry stepped down to the sidewalk. One of the remaining officers shined his flashlight ahead of her and her heart sank.

"He got me again." They peered at the deep scrapes. The ambulance's rotating red lights streaked through the dark, its intermittent beam emphasizing the damage with each flash. Terry continued, "My car was vandalized two other times. I have security cameras now, so this should have been recorded. I'll find out how to get the tape to you."

The officer nodded and followed her back to the house. "Why do you think he did this?"

Terry closed the door on the fading wail echoing behind the departing ambulance. She paused, glanced at the officer's nametag. *J. Philbin*. She then said, "The car vandalism started after I took on a client in a civil matter. Long story short, O'Grady had defrauded her on a purchase, which also led to criminal charges. The indictments came out today and I guess he turned himself in. He was also recently served with papers for the civil suit."

Officer Philbin nodded. "He probably made bond and came straight here."

"When I woke up and felt the cold…" Terry paused. She couldn't explain that she suspected one of her ghosts was roaming the house. "I found the door open. I realized that I had gotten distracted when I came in and must not have shut it securely behind me. As soon as I shut the door, I saw the wet footprints and he attacked me." She provided more details as the officer asked questions for the report.

"You had quite an ordeal tonight. Are you going to be okay? Can I call someone for you or take you somewhere else?"

Terry shook her head. "I'm waiting for my fiancé. His flight was delayed but he'll be here soon."

The officer sealed the screwdriver into an evidence bag. "I'm almost finished here, and then I'll meet my partner at the hospital. Once O'Grady is released, he'll be booked at the station. I think between this and his other crimes, bond will be pretty high. I doubt if he will be out anytime soon."

Terry shivered. *I hope he can't walk anytime soon, either.* She pointed to the stilettos resting against the baseboard, where she'd kicked them before the police arrived. "Do you need to take my shoes as evidence? I kind of nailed him in the—crotch."

Trying to suppress a laugh, the officer shook his head. "Those things should probably be classified as lethal weapons. But I don't need to take them." He snapped a few more pictures around the disheveled parlor. Then he scribbled in his notebook, and gathered his things. "I'm done here. The detectives will follow up, but you've given a very detailed statement. You'll be a great witness."

"You've been very kind, Officer Philbin. Thank you for everything."

As soon as the officer left, Terry closed and double-checked the doorknob to be sure the locks secured in place. She then pressed her forehead against the door frame and gathered her wits.

It would serve no purpose to call her family at that hour. Although she'd catch flak for not calling about the encounter with O'Grady, it could wait until daylight.

She did call Kyle. Hampered by the increased snow, he had only reached Richmond by the time she finally had the chance to call. She gave him a brief synopsis of Abigail's appearance and assured him that she was fine and safe. Knowing he was in the company of others, she added, "There were other—events, but I'll tell you later."

"Why don't you go to the apartment?" he asked.

"I locked the spare key inside the apartment," Terry said.

"I forgot you mentioned that earlier. How about going to your parents' house?"

"I'd rather just stay here until you get home. I don't want to worry anyone."

"I'll be worried."

"Please don't be. There's nothing here that will hurt me now. See you soon." Terry hung up the phone and went to the bedroom. She gathered her delicate lingerie, now tainted by the encounter with O'Grady, and trashed it in the kitchen waste can, resisting the urge to spit. She put water in the tea kettle and placed it on a back burner. While the water heated, she straightened the parlor.

"I remember that night now and what happened." The ethereal voice crackled with static.

Terry jumped and spun around to face a fractured blue blur lighting the parlor. The image flickered and faded once before the bluish form turned human. Therésé stood before her, a shawl draped across her shoulders, snowy white hair framing her wrinkled face.

Relief at the sight of Therésé overcame the startled pounding of Terry's heart.

"I'm so glad to see you!" she cried. She threw her arms around her ancestress' neck. "Where have you been? I did not know if you would return."

Therésé shook her head. "I have been trapped between our worlds. It is like being in a dark room, with nothing but occasional light coming through a window. I could see you but I could not reach you. I struggled to cross through one more time."

"Abigail appeared. She did not harm me but she frightened my attacker."

This time, Therésé head bobbed up and down. "I saw her. I could not reach you. Since our deaths, I have never crossed paths with her spirit until that time in the attic. When she formed, I could not appear, but I could prevent Kyle from falling down the stairs. Abigail was always trapped on her own side of..." She raised her shoulders helplessly.

Terry reached for the older woman's hand. "I've been waiting for you to finish telling me about the night you came back. I need to know what happened when you went to the outside building. Someone grabbed you from behind. But you left before you could tell me what else happened that night."

"Yes, that is right. Someone grabbed me from behind. Just like what happened to you tonight. I was held against a hard chest, the man's hands clamped over my mouth. I was frozen with fear." Theresé placed both of her hands across her mouth, eyes wide in horror as her memory replayed the incident. Her image wavered.

Unsure if movement would cause the image to fade further, Terry held her breath and waited.

When Theresé lowered her hands, she studied the weathered skin on her splayed fingers. She dropped her arms to her sides. In a shaky voice, she said, "It's harder to cross over to your side now. I knew not if I would be able to come back this time. But I fought my way back to you. I need to tell you what happened."

Terry took one of the weathered hands in hers and led the aging woman to the sofa. They sat side by side.

After a protracted sigh, Theresé continued, her voice stronger. "I remember everything about that night now." Eyes distant, Theresé lifted her palm as if pushing the door inward.

Her preoccupied look worried Terry. The old woman seemed feebler than ever before.

"I struggled to break free of the man's grasp, but then he whispered and told me to calm down. His voice was hoarse but I immediately recognized it was my brother Louis. We could not see each other in the dark so he did not know me. He said he would release me but if I made a noise, he would kill me. I nodded to show I understood and he slowly removed his hand. I turned and whispered his name, throwing my arms around his neck. He recognized me then, and gathered me close. I explained why I had come."

Terry remained motionless, still afraid to move and lose contact with the spirit.

"Then Louis told me what happened. After he helped James and Lizzie get away safely, he remained behind to keep their cover. But he wanted to check on Mama and Grandpapa before he returned to his unit. Inside he found Mama had fallen to the bottom of the stairs. Mama managed to tell him that she had found Abigail in the act of trying to kill our grandfather. He realized our mother and Abigail had engaged in a confrontation, the same one you and I saw in that image. Mama died in his arms, her blood covering his hands. Then he heard a noise above him. It was Abigail, her body distorted as she lay sprawled on the floor at the top of the stairs. She was injured, but still she said ugly things about our mother. Louis pressed his hand on her throat until she died."

The clock struck twelve, and both women turned to face it, gripping hands. Terry held her breath as she waited, wondering if some time warp would send them back to the past again. She exhaled a ragged breath when nothing happened.

With a strained voice, Theresé continued. "Louis found Grandpapa weak and near death. When we went back in time, we looked down on that scene as well. Do you remember?"

Terry nodded. *How can I ever forget?*

"Grandpapa told my brother to bury Abigail in the backyard by the new magnolia tree. He could do nothing to help, but planned to tell the doctor that he had heard the struggle between his wife and daughter-in-law. He would say Abigail fled in the night after murdering our mother. Sadly, when Louise finished and returned to our grandfather, he found him already dead. We…"

Whistling from the kitchen indicated water had come to a boil in the teapot, but Terry ignored it, fearful any movement would cause her ancestress to disappear. The incessant shrill of the teapot broke Theresé's concentration. She frowned as if noticing the sound for the first time, and looked toward the kitchen.

"I need to turn that off before it burns up," Terry said, scrambling to her feet. "Do you want some tea?"

Theresé nodded. She shivered and drew her shawl closer.

"I'm so cold. So tired and so cold."

Terry dashed to the kitchen and turned the knob off under the burner. She grabbed two mugs from the cabinet, clanking the ceramic together in her haste. Her shaking hands sloshed water as she poured. Not bothering to wipe the counter, she carried the steaming cups to the parlor and set them on coasters.

Therésé wrapped her fingers around one mug, and said, "I kept Louis's secret for years. Not even Papa knew what my brother had done. We told our father that Mama died peacefully in her sleep, as did Grandpapa, and we kept that story until we died. I am ashamed to say that I felt no remorse in hiding what he had done. Abigail was a wicked woman most of her life. But poor Louis. At first, he said he did not care. However, his guilt soon became a burden. He tried to make amends by becoming a physician to heal lives. He hoped by saving a life he could make up for taking one. He never seemed to find the peace he sought in his life." A veil of bewilderment settled in her eyes, and she frowned again.

Terry leaned forward in concern and covered the old woman's hands in hers, rubbing gently to warm the cold skin. *Could ghosts have memory problems as they aged?* More worrisome to Terry than Therésé's' mental state, however, was the appearance of a soft aura flickering around the colonial woman. Not since Therésé had taken on a human shape had the ethereal glow surrounded her. She feared Therésé might return to her ghostly form before finishing the story.

"Therésé? I'm a little confused. I understand you are telling me something else happened, but I don't know what it is." Terry prodded, voice soft.

Tears rolled down Therésé's cheeks. "One day, Abigail had someone plant a magnolia tree. It wasn't very big yet, and I can remember her evil face watching the gardener plant it. In the dark of night, Louis buried Abigail beside that magnolia sapling. The rain had stopped and the moon gave him some light. Then he hid in the kitchen to plan. He was becoming desperate, but my arrival provided the perfect cover. We devised a story. Louis could not report the incident because there was no reason for him to be at our grandfather's house. And he would have to account for his absence from his unit. He was already covered in our mother's blood and dirt. We ran down the alley to another one that runs close the tavern. I bound and gagged him, and pushed him down a small gully under some bushes. He would tell whoever found him that he had been knocked unconscious by the escaping traitor, James, and left for dead. We hoped his dear friend would forgive being used this way. I would enter Grandfather's house, find him and Mama and run to the doctor's house."

Theresé broke into sobs. "In spite of knowing what to expect, I became hysterical at the sight of my beautiful mother lying dead on the floor. I ran screaming from the house. When I arrived at the doctor's house, I did not have to convince him of my shock. He had known of Abigail's previous attempt to poison my mother. When the constables came, they concluded that Abigail had killed Mama, and perhaps even Grandpapa before fleeing. Louis's involvement was never discovered. Grandpapa and Mama were buried side by side in the back yard, far away from the magnolia tree where the Wicked One was buried. I came here to live out my last years with Celestine's family. After I died, my body was taken to New England for burial near my father, but my soul remained trapped here, between the past and the present. My spirit wandered, not in fear or darkness, but also not in peace. I could always sense my mother's presence nearby. But one day I could not feel her. Why?"

"P. Roker and C. Roker," Terry murmured. "You had them buried in the back yard of this house, right?"

Theresé nodded.

Terry jumped to her feet. "I know where Clothiste is!" She danced a short jig and knelt before Theresé with a smile. "I know where your mother is, Theresé. Many years later, your great-granddaughter Celestine moved two family graves to the Catholic cemetery. Graves marked with only initials of the first names. Everyone just assumed they belonged to Celestine's great-grandparents."

Theresé's form strengthened, and she was the young woman Terry had first seen.

Terry gripped Theresé's hands in hers and continued, "I am Celestine's descendant, and she is yours. That makes you one of my great-grandmothers. I don't know how many, six, I think."

Theresé struggled with her memory. "I married Antoine LaCroix. We had one daughter, Antoinette, named after him. I outlived my husband, my daughter, and even my granddaughter. I came to live in Celestine's home—this house—in my last years. I was an old woman in body, but my mind lived in the summer we spent in this house. The summer I lost my mother."

"But she is not lost now, Theresé. I know where she is. I can take you to where she was re-buried."

Theresé smiled and shook her head. "No, you won't have to. I know where she is now. You helped me find her. She waits for me on the other side. I will join her soon."

"All along, we thought the bones belonged to Clothiste. Then I had special scientific tests done and we learned they did not come from anyone in my family. We buried Abigail's bones properly but in a place far from your mother and grandfather. Now I will put a marker at her grave."

"That is the right thing to do, and very kind of you. We will have peace."

Terry rested her cheek on her many-great grandmother's knee and let the tears fall. She raised her head and said, "I won't see you again, will I, Grandmother Theresé?"

Theresé stroked her descendant's hair. "This is the last time, my dear," she acknowledged with a sad nod. "I will cross the line one more time, to find peace at last. Thank you, Terry. You are a kind and good woman and I am proud of you. Continue to speak for those who cannot. The world needs justice to survive."

The ancestress and her descendant embraced. Translucency engulfed Theresé's figure, but her hands remained firm and solid. Tears streamed down Terry's face, and Therese brushed one away with her knuckle.

"Like Nicole's teardrop." She held it to the light. "Do not weep, child. I am at peace and I will join my sisters soon. But now I must go."

Terry tightened her hold. Therese smiled again and slackened her grip until only their fingertips touched. Then she disappeared.

Terry stood in front of the fireplace for a full five minutes, sobs wracking her shoulders. Tears spent, she straightened and blew her nose. She eyed the scattered antiques.

She moved one candlestick. When nothing happened, she placed it on the mantle.

She gripped the other. The second candlestick delivered only a lukewarm sensation. She glanced down. A weak trail of gray film floated around her legs.

Was Abigail making an appearance? Terry's breath hitched and she stiffened her body.

Sparkles of blue spun over the dark trail. The parlor basked in the glow. The sparkles flittered toward the mist, which then slithered toward the fireplace.

Terry whispered, "Let it go, Abigail. I hope you find your peace."

Hissing as though water had been thrown on flames, the steamy haze dissipated up the chimney flue.

With a gentle snap, the blue light disappeared and the room fell into serene quiet.

Terry whispered, "Goodbye, Grandmother."

She left the room, turning out lights as she went.

***

"How far have you gotten now, Kyle?" Terry asked. She peered out the window for signs of headlights.

"Five minutes away, Terry. Coming down London Boulevard now."

"I'm waiting." Although she'd exchanged several phone calls with Kyle, she'd refrained from telling him the events of the evening. In a cold car full of strangers and weather issues, the last thing he needed was to be saddled with worries.

The minute she spotted the beam of the headlights, she locked the inn door behind her and walked down the steps. Kyle jumped from the car and spoke to the occupants, then removed his suitcase from the trunk. He called one more farewell and met Terry on the sidewalk.

He wrapped his arms around her and exclaimed, "Baby, it's cold out here! We finally got the heater going but…"

Terry clung to him, a small sob escaping.

Alarm shook his voice. "What is it? Is your mom okay?"

"Everyone's fine. I-I've got a lot to tell you, Kyle." She grabbed his hand. "Let's get inside your apartment."

***

"The bastard!" Jaw clenched, Kyle flexed his fists. Terry curled beside him on the couch, head on his shoulder, and entwined her fingers with his. The level of his anger surprised and concerned her. She had never seen him mildly annoyed, let alone angry. "He didn't hurt me," she said. She squeezed his hand reassuringly.

Kyle raised one eyebrow and tilted her chin to study the bruise. He said nothing.

"Okay, he pushed me and I fell. But he came out on the wrong end of my shoe. I'll have to wear a lot of make-up or it'll look like you did it."

"Never! A man who hits a woman is a low-life coward. And the bastard cost me my fantasy welcome home."

Terry shuddered. "Mine too. But there will be other opportunities."

CHAPTER 24

Kirby Lawrence circled the block several times before finding a place to park. He felt a little silly walking down the street dressed in his costume as a colonial British officer. He passed several other pedestrians, who nodded and smiled, apparently undaunted by his unusual attire. He recalled that on a number of occasions after working late at the Naval Medical Center, he had seen colonial re-enactors strolling along High Street in celebration of local events.

The heavy black boots he wore created a low thump with each step he took. The limp was barely noticeable anymore. Surprisingly, he ran easier than walked. He still heard the slight difference between the sounds of each footstep. The replica saber he wore at his side clinked in an irregular rhythm, matching his irregular gait.

"*Louis.*"

It was only a feathery whisper, but the word seemed to dance across the air.

He spun on his heel in a 180° arc, peering down the dark sidewalk to see who called.

No one was there.

A crisp breeze picked up, swirling brown leaves across his path. He drew his lapels tighter. In spite of the wool jacket covering his long-sleeved white shirt, a shiver rippled down his spine.

He continued his walk toward the inn. Dried foliage crunched under his feet—a crisp clean snap as his good leg swung forward, a slight scrape as his other boot dragged across

261

leaves.

"*Louis.*"

He stopped, sure he had heard the voice in spite of the music and laughter emanating from the B and B. Trees rustled, sending dried leaves swirling around him.

A mother's voice called out over the din. "Stop running, Tanner!" A little boy in full speed ahead came to an abrupt halt in front of Kirby. Dressed in a colonial drummer boy's outfit, the boy banged the drum with petulant thumps. He turned pouty eyes toward Kirby.

"You wait right here for your dad, young man." Beth said as she reached her son's side and touched his shoulder.

She turned her gaze to Kirby and said, "I'm sorry. He's not happy about his costume."

"It's stupid!" Tanner banged the two drumsticks on the rim to emphasize his distaste. "I wanted a sword."

Kirby dropped to one knee in front of the little boy. "Do you know that drummer boys were very important during the war? They were almost more important than the officers."

"Why?" Tanner thumped listlessly, a skeptical look crossing his face.

"Well, you see." Kirby adjusted his kneeling position, sword clanking. "The drummers and other musicians provided an important service during the old wars, long before there were telephones or radios that made it possible for soldiers to be in touch."

"My dad's fire truck has a radio and they talk to each other."

"That's right. But since the army didn't have that kind of equipment back then, the officers needed some way to send commands to their troops. So they needed drummers and pipers to sound the commands. That's why they didn't carry guns. They used their instruments to send the general's orders. Other drummers or pipers further down the line would pick up the signal until it reached the ears of all the soldiers. The drummers had to learn special beats and drum rolls to tell soldiers things like when to turn right or left, or to load their muskets. Another reason the army needed musicians to play for them was to keep the soldiers' spirits up during the war, or to show the citizens what a strong army they had."

"Really? Did they have swords too?" Tanner thumped once.

"No, they didn't carry swords because they were so young. In fact, their coats were different from soldiers so that if the enemy captured the musicians they would know that they did not carry weapons."

"Awww, no fair."

"*But*…the drummer boys, the pipers and the bugle boys, they were really the bravest of all."

"Why?" Tanner tap-tapped on the drum.

"Because they didn't have any weapons."

"Hey, cool! The big men had guns and swords and the little kids didn't?" Tanner thumped both wooden drumsticks on the plastic replica drumhead.

"That's right. But you could help us out tonight, like the drummer boys did. You can announce your parents' arrival to the party. Just tap "ta-thump, ta-thump, ta-thump, thump, thump" on your drum. Can you try that?"

Tanner nodded. He slipped his hand from his mother's grasp. Balancing the drumsticks in either hand, he tested a beat. Kirby repeated the rhythm. Tanner followed the tempo until he had the pattern down.

"Are you Louie?" Tanner asked. He rolled through the drumbeat.

Startled, Kirby glanced over his shoulder. *Had the boy heard it too?*

"I heard the lady call you." Another drum roll.

Connor arrived before Kirby could answer, leaves crunching under the boots of his Union Army uniform. "I had to park way over on Green Street." He knelt beside his son, listening to the taps. "What have we here?"

"I'm gonna announce your arrival." Tanner turned toward the porch steps, banging out the eight-beat cadence. Ta-thump, ta-thump, ta-thump, thump, thump.

The two men stood. Kirby nodded toward Tanner. "I was just telling him how important the drummer boys were to the officers during the war."

"Well, he's in a better mood now," Connor laughed. "Did you tell him the drummer boys probably emptied the general's chamber pot during the day?"

"I did leave that part out," Kirby said with a laugh. He extended his hand and Connor gripped it.

A single blue spark snapped in the dark when their palms touched. Both men drew back.

"Sorry about that, man." Connor laughed. "Happens in my family a lot."

Kirby brushed his palm along his coat.

"Thank you for calming our son down," Beth said. She'd dressed as a southern belle, the hoop skirt hiding her baby bump. "We may be able to enjoy ourselves now."

"My pleasure." Kirby followed Connor and Beth up the stairs behind Tanner's increasingly louder ta-thump, ta-thump, ta-thump, thump, thump.

Kirby entered the parlor to the party in full swing. "Thriller" echoed from unseen loudspeakers. Costumed guests glided around the room. Most people dressed in period costumes reflecting past eras, but several swashbuckling pirates and a lone Scotsman in kilt and sporran infiltrated the crowd.

A tall redhead wearing an eye-catching steampunk outfit strolled around the room, greeting guests. Kirby barely recognized her as the woman who owned the café. She looked like something out of a sci-fi western. She wore her hair piled high, topped with a little top hat from which a single black feather jutted. Buttons shaped like gearwheels lined the front of a red leather bustier. Her black taffeta skirt was hitched above one knee, revealing a long leg covered in black nylons. Following behind her was a man in a black jacquard waistcoat with tails, gold brocade vest and satiny puff tie. The occasional tug at his collar indicated a less than comfortable steampunk companion. Still he laughed and exchanged friendly words with guests.

Mary Jo glided before Kirby, smiled, and extended her lace-gloved hand. "Welcome to Clothiste's Inn, Commander Lawrence. Thank you for coming. This is my fiancé Chase Hallmark."

The men shook hands.

"I'm sorry my fiancée couldn't be here," he said. "She has frequent migraines." *Actually, the bitch threw a temper-tantrum and refused to come.*

Mary Jo linked arms with Kirby and said, "Let me show you to the buffet area." She drew him toward the dining room. A steady stream of partygoers filed between the table and buffet piled with plates and platters of food.

Hannah wound through the queue and called to Mary Jo. She wore a lime green sweater with a fluorescent orange pumpkin on the front. Above a scowling jack-o-lantern black glitter spelled out the words, "This IS my costume." She tapped Mary Jo's arm and held up her camera. "I wanna get a picture of you and the others," she rasped, inclining her head toward the parlor.

"Kirby, if you'll excuse me, I'll leave you and Chase to commiserate over your costumes."

Chase tugged at the stiff collar at his neck and said, "This tie comes off in five minutes."

Terry laughed and followed Hannah's neon sweater.

"I think our ancestors would be proud of us, don't you?" Terry linked arms with Stephanie and Mary Jo.

"Absolutely," Mary Jo replied.

"Hold still, you three." Hannah held her camera and snapped a photo. She snapped two more in quick succession and turned to take a picture of a guest dressed as Abraham Lincoln.

"This is so much fun." Stephanie hopped from one foot to the other in excitement and then grabbed Terry's arm, pointing down. "Are those stilettos under your gown, Terry?"

In unison the women peered at the points peeking from the hem of Terry's blue silk gown. She lifted the skirt a bit higher to reveal the powder blue suede shoes.

The trio burst into peals of giggles as they turned to face the unlit fireplace, crinolines of their collective colonial, antebellum, and steampunk Victorian dresses rustling.

"Oh, look at our necklaces in the mirror," Terry said when she straightened her head. "They sparkle in the light of the chandelier."

"That chandelier is actually behind us," the pragmatic Mary Jo pointed out. "But you are right, they do seem to light up, don't they?"

Stephanie stood on tiptoes until she could see her pendant.

The women pressed their heads together at their combined reflection. For a brief moment, the jewels in their pendants twinkled. The sparkles danced toward the mirror and disappeared. The jewels returned to normal.

Terry smoothed the satin of her Colonial gown and glanced around her self-consciously. Party guests seemed oblivious to the three women grouped together. She giggled and whispered, "If anyone is watching us or listening closely, they'll be calling for the men in green coats."

The lively rendition of "Ghostbusters" filtered through the air and the trio burst into laughter.

Mary Jo drew her friends away from the mirror, suddenly serious. "I think our ghosts have finally left the building," she said.

"I hope so." Tears brimmed in Stephanie's eyes. "Nicole found her necklace, Marie Josephé her heart, and Theresé her mother. I hope they have peace. Even Abigail. She was cruel and wicked. Although she died violently, maybe she can rest now that her body was discovered and buried properly."

"It was good of you to bury Abigail's bones, Terry," Mary Jo said. "Under the same circumstances, I don't know if I would have been inclined to spend money like that for a stranger's burial."

"You would have too, Mary Jo. I don't know if someone who was killed or died violently ever finds true peace, but Abigail is far away from my family now. Even now that I know who she was and her history, my conscience would not have let me do otherwise. And after all, she was married to our ancestor Phillip."

The last notes of "Ghostbusters" faded as the three women hugged each other and separated to mingle with their guests.

Terry sought Kyle, resplendent in a George Washington costume. He leaned against a wall, having made short shrift of the powdered wig and tricorn hat. He held out his hand and she drew him to the empty hallway between the innkeeper's suite and the kitchen.

"I need a break. People seem to be having fun. I'm so happy everyone got into the spirit and wore a costume. Even Hannah." They laughed at the green-clad sprite working the crowd with her camera.

He leaned close and murmured, "I'm actually looking forward to when the party is over."

"And why is that?" Terry swayed her hips in a quick but seductive move.

"That Colonial Room upstairs is calling us."

"Is it now?" She turned and circled his neck with her arms.

"Yep. And I seemed to notice a well-turned ankle a few minutes ago when my fiancée was showing off a new pair of high heels. Blue heels, I do believe."

"Powder blue, to be specific."

"Yep. Powder blue at the end of long bare legs. Which would look great under a tan overcoat." Kyle nipped her lip.

Terry threw back her head and laughed wickedly. "How about a silk dress?" She brushed her lips across his cheek and whispered in his ear, "These legs are commando all the way up."

***

Tanner walked up to Kirby empty-handed. His mother had long ago confiscated the drum and sticks. He stuck his lips out in a pout and asked, "I'm bored. Can I see your sword?"

"Well, I think your mom might not like that. It's not real

anyway. It's only a replica."

"Oh." Tanner took the man's hand, and studied the emerald ring. "Is that a girl's ring?"

Kirby laughed and picked the boy up. He held his ring toward the light, the stone's green facets twinkling in the light. Tanner's gaze followed Kirby's movements.

"Not at all. This is a man's ring, and it's very old. It's been in my family for generations. Well, just this green stone, which is called an emerald, has been. A long time ago someone in my family owned it but lost the metal part. My grandfather had the emerald mounted onto a new ring. He gave it to his son, my father, who then gave it to me. One day I will give it to my own son."

Tanner nodded knowingly. "My Aunt Terry has an old necklace. And Aunt Stephanie founded Nickel's necklace, and Mary Jo founded Marie Jo-fesses too."

"That's very interesting. Are you having fun?"

"Aye, Aye, sir!" Tanner snapped his fingers to his forehead in salute.

Kirby realized Tanner was looking straight ahead and his gaze followed Tanner's. On the fireplace wall, a gilded rectangular mirror presided over the candlesticks and bric-a-brac on the mantle.

The looking glass shimmered. His face and Tanner's changed. Another man and boy faced them in the mirror.

"Hi, Louis," Tanner said, maintaining the salute while waving with his free hand. He drew out the second syllable, the word sounding like, "Lou-weeee." The boy shimmied from Kirby's hold and stood in front of the fireplace. He broke his military gesture with a long swipe of his hand and dashed toward the dining room.

Before Kirby could glance back to the mirror, Terry strode beside him, skirts rustling.

"Thank you for coming by the open house," she said, and offered him a glass of champagne. "Congratulations on you and your fiancée being our first guests."

"I didn't realize at the time I made the reservation that we were your first official guests. I'm sorry she couldn't make it tonight." *Not really. I'm having more fun without her.*

"We have one other couple coming but only on Saturday night. Nothing else is booked in November yet. We are full almost every weekend in December, though, I'm excited to say."

"That's great. We look forward to it. This house fascinates me. It has since the first time I passed it."

"Really?" Terry glanced around. "What intrigues you the most?"

Kirby shrugged. "I don't know. It just draws me in, like I belong here. Maybe it's the Colonial setting of this room and me wearing this costume, but it feels so authentic."

"We used a lot of period pieces to decorate. My great-aunt had so many old things crammed in the attic, heirlooms handed down through the generations. Even ghosts. Maybe I shouldn't tell you that."

"Ghosts, huh?" Kirby faced crinkled with a smile, then his expression grew serious. He ran his fingers across the mantle with silver candlesticks and an ornate clock. "Aren't you worried about these antiques being stolen?"

"We're keeping our fingers crossed. I noticed you were very interested in that mirror." Terry motioned with a tilt of her glass.

"It's very unique." Kirby couldn't very well ask her if it was haunted. "Is it a Halloween prop? A hologram mirror?" He glanced in the mirror, his face and Terry's reflecting back.

Terry shrugged. "No, just an antique we found in the attic. Promise me you won't slip it in your luggage when you're here."

Kirby lifted his hand in a Boy Scout salute. "Scout's honor," he promised.

Terry laughed. Kyle called to her as another guest arrived and she said, "Excuse me, please. The father of our country—and my future children—has summoned me."

"Well, then, you mustn't keep the good general waiting." Kirby bowed. "Thank you again for inviting me to the party."

"My pleasure." Terry dropped to a curtsy, gathered her satin skirts and swished through the throng to meet George.

Kirby took a sip of champagne and glanced back to the mirror. The glass quivered and darkened. Kirby glanced around the room. Party-goers fully engaged in deep conversations seemed oblivious to the strange activity.

The face appeared again, this time without the child. Wending through the throng to look closer, Kirby kept his gaze glued to the man in the mirror. This time the image beckoned him closer. Kirby eased up to the mantle, and skimmed his fingers along the glass. The likeness in the mirror matched Kirby's movement, sweeping from side to side.

When Kirby's fingertips brushed the bottom of the frame, the shiny surface undulated like a stone skipping over a calm lake. The solid finish gave way to a quivering void.

The surrounding sounds of laughter and chatter disintegrated to a silence that roared in his ears.

A set of fingers reached through the slim portal of another world, pressing his. Kirby drew back his hand as if burned, but not before he caught the glimpse of an emerald ring, not unlike the one he wore.

Except blood smeared the stone.

He stepped back from the hearth, rubbing his trembling hand along his thigh. He glanced down. His fingers were clean and dry, and left no stain on his breeches. Stunned, he glanced around the room at guests clumped in small groups. Mouths moved but he heard nothing. Not one person glanced in his direction or seemed aware of anything amiss.

Sound suddenly returned to his ears.

Creedence Clearwater Revival's version of "I Put a Spell on You" played through the speakers.

When the bluesy song faded out, a temporary lull of silence allowed the chatter and laughter to penetrate his hearing. The gentle clink of glasses and china provided a different musical background.

He glanced at the mirror once more. His reflection stared back at him as a new song started.

His dropped his gaze to the ornate clock just below the frame.

Something Wilson Pickett was singing about the midnight hour had just caught his attention.

EPILOGUE

Separate bolts of red, white, and blue spiraled on their upward journey towards the stars. Far above the horizon, the twirling sparkles stopped and formed the figures of three young girls.

The sisters joined hands, laughing as they danced in a circle. They glanced once toward earth and then back at each other.

The figures merged into a cloudburst of sparkling lights that headed toward heaven.

As Nicole's happy giggles faded to silence, a solitary shimmering teardrop fell to earth.

TERRY'S FAMILY TREE

Elisabeth (unk 1st wife) m. PHILLIPE DE LA ROCHER
(aka Phillip Rocker) m. Abigail Weldon (2nd wife)
/
(1743-1812 age 69) ETIENNE DE LA ROCHER m.
CLOTHISTE JANVIER (1748[2]-1781 age 33)
/
THERESÉ MARIE LA ROCHE (1764-1861 age 98) m.
Antoine Dubois
/
ANTOINETTE DUBOIS (1787-1814 age 73) m.
Richard Plunkett
/
JENNIE PLUNKETT   (1812-1841) m. Pierre
Longchamps (1809-1860)
/
CELESTINE LONGCHAMPS (1841-1937-age 96) m.
Frank Wyatt (1840-1890), m. Ellis Harper
/
HENRY WYATT (1861-1899) m. Mary Hardy
/
PETER WYATT SR. (1907-1979) m. Priscilla Garwood
/
PETER WYATT JR. (1933-2000) m. May Lindle
/
JOAN WYATT (1954-) m. Charles Dunbar (1952-)
/
TERESA "TERRY" DUNBAR (1985-) engaged to KYLE

[2] Kyle and Stephanie's research uncovered several incorrect birthdates in Stephanie's original records. Clothiste was actually born in 1748. Louis was born in 1763, Theresé in 1764, and Marie Josephé in 1765.

Allie Marie

AVERY (1984-)

TURN THE PAGE FOR A SNEAK
PREVIEW OF
HANDS OF THE HEALER
THE CHRISTMAS EMERALD
BOOK 4 OF THE TRUE COLORS SERIES
COMING IN 2016

PROLOGUE

Louis
Somewhere in time

I do not regret killing men on the battlefield. I was a soldier and it was my job. I had to kill a number of men in the call of duty.

But there is one death I cannot shake from my memory. It haunts me.

I committed murder one night.

I pace the dark room. A few steps in any direction and I am face-to-face with a cold dank wall.

I'm trapped—caged like a miserable animal.

Sometimes light shines through a small window in the wall. I race to look into the light.

But it is dark when I reach it. My hands roam in mad desperation but I cannot find the casement.

The room spins.

It always does.

Total darkness surrounds me. The window will not reappear on the wall I face. I have scoured every inch of these barriers with my fingertips. Side to side. Top to bottom. Yet I cannot find the opening for a door or window.

I never do.

A brilliant yellow square gaps in the wall. Light comes in but I know if I look through it again, I will see the same scene, the one I relive over and over. It will be the murder.

It always is.

But tonight. Tonight, the lights of three short flashes appear in the wall. At first I am reminded of the night I killed the soldiers.

But this is different and that memory quickly fades. For the first time *in centuries I feel a moment of peace.*

A swirl of red, white, and blue sparks explodes through the opening and fall around me like snowflakes.

I hear my sisters' laughter.

Just as snow melts on warm ground, the sparks fade away, the laughter with it. I plunge into darkness again, and the spinning continues.

Does the room rotate around me, or do I spin head over heels? I cannot tell.

The spinning stops abruptly. I hear music and voices. Dazzling pinpoints of green light spring from a new gap, stunning hues dancing along the walls around me. I see blurry images.

A boy's laughter fills my ears. My son?

His boyish voice sings out, "Lou-weeee!"

Why does my son call me by my given name instead of Papa?

I reach the window just as the boy waves. He and the man disappear.

Come back! *I shout, but the words are only in my head.*

The window shutters and once again, I am plunged into darkness. The room whirls and I close my eyes. Behind my lids, tiny green sparkles explode. Echoes of light instead of sound.

In desperation, I run my hands over the wall. I reach the corner and turn to the left. I repeat this all around the room until I am back where I started.

Or I think I am. How can I tell? Nothing changes.

A sudden burst of light pours through the small rectangle in the dark. I fling myself in front of it before it can leave me again.

The window has become a watery mirror. I see a man on the other side. He wears a redcoat uniform. The face stares back at me. At first, I think it is my face.

Am I looking at my own reflection?

Or is this the face of the one who will free me from my hell?

I can see him through the quivering opening. I motion the man closer. Simultaneously, we move our hands from side to side across the clear surface.

Then I push my hand forward—and my fingers plunge through the looking glass.

ABOUT THE AUTHOR

Author Allie Marie grew up in Virginia. Her favorite childhood pastime was reading Nancy Drew and Trixie Belden mysteries. When she embarked on a new vocation writing fiction after retiring from a career in law enforcement, it would have been understandable if her first book was a crime story. Researching her own family tree inspired her to write the True Colors Series instead. The other stories are patiently waiting their turn.

Her debut novel, *Teardrops of the Innocent: The White Diamond Story*, was a 2015 New England Readers' Choice Award Finalist in paranormal. The second in the series, *Heart of Courage: The Red Ruby Story* released in May 2016. Following the February 2017 release of the third book, *Voice of the Just: The Blue Sapphire Story*, the fourth book, *Hands of the Healer: The Christmas Emerald*, is slated for release later in 2017.

Besides family, her passions are travel and camping with her husband Jack.

CPSIA information can be obtained
at www.ICGtesting.com
Printed in the USA
LVHW081802091019
633690LV00011B/789/P